Good Karma

Also by Donya Lynne

All the King's Men Series
Rise of the Fallen
Heart of the Warrior
Micah's Calling
Rebel Obsession
Return of the Assassin
All the King's Men - Prequel

Good Karma

Donya Lynne

Good Karma

Donya Lynne

ISBN: 1938991052

ISBN 13: 9781938991059

Cover art by Reese Dante.

Edited by Laura LaTulipe

Dedication

To anyone who's ever felt like they didn't fit in.

Acknowledgements

This book has been two years in the making. During that time, there have been countless eyes and hands who have participated in making the book what it is today. Thank you to my incredible team of beta readers. Your feedback encouraged me to keep moving forward, constantly rewriting and tweaking until I was satisfied with the story. Thanks also to the Heart of the West RWA contest. The judges' feedback was vital in my decision to rewrite the original draft. There are so many people who, in some way, made this book possible that there's no way for me to list them all without worrying I've left someone out. This book was truly a team effort, so to all who've played a part, my sincere thanks.

A Note from Donya

Only through fire does one find rebirth. Only through the trial of suffering and forgiveness does one find true happiness and peace. The Strong Karma Trilogy is a sensual and erotic journey of story and character evolution through adversity, torment, and eventual jubilation. Each book unravels one segment of the complete tale, and each novel comes to a definite conclusion, building on the next to weave an inspiring, heart-warming (and, at times, heart-breaking) love story between two people who must come full circle within themselves before they can embark on a lifetime with one another. Often humorous, often gut-wrenching, and always steamy, the Strong Karma Trilogy promises that everything ends as it should. All you have to do is believe. I hope you enjoy this deeply personal series, which has been a true labor of love.

Chapter 1

No matter how much you regret, how angry or sad you become, your yesterdays will never return. The world of "should have" or "could have" or "if only would have" is a world of pointless suffering.
-Doe Zantamata

Cinderella, meet the palace.

"Stop staring," Daniel said, holding out his arm.

Karma snapped her mouth closed and tossed her hair as she flung her arm around his. "I'm not staring. I'm...*admiring*."

Even so, she gazed wide-eyed at the gilded opulence of the Palmer House Hilton's breathtaking lobby. There were so many rich details everywhere she looked, including in the magnificent frescoed ceiling. No doubt she could spend all day in the lobby alone and still not see all the architectural and artistic marvel.

He patted her hand. "If you say so, dear."

Karma didn't miss the irony. Being Daniel's date was the most action she'd seen since her freshman year at Purdue, and Daniel was gay.

What was wrong with this picture?

With self-conscious fingers, she caressed the smooth, red satin that fell over her body like melted silk. When had she worn anything more luxurious, more decadent, more provocative?

More red.

The cowl-neck dress salaciously exposed her shoulders and was such a vibrant shade that the word red didn't do it justice. It was red times infinity, vivid and bright. An explosion of shimmering, liquid crimson that commanded attention, stopped traffic, and bellowed, "Look at me!"

In other words, not at all what she was used to wearing.

The only item in her wardrobe that wasn't the shade of a bruise or the epitome of the word neutral was a yellow Purdue University T-shirt she'd bought in college. Hanging the dress among all that dullness would be like plopping Carmen Miranda into a room full of nuns.

"How was Zach when you called him?" Karma tried her best to own her new look and forced herself not to stare at the floor as Daniel navigated her through the lobby.

"He's better." Daniel guided her between two cushy easy chairs. "Miserable, but better. He said he wishes he could see you in this getup, though. I promised to take pictures."

Zach was Daniel's husband, and by all rights, he should have been the one on Daniel's arm tonight, not her. But Zach had come down with food poisoning, and since Daniel hated going anywhere alone, he had turned to her in a panic, begging her to be his date, promising to cover all her expenses if she attended his sister's big debut with him.

At the time, Karma hadn't realized "all her expenses" would include a new designer dress, a gold clutch to match a pair of strappy Jimmy Choos, and a merino wool wrap the color of cappuccino. Altogether, her expenses totaled three thousand dollars, and that wasn't including the trip to the salon this morning, where Daniel and his sister, Sonya, had used their power and influence—and even more of their family's fortune—to give her a drastic makeover. Hair, makeup, mani-pedi. Karma barely recognized herself.

"You really didn't have to do this, you know." She gestured to her dress.

"Sweetie, do *not* even worry about it." He waved her off, just as he had the first half-dozen times she'd tried to tell him he'd spent way too much money on her.

"But…twelve *hundred* dollars?" She had almost swallowed her tongue when she saw the dress's price tag.

"Oh, honey, I can afford it. And you saved me from attending Sonya's big debut stag, so buying you this *magnificent* dress—if I do say so myself—is the least I could do. Besides, you're my best friend, and your wardrobe is depressing." He mock-shuddered. "It could use a splash of color." His fist popped open on the word *splash*. The gesture simulated more of an explosion, which was probably more appropriate. Then he brightened as if he'd just had a fabulous idea. "In fact, when we get back to Indianapolis, I'm taking you shopping. You need some new clothes to go with the new you." He snapped his fingers as his gaze danced over her face and hair.

Why did she suddenly feel like Frankenstein's monster, only prettier?

"Fine. But I'll use my own money from now on."

"Awe, you're no fun." He led her toward a wide, regal staircase along the far wall.

Saying yes to a trip to Chicago had been easy. In college, she and Daniel had spent at least one weekend a semester in the city, which was his hometown, so making the trip was like old times, even though old times had ended only a couple years ago. Now she wondered if she would owe him for the rest of her life. After all, she didn't come from wealthy blue blood like he did, and there was no way she could afford digs like this on her miniscule executive assistant's salary.

She tightened her hold on Daniel's arm as they started up the stairs. "I wish you could have found me more practical shoes." Navigating on such high heels was proving to be quite the challenge.

"Nonsense. This dress calls for extraordinary shoes. And nothing extraordinary comes shorter than three inches."

"These feel more like four." She wobbled and whipped her other hand around to clutch his sleeve so she didn't fall.

Daniel smirked. "Try three and three quarters."

No wonder she could barely walk. "You're trying to kill me, aren't you?"

"Death by fashion. No better way to die." When they reached the landing, Daniel guided her toward the elevators, where they rode to the fourth floor.

If she had thought the lobby was beautiful, the ballroom where the main event was taking place was beyond exquisite. Everything sparkled and appeared coated with gold, but the illusion was only a trick of the lights and glittering stemware.

Daniel bent toward her as he helped her out of her wrap. "You look like sweet little Alice after she's fallen down that magical rabbit hole, all starry-eyed and gaping." Then he draped her wrap over his arm and patted the fabric. "I'll check this. You just stay here and stare. I'll be right back." He hastened down the hall toward the coat check.

Karma blinked and watched after him as she ran her palm up and down her bare arm, feeling naked without her wrap—and embarrassed she'd been caught ogling the ballroom like an open-mouthed toddler in Willy Wonka's Chocolate Factory. But she had never seen anything like this place. The historic hotel was a standing work of art in and of itself. The perfect location to hold a charity event for the Arts Coalition.

Throughout history, celebrities and dignitaries had stayed and performed in the Palmer House Hilton, and she could see why. The hotel was magnificent. Who wouldn't want to cozy up to all this grandeur? But while such guests might have thought it was them who graced the hotel with their presence, she felt it was the other way around. The hotel was the greatest celebrity of them all, gracing all who entered with *its* presence, graced by none, and making everyone within its walls a celebrity by association. Karma certainly felt like a Hollywood starlet just being here, even though in the real world she was a big fat nobody. Such was the magical spell of the Palmer House Hilton.

As she waited for Daniel outside the ballroom entrance, a dozen pairs of men's eyes turned toward her. These were men way out of her league, some with women on their arms, some without, but all dressed in suits worth more money than she earned in a month. Talk about intimidating. And yet, an unfamiliar thrill shot through her blood from the attention.

Daniel rejoined her and took her hand. "All set. You ready to explore Wonderland?"

"Huh?" She frowned up at him.

He laughed. "Alice? Wonderland?" He gestured into the ballroom, apparently having way too much fun at her starry-eyed expense.

She made a blasé face. "How about you stop giving me a hard time and help me find a glass of champagne?" If she was going to play starlet for the evening, she was going to drink like one.

"Well, well." He arched one of his perfectly groomed eyebrows. "Certainly, *madam*." He bowed his head and led her inside.

"That's more like it." She clutched his hand as the vibrant energy of the room invaded her. She could almost feel the money, the prestige, the sexy influence of so many powerful people in one place. The weighty stature of those in attendance seemed to add another layer to the paint on the walls. It infiltrated the air and covered all the surfaces. It was an invisible guest making its way around the room, infecting everyone.

"You belong here, Karma." Daniel squeezed her hand.

Startled, she turned and met his coffee brown eyes. "You're joking, right?"

He shook his head. "For once, no." His gaze ranged her face then down to the dress that made her feel like a spotlight was shining on her. "You clean up well, Karma. Very well. You're the prettiest girl here." He examined the room. "But, damn, the way all these men are looking at you is giving me a complex." He ushered her in the direction of the bar.

She had to admit she did feel different. More alive. Maybe even a bit audacious, like she might actually be able to pull off the celebrity status in her fantasies. She bit her bottom lip and glanced over her shoulder, catching the eye of a handsome, older man who was chatting with another couple. His gaze swiftly appraised her as she passed, and he smiled. Trying not to giggle, she turned back toward Daniel. A part of her liked the attention, but she had no idea how to react to it.

Was her sudden sense of adventure a result of all the designer bling? The fact she was in unfamiliar surroundings that beckoned her fantasies? Or was her shockingly red dress the cause? After all, red was the color of passion and danger. Perhaps she was subconsciously connecting with her attire and absorbing its influence, becoming someone else, but who? A vixen? A daredevil? A woman snared by her desires? And if so, what exactly *were* her desires? Her life had been so bland up to this point that she hadn't given them a lot of thought.

Now, in one night, wearing a bold dress and towering shoes—both of which were completely outside her comfort zone—she dared to imagine she could be someone else. Someone bold, who took risks, who was maybe a tad reckless. No longer did she fall into the dependable, responsible mold she had clung to her entire life.

As Daniel ushered her toward the bar, she noticed the way the men in her path covertly—or even flagrantly—stared at her. One tipped his drink. Another raised one eyebrow and offered an appreciative nod. All the attention made her cheeks heat, and her fingers played over the low neckline of her dress as her gaze flitted from one man to the next.

No one had ever stared at her. At least not like that. But in the short distance it took to reach the bar, Karma caught at least a half-dozen men undressing her with their eyes. The attention was unnerving, yet exhilarating. For the first time, men didn't see her as one of the guys, their buddy, their pal they could hang with after a softball game or eat pizza with and tell crude jokes around.

Tonight, she was a goddess, and a strange inner voice she had never welcomed before preened and sighed delightedly at being freed. Who was this new woman emerging from her body? This courageous woman with a new outlook, who enjoyed being gawked at in a way old Karma had never experienced nor appreciated?

Back in Indianapolis, she was forever destined to be the bridesmaid but never the bride, but not here. Not in Chicago. Tonight, she felt like a movie star, the one woman in the room all the men wanted to ask to dance, kiss, whisk away in a magical carriage. She was Cinderella.

Beside her, Daniel casually glanced around as he lifted a glass of champagne. Under his breath, barely moving his lips, he said, "Girl, you've got every man within twenty yards wishing he'd come alone tonight, and every woman wishing you hadn't come *at all*." He caught her eye with a devilish wink and took a sip of his champagne. "See what a little makeup and a new hairstyle can do? Oh, and of course, a dress that's not part of some boring business ensemble." He half-rolled his eyes as he looked away.

Karma giggled, unable to stop the giddy, surprising rush of excitement tugging at a part of her that she hadn't known existed. A part that wanted the attention…that wanted these men to desire her and these women to be jealous of her. She had never been the source of a woman's jealousy, nor the reason for a man ignoring his date.

"Come on," Daniel said, taking her hand, "let's find the casino room. I'm sure to win big with you distracting all the men. Do you think I can get you to flash some leg?"

"Daniel."

"Just kidding."

Karma snatched a glass of champagne and welcomed this new personality clamoring for the spotlight. For just one night, she could live the fantasy. She could be Cinderella. Soon enough, she would return to Indiana, to the ho-hum job not in her field of study, to the only town she had ever called home, and tuck this newfound side of her personality back into its closet.

But for now, she would enjoy the fairy tale.

Chapter 2

I cannot always control what goes on outside. But I can always control what goes on inside.
-Wayne Dyer

In his suite, Mark Strong shrugged into his Armani tuxedo jacket. He rented a room at the Palmer House Hilton every year for the Chicago Arts Coalition's annual charity benefit. Better to do that than drink and drive. And he knew tonight he would be drinking. That was a given at this event.

After a quick adjustment to the cuffs of his crisp white shirt, Mark smoothed his palm down his tie then made his way from his suite to the fourth floor, fashionably late.

The entire floor had been reserved for the benefit, an event he had been attending since he was a teenager. Of course, back then, he'd been with his parents. At thirty, he no longer needed a chaperone.

In the exhibit hall, a variety of portraits, paintings, sculptures, and other works of art were on display, and a string quartet played on a small stage against one wall. In the Red Lacquer room, a mock casino had been set up for the evening, where those with a taste for risk could sate their demons for a good cause, as well as the chance to win one of the glamorous door prizes being given away.

But the main action was in the Grand and State ballrooms, where food and drink coursed among the partygoers in the hands of black-tied wait staff, and where Chicago's social elite mingled. While the allure of gambling was tempting, Mark would remain in the main ballroom for now and fulfill his social obligation, hobnobbing with politicians and socialites, as well as the members of his parents' dance studio, who were old friends he had known since childhood.

With a friendly nod, he plucked a flute of champagne from a passing waiter's tray and eased into the crowd. A quartet of guitarists on the stage began playing a slow, Spanish tune perfect for a sensuous rumba. If only he had a date, he might have swept her onto the dance floor to give his retired moves a wake-up call.

Turning away, he navigated the crowd, stopping occasionally to converse and shake hands. The music created a gentle ambience within the warmth of shimmering, burnished gold walls and sparkling chandeliers. Candlelit table lanterns and fern fronds added an elegant touch to an already decadent room.

"Mom. Dad." He stepped between his fashionably attired parents standing beside one of the cocktail tables in the reception area. "You look good." He shook his dad's hand then kissed his mom on the cheek.

"So do you, honey." His mom fiddled with his tie. "You're so handsome in your tux. Where's Abby?" She frowned and looked around.

He cleared his throat and briefly turned his attention to the crowd. "Abby and I broke up." He downed a healthy swallow of champagne.

A note of disappointment crossed his mom's face. "Oh."

By now, she had to be used to the revolving door of women who came into his life then exited a few months later. Mark didn't do commitments. Not anymore. The only meaningful relationship in his life had fallen apart in grand fashion six years ago, and he'd been trying to make up for his shortcomings ever since.

"I'm sorry to hear that." She stared into her wine glass. "Abby was a nice girl."

All the women he dated were nice. Educated, well appointed, and sophisticated. What every man of means looked for in a woman. They just weren't for him. Or, rather, he wasn't for them. He wasn't good for any woman now. Not after the nightmare of his past, which had messed up his head to the point he couldn't even set foot in a church anymore.

Mark averted his gaze to the clusters of people gathered among the impeccably decorated tables. "It just didn't work out between us." He took another drink of champagne. The alcohol would help him get through the evening. "Is Carol dancing the exhibition again this year?"

"No, not this year," his mom said flatly before quickly taking a sip of wine.

His dad forced a tight grin. "Sonya is."

Mark scrutinized his parents' truncated reactions. Then again, Carol wasn't a cozy topic of discussion between him and his parents.

"Sonya? That's an interesting choice."

Carol was the most decorated dancer at his parents' studio. She had performed the exhibition for the past five years. She was in her prime and a three-time Professional Latin Ballroom Champion. Why would Sonya take Carol's place? Not that Sonya was a poor choice. She was adequate for the task and a rising star at the studio. In fact, she had recently won her first competition.

"Yes, well, Sonya has really impressed us." Mom took another hasty drink of her wine, glancing away.

"Will Carol be here?" Mark finished his champagne and grabbed another from a passing tray.

His mom shifted uneasily and looked at his father. What was with all the cloak-and-dagger?

"I think she and Antonio will be here, yes," his dad said with an edge of discomfort.

Antonio. Carol's dance partner. Her husband. A woman thief. But then, that wasn't really fair. What had happened wasn't Antonio's fault. He'd just been the benefactor.

A hand clapped down on Mark's shoulder. "Hey, Mark."

He turned to find his best friend, Rob, had joined them. "Hey, buddy."

Rob shook hands with Mark's dad and kissed his mom on the cheek. "Good to see you again, Mr. and Mrs. Strong."

"Likewise," his mom said. "You look good, Rob. Have you been working out?" She appeared eager to change the subject, which curdled Mark's nerves.

"I've been hitting the gym pretty hard lately." Rob eyed Mark. "Your son has been kicking my ass on the courts, so I needed to get a leg up somehow."

"Oh really?" His dad chuckled. "I always thought he had the talent to play in the pros."

Mark gave his dad a good-natured but cynical look. "You know I'm too short."

"Too short? You're six-two, son."

"Yeah, too short." Mark laughed. "Some of those guys are over seven feet tall."

"Oh, but you were talented enough. Look at Michael Jordan. They said he was too short, too."

Mark glanced around the room and sipped his champagne. "I'll stick with consultant work."

"Speaking of, how is work?" his dad asked. "We haven't seen you in a while."

"I just finished an assignment a couple of weeks ago in Wisconsin."

"And now what?" His father swirled the wine in his glass.

"I'll be heading down to Indianapolis on Monday." Mark's eye continued to rove the room. Just hearing that Carol was attending the benefit had him on high alert. Mark lifted his glass only to find it empty. Again. But then, they were barely filling the flutes halfway.

"Indianapolis, huh?" His dad flagged down a waiter after noticing Mark was dry. "Weren't you just there for March Madness?"

"Yes." Mark drove down to Indy almost every year for the NCAA basketball tournament.

"And now you're going down for a job just in time for the Indy 500. How's that for luck?"

"Yes, but I doubt I'll get to the race. I'll be too busy."

"You can always come back to the studio." His mom ran the tip of one elegant finger around the rim of her wine glass. "At least then you could stay in one place."

It was an old joke. Mom always teased him about returning to the family business even though she knew he wanted to make his money the way Grandfather had, through strong business acumen. Granddad's shrewd talents in business had allowed his mom to follow her dreams of becoming a professional dancer…and for Mark to receive a multimillion-dollar trust. The least Mark could do was build a name for himself to pay homage to one of the greatest men he had ever known. Besides, with Carol working and training at the studio, there was no way Mark would set foot in the place.

"Uh, no, Mom. I'll leave the salsa and cha-cha to you and dad." *And Carol.*

"You're welcome any time, you know." Mom knew why he didn't visit the studio anymore, but they never talked about it. She was good at dancing, whether literally or figuratively, around sensitive subjects best left untouched. "I'm sure your dancing hasn't gotten *that* rusty, has it?"

He leaned in and kissed her cheek. "Actually, yes. I haven't danced in a while." He had left dancing behind to earn his master's at the University of Chicago's Booth School of Business, one of the top business schools in the country. His mom had been disappointed about that at first, but now she seemed content with his career choice, if a little sad he hadn't pursued dancing.

The four chatted a while longer, then Mark and Rob broke away and settled at the bar.

"So, you and Abby broke up." Rob flagged down the bartender. "Corona, please."

"Yep." Mark leaned against the bar and faced the room.

"Seven months. That's a new record for you."

Mark blew out a puff of air. "I guess." He didn't normally date a woman more than three or four months. Longer and they started itching for more, clinging…as Abby had begun to do.

But Mark had to admit, he had enjoyed the steady constant Abby had brought to his life. He hadn't needed to go through the tedious getting-to-know-you bullshit that bouncing from one relationship to the next entailed. And Abby really was a nice girl. He hadn't wanted to hurt her. Still, he should have ripped off the Band-Aid months ago instead of letting her end it. He would never make *that* mistake again.

"What happened this time?" Rob nodded to the bartender as he took his beer, then turned around and joined Mark, gazing at the mingling crowd.

"Same ol' same ol'," Mark said. "We had an argument last night." He chuffed. "Seems she was more into our relationship than I was. Asked if I was ever going to ask her to move in. I told her no. Then she asked if I ever plan on marrying her." Mark took another drink.

"Another no," Rob said, glancing down at his Corona.

"Yep."

"I guess that didn't go over well."

Mark shook his head. "Nope."

Even now, remembering how Abby had broken down in front of him killed him. He knew that kind of hurt all too well. Sure, maybe he knew it to the power of a hundred, but that didn't mean Abby's torment was any less agonizing to *her*. She didn't need to know the level of suffering he had endured in the past to know that his not wanting to marry her now hurt like hell.

He took another gulp of champagne but kept his exterior dull and emotionless. This was his burden to bear, no one else's.

"Yeah, well," Rob said, "maybe that's because you never told her you didn't want a serious commitment. You ever think about that?" Rob pushed the lime wedge into his Corona then tipped the bottle for a swig.

Rob had a point. Mark didn't want commitments from the women he dated. They were simply stepping-stones. But to where?

"I don't know, Rob. Maybe."

He had been committed once. He had been in love. The house, the wife, the kids, the white picket fence…the golden retriever…all of it had been within his grasp. The term "family man" had defined him to a T. But then that train pulled out of the station without him and left him scratching his head like a fool, and he blamed himself for the failure. If only he had been more attentive, more selfless. If only he had sought to give *her* pleasure as much as he had sought to fulfill his own—to include her more than he had—then maybe he wouldn't be where he was now, which was in a never-ending cycle of women he could never get close to, and who he didn't let get close enough to him to break his heart if and when they left. And they *always* left. They always had and always would. Nowadays, he kept women safely at arm's distance. That kept things simple and harmless. No complications. No pain. No chance for another heartbreak.

But he didn't let his trysts be a waste of time. Somewhere deep inside, in a place he refused to acknowledge but knew existed, he hoped for a second chance at happiness. If he got it, he didn't want to make the same mistakes, so he dated to practice being the kind of man a woman wanted. Practice makes perfect, as they say, and he was an overachiever that way. A perfectionist. But apparently he had become too good at giving women what they wanted and needed, because for the past couple of years, every woman he dated wanted him to pop the question. Perhaps he was going about this all wrong.

"Maybe you're right," he said to Rob. "Maybe I need to change my approach."

"Hell yeah, I'm right," Rob said like a wise guy, clapping him on the shoulder. "I'm always right."

"Modest, too." Mark tipped his head toward him.

Mark had enjoyed his time with Abby the same way he enjoyed his time with every girl he dated, but he had to admit that telling his past girlfriends up front that he wasn't a commitment kind of guy probably would have saved everyone some grief. He liked dating, and, like any hot-blooded man, he enjoyed the sex. He just didn't want to settle down.

Was he wrong for how he felt? He wanted it all—the dating, the love, the sex, the intimacy. All of it…*except* the commitment. And he enjoyed making a woman feel good about herself. Too many women seemed to suffer some blow to their self-esteem, just as he had, and giving them a little pleasure and a boost to their confidence always made him feel better.

He was surprised by how many women saw themselves as less than they were. Even the beautiful ones. *Especially* the beautiful ones. They got in their own way when it came to men. Even Abby, as pretty as she was, suffered from self-doubt. In hindsight, her insecurity was what had attracted him to her, because he had a soft spot for people—not just women—who, in one way or another, battled inner demons…probably because he had battled his own all his life and could relate. And because he was who he was—and because he never wanted to fail again—he took it as a personal mission to bring these women out of their shells. Give them joy, pleasure, a little happiness. He studied them, because…well…that's just what he did. He studied everyone and everything. Including women. What made them tick? What did they want? What were the best ways to give them pleasure? How could he bring this one out of her shell while taming that one's wild side? He was a student studying for his master's, and women were the subject. But would he ever write his thesis and graduate?

But it was more than that. Mark was a man with something to prove. That he could make a woman feel beautiful and special, and that he wasn't the selfish bastard he had once been.

"Well, look at it this way," Rob said, "now that you're single, there's nothing stopping you from having a wild night with one of these fine ladies before you leave for boring old Indianapolis." Rob lifted his beer and waved it in an arc toward the crowd.

"You know that's not who I am." Mark didn't do casual the same way he didn't do commitments. He lived in the halfway between the two. Casually committed? Was that even possible?

"Yeah, yeah. You and your mighty principles." Rob grinned, glanced away, and then his eyes went cold.

"What?" Mark turned to find what had spooked Rob.

And there she was. Carol. The reason why he hadn't had a relationship that lasted longer than four months—with the exception of Abby, of course—for the last six years.

His heart skipped a beat as it always did when he saw her, not because of how beautiful she was, but because of the traumatic reminder of the past. The humiliation still felt fresh, as if what she had done happened only yesterday. A wave of nausea swept through his body. His pulse raced, and he quickly downed a gulp of champagne. A nice buzz was setting up shop in his brain, which was perfect. He would need it to get through the rest of the night.

Carol laughed at something Antonio whispered in her ear, and that's when he noticed the bump. The one her right hand caressed with the love and affection every mother would show her unborn child. So that's why Carol wasn't dancing tonight…and why his parents had behaved so strangely when he'd asked about her.

Carol was pregnant. How about that?

Rob said nothing. God love him. He knew without Mark having to say it that seeing Carol pregnant devastated him.

Mark turned away, cleared his throat, and drained the rest of his third glass of champagne.

That was supposed to have been his life. His baby. His wife. His fucking white picket fence.

For a second, Mark thought he was going to be sick, but he forced himself to breathe and pushed back his emotions—as well as the bile rising in his throat.

"Hey, man. I'm sorry," Rob said quietly.

"About what?" Mark squared his shoulders and faced the room again as if nothing were wrong.

Rob glanced down, fiddled with his beer bottle, then looked at him. "It's not fair."

"What? That she's pregnant." He huffed and shrugged as if it were no big deal. "Good for her. She'll be a good mom. And Antonio…yeah…well…he'll be a good dad."

"This is me you're talking to, Mark." Rob gave him a look that said he wasn't buying Mark's line of shit.

Mark shrugged again. "I know. But I'm good. Really." He clapped Rob on the shoulder and waved for the bartender to bring him another of those half-glasses of champagne, which he downed in one gulp. "Excuse me." He smiled at Rob then walked away.

With measured steps, he left the ballroom, made his way to the elevator, rode to the floor of his suite, unlocked his door, entered, took off his tie and tuxedo coat, and carefully hung both over the back of a chair. Then he slid into the bathroom. As he unbuttoned the cuffs of his starched shirt, he stared at his reflection in the mirror. Where had his life gone so wrong? How had he failed so miserably? Why hadn't he been able to make Carol happy? Just…why?

Resting his head against the cool glass, he closed his eyes and held his breath.

One count.

Two.

Three.

Pain knifed his heart as he lost the battle.

He collapsed in front of the toilet and gripped the sides as he threw up. The champagne, his dinner…his heart and soul. He was shredded, wrecked beyond repair.

After the retching ceased, he leaned against the side of the bathtub, his face in his hands, tearless sobs jerking his body as he gasped for air.

Fuck! He thought he'd been getting better, but like everything else in his life, that had only been a lie. He was no better now than he had been then. Damn her! Damn her to hell for doing this to him!

Seeing Carol pregnant had destroyed him all over again.

Chapter 3

A ship in a harbor is safe, but that's not what ships are built for.
-Grace Hopper

Karma fidgeted on the high seat at the blackjack table and tugged the hem of her dress. She felt like an underdressed beacon, and, as in the ballroom earlier, men eyed her with barely veiled precision, as if they were trying to decide how best to get her out of her dress.

She picked up one of the round, plastic chips from her dwindling pile and worried the tip of her manicured nail in the grooves around the edge. Daniel had bought her five hundred dollars' worth of chips—the lifetime debt continued to mount—and had joined her at blackjack for a while before venturing off to play poker. He was a virtuoso at Texas Hold'em while Karma's knowledge of poker extended to knowing that a deck of cards was involved. Blackjack, on the other hand, she could manage. She had to be able to count to twenty-one, and that was about as much as she needed to know.

The dealer dealt her a pair of cards. Fourteen. She tapped the table for a hit. She was dealt an eight. Bust. Her stack of chips grew even smaller. She was losing more than she was winning, but it was all play money, anyway. No one would get rich in this casino. Chips were bought with money, which went to the charity, and winnings were cashed in for tickets to enter into the drawings for the prizes, one of which was a Caribbean cruise for two on a semi-private, luxury yacht.

Wouldn't it be something if she won that?

But if she did, who would she take with her? She would probably just give the tickets to Daniel and Zach. Maybe that would be enough to ease her conscience over how much Daniel had bankrolled for her to come tonight.

Mark entered the Red Lacquer Ballroom, a glass of scotch in his hand. The evening had graduated from champagne to something stronger, despite his gastrointestinal overload an hour ago.

After losing control over his emotions—and his dinner—he had pulled himself together, washed up, rinsed out his mouth, changed his shirt, and donned his jacket and tie once more to continue his evening. Avoiding Carol was of utmost importance, though, which had led him to the makeshift casino. Carol wouldn't dream of gambling and would stay firmly rooted in the main ballroom.

If only Abby had waited a few more days to break up with him, she would have been on his arm tonight. Her presence would have offered a buffer against Carol's mental onslaught, and his feelings of vulnerability and exposure might not have surfaced. Being alone was like announcing to Carol that he hadn't moved on, which he hadn't, but he didn't want to admit that…to her, himself, or anyone.

He killed the drink he had been nursing for the last half hour and fought to clear his head as he set his empty glass on the bar. "Scotch," he told the bartender. "Double." He scanned the room. He didn't want to be alone. Not now. Not tonight. But he wasn't one for casual flings and one-night stands, so where did that leave him?

Rob's words came back to haunt him. *There's nothing stopping you from having a wild night with one of these fine ladies.* That was Rob, not him, but right now, the temptation to let go of his control was almost overwhelming. He was beyond frayed, and the idea of female companionship appealed to him more than usual now that Carol had shocked his system.

He really needed to get his shit together. Come to his senses. Put aside this idea of finding a suitable woman and losing his loneliness inside an evening of unbridled passion. That wouldn't do anyone any good, and he knew himself well enough to know if he did that, he would just feel worse in the morning. Maybe he should just leave before he did something stupid. Head home…call it a night…throw in the—

His gaze landed on *her* and every rational thought screeched to a halt.

Standing a little taller, he lifted his freshly filled glass to his lips as he took in her statuesque form. Even sitting, she held herself like a queen. Wait. Perhaps not a queen, but a princess meeting the public for the first time, with an air of insecurity over a layer of confidence. Or was that a show of confidence over a core of insecurity?

The way she smoothed her hand self-consciously down the skirt of her magnificent red dress, the way she nibbled the inside of her bottom lip as she hesitantly glanced over her shoulder, the way her fingers fidgeted over the chips stacked in front of her, and how her feet twitched in time to a silent beat…this was a woman not accustomed to her surroundings or her effect on men. But Mark's sharp eye caught every revealing nuance in her body language. She wasn't used to wearing such provocative clothing, such decadent high heels. She seemed completely unaware that she was the sexiest woman there, as if she held no understanding of her own appeal or how she drew men's gazes the way strawberry blossoms drew bees. She had the eye of every man in the room—including his—and yet she sat alone.

What a crime.

Intensely intrigued, Mark's innate desire to understand the unknown perked to life. Why was such a stunner alone?

No matter. He could remedy that.

Mark made his way across the room, watching her, studying her.

And that dress. Such a shimmering, vivid red should be illegal. Her auburn hair was pulled over one shoulder to expose the nape of her neck and shoulder blades. If he had been her date for the evening, he wouldn't hesitate to walk up behind her and drop a kiss on that alluring expanse of skin. Everything about her, right down to her pretty feet in those strappy gold shoes, beckoned.

Mark didn't know if it was the alcohol, his need to find companionship to dull the ache in his chest, his recent breakup with Abby, or if this woman was simply a mythological siren come to steal his heart. With just a glance, she had pushed his sorrow into the background and awakened his primordial need to explore.

The seat beside her became available, and he eased onto it before placing a hundred-dollar chip on the table, stealing a peek at her cards as she looked at them. The dealer dealt him in.

She didn't seem to notice his presence as she tapped the green felt beside her pair of cards.

"I wouldn't take a hit on that, if I were you."

She turned and visibly caught her breath. Her pale green eyes widened briefly then her lashes fell as she looked away. "Why not?"

He shrugged. "Just wouldn't."

She bit her lip and smiled then turned toward the dealer and tapped the table with her delicate finger, anyway.

Such bravado. He licked his lips and fought back a smile as he glanced into his drink.

The card she received put her over twenty-one.

He collected his winnings from the dealer and sipped his scotch. "Told you."

Her eyes sparkled when she looked at him again. "Well, it's for a good cause, right?"

"That it is." Mark recognized many faces here tonight, but not hers. "My name is Mark Strong," he said as he accepted the next deal.

"What's yours?"

"Karma." Once again, she smoothed her palm down her skirt then motioned as if out of habit to tuck her hair behind her ear, even though it was already draped over her other shoulder, giving him a peek at her elegant neck.

"Do I make you nervous, Karma?" He tapped the table for a hit.

Karma quickly dropped her hand back to the table with a slight flourish. "No."

But Mark could tell she was as attracted to him as he was to her.

They played two more hands in silence. On the third, Mark said, "Want to make it interesting?"

She turned curious yet emboldened eyes toward him. "Interesting?"

"Yes." He nodded toward the cards they had just been dealt. "If I end up with the better hand, you have to dance with me." He dared to take her back into the main ballroom, to dance with this splendid woman in front of God and everyone. In front of Carol.

Her gaze caressed his face then dropped to his chest before meeting his eyes again. "And if I have the better hand?"

"What would the lady like?"

She took a moment, looked at her cards, and then met his gaze as she bit her lip. Daring and something else, something bordering on excitement, flickered in her eyes. "If I win, you have to buy me a drink."

"It's an open bar."

Her gold hoop earrings brushed against the smooth, flawless skin of her neck as she giggled bashfully and glanced away. "Well then…" She thought for a second. "If I win, you have to have a drink with me."

"In that case, it sounds like a win-win all around." He could barely take his eyes off her. She was like no woman he had ever seen. So striking. She was like a majestic greyhound, long and slender, with simple elegance and understated beauty that outshone even her attire. Yet, there was a vulnerability and innocence in her eyes that belied the dress, the shoes, the way her hair fell seductively to one side. Karma was a dichotomy, two extremes tied into one.

His lips twitched as she took a hit on her cards. He wouldn't have asked for another if he had been dealt her hand, which he had peeked at, but so much the better for his odds.

He stayed. His hand was already a keeper. Queen of hearts alongside the ace of diamonds.

Her shoulders slumped momentarily after the dealer dropped her next card in front of her. King of spades.

"Bust." She turned toward him. "I guess you win."

"I guess I have." He nodded toward the dealer, collected his chips as she did likewise, stood, and adjusted his jacket before holding out his arm. "Shall we?" He bobbed his head in the direction of the main ballroom.

She hesitated briefly then carefully dismounted the high chair and wrapped her arm around his. Her awkward mannerisms, and the way she bobbled on her—yes, those were Jimmy Choos—made her that much more intriguing.

Once she steadied herself, he led her back into the ballroom. Whether Karma ended up in his suite or not, the evening had just taken a turn for the better.

Karma couldn't believe this was happening. A handsome man had really just asked her to dance.

Under his tuxedo, Mark's arm felt strong, powerful, the arm of a man who took care of his body. He led her out of the casino to the dance floor in the main ballroom. A live band played easy jazz, and they began swaying back and forth in time to the music, another couple among many.

She really was Cinderella, this was her ball, and Mark stood in as a worthy prince.

"So, Karma, what do you do? Wait, let me guess. You're a model." One corner of his mouth rose as if he was only teasing. His dark green eyes bore into hers with such intensity that she couldn't look away.

"How did you know?" Fine. He was teasing, but why not play a little? After all, she was someone else tonight, wasn't she? Let Mark think she was a model if that's what he wanted to believe. Besides, after tonight, she would never see him again. For a few hours, she could pretend she was someone exciting, someone important, someone worthy of a handsome, charismatic man.

His eyebrows lifted as his grin widened, and he looked away as if suppressing a thought. For a while, they merely danced. Mark's subtle cologne infiltrated her senses, and the hard lines of his body beneath his jacket became impossible to ignore. He felt sturdy, rugged, like a man who got what he wanted and didn't let go until he was finished.

She skimmed her left hand from his shoulder to his chest and studied her slender, pale fingers against the stark black of his tuxedo.

Warmth emanated from under all that rich wool, and she brushed her hand back and forth across the firm swell of his pectoral, which felt solid and firm. She stilled her hand and pressed her fingers against the fabric, enjoying the subtle curve of his chest against her palm. What did Mark look like undressed? She could bet he looked as impressive as he felt.

His hold around her waist tightened, and he pulled her more firmly against him, snapping her from her fantasy. She glanced up at his face. He was watching her, eyes narrowed, his lips curled with amusement. Then his gaze dropped briefly to her hand.

Oh God! He had caught her feeling him up.

Heat flooded her cheeks, and she hastily returned her hand to his shoulder.

After several long, awkward moments, he said quietly, "You're not a model." His rich, deep voice smoldered.

Warmth spilled through her body like melted butter. It was a feeling she had never experienced, and it made her breathless. "What makes you say that?" She wasn't ready to concede the game.

He held her fully against him now, his face only inches from hers, his eyes drilling holes into her soul.

He released her hand, and his gaze followed the tip of his finger as it trailed down the side of her neck to her shoulder. "Call it a feeling."

Heat bloomed between her legs as he called her bluff, and she shifted uneasily at the foreign sensation. Part of her wanted to run, but the other part—the stranger inside her—desperately wanted to explore these new feelings Mark was awakening. Without a doubt, he was the sexiest, most attractive man she had ever laid eyes on. From the first moment she gazed into those dark eyes at the blackjack table, she knew she was in the presence of a man who knew pleasure and power.

Unbidden, her fingers curled against his shoulders. She wasn't used to men touching her this way, speaking to her in hushed, intimate whispers.

The tip of his finger glided up her shoulder to her neck. "You're not accustomed to wearing such provocative clothes, such scandalous shoes." Not a question, but a statement of fact. He knew. He saw right through her. His fingertip grazed across her collarbones. "You're not used to men looking at you." His lips brushed against her cheek, right beside her ear. "And you have no idea how incredibly sexy you are, do you?"

Her breath actually hitched as tiny, warm explosions lit her belly.

"I'm sexy?" The question whispered from her lips before she could think.

Mark pulled back, wearing a knowing grin. "A model wouldn't even ask that question." He paused then said, "And a model would be comfortable in the spotlight. You aren't."

She couldn't answer, could hardly move. She was way out of her league but refused to surrender.

Mark let out a quiet breath, not quite a sigh, but not a full exhale, either. "I don't know who you are, just your name. But what I do know is that you're the most beautiful woman here, and you're dancing with me, and every man in this room wishes he were in my shoes right now." His eyes lifted and scanned the vicinity as if proving to himself that what he said was true. Then he met her eyes again. "That's all I need to know."

She was in deep. So very deep. He was a stranger, but he had called her beautiful. No one had ever called her beautiful before. And he implied that she had bolstered his ego by dancing with him and no one else. When had she ever boosted a man's ego?

Tonight, this dress, and all that went with it, truly was magical. For a few hours, she was living a life she had only imagined.

She'd only just met Mark, and yet she was snared irrevocably and unapologetically in his web with no desire to free herself. Let her be caught. For tonight, just this once, let her be captured by the decadence of a glance, the thrill of a touch, and the scent of his cologne on her skin.

Chapter 4

Go for it now. The future is promised to no one.
-Wayne Dyer

Karma was everything Mark liked in a woman. Innocent. Sweet. Shy.

The moment he touched her and wrapped his arm around her slender waist, a spark had ignited. One that persisted and intensified the longer they danced. She smelled of wild flowers and fresh undertones, like petals floating down a mountain stream. And her skin. It was so smooth, so pristine. She really could be a model if she wanted, but he had only been joking when he asked if she was. He had already known she wasn't.

Why had she lied about that?

Rather than make him angry, the deception deepened his curiosity.

"How about that drink?" he said when the song ended.

"Even though you won the wager?" Purity, as well as curious desire, shone from her luminous eyes. From the way she looked at him and tried to hold herself the way a worldly woman would—operative word being *tried*—Mark got the feeling it wasn't just her outfit and all the attention she wasn't used to, but men showing their interest, as well.

"Yes, I did, but that doesn't mean we can't both get what we want." He guided her from the dance floor, more intrigued by the second. Who was this splendid, naïve butterfly who seemed both eager and terrified to open her wings?

At the bar, he ordered another scotch on the rocks and champagne for her.

"Have you seen the exhibits?" He took her hand and scanned the room. Carol was nowhere to be seen, but the way Karma's hand fit so nicely in his, he didn't care. He studied their connection. Her French manicure gleamed in the soft lights, and her warm hand offered security.

Strange that *she* would make *him* feel safe. Shouldn't it be the other way around?

"No, I haven't." Her delicate fingers squeezed his.

He nodded in the direction of the exhibit hall. "Then let me give you the tour."

Karma felt like she'd stepped into a whirlwind and been carried off to Oz.

Mark knew his way around. Clearly, he was more deeply connected to this charity event than as a mere philanthropist. He knew the names of the artists, musicians, and dancers. In fact, he knew Sonya, a snippet of knowledge Karma didn't reveal they shared.

Maybe she was being selfish, but something about sharing him with the normalcy of her life felt wrong. What she had with Mark was a fantasy, and fantasies weren't meant to be shared with the real world. They were surreal, an illusion, *private*. Perfect. And that's how she wanted to keep him.

Karma followed him from one display to the next, listened to him tell a personal story or provide an odd fact or two about the artists, watched his face light with a charming smile as he recalled a funny anecdote. Other guests stopped him periodically to say hello. Everyone seemed to know him. He always introduced her then smoothly moved them along as if working toward a destination.

After thirty minutes, he wound them out of the exhibit hall and back toward the casino room.

"How do you know all these people?" she asked. Daniel still played poker at the corner table across the room, oblivious to her wanderings with the enigmatic, yet remarkable Mr. Strong.

At a high-top cocktail table tucked in the shadows, Mark leaned on his elbow and faced her. "I grew up around them. I've known some of them since I was six years old." He traced his fingers down the short sleeve of her dress and stepped a little closer.

A shiver raced down her spine and she lifted her glass for a drink before she realized it was empty.

Mark didn't seem to notice. "Have you ever been to Vegas?" His gravelly voice stroked her senses.

"No." She imagined this was how the sheep felt right before the wolf attacked. "Why?"

"Your dress reminds me of a club called LAX inside the Luxor." His fingers tugged gently at the hem of her short sleeve before he swept his hand to the small of her back.

"How so?"

He grinned and glanced down at her dress. "Like LAX, your dress is very red." He drew his gaze back to her face and stared at her mouth for a heartbeat. Then, without warning, he tilted his head to hers and kissed her.

Karma's knees almost gave out. His strong lips and the way the tip of his tongue teased hers turned her legs to Jell-O, and she had to grip the lapels of his jacket to keep herself upright. He seemed to instinctively read her reaction and pulled her closer, steadying her with his body.

With a strained exhale, he broke away, circled the room with his gaze as if making sure no one was near enough to steal her away, then dragged her from the table and into the shadowy corner. Her back hit the wall. Then, with even more urgency, his mouth found hers again, and a quiet moan broke in the back of her throat as her knees threatened to buckle once more.

Behind her was the wall. In front of her was a different kind of barrier. One that was just as solid and pulsed with fiery heat. She was trapped, but in no way did she want to break free. Let her remain confined.

His body pressed against hers as he tilted his head, deepening the kiss, and her right hand found the back of his neck. Her fingertips dipped into his short, thick hair.

She had never been kissed like this. Never with such passion and yearning.

"Come to my room." He spoke fiercely against her mouth, and his dark eyes blazed into hers. "It's quieter."

She stared into his eyes, which radiated the same fire she felt deep in her core. For a long, breathless moment, she got lost in their green-grey depths. "Okay." Under his heated influence, it was the only answer she could come up with.

He wrapped his hand around hers and led her back into the hall. Her legs were still so wobbly that she almost tripped over her own feet as she followed him to the elevator. Damn these high-heeled shoes. They didn't help.

Sexual tension spiked the air, and the hairs on her arms stood on end. What was she doing? After that kiss, what did she think would happen once she got inside his room? Just a little quiet conversation?

She'd always been taught not to be reckless, not to go to rooms with strange men, to play it safe. Until now, that's exactly what she'd done. She had always taken the safe route, never the risky one. Mark was risky. Going to his room was risky. And yet, she couldn't stop herself. Tonight, she wanted the risk. She wanted to lay down a five-hundred-dollar bet on Mark Strong and spend a few brief hours savoring the winnings. Tomorrow, back at home, after the glass slipper broke forever, she could return to the status quo, but not now, not as Mark swept her into the elevator, into his arms, and weakened her knees with another searing kiss that short-circuited her thoughts and sent static through her veins as the doors whispered closed.

As the elevator started its upward journey, to a destination fraught with uncertainty and the promise of ending her six-year sexual drought, Karma felt her heart slip further out of her protective grasp as Mark's masterful lips whisked her away from reality.

She was fully immersed in the fantasy.

Mark couldn't get enough of this extraordinary woman. He hadn't meant to kiss her, but the lighting had lit her face in just such a way, and her full, pretty lips had been too inviting. Before he could stop himself, his mouth had met hers, and their kiss had been glorious.

She tasted of champagne, and the way she trembled against him and clung to his jacket so she didn't collapse in a weak-kneed heap expressed all Mark needed to know about her inexperience. Such a stunning woman, wearing a stunning dress, who could capture every eye in the room, and yet Mark would bet every dollar in his bank account that she hadn't had more than two lovers, maybe not even more than one. She had certainly never been kissed like this.

The elevator doors opened. With his mouth still locked to hers, he practically lifted her off the floor and carried her into the hallway. He had to know her secrets and understand her duality. How could she look the way she did and still be so innocent? And why, if she was so innocent, had she come upstairs? More importantly, why was he allowing it?

He fumbled for his key, unlocked the door, spun her inside, and kicked the door closed.

Why was he doing this? This wasn't how he handled himself, and it wasn't how he handled women, especially women as precious as Karma. And she *was* precious. Everything about her except her wardrobe cried that she wasn't this kind of woman. The same way he wasn't this kind of man. She deserved better than to be treated like some random one-nighter, and yet he couldn't bring himself to stop and be the gentleman he had taught himself to be in the last six years.

He pressed her against the wall, drank her in, devoured her lips, and slid his tongue over hers.

He unbuttoned his tuxedo. Her hands slid inside, and her nails scratched his chest as her fingers curled against his shirt, making him groan as he dropped the jacket to the floor.

Karma eased his ache and abolished life's bitterness. Something about her called to his basic, primitive need for connection, and he was drawn in as if by gravity, unable to pull away. Parts of him that had been cold for so long finally warmed.

He skimmed his hand up the front of her dress. He wanted to lose himself in her virtue, revel in her purity, and forget how horribly the night had started, as well as the loneliness of the last six years.

But as his palm swept under the slight swell of her breast, her breath hitched, and she froze.

Jolted from the intoxicating moment, he pulled back and looked down into her suddenly lucid eyes. The innocence was still there, but her fearless spirit was gone, replaced by what looked like panic…or perhaps dread.

Oh God, what had he done? How had he let this happen?

In a blink, their magical evening blew away like vapor. She looked like a scared rabbit as she slowly released his shoulders and crossed her arms over her chest as if to shield herself, but could he blame her? He should have known better than to take her to his room, to move so fast. He was in no frame of mind to be taking up with a woman tonight, anyway. Damn Rob for putting the idea in his head in the first place.

He blinked, and the last of the enchanted haze cleared.

"I'm sorry. I shouldn't have…uh…" But really, what could he say? The damage was done. He had become the very thing he had sworn he would never be.

Glancing toward the windows beyond the bed, he took a deep breath and felt clarity rocket back to his senses. Like a selfish pig, he had brought Karma to his room to rid himself of the loneliness and sorrow of the past twenty-four hours. His breakup with Abby. Learning that Carol was pregnant. The reminder that the life he should have had now belonged to someone else. He had been ready to use Karma to help him forget the destitution of his life. For what? All he would have gained by taking advantage of her was a stack of lies, to awaken tomorrow and still be the same pathetic, lonely man he had been two hours ago. Sleeping with her wouldn't have fixed anything.

What kind of self-centered asshole did that? Used such a sweet, delightful woman as a means to an end? This certainly wasn't the type of man he had aspired to be. If she hadn't stopped him, he would have embodied all that he had promised not to become.

"I…I'm sorry," he said again. The guilt was almost crippling.

"I…" She blinked rapidly and glanced toward the door. "I have to go." She pushed past him and skittered out of his room.

The door clicked shut behind her, and he fell against the wall, eyes closed. He blew out a heavy sigh. Damn, he really needed to figure his shit out. Maybe, if given enough time and space—from Carol, from Abby…from Antonio—he would remember who he was and be okay again. Yeah, right. It had already been six years, and he was no closer to being okay than he had been the day his world had turned upside down.

After almost a full minute, he sighed, smoothed his hands down his face, and bent to retrieve his jacket from the floor. Then he trudged toward the bed.

Alone.

But with the taste of Karma's champagne kisses still on his lips and her fresh, floral scent still in his nose.

If only his life weren't such a mess.

He had really liked this one. Something about Karma had been different.

But now she was gone, and maybe it was better that way. He was in no position to start another relationship when he would be gone for the next four to six months on business.

With a sigh, he sat on the bed and stared out the window.

Yes, it was better that she had left.

Now if he could just make himself believe that.

Chapter 5

Action brings reaction.
-Author Unknown

On Monday morning, Karma brushed her fingers down the red satin dress now hanging in the back of her closet like a diamond in a sea of coal. The majestic garment had to be giving her dark slacks, dark blazers, and white blouses an inferiority complex. She could relate.

Saturday night's fantasy was over. She was back in Clover, a northern suburb of Indianapolis. Back to reality.

Good-bye, Cinderella.

She hadn't even had a night of passion with her prince before returning to her humdrum existence. Unwelcome childhood memories she thought she'd left behind had reared up and interfered, just as they always did in the pivotal moments of her life. Obviously, she wasn't as bold as she thought, or as over her insecurities. At least she still had that first kiss…and all the kisses that had come after. Her prince had given her the most glorious night of her life, even if it hadn't ended in his bed. But she would always remember the way Mark had kissed her with abandon, held her with the unabashed yearning of a man lost to his libido, and literally swept her off her feet. She had replayed every sinful, decadent moment at least a hundred times in the past thirty-six hours. Unfortunately, she would never know what Mark looked like under that tuxedo. He was there. She was here. She hardly knew anything about him, and she hadn't told him anything about her. Their evening was destined to become just a memory. But what a wonderful memory it would be.

Well, except for when she bolted from his room like a scared rabbit.

After hurrying back to the elevator, her hands had trembled as she pushed the elevator button for the fourth flour, returning to the downstairs ballroom just as Sonya had been about to perform.

Daniel spied her in the crowd and scooped her to his side. "Where have you been? I looked everywhere. You almost missed her." He waved toward the stage as Sonya's dance partner led her to the center.

Tongue-tied, she shrugged. "I went to the restroom."

The lie came as easily as she'd gone upstairs with Mark.

But yesterday morning, on the drive back to Indy, she had leveled with Daniel and told him the truth.

"Karma!" he'd said, eyes wide and mouth opened in astonishment. "I didn't know you were such a wild woman."

"I'm not." She frowned and looked out the window.

"What do you mean?"

"I chickened out."

"You what?"

"I got up to his room, and everything was great, and then…" She thought about how Mark had pressed his hand against her breast, and her breath caught in her throat all over again. "I just couldn't."

"Why not? What happened?"

She turned her attention to the passing cornfields being plowed for planting, still feeling Mark's arm around her waist and the way his dark eyes had consumed her. That exhilarating free-fall feeling shot through her belly the way it did every time she recalled the way he kissed her. How could she admit the truth? That as soon as Mark's hand had touched her breast, the taunts of her brother, his friends, and her classmates from grade school had exploded inside her head. In that instant, the last thing she had been capable of was undressing in front of him. Damn her stupid brother and his damn friends for messing up her mind like that. And damn her for allowing them to still have such an insidious effect on her.

"It doesn't matter," she had said softly as she touched her fingertips to her lips. She could almost feel Mark kissing her, could still taste the scotch he'd been drinking.

She and Daniel hadn't talked about the incident the rest of the way home, but if Mark were a drug, she would gladly take another hit.

Even now, as she caressed the satin and mentally returned to Mark's room, she regretted running away. What if she hadn't been spooked? What if her childhood memories hadn't ruined the moment? Would Mark have made love to her? It had been years since she'd had sex. And it had never been that great. In fact, it had downright sucked. Mark hadn't seemed like the kind of man who sucked at sex. On the contrary, he seemed more than capable at giving pleasure, and she had definitely felt all kinds of yumminess happening inside her body just from his kisses. Mark certainly could have given her what her first two lovers—and she was being generous using that term for Brian and Richard—had failed to deliver.

A wistful smile touched her lips. For one night, she had been desirable. She had almost succeeded in becoming someone else, but the good girl inside had stopped her from letting go of reality completely.

If she had a second chance—a do-over—she wouldn't run. She would embrace it and not let her inexperience and the past scare her away. Things had just moved so quickly, and she hadn't been with a guy in so damn long that she'd frozen up like a dummy. The same way she had the first time a boy kissed her.

What a nightmare that had been. She'd been in ninth grade and a member of the cross-country team. It had been late when the team returned to school after an away meet, and she and a boy named Tony went to get something out of his locker. She liked Tony, and she was pretty sure he liked her, too, so she was excited he had asked her to go to his locker with him. As she waited, he pulled out a couple of books, his back to her. Then, out of nowhere, he spun and smashed his mouth against hers. Her eyes shot open wide, and she locked up like a switched-off C-3PO, arms and legs rigid, unable to breathe, unable to move. Not even her mouth. Her mind screamed to kiss him back, but her lips refused. They formed a tight O like on a blow-up doll and rebuffed any attempt to unknot, even when Tony shoved his tongue against them over and over.

It had to have been the worst kiss in the history of bad kisses, but she had still floated out to her mom's car afterward. Up to that point in her life, she had never felt anything more titillating, more exciting, more arousing.

But she'd been a silly kid, and so had Tony. He had pattered around after her a couple more weeks, but she had no idea how to talk to him anymore. She still liked him, but she didn't know what to say, and she certainly didn't know how to act. Tony must have gotten discouraged, because he eventually stopped coming around, and in that silent way that kids drift away from what scares them, she drifted away from Tony.

He never tried to kiss her again, and a few months later, he had moved on to another girl. One who probably hadn't turned into a stupid, lockjawed robot when he put the moves on her.

In a lot of ways, she was still that scared little girl. Terrified of boys, unsure what to do, how to act, what to say. Exhibit A, Saturday night with Mark.

With a sigh, she slid the dress inside its garment bag and sealed away her fairy tale once and for all. Then she plucked a chiffon blouse and a navy blue blazer and slacks from their hangers and headed back into her bedroom.

Back to reality.

An hour later, while Karma fixed a cup of tea in the break room, her friend and coworker Lisa corralled her. "Welcome back from vacation. How was your trip to Chicago?" The glint in Lisa's eyes as she poured her coffee gave away that she had already talked to Daniel and knew all about Karma's escapades.

"Fine." Karma furtively slid past her and out the door.

"That's not what I hear." Lisa tagged along.

"Don't you have work to do?" Karma glanced over her shoulder. "Humans to resource or something?" Lisa was three years older than Karma and worked in Solar's Human Resources Department.

"It can wait. Hearing about your steamy Saturday night is way more exciting."

They made their way upstairs to Karma's desk.

"There's really nothing to tell." She wanted to put the incident behind her. Saturday and her waltz through fantasyland were over. She couldn't dwell on what could have been…or even what *had* been, no matter how incredible it was. Doing so would be unhealthy and only distract her, especially when there was no hope of ever seeing Mark again. He was a fleeting moment in time. A blip on her radar of good judgment.

Lisa sidled up to the counter in front of her desk. "That's not what Daniel said."

Karma opened her e-mail and winced at the more than three hundred unread messages. This was the problem with taking a week's vacation. She'd need another vacation to recover from this one.

"And what did Daniel tell you?" she said, abandoning her overflowing inbox.

"That you were the most stunning woman in the room. And I believe it. Daniel texted me a picture of you in that *amaaaaazing* dress. Girl, that picture didn't even look like you. So sexified." Lisa sipped her coffee, her brown eyes twinkling. "*Aaannnd*, Daniel told me you had a little mini tryst with some hot, mysterious man." She coyly lifted one shoulder as she offered Karma a sidelong glance.

"He was nobody." Karma concentrated on a stray tea leaf floating in her mug.

"Uh-huh. That's why your face just turned as red as that dress you wore Saturday night."

There was no way Karma could hide the effect Mark had had on her—that he was *still* having on her. Men like him, who were urbane and held themselves in a calm yet controlled way that deigned the world as theirs, weren't easily forgotten. In Chicago, they were probably the norm, but in Indiana, where conservatism ruled and false modesty was a way of life for the wealthy, she had never come up against a man like Mark, and she had certainly never imagined catching such a man's eye.

Lisa checked her watch. "Well, you can tell me all about him later. I've got to get back. Some consultant is coming in today and I need to print off a few personnel reports for him."

"Consultant?"

Shadows crossed Lisa's face. "I found out Friday."

Karma knew a consultant coming in wasn't good news. This could mean layoffs.

"He'll be working with Don," Lisa said, hugging her coffee mug inside her palms.

Don Jacoby was the Director of Operations and Karma's boss.

"Great," Karma said. "That means *I'll* be working for him. Just what I need. Not that I'm already behind since Jolene doesn't pull her share of the weight in *her* department."

Lisa smiled sympathetically. "I know. But look at the bright side. Maybe this consultant will see what's going on with Jo, and if he recommends letting anyone go, it will be her." Her cheery smile was almost comical.

Lisa's ability to see the silver linings in all bad situations was refreshing, and Karma was grateful for her optimism. "I can only hope."

Jolene was an expert at skirting her work, which meant the sales managers often came to Karma for administrative support. Don understood the situation, and as long as his work took priority, she was free to assist the sales teams when necessary.

Still, the dysfunction added to an already defective relationship. Jolene was best friends with Karma's brother and sister-in-law and had been since they were kids, which meant she had been part of the posse that had made her childhood a living hell. The ramifications of which Karma was still feeling as an adult if her rapid exodus from Mark's room Saturday night was any indication.

As if all that wasn't enough, Jo was also the office's biggest gossip.

"Good morning," Jolene said, coming around the corner.

Speak of the devil.

Jo's gaze remained glued to her cell phone. Her long blond hair flowed like a cape behind her and her abundant breasts jiggled under a top that looked one size too small but perfect on her.

Karma exchanged glances with Lisa as Jolene passed and disappeared down the hall toward the Sales Department. Jo hadn't even looked at them. Thank goodness, or Karma might have laughed.

"Okay, girl. I'll talk to you later." Lisa cradled her coffee and headed back toward the stairs. "Remember, you owe me all the sordid details."

"Yeah, yeah." Karma waved her off and dug into her e-mail.

At eight fifty-five, just as Karma sat back down at her desk from making another cup of tea, her phone rang. It was Nancy from the front desk.

"Yes?"

"Don's nine o'clock is here."

Karma rolled her eyes at the obvious flirtatious drawl in Nancy's voice. Apparently Mr. Streamline-The-Jobs-Right-Out-The-Door-To-Get-Solar-Back-In-The-Black was also Mr. Catch-Nancy's-Eye. But then, what warm-blooded man with an ounce of sex appeal didn't catch Nancy's eye? She was a cougar who hungered for young man blood.

"I'll be right down." She hung up and poked her head into Don's office. "Your appointment is here. Are you ready for him?"

Don looked up from his tablet. "Yes. Absolutely. Thank you." He quickly began tidying his desk.

Even Don seemed a little nervous, but that was understandable. This guy was coming in to plow through Don's domain and pick the meat of his department from its bones.

She reached the top of the stairs and tugged at the hem of her blazer as she peered over the railing. Just her luck, their visitor was under the stairwell so she couldn't steal a peek at what had so obviously caught Nancy's eye.

As she descended, she glanced at Nancy, who sat at the reception desk, smiling coyly, her gaze locked like a viper's on the area under the stairs. Did Nancy know no shame? She wasn't even trying to hide her lust.

Susan from Accounting walked past, her cheeks flushed, a girlish grin toying her mouth. Her eyes flicked sideways as she passed by the hidden alcove.

What was with everyone? What was she about to see when she turned the corner? The way Nancy and Susan practically drooled over the consultant, she was starting to get a little nervous.

She reached the bottom step, turned, took a few steps, and nearly tripped over her half-inch heels.

Oh. My. God.

It was her prince.

Chapter 6

Forget the fairy tale.
-Author Unknown

Mark wore a tailored, navy pin-striped suit that fit his athletic build even better than the tuxedo he had worn on Saturday. His dark brown hair was slightly mussed but not messy, and he was just as sexy today as two nights ago, flipping casually through the latest issue of *Sports Illustrated.*

Karma gathered herself. "M-Mr. Strong?"

"Yes." He spun toward her as he closed the magazine and dropped it on the lobby table. Then his eyes narrowed and his brow furrowed. It was the expression of someone who knew her but couldn't quite place her face. "Have we met?"

Was she so different in her real clothes that he didn't recognize her? With her real hair and her real shoes? She had recognized him immediately, but he didn't know who she was, even after how intimate they had become with one another. She glanced at the floor and smoothed her palms over her blazer as much to dry them as to find something to do with her hands.

When she met his gaze again, she saw realization dawn in his expression. The hard line of his brow softened and rose briefly before crinkling in awareness.

He cleared his throat, straightened his tie, and smiled. "Small world."

"Yes, it would seem so." She held out her hand. "I'm Don's assistant, Karma Mason."

The ruse of being a model was officially over, not that he'd believed her in the first place. She was a whole lot of nobody special. She wasn't a model or a rich, Chicago socialite, or even Cinderella. She was Karma, executive assistant by day, wannabe journalist by night, and about as conservative as Mother Teresa, even if her innermost thoughts seemed to have taken a more liberal track in the last few days.

Mama T would not approve.

Mark's brow ticked with awareness, and he took her hand as he tilted his head slightly to one side. "Pleased to *finally* meet you, Karma."

The choice of his words, as well as his inflection, made it clear he referred to the fact that he had never actually gotten to know her, just as she had never really gotten to know him. So much for charades, because there was no way to hide the truth, anymore.

His gaze swept with swift efficiency down her body and back to her face. The once-over took all of a second, but she felt stripped on the spot, as if he were kissing her again, right there, in Solar's lobby, casting away her logic and reason with little more than a glance.

She gestured toward the stairs. "I'll take you up to Don's office." Forcing her feet to move was like slogging through mud. Or maybe nearly set concrete.

"Karma," he said thoughtfully as they started up the stairs. "So, you're Don's assistant?"

"Yes." She took hold of the railing, willing her legs to stay under her.

"You know, I recently met a woman named Karma. She was…intriguing."

Oh boy. Breathe, just breathe.

Heat flooded her face. "What a coincidence." Her wobbly legs threatened to give out. Mark was so not what she'd expected today. She had thought she would never see him again, yet here he was, in her world instead of his.

This was no longer a fantasy. It was a nightmare.

When Mark had arrived at Solar this morning, the last thing he had expected was to come face-to-face with the woman who had captivated his thoughts the better part of yesterday. He had felt awful about how he had treated her Saturday night and had racked his brain to figure out a way to learn her identity and how he could reach her to at least send a note of apology. He never imagined he would actually see her again. And now, here she was, leading him up the stairs to meet with Don Jacoby…apparently her boss. Talk about your strokes of luck.

He trailed behind her, studying her mannish suit, the unremarkable, low-heeled patent leather shoes, and the tight chignon holding all that beautiful hair in a bundle that denied its glory. Her story and everything about her was beginning to make sense. Her innocence, her mystique, the way she had seemed so unsure in that dress. And yet, the dress and the strappy gold stilettos had seemed to fit her personality better than this masculine garb and clunky footwear.

"So, not a model," he said at the top of the stairs as he fell in beside her.

Her cheeks flushed. "No, not a model." She lowered her gaze to the floor then started down the hall.

The self-conscious gesture tugged at his curiosity. Seeing her here, in her regular surroundings, wearing what he could only guess were her regular clothes, with her hair pulled into what was probably her regular hairstyle, he couldn't integrate the woman in front of him with the woman he had met this past weekend. They were two totally different people sharing one body. Which persona was real? Which one was a front?

"Nothing wrong with that," he said. "Models are too high maintenance, anyway." He had dated a model once. Never again.

She looked up at him. "High maintenance?"

"Absolutely." He lightly elbowed her arm. "Being an executive assistant is much better."

Biting her bottom lip as she smiled, she turned her attention to the front again.

Life had given him another opportunity to set things right. To apologize and behave like a gentleman instead of a heathen ass.

"Karma, I wanted to—"

"Mark, good to see you again." Don walked around the corner, hand outstretched.

Mark had met Don only once, during his off-site meeting with Solar's executive team a few weeks ago.

His apology momentarily interrupted, he shook Don's hand. "Likewise."

Don led him away from Karma, toward his office. "Can I get you a cup of coffee? Water?"

"Coffee's fine." He glanced over his shoulder, wishing he'd had just a few more seconds with Karma.

Don turned toward her. "Karma, could you please grab Mark a cup of coffee? Thank you."

Under the circumstances, with his apology still sitting on his tongue, Mark hated that Karma now rushed away to fetch him a cup of coffee like some waitress. It smacked of salt on a wound. Mark would have preferred helping himself, but he followed Don into his office, set down his briefcase, and unbuttoned his jacket as he took a seat.

A moment later, Karma appeared beside him, holding a steaming mug of coffee. She handed him cream and sugar separately. "I didn't know how you take it."

"Black, one sugar," he said, mesmerized by her pale green eyes the same way he had been Saturday night. "But this is perfect. Thank you."

With a polite nod, she turned and exited the office, closing the door behind her.

As he and Don forged past the usual pleasantries and started in on the business at hand, he vowed to follow up on that apology as soon as he got the chance. Life had given him a second opportunity to make things right, and he refused to waste it.

Chapter 7

One of the essential principles for living an aspired life is to remember that our desires don't arrive on our schedule. They arrive when they're supposed to.

-Wayne Dyer

Karma collapsed into her chair, picked up her phone, and dialed Lisa's extension.

"Hey," Lisa said over the line. "What's up?"

"It's *him*," she whispered.

"Who's him?"

"The *consultant*." Karma glanced around to make sure no one was listening. "It's him, the guy I met Saturday night."

Lisa took a moment to make the connection. "WHAT?" She quickly lowered her voice. "Are you serious?"

"Yes. What do I do?"

Lisa paused then giggled. "Go home and put on that incredible dress."

"I'm being serious." How could Lisa joke at a time like this? "I am so screwed."

"Whoa, hold on, just wait a minute. You are not screwed."

"But—"

"Karma, listen to me." Lisa's voice grew softer. "No one else knows. Just you, him, Daniel, and me, and I'm not going to tell anyone."

"But what if someone finds out?" She sounded as panicked as she felt.

"Now, just relax. Take a deep breath, Karma."

She forced herself to inhale heavily then blew out a loud breath.

Lisa continued. "You two didn't do anything wrong, and so what if you did?"

"But—"

Lisa cut her off. "Uh-uh. No. You've done nothing wrong, and you're not going to get in trouble."

Karma lowered her voice even further. "This is a nightmare."

Lisa laughed.

"You think this is funny?"

"Actually, yes. You're freaking out over nothing."

"This isn't nothing. This is a man I kissed, who took me to his hotel room." A man she would have slept with if she hadn't been such a chickenshit.

"More power to you, sister."

"Lisa!"

"Oh my God, girl. Go for it. He's here. Don't you think this is a sign?"

"A sign? Yes, it's a sign I never should have gone Saturday night."

Lisa sighed. "You're hopeless. No, what I mean is don't you think it's a sign that the two of you were meant to hook up? I mean, you met Saturday night in Chicago, and now he's here. Don't you think that's more than just a coincidence?"

Lisa and her signs. Like Daniel, she was forever thinking life was one constant circle of signs and metaphysical influence.

"What about the nonfraternization policy? Shouldn't you be telling me to stay away, not hook up with him?"

"Are you kidding me? Hell no. And you know how lax the company is about that stupid policy. If you want him and he still wants you, I say go for it. I won't tell anyone."

True. The company all but referred to their nonfrat policy as more a guideline than a hard and fast rule. Still, Karma couldn't imagine "going for it." That wasn't how she behaved, at least not in the real world. Sure, just this morning she had wanted a second chance, but that was before her prince had turned into Solar's new consultant. This fantasy had just taken a very real turn.

"I can't do that." She sounded more like she was trying to convince herself than Lisa.

"Oh, Karma, live a little. Have some fun for a change. Just keep it on the down-low."

Karma shot a glance to Don's closed door. "Aren't you supposed to advise against this sort of thing?"

"Not when it's you we're talking about."

"What's that supposed to mean?"

"Just that I have your best interests in mind before Solar's. And I think you need to go for it with this guy. There's a reason he's here. It's a sign, I'm telling you."

"I don't know, Leese." She didn't want to put any credence on the *it's-a-sign* theory.

"What's not to know?" An exaggerated sigh came through the line. "Just...okay, all I'm saying is to keep yourself open to the idea. It could be fun, and I saw that smitten look on your face when we were talking about him this morning." Lisa made a breathy noise. "And Lord knows you could use a little bow-chicka-wow-wow."

"Oh my God, really?"

"Oh, you know what I mean."

Yes, Karma knew all too well what Lisa meant. If a woman could become a born-again virgin, she *was* one.

"You're not helping, Leese."

"I am so. You're just not listening."

"I gotta go." This conversation was going nowhere.

She hung up and stared at the closed door again. Behind it, not even twenty feet away, was the most captivating man she had ever met. A man she had lied to, kissed, and almost done unspeakable things with in his hotel room. But also a man she had fled from like a silly adolescent girl when things had gotten too hot. Just like she had done to Tony back in high school.

She dropped her head into her hands.

God, shoot me now.

At four thirty, Karma wrapped up the day's work and prepared to go home. Mark's arrival, which felt more like a head-on collision, had left her mentally exhausted, and all she wanted was to escape to a pair of sweats, an oversized T-shirt, and an evening on her couch.

Just as she was filing the final operational report from last week, Mark stepped out of the conference room, which had become his makeshift office. "Karma, do you have a minute?"

She glanced toward Don's closed door. He had left fifteen minutes ago to take his wife to the airport, so only she and Mark remained. "Uh, sure." She closed her e-mail and followed him into the conference room.

The door latched quietly behind her as he closed it.

"I wanted to talk to you about Saturday night." He took a seat.

Of course he did.

She sat down, folded her hands in her lap, and closed her eyes for a moment to gather her courage to face the elephant that had stood between them all day. He was probably upset that she hadn't told him the truth about who she was. If she had been honest, maybe he wouldn't have walked into Solar deaf, dumb, and blind, and she wouldn't have been caught off guard.

"I'm sorry," she blurted at the same time he did.

Her cheeks heated and she looked away as he smiled.

"Why are you apologizing?" he said. "You didn't do anything wrong."

"I lied about who I am."

"You *innocently misled* me." He sounded like a lawyer leading his witness.

"Same thing."

He paused then said, "I think you already know that I knew you weren't a model." His dark, benevolent eyes softened what could have been a much harder blow under the circumstances.

All she had wanted was to pretend to be someone else for a night. If she had known what the consequences of her actions would be, she would have reconsidered her behavior.

"But that's not what I want to talk to you about." He cleared his throat. "I wanted to apologize for how I behaved. With you, I mean."

This was surprising. "Why?"

He sighed. "I never should have taken you to my room. I made assumptions and moved way too fast." He met her gaze with sincerity. "Yes, I found you attractive, and yes, I enjoyed our time together, but taking you to my room like some one-night stand isn't who I am. It's not who I aspire to be, and you deserve better than that." His lips pressed into a thin line. "I don't normally treat women so casually, Karma, and I just wanted to apologize for my behavior." He took a moment to study her.

All she could do was stare.

"And I'd like to make it up to you. Let me take you to dinner and show you that I do know how to behave myself while in the company of a beautiful woman." He grinned and one lone dimple creased his right cheek.

He wanted to take her to dinner? This just got better and better. Lisa's words crept back into her thoughts. *Go for it.* Was she really considering doing just that?

"Tonight?"

"Actually, tonight I'm meeting your boss for dinner, but if you're free Friday night, I've made reservations at St. Elmo's." Then, as an afterthought, "I never miss an opportunity to eat at St. Elmo's when I come to Indy."

Tonight, Friday night, who cared? All that mattered was that he was asking her out. Well, asking her to dinner. This wasn't a date, just him atoning for whatever guilt he might be harboring about this weekend.

Still, Karma had thought all the embers of Saturday night's fairy tale had turned to cold ash, but apparently, one still smoldered. Mark had used that word again—beautiful. And with that one word, the evening, the dress, the shoes, and the magic all flared back to life. Once more, she was Cinderella, and how could Cinderella say no to her prince, especially after he'd just called her beautiful again?

Chapter 8

Serendipity: The effect by which one accidentally stumbles upon something truly wonderful, especially while looking for something entirely unrelated.
-Author Unknown

On Tuesday morning, Karma was making a mug of tea in the break room, her mind backtracking to Saturday night in Chicago, when Mark walked in and placed a couple of bottles of juice in the fridge.

"You should label those," she said, shoving aside the memory of his kiss. "Otherwise, they might not be there when you come back for them later."

"Thanks for the tip." He cozied up beside her and poured a cup of coffee. He smelled clean, like soap and aftershave, and his hair was slightly damp. "You wouldn't happen to have a Sharpie, would you?" How did every word out of his mouth sound like a come-on?

She opened a nearby drawer. "We keep some in here."

He pulled out a marker, returned to the fridge, and marked his initials on the caps of the bottles. Then he tossed the marker back in the drawer. "By the way, good morning." He added a packet of sugar to his coffee.

"Good morning." She lifted her tea, blew on it, and took a sip. Pleasant tension settled between them, as if he were remembering their time together in Chicago, too.

After he stirred the sugar into his coffee, he flipped the stir stick into the trash, picked up his cup, and followed her out.

"Do you think you could recommend a few local restaurants?" he said. "I haven't had a chance to stock my kitchen, yet, and could use some suggestions so I don't get stuck in a rut."

"Kitchen?"

"Yes. My company set me up in a condo while I'm here."

"Oh, okay. Sure, I could recommend a few places. What kinds of food do you like?"

They reached the stairs and headed up. "I'm pretty flexible. Maybe something unique to Clover. Little mom-and-pop places or specialty spots unique to the city."

"Okay. I'll make a list for you." Why did she feel like they were making small talk for small talk's sake?

At her desk, he departed for the conference room, and Karma

stared after him. Should she seek cover or stand in an open field waiting for lightning to strike? Because that's how it felt to be around him.

After Pilates Wednesday night, Karma swung by her favorite pizza place, Greek Tony's, for dinner. The quaint dive didn't look like much, with Formica tables, wood paneling walls, and a mish-mash of mirrored pictures depicting various brands of beer alongside portraits of local sports teams the small restaurant had sponsored over the years. But you couldn't beat the food. This was the real deal. The best pizza and Italian subs in Clover.

"Hi, Andrew," she said to the twentysomething behind the counter. She was on a first-name basis with most of the staff, and Andrew was her favorite. He was always quick with a smile and knew what she ordered by heart.

"Hi, Karma. The usual?" Andrew didn't even wait for her to agree before he started entering her order.

"Please. Thank you." Karma pulled out her credit card, paid, and then took her small cup to the soda fountain and filled it with cherry Coke.

When she turned and looked for a place to sit, she smiled when her gaze met Mark's. He was sitting at a table along the wall, watching her. It was as if fate was trying to send her a message. He just kept popping up everywhere she went.

Ugh. She was starting to sound like Lisa. *It's a sign!*

He waved to the empty chair across from him, and after a heartbeat's hesitation, she decided to join him. They hadn't talked much the past three days, but she had begun helping him pull reports and work up correspondence. There was no reason why she shouldn't share a table with him.

"Wow, our second date, and I'm not even trying," he said with a smile as she approached.

"Is this a date?" She took a seat.

He laughed. "Sure. Why not?" He took a bite of his sandwich.

"What have you got there?" She nodded toward his sub and sipped her Coke.

He wiped sauce from the corner of his mouth, chewed, and swallowed. "Stromboli."

"I've never had it, but I'm sure it's delicious."

"It is." He took another bite. "Want some?"

"No, that's okay."

"No, really. You should try it."

She bit her lip. "Okay, why not?"

He tore off a messy chunk dripping with sauce and held it across the table. Obviously, he intended to feed her. With a nervous little chuff, she leaned forward and opened her mouth. He popped the bite between her lips then sat back.

"Well?" he said as she chewed.

She finished the bite and swallowed. "It's good, but then, it's Tony's. Everything's good here."

"Well, when you wrote 'best pizza in town' beside their name on the list you gave me, there was no way I could resist."

"You like pizza?"

"I like Italian."

She took a closer look at him. He had the right features, the dark hair, and a slightly olive complexion. "Are you Italian?"

He swallowed another bite. "Half. My mother is Italian, but you'd never know it listening to her talk. Her English is perfect. You only hear the Italian influence when she says things like 'mozzarella' or 'bruschetta.'"

She liked how he said both words with a foreign accent. "Do you speak Italian, too?"

"Yes, but I'm out of practice."

"Say something."

He thought a moment. "*Mi piace passare del tempo con te.*"

Who would have thought a foreign language could sound so sexy? "What did you say?"

"I enjoy spending time with you."

She smiled as her cheeks flamed.

"*Sei carina quando arrossisci.*"

She giggled even though she had no idea what he'd said. It just sounded like something that would make her giggle. "What does that mean?"

"You're cute when you blush." Then he said, "*Mi piace farti arrossire.*"

"What did you say?"

His eyes twinkled. "I like making you blush."

Warmth filtered down to her neck as she hid her face. "How do you say 'you're good at it'?"

He laughed. "*Sei bravo a farlo.*"

"Well, *sei bravo a farlo* then."

"*Si. Grazie.*"

"I can tell I'm going to have to learn Italian."

"It's not too hard."

"Says one who already knows the language."

Andrew appeared with her sub and set it in front of her then headed back behind the counter.

Mark nodded toward her sandwich. "So, what's 'the usual'?"

Obviously, he had heard the exchange with Andrew when she ordered.

"Meatball sub."

"I would never have guessed that."

"Why not?"

"You just don't seem like a meatball sub type."

"What type do I look like?" She blew on the edge of the sandwich before taking a cautious bite, trying not to burn her tongue.

"Salad. Sushi. Tofu."

She wrinkled her nose. "Tofu?"

"I guess that's a no?"

"Yes, that's a no. I prefer real meat."

He nodded toward her sub. "I can tell. That looks terrific."

"Want a bite?" She cut off a piping hot piece and blew on it then held it out just as he had done for her. He leaned forward and gingerly took it into his mouth.

"So? What do you think?" Karma bit off another chunk.

"I think I'll have to get that next time. That's delicious."

"I know, right?"

They ate in silence for a moment.

"So, your mom is Italian. What about your dad?"

"He's got some Italian in him, too, but he's mostly Greek. What about you?"

"English on my mom's side, mostly German on my dad's."

They made more small talk as they finished their meal, then Mark sat back. "So, what do you do for fun?"

She shrugged. "I usually just hang out with my friends." *Lame.* He was probably used to going to parties and social events every other night.

"And where do you go?"

"Mostly, we just stay in or go out to eat."

He stood and gestured toward the door. "Come on. Let's go." He had a presumptuous expression on his face.

"Where?"

"It's a surprise."

"I don't know. I should probably just go home."

"And miss the fun. No way. Come on." He nodded toward the exit. "Come with me. It'll be fun, I promise."

She sighed and bit her lip. Should she go with him? Her cautious side sat on one shoulder, legs crossed, admonishing her for even considering it. On her other shoulder, her new goddess side she had discovered Saturday night hopped up and down, pumping its little fist. "Go, go, go!" it seemed to be saying.

The goddess won.

"Okay, sure, why not?" Once more, she went against everything she'd been taught. *Don't go to strange men's hotel rooms. Don't get into a strange man's car.* But Mark really wasn't a stranger, anymore. Not really.

He drove her toward downtown Clover and parallel parked along the packed road in front of Finnigan's. Loud music poured into the street when someone opened the door.

A sign out front read Ladies Night. Another read Karaoke 7-11PM.

"What are we doing here?" Karma said.

Mark held the door for her then followed her in. "I passed by here on my way to dinner and thought it looked like fun."

Music blared. The place was packed for a Wednesday night.

They managed to find a small, vacant table crammed in the back corner.

"Stay here. I'll get us a couple of drinks," Mark said as she sat down. "What would you like?"

"Virgin daiquiri." She had to drive later, so it was non-alcoholic for her.

He gave her a look. "Oh come on. Just one drink. It'll work out of your system before you drive home. Live a little. Have some fun."

She nibbled her bottom lip then said, "Okay, a margarita." The list of things she'd been taught not to do but did anyway continued to grow.

"Be right back." He disappeared into the crowd.

Finnigan's was abuzz with laughter and music, and drinks were flowing, making the men bold and the women daring. A couple of platinum blondes with obvious breast implants hawked Mark as he made his way to the bar, and a stab of jealousy sent green-eyed shards through her blood. As if she had a right to be jealous. The taller of the two touched his arm to get his attention then said something. He smiled politely and shook his head before continuing to the bar.

Whatever he told them left them with disappointed faces.

Good for Mark.

She settled into her chair. While waiting for him to return, she checked her watch. Seven thirty. It seemed that the karaoke was in a break, or maybe it just wasn't late enough for the patrons to be drunk enough to have the guts to sing.

Karma had always said she wanted to try karaoke, but every time she got a chance, she chickened out. She'd been told she was a good singer, but the idea of singing on stage made her squeamish. Singing in front of friends was one thing, but in front of strangers was another. What if she messed up? What if she sang off-key? The fear of embarrassment was greater than her desire to let loose, so karaoke remained on her bucket list.

Where was Mark? He had been gone an awfully long time.

She had just begun to search the crowd by the bar when the music cut off and the spotlight shone on the stage.

On Mark!

She gasped and sat forward as the music for Pharrell's "Happy" started. Behind him, on a large screen, the video began to play, but all eyes were on him.

He started to sing and every woman in the bar fixed him in her sights. A split second later the place erupted into a frenzy. Mark could sing. And he could dance. And for a man with such a deep voice, he had a hot falsetto. Every woman in the room, including her, fell a little bit in love.

She could only sit, stunned, and watch, mesmerized by his loose hips and fast feet. By the end of the song, most of the bar's patrons were on their feet, singing along, dancing and clapping. Then the cheers and whistles rose again as he bowed and waved to the crowd.

For about a minute, Mark was the star of the evening as he forged his way through the crowd to their table, drinks in hand. He set hers in front of her.

"That was great," she said as he sat down. "I didn't know you could sing."

"Double threat. Dancing. Singing." A thin film of perspiration coated his forehead. "My parents are professional dancers."

Well, that explained his moves. Apparently, some of Mom's and Dad's talent had rubbed off.

"Well, everyone loved you." She sipped her drink.

"And they'll love you, too."

"Huh?" She wasn't sure she'd heard him right.

"You're next," he said.

"What?" She froze mid-sip as what felt like ice water broke through her veins.

He gestured toward the stage, grinning wickedly. "You're up. They're waiting for you."

"WHAT!" This was what she got for getting into a strange man's car, going to his room last Saturday night, and agreeing to drink alcohol when she would have to drive later. Punishment.

He laughed. "Oh go on. It'll be fun."

"I can't—"

"Yes, you can. The words are right there on the screen. It's easy."

"Mark." She was whining, but she didn't care. "Are you trying to humiliate me?"

He shook his head and squeezed her hand. "Oh come on. It's not that bad."

"Yes it is." What he was asking was the equivalent of throwing her into the ocean without a life preserver when she didn't know how to swim…in the middle of a hurricane.

"Oh, go on. You know if you don't you'll regret it."

A spotlight turned on her.

"Don't make me do this," she said.

He pointed toward the stage. "They're waiting. No one else can go until you do." He took her hand and helped her out of her seat.

"Mark, no…"

"You'll be great." He gave her a gentle nudge, and she nearly tripped over her own feet. "Come on, everybody," he yelled into the crowd. "Give her a little encouragement. It's her first time."

Really? He had to make virgin references at a time like this?

But the crowd cheered. A couple of men beside her clapped her on the back. "You'll be fine," one said.

"Just try to imagine everyone naked," said the other.

"I don't think that'll help." But she was walking now.

Toward the stage.

All eyes on her.

The spotlight warm.

This had to be how death row inmates felt on their final walk to the electric chair…or however they did that sort of thing now.

The walk took far too little time, and the next thing she knew she was in front of the DJ who was working the karaoke setup.

"What am I supposed to sing?" she said.

"What would you like?"

She shrugged. "I have no idea." Her voice broke and sounded a little higher than usual. "I've never done this."

"How about 'Royals' by Lorde?" he said. "It's usually a good one for first-timers. Easy. Slow. Kinda one note."

She knew that song. She had sung along to it on the radio a few times. "Okay." Maybe this wouldn't be so bad.

"Just watch the monitor. The lyrics will come up for you a couple of seconds before you need to sing them."

"Okay," she said again. *God, kill me now.*

He smiled. "You'll be fine. Just relax." He winked and nodded toward the stage, indicating she should get ready.

Uh-huh. Relax. Learning how to breathe underwater would be easier. How had she let Mark talk her into this?

Her heart raced, her palms were sweaty, and her whole body trembled, but she managed to make her way to the microphone.

The music started. With the light shining in her eyes, she could barely see Mark all the way in the back, in the shadows, but could tell he was sitting with his arm over the back of the chair she had just vacated.

Her voice shook as she sang the first line, but at least she was on key.

She continued and fell a little off-key on the second line when it dipped into her lower register, but she was back on track when she sang the third line.

As she continued to sing, she began to relax. In the front of the crowd, by the stage, a couple of men watched her appreciatively, a glint in their eyes. Their suggestive gazes reminded her of Saturday night, the red dress, the way the men at the benefit had appraised her.

And then something wondrous began to happen. She began to enjoy herself. Maybe it was the adrenaline, or the spotlight, or the crowd swaying and singing along with her, or maybe it was the fact that her goddess alter ego—the one she discovered in Chicago and who relished the attention—was dancing and laughing inside her mind. Whatever the reason, with every line she sang, she fell a little bit more in love with being on stage.

She fed off the energy of the crowd, off the electricity of the room, off the intensity of her own adrenaline.

By the time she reached the final chorus, she was holding the audience in the palm of her hand and didn't want to leave the stage.

They cheered for her. They whistled and cried for more. She covered her face with one hand, trying not to laugh, then set the microphone back on the stand and headed toward the steps.

The DJ high-fived her. "That kicked ass!"

Now she did laugh, pure elation singing from every cell in her body. Then she darted into the crowd, back to her table and into Mark's arms as he scooped her up and hugged her.

"That was incredible," he said, setting her down.

"Oh my God, I can't believe I did that." She clapped her hands on the sides of her face, too torqued up to sit. "That was so awesome! I've never done that before. Can I go back up there? Can we do it again? I want—"

His lips crashed down on hers, and her soul lit like a supernova as her rambling thoughts ceased, replaced by a whole lot of Mark. Every part of him invaded every part of her for what felt like a very long time. When he finally pulled away, they were seated, and she was in his lap, but she didn't remember sitting down.

"Uhhh…" His eyes twinkled mischievously. "Sorry?" His apology lilted like a question as his gaze searched hers. He looked like he was barely suppressing his surprise at his own actions.

His arms held her tightly, his hands pressed securely against her back.

"Wow," she said flatly, awestruck and numb. She touched her fingertips to her lips, which lifted slightly at the corners as she gazed into his eyes.

He stared at her mouth for what felt like a minute, his eyes dazzling with mischief. "That was nice."

Nice? Try hot. Smoking. Sizzling.

He gently lifted her off his lap, and she managed to find her own chair again.

"That was out of line, wasn't it?" He pursed his lips as if stifling a grin.

"Um…" Her heart raced, her mind leaped with a hundred torrid thoughts, and every fiber in her body vibrated. And yet she couldn't speak.

He straightened his shirt and took a deep breath. "I promise to behave now." He crossed the tip of his index finger over his heart. And were his cheeks flushed?

Karma turned her attention back to her drink and the stage, but his kiss continued to burn its way through her body, making her breathless and aroused. She glanced at him out of the corner of her eyes. That's when it hit her. She didn't want him to behave. But did she really want him to *misbehave*? That could pose a problem now that they worked together.

With one kiss, Mark Strong had flummoxed her…and excited her.

And damn her, she wanted more.

Chapter 9

Don't forget to love yourself.
-Soren Kierkegaard

Thursday night, Karma was cleaning up dinner dishes, still daydreaming about the night before…and the Saturday before that…and all the wonderful moments she'd spent with Mark so far. The way his lips had felt against hers. The way he looked at her. The way his hand had felt on the small of her back. The dusting of dark hair on the backs of his hands.

She wanted to slowly unbutton his shirt and run her hands over his chest and down his stomach…see if he had dark hair everywhere. What if he did? What would that feel like against her fingers? Would it be coarse or soft? Thick or, like on his hands, only a dusting? He probably had a nice stomach, too, ribbed with muscles. She already knew he had a nice chest. His pecs were firm, raised, and sexy. She was into chests. And arms. And hands.

God, she could *not* get that sexy man out of her mind, and now she was aroused. Again. The way she had been every night since Saturday.

Checking the clock, she saw she had just enough time before the game started to slip in to her bedroom, lie back on her bed, and imagine Mark Strong pulling her against him the way he had when they'd danced. She imagined what might have happened in his hotel room. He would have undressed her, taken off his shirt, slipped his hands up her thighs. Would he have licked her? There. Right between her legs. She had never experienced that before, but she wanted to. Would Mark have given her that?

As she imagined all that Mark could do to her, her arousal grew. She was wet and slick, and she fantasized that her finger was his tongue. Just the thought was enough to send her over, and she gasped and shuddered into the fantasy.

Sex with herself was safe for sure, but she was growing bored with safe sex.

She wanted something dangerous. Something hot. Something purely Mark Strong. On the conference room table. Or in the chair.

Now *that* was something to think about!

Gathering herself, she straightened her clothes and returned to the kitchen, her body warm and tingly, a smile on her face.

She'd just finished popping a bowl of popcorn and was on her way to the living room when her phone rang.

She dashed to answer it. The caller ID showed her dad's name.

"Hi, Dad." She flopped onto the couch and crossed her legs under her, resting the bowl of popcorn in her lap.

"Hi, sweetie. What are you up to?"

"Just sitting down to watch the game." Telling her dad about her oh-so-naughty thoughts of the dapper Mr. Strong was so not going to happen.

"It should be a good one tonight. Game seven." Like her, Dad was a huge sports fan, and the Pacers were playing tonight. Daddy-o was over the moon they had made the playoffs.

"Yep." She grabbed the remote. "I'm turning on the TV now."

They talked basketball for a few minutes then her dad said, "You up for a fishing trip Saturday?"

"Sure." Karma was horrible at fishing. She couldn't even tie a knot in the line. But she enjoyed driving down to Peterman Lake with her dad two to three times a summer. They spent the day on the water, catching mostly nothing and a sunburn. But the real enjoyment wasn't in hooking fish. It was the time they spent together, not even talking, eating ham and cheese sandwiches on Wonder Bread and sipping iced tea from Ball jars.

"Good. I'll pull out your rod and tackle box. Looks like it's going to be a great weekend."

Despite their differing opinions of the world and of her path in life, she was super close to her dad. He was her hero. Her rock. The most important man in her life, who had taught her how to ride a bicycle without ever putting on training wheels, who had taught her how to plant and tend a garden, fly a kite, change a tire, and gap a spark plug. He had also taught her the principle of work first, play later.

Only, all Karma ever seemed to do was work. She thought of Mark. Maybe it was time to play a little.

"So, how's everything else?" her dad asked.

"Good. Nothing new." Aside from Mark and all the excitement he'd brought with him, the rest of her life remained pretty boring.

"When is some nice boy going to snag you up?" Her dad still teased her mercilessly about "boys."

She laughed. "When are you going to start referring to them as *men*?" Skirting the question was better than telling him she *had* met a man. A very virile man she was still uncertain about, but a man nonetheless, who rocked her world without even trying.

"When one grows a pair and asks you out." Her dad was incorrigible, but that was one of his most endearing qualities.

"You know, most fathers are more worried about keeping their daughters safe from *boys*," she said. "If you were normal, you'd think of my singledom as a good thing instead of trying to marry me off."

"Is that how it works?"

"For most dads, yes."

"Good thing I'm not normal, huh?"

"That's true. No one can ever blame you for being normal, but that's what I love about you." She and her dad were *likethis.* Tight. Two fingers crossed. Still, she didn't tell him everything. In some cases, it was better that way.

Case in point, she would keep Mark to herself for a while.

"Okay, honey," her dad said, "the game's getting ready to start, so I'll let you go. I just wanted to line things up for this weekend."

"I'll see you Saturday."

"I'll bring the iced tea."

"And I'll bring the sandwiches."

"Love you," Dad said.

"Love you, too."

She hung up, increased the volume on the TV, and settled in for the end of the pregame, trying not to remember that tomorrow was the day Mark was taking her to dinner. If she thought about that fact too much, she wouldn't get any sleep tonight.

Chapter 10

You don't need to take revenge. Just sit back and wait, because karma will get hold of those that hurt you and, if you are lucky, God will let you watch.
-Author Unknown

On Friday, around four o'clock, with her nerves creeping in over tonight's dinner, Karma snuck a peek into the conference room. Mark was bent over his laptop, chin resting on his fist. The sleeve of his light-blue dress shirt stretched against his biceps, and his short, dark hair appeared slightly tousled. Karma had noticed earlier in the week that he had a habit of raking his fingers through his hair when he was on the phone or deep in thought.

"Hi, Karma!" Jolene startled her as she bounced up to the desk and slapped her hands on the counter as if she were trying to draw as much attention to herself as possible.

"Jo?" This was a surprise.

"Is he busy?" Jo's gaze darted toward the conference room.

Ah, so there it was. The real reason for Jo's visit.

"Um…" Karma looked toward the conference room, searching for any reason to turn Jo away. Not that Karma had any right to keep her away from Mark, but… Okay fine. She was jealous. All week, she'd had Mark to herself, and now here came Jolene. Beautiful, busty, little Miss Hot Body, in her barely there blouse and up-to-there skirt.

Jolene leaned in and whispered, "Does he have a girlfriend? I heard he doesn't. Do you know?"

Cold dread and defeat sank like lead inside Karma's stomach. Jo was the kind of girl men didn't say no to. If she had her sights set on Mark, the game was already over.

"I don't know," she said quietly. "I…I don't think so."

Why fight it? Jolene was everything Karma wasn't. Jo had never had to work for attention her entire life. She walked in a bar and men lined up to buy her drinks. She got sick, and men fought to hold back her luxurious blond hair.

Jo giggled quietly. "He's so slammin' hot."

"I hadn't noticed."

Jo was already quick stepping away from Karma's desk, aimed like a laser toward the conference room.

Karma's shoulders sagged. Well, having Mark to herself had been fun while it lasted. Her stomach sank as she watched Jo stop a few paces from the doorway, fluff her hair, and then move in for the kill. Jo was the kind of girl Karma imagined Mark would normally date. She was Barbie. He was Ken, except Ken had never been *that* sexy. Ken only alluded at sexy. Mark was the real thing.

Jolene knocked on the door. "Excuse me, Mark?"

Mark turned, briefly caught Karma's eye, then looked at Jolene. "Yes?"

"Hi. I'm Jolene. We haven't met, yet." Jolene fell into her patented come-hither pose. Breasts high, shoulders back, chin down so she could bat her lashes at him. She tilted her head so that her long, blond hair fell to the side.

"Mark." He stood and shook her hand.

Jolene let hers linger a couple of extra seconds in his then let go.

"You're the sales admin, right?" Mark said.

"Yes." Jo brightened as if the fact that he knew what position she held meant he had been checking her out, too. "If you ever need anything…sales reports, sales data…anything at all, I'm your girl."

If Jo even knew how to pull a sales report, it would be a miracle. Karma was the one who pulled those reports and manipulated the data for the sales staff, not Jolene. In truth, Jo should have been fired a long time ago. The only reason she was still around was because her boss drooled after her, and she flirted incessantly to keep him wrapped around her little finger.

Mark smiled politely. "Well, I've got all the help I need, but thank you." He gestured toward Karma. "Karma takes excellent care of me."

Karma's face heated at the compliment, and she sat a little higher. Jolene shot her an icy look.

"Well, of course," Jo said. "Karma's such an eager beaver." She laughed drily then turned back to Mark and fell into her come-hither pose again, undeterred. "But hey, a few of us are going for drinks after work. Would you like to join us?" Her tone suggested more than just drinks.

Karma held her breath. He already had plans with her, but he could easily change his mind and go with Jo.

"I'm sorry, but I already have plans," Mark said. "Maybe another time."

Karma breathed a sigh of relief and smiled. There was something satisfying about seeing Jolene get turned down, especially by Mark. And the fact that Mark was honoring his plans with her when he could have bailed and had drinks with Jo made Karma respect him that much more.

"Oh." Jolene sounded despondent. This had to be the first time a man hadn't fallen for her charms. "Okay. Another time then."

"Perhaps. Nice to meet you, Jolene."

Karma glanced at Mark out of the corner of her eye just as he glanced toward her. "Karma, do you have a minute?"

She hopped up with a bit more pep in her step. "Sure." She grabbed her notebook and headed toward the conference room.

Jo turned, scowled, then slinked off, dejected.

Mark waited until Jo was gone, then said quietly, "That was interesting."

Karma clutched her notebook against her belly and bit the inside of her bottom lip. "Jo thinks you're the bee's knees."

Mark laughed. "The 'bee's knees'?"

"Well, I'm paraphrasing. That's not exactly how she phrased it. I think her exact words were 'he's smokin' hot.'"

"I see."

She glanced at her shoes. "I can't believe you told her no."

"I already have plans with you."

"You could have cancelled."

Mark didn't respond until Karma met his gaze again. Then he glanced past her as if to ensure they were still alone, leaned forward, and said, "I don't cancel on someone unless I have good reason to. And drinks with Jolene isn't good reason."

"Most men would disagree with you."

Mark frowned, looked out the door again, and shrugged with a subtle shake of his head. "She does nothing for me."

Karma opened her mouth then flapped it shut like a fish breathing out of water. Had Mark really just said Jo did nothing for him?

"She's an open book." He rocked back in his chair, his gaze boring into hers. "I prefer women who aren't so…obvious."

Karma fidgeted and scratched the toe of her shoe on the back of her ankle. "It's just that I've known Jolene a long time, and men always look twice at her."

Mark studied her for a moment then sat forward. "Let them. But I happen to think there's only one woman at Solar who's worth looking at more than once."

If her heart could have stopped without killing her, it would have. "Oh? Who?" She could barely speak, her words wisping out on a breath.

With a grin, Mark leaned back once more. "I'm looking at her."

"Oh," was all she could say.

"By the way," he said, "I've been meaning to tell you that you look very nice today. That's a pretty color on you."

She wore a simple, magenta button-down blouse she had bought during an impromptu shopping trip with Daniel and Zach earlier in the week. She had paired it with black slacks and the black shoes she had worn on Monday.

"Thank you."

Mark's eyes narrowed. "Although…" His mouth curved into a crooked grin. "That blouse would look so much better if you unbuttoned one or two buttons."

Karma's pulse quickened at the thought as she lifted her hand to her collar. If she unbuttoned it, wouldn't that show too much skin?

"Just a suggestion," he said as if noticing her sudden discomfort. "But that blouse is made to be unbuttoned. Trust me." He smiled then turned back to his laptop, casually dismissing her.

She returned to her desk and slowly sat down. A cauldron of sensations stirred and bubbled inside her. Excitement, daring, fear. She glanced at Mark. He was focused on the screen of his tablet, seemingly oblivious to the storm he had awakened inside her.

Why did she suddenly feel like one of Pavlov's dogs? Mark acknowledged her blouse with positive reinforcement, and now all she wanted was to please him more. If she did, would he keep paying her compliments?

Yet, she hadn't expected him to say something like *that* about her blouse. His words seemed so innocent, but the tone of his voice, as well as the way his eyes glinted, oozed a subtle sexuality she recognized as purely Mark. After their trip to Finnigan's, as well as a few innocent conversations at the office, she had learned that nothing about him was overt. Every move, every suggestion, came disguised as an innocuous expression meant to provoke a response. For all its apparent innocence, Mark's suggestion to unbutton her blouse may as well have been an outright challenge. It was as if he wanted to see if she had the guts to push out of her comfort zone.

For several minutes, she sat at her desk, unmoving, her mind racing. Mark was busy typing away, calm as could be, while she broke out in a sweat over something as simple as unfastening one or two tiny buttons. What the hell? Was this really such a big deal? Women wore more revealing blouses than hers—unbuttoned or not—all the time.

She looked down at her blouse. Maybe it *would* look better

unbuttoned. She would certainly look less like a nun. But then she risked showing off her scant cleavage. Cleavage? Who was she kidding? She needed the help of a Wonderbra stuffed with Beyoncé's ample curves to give her cleavage, which implied mounds of flesh pushed against each other. What Karma had up top could not be described as mounds of flesh. Her childhood classmates had made that abundantly and repeatedly clear.

She looked around the open space surrounding her desk. No one was watching. Why not take a chance? Grow up a little? Put the insults of her youth behind her once and for all. Memories of Jolene and her brother laughing and making fun of her flashed through her mind, and she frowned before glancing down the hall in the direction Jolene had gone a few minutes ago.

The resulting jolt of anger provided motivation.

Just do it, for God's sake!

She rapidly unfastened the top button, then the next one.

There. Take that, Jolene.

She had gotten over feeling exposed in the red dress last Saturday night, and she would get over feeling exposed in her blouse. Nothing to it.

A few minutes later, Mark packed up his laptop and grabbed his jacket.

He approached her desk. "Karma, do you think you could recommend—" His eyes dropped to the open collar of her blouse. His brows gave an upward tick, as did the corners of his mouth, and he stepped closer to her desk as he lifted his gaze to hers and cleared his throat. "I'm hoping you could recommend a gym. Maybe one that has basketball courts?" His eyes drilled hers with obvious delight.

She took a shaky breath, certain that her blouse had fallen open to reveal her breasts, but she refused to fidget or cover herself. "The gym I use has four full basketball courts." Her mouth suddenly went dry. It was like she had a mouthful of cotton.

"You work out?" A note of approval lilted his voice.

She nodded and maintained eye contact, quelling her nerves as she peeled her tongue from the roof of her mouth. "Yes. Yoga and Pilates three times a week."

He offered an appreciative tilt of his head. "Nice. I try to run a couple of miles a day and do some weight lifting. Do you ever lift weights?"

She shook her head and worried the tip of her right thumb over the fingernails on her left hand. "No, not really."

Mark adjusted his bag over his shoulder. "You should give it a try." He lowered his voice. "Some men find it sexy." His gaze flashed to her blouse again.

Karma caught her breath, and her skin prickled with heat.

He grinned, his eyes twinkling. "Not that you need to worry about that."

Mark was purposely trying to unnerve her. But he could be so alluring like this, playful and flirtatious.

She bit the inside of her lip.

"Forgive me. I'm embarrassing you." But he didn't sound like he really wanted forgiveness. It was obvious to Karma that he knew exactly what he was doing and felt no remorse whatsoever. To him, this was a game, and he was the master. And yet…she still wanted to play.

"You're not embarrassing me." But the flames running down her neck said otherwise. She couldn't even hide behind her hair, because it was pulled into her usual chignon.

He looked much too pleased with himself as he adjusted his bag once more and checked his watch. "Well, perhaps you could give me the name of your gym? I'd like to check it out."

As she grabbed a small notepad, she stole a glance at her blouse. Whew! Still covered. She scribbled down the name then tore the slip of paper from the pad. "They offer temporary memberships, and it's only about five minutes from here, so it's convenient."

"So it is." He folded the square of paper before tucking it into his palm. "I'll check it out next week. Who knows, Miss Mason, perhaps I'll see you there some night after work."

Mental note: Look good at the gym. "Maybe you will."

Then he leaned closer and whispered, "I'll see you in a bit." With that, he turned and left.

Karma stared numbly down the empty hall as if she could see the pheromone trail Mark had left behind. She had a feeling things were about to get interesting in her boring little world. And maybe, if she was lucky, Mark would misbehave again tonight.

Chapter 11

No matter how hard the past, you can always begin again.
-Buddha

By six thirty, Mark had found a parking garage near St. Elmo's in downtown Indianapolis. He and Karma had chatted non-stop on the drive down. She'd asked where he was staying, and he'd informed her that his company had set him up in a condo. It was more cost effective than a hotel. They'd reminisced about their trip to Finnigan's Wednesday night, and about how they both shared a love for jazz, as well as for watery locales. She'd told him that her dream vacation would be to a tropical island with white sand beaches and water so clear she could see all the way to the bottom. However, for all their easy conversation, she seemed reserved, as if she still needed time to get used to being around him.

When they got out of the car, they were met with the savory aroma of grilled steak, barbecue, and a myriad of other mouthwatering scents. They were smack in the middle of what Mark referred to as Food Alley. Three city blocks of every kind of restaurant imaginable.

A warm, blustery breeze tore between the tall buildings as they walked the short distance to St. Elmo's. He opened the door, stepped aside to let her enter, then navigated her through the Friday night after-work bar crowd as the hostess led them to an intimate table for two along the wall.

After ordering them both an appetizer of shrimp cocktail, he rested his elbows on the table and laced his fingers together. "So, I'm dying to hear how an executive assistant from Indianapolis ended up at an arts benefit in Chicago last Saturday night."

"My friend Daniel took me."

"Boyfriend?" He hoped not.

She grinned. "Daniel's married."

Mark breathed a sigh of relief.

"To another man," she added a moment later.

"Oh. I see."

Karma giggled.

He chuckled, feeling a little foolish. "I guess I asked for that."

The server returned, filled their water glasses, and took their orders.

"So, how did you and Daniel meet?" he asked, then sipped his water.

"I've known Daniel since college."

"Where'd you go?"

"Purdue."

"You went to Purdue?" This was an interesting twist. He wouldn't have imagined that a Purdue graduate would become an executive assistant. But with the job market the way it was, he had seen stranger things. He had an acquaintance who held a master's degree and now worked as a greeter at Walmart. Times were tough, and people had to do what they had to do to get by. "What did you study?"

"I thought I was going to be a civil engineer my freshman year, but changed my major to mass communication with an emphasis on journalism after the first semester."

"That's quite a shift, isn't it?"

"My dad wanted me to become an engineer more than I did. I had the aptitude and the grades for it, but not the passion."

There was something to be said for passion in one's job. Without it, work became toxic drudgery. With it, work became the nectar of life.

"And you have a passion to write?"

Her whole face lit up. "Yes."

"Then why aren't you doing that instead of working for Solar?" Clearly, her heart lay with the written word, not administration.

Defeat replaced joy and her shoulders sagged just enough for him to notice. "I had a job lined up at the local paper after I graduated, but they withdrew their offer. The economy couldn't support the employees they already had, so they couldn't add one more. In fact, they laid off a few." She lifted her hands, palms up, and then dropped them to the table. "After that, I couldn't find work in my field. I needed a job, and Dad knew Don. His assistant had just resigned, so he agreed to interview me. We hit it off right away."

"How long ago was that?"

"Two years," she said.

"And that makes you, what? Twenty-four? Twenty-five?"

"Twenty-four." Her cheeks flushed as she bit her bottom lip and offered him a suppressed smile.

"Young and hungry. Willing to do whatever it takes. I was like that at twenty-four." That had been before hell had descended on his life.

"How old are you now?" From the confusion in her expression, she looked as though she didn't think he was much older than she was.

"Thirty."

"Oh." She looked surprised.

"How old did you think I was?" This should be good.

She fiddled with her cloth napkin. "I don't know. Maybe twenty-seven."

Silence descended between them again, and Karma nibbled her lip as she glanced away. Her bashfulness was adorable. For several seconds, he said nothing, content just to admire the way her cheeks remained flushed, as well as her nervous habit of tapping her pretty fingernails on the tablecloth.

"So," he finally said, leading her back into conversation, "you found your way to Solar and became Don's assistant."

"Yes. It's not what I went to school for, but I like it, and I'm good at what I do."

There was a subtle note of reticence in her tone.

"But…?"

"But what?"

"But you don't see yourself doing it forever, do you?"

Her expression told him he'd hit the nail on the head. "I know there's something else out there for me. I just don't know what it is or when I'll find it."

"You'll figure it out when the time is right. Everything in its own time." He paused. "But, you know, you don't have to be a journalist or a reporter to write. You just need a pen and a piece of paper, or perhaps a blog. It could be a private blog only you see, or you can write under a pseudonym. There are plenty of options for you to express your passion."

She appeared to contemplate that for a moment, a glimmer of inspiration in her eyes.

When she didn't reply, he pushed their conversation back toward how she had found her way to Chicago. "So, you met Daniel at college."

"Yes." She perked up with the change in subject. "We took a creative writing class together freshman year. Hit it off immediately, much to my parents' dismay. Don't get me wrong, my parents are good people, but they're just really conservative, especially my dad. Homosexuality isn't exactly a popular subject with them, so they were a little surprised when I told them about Daniel." She seemed to be on a roll now, talking animatedly. "But I liked him, and Mom and Dad accept him now, because they see how good we are together. He's the brother—or rather the sister…" She hesitated, giggled, and then said as an afterthought, "He says he's my sister." She laughed again. "Anyway, he's like the sister I never had wrapped inside the package of a best friend. But he's from Chicago, and his sister is a dancer. As a matter of fact, she danced the exhibition Saturday night."

"Sonya?" The world they lived in grew smaller as the six degrees of separation between them narrowed.

"Yes." She sipped her water. "I should have told you when you said you knew her, but…"

"But…?" He prompted her to continue.

"I didn't want to." She forced a thin, sheepish smile. One that conveyed secrets and a touch of guilty indulgence.

"Why not?"

"Because…" She sighed and looked down. "I was enjoying myself too much."

It wasn't much of an answer, and Mark got the impression she wasn't giving him the whole truth. And the only reason she wouldn't want to reveal the truth was because doing so would reveal more about her than she wanted him to see. A vulnerability perhaps? Or maybe she wanted to deny her true feelings because they frightened her, and now she was hiding from them.

Hiding was a terrific way to keep from facing fears. He should know. He was still hiding from his. It takes one to know one. Wasn't that how the saying went? Well, Mark could definitely see himself in Karma, even if he didn't want to acknowledge his own faults.

"Anyway," Karma said, "Daniel's husband got sick and couldn't attend, so he begged me to go instead. That's how I ended up at the benefit."

"Fortunately for me, you did." He leaned toward her. "That dress you wore was stunning." He briefly took in her magenta blouse. She had rebuttoned one of the buttons, much to his dismay. Still, it was an improvement over the boxy, mannish suits she had worn the rest of the week. Her work attire was such a vast contrast from Saturday night's striking dress.

Karma blushed and glanced away. "Daniel bought it for me. His family's rich, and he insisted on buying it. He said it was his way of saying thanks."

"That's some thanks. It definitely caught *my* eye." And everyone else's at the event. The question now was, how had she gone from wearing a dress like that to frumpy suits? He didn't think he would be able to end the evening until he had an answer, or at least a more definitive theory.

Their shrimp cocktail arrived, and they took a short break from talking to eat.

After eating half his shrimp, he dabbed his fingers on his cloth napkin and took a sip of water. "I'm curious about one thing, though. Why the ruse about being a model? I was only joking when I guessed that as your profession, but then you played along." This one small infraction had intrigued him more than anything else.

Color touched her cheeks, and she shrugged as she glanced toward the bar. "I don't know."

"You had to have a reason. What was it? I haven't been able to figure it out." But he had a few educated guesses.

Karma swirled one of her shrimp in her sauce, eyes downcast. After a long moment passed, she finally said, "It's not very glamorous." She met his gaze. "Being an executive assistant."

He fished the last shrimp from his glass. "Why is that important?"

Another shrug. "It just didn't seem…I don't know…impressive enough."

He wiped his fingers on his napkin. "For every day, or just for Saturday night?"

She nodded at the latter. "Mostly Saturday." She sighed and got a faraway look in her eyes. "That place, that hotel…it was so fancy, and I'm so…"

"So what?"

"So ordinary."

He fought back a laugh. "I can assure you, in that dress, in those shoes, looking the way you did…you were definitely not ordinary."

"Well, that was all just the façade."

"And what a lovely façade it was."

She shook her head. "Maybe I looked like I fit in on the outside, but inside, I felt…" She looked lost for words.

"Plain?"

Her gaze fell to the table. "Yes."

"And you wanted to be *not plain*, is that it?"

She nodded. "Yes."

"And who were you trying to impress with your make-believe alter ego?"

She met his gaze for an instant before looking away again, and the color in her cheeks deepened. For several seconds, she didn't say anything. Then, "You, I guess." She looked at him, and modesty pulled at her tender features.

He pushed his empty cocktail glass aside then reached across the table and tucked a strand of loose hair behind her ear.

"I'm flattered." He crossed his forearms on the table. "But you didn't need to try to impress me. I was already impressed, whether you tried or not. And to be honest, I was more concerned about impressing *you*." He chuffed as he recalled how poorly he had treated her. "Something which I failed miserably at, by the way."

"No you didn't." She spoke up quickly. Almost too quickly. "You didn't fail. I was impressed." Her kind smile and the way her eyes sparkled warmed his heart.

"But I scared you."

"No." She shook her head.

He was confused. "I must have. You left my room so suddenly. And I'll be the first to admit you had every right to. I was way out of line."

"That was me, not you." She closed her eyes and lowered her face into her hand. "I feel like such an idiot. I just…yes, I got scared, but…" She blew out a nervous breath. "Trust me, it wasn't you. That was all me, okay? Not you."

He didn't understand, but she clearly wanted to assure him her quick departure hadn't been his fault. Whatever had made her flee his hotel room had been her doing, not his, and now he was even more curious. The more time he spent with Karma, the more she puzzled him. And Mark liked puzzles. Especially ones that came in a pretty little package with pretty green eyes and a heart-shaped mouth.

She seemed like a woman on the cusp of letting go but didn't know how. She was innocent yet audacious. Sweet yet bold. A woman unaware of her allure, but who wanted to learn.

He could show her how to let go. He could teach her to embrace her charms. He *wanted* to. This was what he had spent the last six years mastering, this art of love and seduction.

He leaned forward, closing the short distance created by the small, white-clothed table. "You're not used to men kissing you the way I did, are you?"

She blushed. It was adorable and endearing the way she kept doing that. She dropped her gaze to her hands again and didn't say anything.

"Is that it?" He didn't need an answer. Her silence and the way she refused to meet his eyes already told him he was right.

"Yes," she said quietly. So quietly he almost couldn't hear her over the crowd near the bar.

A few more pieces in Karma's puzzle fell into place.

Chapter 12

Don't let your fear of what could happen make nothing happen.
-Doe Zantamata

After dinner, Mark suggested they enjoy the city and take a walk, and since Karma didn't have anything waiting at home but the couch, a pair of sweats, and a Friday night movie, she figured why not? So, they ventured out and eventually found their way to the Circle Center Mall.

As they passed the entrance to Carson Pirie Scott, a pretty blouse caught her eye, and she stopped to take a closer look. Until last weekend, she hadn't realized how long it had been since she'd gotten a real haircut or shopped just for fun. Focused on school and work for the past several years, shopping and tending to her appearance had fallen way down on her list of priorities. Even two years out of college, she still lived according to comfort instead of style. Not that she had ever been much of a fashionista, but at one time, she had actually been interested in makeup, trying to style her unruly hair, and buying cute outfits once in a while. But then came college. While attending Purdue, she had gotten used to pulling her hair back, yanking on a pair of sweats and a sweatshirt, and darting to class without even a glance in the mirror. The habit had stuck. Maybe it was time she broke it.

"This would look good on you," he said, lifting the sleeveless tie-neck top off the rack. The fabric shimmered, an abstract print in shades of coral, tan, cream, and black.

"I like it." She ran her fingers over the material, which felt cool and slick.

There was nothing like it in her wardrobe, so colorful and youthful, yet elegant. Had she really let herself go this badly? Had she ratcheted herself so far down on her list of priorities that complacency had locked her wardrobe—and herself— into a dull, outdated palette?

Mark held the blouse toward her and leaned back, head tilted, as if imagining what it would look like on her. "Would you wear something like this, I wonder?"

The question sounded like a trap.

"Or this?" Mark picked up another blouse. This one was a floral print in muted pastels of slate blue, moss green, and peach on a robin's-egg blue background. Ruffles adorned the front of the blouse beneath the mandarin collar, and delicate brushed metal buttons decorated the placket. "What do you think of this?"

"It's pretty, too." Both blouses were actually quite nice. Not too flashy, they were classic and chic, a nice halfway point between her usual attire and the crimson dress she'd worn to the benefit.

"You should try them on." Mark spied fitting rooms nearby and gestured. "I'll find you something else to try on with them."

She laughed. Most men hated shopping, and yet Mark looked right at home as he began rifling through the racks.

"What?" he said, grinning crookedly.

"I just…" She snickered and shook her head. "I've just never met a man who looked so comfortable shopping. Especially in the women's section."

"Well, I'm not like most men, remember?" His jazzy smirk made her giggle.

"I can see that."

He continued flipping through blouses, suits, and skirts. "Go on. Quit staring at me and try those on." He waved her toward the fitting rooms.

"Fine. Knock yourself out." If he wanted to play her personal shopper, she wouldn't stop him.

She took the two blouses into the fitting room, peeled out of her shirt, and slipped into the breezy, sleeveless floral print blouse. The fabric whispered over her skin like sheer curtains over an open window. She even breathed more easily.

When she stepped out of the fitting room, Mark was waiting nearby holding a tweed, off-white pencil skirt and matching jacket.

"Oh, now that's attractive." Mark set the suit on a chair and approached, admiring the blouse as she turned and faced the mirror. "See how it tapers at your waist and flairs gently at the hips?" He stood behind her and skimmed his palms lightly around her midsection.

Karma's pulse skipped a beat, and she shivered. "It's nice." Was she referring to the blouse, his hands on her waist, or both?

He grinned at her reflection then returned for the suit. "Here. Try this on with it. I guessed a size four."

He'd guessed her size in one shot. "How did you know?"

"I know women's bodies."

How was that for a loaded statement? "Did you really just say that?" She fought not to show her amusement.

He held up his hand. "Now, wait a second. Before you go making snap judgments, what I mean is, my mom is a professional dancer, and, as her only child, I got the special honor or learning how to sew and alter costumes." He handed her the suit. "At the time, I thought it was cruel and unusual punishment, but as I got older and began helping my parents at their dance studio, well..." A mischievous smile tugged at the corners of his mouth. "Let's just say it's good to be a heterosexual man who knows how to sew in a room full of half-naked women. I learned quickly what looks good on a woman. And, for the record, that's why I look so at-home shopping for women's clothes. Mom insisted I tag along on her shopping trips."

"I think thou doth protest too much."

He bit back a smile. "Just dedicated."

"I see." Karma inspected the skirt and matching jacket. "And now *I'm* your little project, is that it?"

He paused for a heartbeat before answering, his voice deep and sensual. "Only if you want to be."

Why did she get the feeling his simple statement was more like an iceberg? Only a little was evident above the surface, but the real meaning remained hidden in the words he hadn't spoken.

Feeling like she was being hunted, Karma disappeared into the dressing room and came out a few minutes later, wearing the suit. Mark glided up behind her like a predator.

"Ah, now this is nice." His hands were once again on her waist. "See how the jacket accents your figure? And how the skirt hugs your thighs and hits just above your knee, making you look classy and sexy all at once. This is what they call a power suit."

"Why is that?"

His lips twisted and lifted at one corner. "Because one look at you in this suit tells every man in the room who's *really* in charge, even if they don't want to admit it."

His voice drifted into her soul and began to peel away her coveted sense of reasoning, and a slow, warm churning began to swirl low in her belly.

"I see," she said softly. "And what kind of shoes would you recommend for such a, um, *power suit*?"

His gaze dropped to her bare feet, and a soft, pensive sound—not quite a moan—escaped his throat. His hands briefly tightened against her body. "Dark grey or black. Something that shows off your toes." He took several deep breaths, gently leaned against her back, and rubbed his palms up her arms to her shoulders then back down to her hands. "You have beautiful feet."

The innuendo in his tone made a starburst of heat explode in her abdomen, low enough that it licked between her legs and down her thighs. There was something prurient and provocative in his tone…and utterly addictive.

He remained behind her for several seconds, his fingers playing over hers as he stared at her reflection. Then he grinned sheepishly and took what appeared to be a forced step back. "I should probably let you change." He pointed behind him, toward the racks outside the fitting room. "I'll wait over there." He turned and left her alone, breathless, speechless, and with warmth pooling between her legs.

Less than fifteen minutes later, she and Mark left the mall and made their way toward Monument Circle. He carried her shopping bag, which contained her new suit, the two blouses, and a pair of black, platform, peep-toe pumps he had helped her select. He was such a gentleman. She hadn't even asked him to carry the bag. He had simply taken it from the clerk after she'd paid, as if doing so was standard operating procedure.

Once they reached The Circle, they stopped at a chocolate cafe and bought a small bag of milk chocolate butter toffee, then made their way back to the parking garage as they nibbled their treats.

Being with Mark was easy, not like it usually was with handsome men. Usually, she got tongue-tied and suffered a loss of words, but there was a gracious quality about Mark. A depth of character that both put her at ease and intensified her awareness, as if every nerve ending sparked to high alert around him. Instead of overpowering her, he enlivened her.

He spoke of the simple architecture of the city, commented on the unique brick roadway of The Circle, and remarked on how impressive Lucas Oil Stadium was. He was a big football and basketball fan, a fact he and Karma shared, and the conversation easily turned toward sports, which dominated the discussion all the way back to the car.

He set her bag in the backseat but didn't move to get behind the wheel. Instead, he took her hand and led her toward the western-facing side of the garage. The sun was just setting.

"It's a gorgeous evening, isn't it?" he said.

She parked beside him. "I love this time of year." A steady, warm breeze blew from the south.

"So do I." He glanced down at the bustling street below.

Rush hour was over, but there was plenty of traffic. Outdoor music played somewhere in the distance. With the Indy 500 at the end of the month, May was a big month in Indianapolis, and there were a lot of festivals and events around the city leading up to the race.

The noise of traffic and the city was oddly soothing yet invigorating. Karma didn't make her way downtown often. It was like a whole other world from where she had grown up in the suburbs. What would it be like to live in the city? Where would she shop for groceries? Would she miss the peacefulness afforded by quiet neighborhoods instead of apartment high-rises?

"Where do you live in Chicago?" She glanced at his profile. He had a strong jaw and prominent chin. When he turned toward her, she noticed that it had a small dimple in the center. She hadn't noticed that before.

"I have an apartment downtown." In the setting sunlight, Mark's eyes were the most striking color. Army green that looked almost grey, with a touch of tawny brown around the pupils. His gaze burrowed in and penetrated her like a stinger, injecting her with warmth that spread through her torso and sent tingles down her arms and legs.

She averted her gaze to catch a break from his severe intensity and the dizzying sensation he ignited with just a simple glance. "Can you see Lake Michigan from your apartment?"

"Yes. I have a balcony that overlooks the lake." She heard the smile in his voice. It was as if he knew why she had looked away.

"I bet that's nice."

"I like the water."

"Me, too."

It was small talk, but it was easy talk, which was all she was capable of at the moment. Even so, she felt the simplicity of their conversation was about to change.

"So," he said, as if on cue, "have I made up for my inappropriate behavior last Saturday?"

She laughed nervously and looked down at the street eight stories below as a strong breeze gusted through the parking garage. "I've already told you…you weren't inappropriate."

He moved closer and lifted his hand to her hair the way he had during dinner, only this time he didn't take it away after tucking a stray strand behind her ear. Instead, he reached around to the back of her head and deftly plucked one of the bobby pins from her chignon. "What about now? Am I being inappropriate now?" He brazenly pulled out another pin.

Her chignon loosened.

She should have told him yes, he was being extremely improper. She should have made him stop and insisted that he take her home. *Should have.* That was her father's voice in her head, but she couldn't say the words. They weren't hers, and they weren't what she wanted. She wanted his nimble fingers in her hair, on her face, her neck, her body.

Falling faster and deeper under his influence, she numbly shook her head as he pulled out another pin. "No, I don't think so."

He grinned and stepped a little closer as his fingers gently fished for the last few pins securing her hair. "How about now?"

Breathless, she could barely speak. "No."

"I'm sorry," he said softly, "but I just can't seem to behave myself around you."

He didn't sound sorry at all.

"That's okay," she heard herself say.

Her hair began to spill over her shoulders as he freed it. "Now, that's better." He tucked the handful of pins inside his pocket then combed his fingers through her hair, lifting it against the breeze. "Much better."

Silence engulfed them as he continued fondling her hair, and the tips of his fingers brushed against her neck in a way that she could tell was intentional. Then his hands fell to her collar, and he unfastened the next button of her blouse, his narrowed eyes sweetly chastising her for having refastened it.

"Uh, I..." She felt obligated to explain that two buttons undone had been a little much for her.

"Sshh." He dressed the collar to reveal more of her neckline.

All she could do was stand in portentous silence, waiting for what he would do next.

"I'm glad you bought that suit," he said a moment later.

"Why?"

His gaze swept down her body then back to her eyes. "I've wondered all week how such a striking woman could wear such a provocative dress then turn around and wear such masculine clothes."

Her cheeks heated, and she began to lower her gaze. Mark slid his index finger under her chin and lifted her face.

"Make no mistake, you're still striking. But that's the thing. You're too pretty for the clothes I've seen you wear this week. The dress was more...you. And the new suit is, too." He paused and slightly narrowed his eyes then flashed a knowing smile. "But you already know that, don't you?"

It was as if he could read her mind. "I…I guess." She knew her old clothes no longer served her. It was definitely time for a change.

He brushed back her hair again as the breeze blew it over her face. "You know, I've learned a few things about you in the last few days, but especially tonight." He smoothed his palms down her sleeves.

"Oh?" She was totally transfixed, locked into submission, eager for him to keep touching her. She shouldn't have wanted that as badly as she did.

He moved closer still, and she felt the heat emanate from his body into hers. "Yes. For example, I learned that you're a very complex woman. More so than most women I've met. But that's what makes you so fascinating." He paused and let his gaze dance over her face. "I've learned that you don't realize how attractive you are, but that you're beginning to learn. That you want to be your own person and not what someone else expects." He examined the side of her neck as he lifted her hair away from her face. "I also learned that you have passion." His voice deepened. "Maybe not so much for the job you have, but for the job you want." He paused and one side of his mouth lifted. "As well as for other things."

Heat flooded her face because she knew exactly what those "other things" were.

He played with her collar again. "I learned that you aren't happy with how you dress and that you want to change." He admired his handiwork as if satisfied with her appearance. Then he pressed closer and leaned down to kiss the wisp of skin between her neck and shoulder. "I learned that you have…lovely feet." His voice hitched as he whispered in her ear. His arm eased around her back.

She swallowed and lifted her hands to his chest, swept away on his voice as she tilted her head back ever so slightly.

"And that you long for excitement." His lips brushed her skin, right below her ear. "You do long for excitement, don't you?"

"Yes," she whispered. Why deny it? He would only know she was lying.

The sky grew darker as the sun dipped behind a building, and the lights flickered on in the parking garage, bathing them in a milky glow.

"You're not used to a man touching you, kissing you…*seducing* you." His hands caressed her back and the sides of her abdomen. "Are you, Karma?"

She closed her eyes. When had she begun breathing so heavily?

"N-no."

"But you want to be seduced. You want to know what it's like." He waited a heartbeat before adding, "You *want* me to behave inappropriately."

It wasn't a question, but she felt compelled to answer, anyway. "Yes." The word barely escaped her throat on a breath. Her fingers curled against his shirt, and she gulped as her eyes blinked heavily.

His lips danced to the other side of her neck, and his arm around her waist pulled her closer. "You're a woman searching," he said softly. "You're a woman trying to find out who she is and where she fits in the world. You yearn for more, hunger for a man to make you feel things you've never felt, but you're afraid because that's not how you were raised, is it?"

He was right. In just a few hours, he really had learned a lot about her.

"You were raised to be a good girl, weren't you?"

Once again, all she could do was nod and cling to him for fear of floating away if she let go.

"That's what I find so attractive about you. It's why I can't seem to stop touching you, misbehaving around you. You *are* a good girl. You just want to be a little bad." He lifted his face and looked her square in the eyes. His lips were almost touching hers.

In the distance, the music changed to something more down-tempo.

"That's why you didn't tell me you knew Sonya Saturday night. Because you enjoyed the intrigue, the mystery. You enjoyed keeping me to yourself and letting me think you were someone you weren't. You liked being a little bad. You liked that no one knew you and that for one night you could pretend to be someone else…to indulge your fantasy to be something you aren't." His lips brushed hers so lightly that she wondered if she only imagined it. "But what if I told you that I think you pretended to be who you *really are*? You just don't know how to be that person in a reality that's been created for you by someone else." Again, his lips whispered over hers, and her eyelids fluttered as she forced herself to inhale. "And your taste for a little bad was why you wore that dress, wasn't it?" His index finger slowly skimmed under her jaw and chin, leaving behind a trail of tiny starbursts. "It surprised you how sexy you felt in that dress. You enjoyed the way all those men looked at you even though you didn't want to. But you did enjoy it, didn't you?"

She could do nothing but stare into his mesmerizing eyes and pant.

"And you enjoyed when I looked at you, too. You liked my eyes on you, appraising you. You didn't want to like it so much, but you did." He paused, and his gaze circled her face before meeting hers again. "You *wanted* the fantasy that I was ready to offer. That's why you don't think my actions were inappropriate. But it terrified you when you had it in your grasp. I see that now." His eyes narrowed. "Something held you back, and I know you had your reasons, but something scared you away. I don't know what that was, but I know it's there." His gaze searched hers as if looking for a chink in her defenses to expose the truth she didn't want him to see.

Everything he said resonated so truthfully inside her there was no way she could deny it. She had a feeling there was nothing he couldn't learn about her if he wanted to.

"You want excitement and passion and pleasure," he said without preamble. "And I can give them to you."

No doubt he could. If how she felt this very moment, pressed submissively against his body and captured by his voice, was any indication, achieving pleasure, excitement, and passion wouldn't be a problem with Mark. But they were in her world now, not his. This was Indianapolis, not Chicago. There were expectations here. She had responsibilities. Recklessness and wild abandon were for her fantasies.

"I…I don't know," she said weakly, reality interfering once more with the fantasy of the two of them exploring the many definitions of pleasure and passion with one another.

A wry grin played over his mouth. "You can be my—how did you put it? 'Little project,' I think is the term you used." He tilted his head to one side. "Would you like that?"

Yes, she would. Very much. She just wasn't sure she could pull it off. Being with him when they worked together would definitely be "a little bad," and the idea thrilled her. But it also scared her.

"What about work?" she said.

"We're both adults. No one at your office needs to know. As long as we're careful."

"What if they find out?"

"Then we'll deal with it."

She bit her lip, wanting to say yes while the practical voice in her head shouted no. "I don't know," she said again.

He pulled back. Not entirely, but enough that instant disappointment rushed in to the places where anticipation had been just a moment ago. "I know it's risky. Yes, I could get slapped on the wrist and lectured about the merits of not dating the employees of the companies I work with. And there's a slim—very slim—possibility my boss would pull me off the assignment if he found out." He shrugged one shoulder dismissively. "But that's a risk I'm willing to take."

"Why? Why risk your job?"

"I wouldn't be risking my job, just a little chastisement." He studied her for a moment. "I met you before I knew we'd be working together. I like you. And I think you like me. Am I correct?"

Her face was perpetually warm. "Yes, but so what? You could get in trouble."

"It would be worth it."

"Worth getting in trouble? Why? Just because we *like* each other?" What was she doing? The devil on her shoulder hopped up and down, yelling at her to shut up already, while the angel nodded chastely and expressed how proud it was of her. If she was being honest, she was kind of on the devil's side, so, yeah, perhaps stopping her protests and looking for a way a relationship with him could work might be a good thing.

Mark reverently caressed her face. "You're a rarity, Karma. You obviously affect me." His arm tightened around her waist once more, and he took a deep, shaky breath. "I can't stop touching you. I can't stop looking at you." A gentle puff of air burst from his nose, making it sound as if he was just as baffled at his reaction to her as she was. "I rarely feel this way about a woman." He sounded like he was talking more to himself than to her. "You excite me. I want to be inside your secrets. I want to share the same breath with you and swallow my name when you whisper it as I'm giving you more pleasure than you've ever known."

The devil shoved the angel off Karma's shoulder and flipped it off as heat spiked inside her body.

"And I want to know what made you run from my room when you clearly wanted to be there."

Karma's pulse raced at the thought.

"You're a mystery, and mysteries intrigue me." Like an artist studying a portrait, he tilted his head to one side then the other. "I can't let you go when I haven't had a chance to solve you."

Karma's mouth fell open on a soft gasp that sounded a little like "oh."

"That's why you're worth the risk, Karma."

She closed her mouth and swallowed. "I see." But she still wasn't convinced this was a good idea.

Mark took a labored step back. "Okay, how about this? I'm driving back to Chicago tonight, just for the weekend. While I'm gone, would you at least consider what I'm offering? We can talk again next week…see what you've decided. How does that sound? Will you at least think about it?"

"What if I say no?" After what he had just said and how aroused she was, she wasn't sure "no" was even part of her vocabulary, anymore.

"I'll be disappointed, but I'll respect your decision and won't bring it up again."

She was thrilled to know he would be disappointed if she declined him, which should have been her first clue as to just how deep she already was.

"What if I say yes?"

Hope flickered in his eyes and that one dimple in his right cheek tugged at her heart. "If you say yes, your fantasies will be my fantasies, and I'll show you how good it feels to be a little bad."

With just a look, Mark could make her feel things she had never felt. With just the subtle inflection of his voice, he made her soul sing, her body warm, and her pulse quicken. She barely knew him, and worse yet, she now worked with him. As Solar's new consultant, he held the authority to destroy her job if he saw fit, and yet, instead of scaring her, that power excited her more than if she had won a Pulitzer.

What was happening between her and Mark felt like the arrival of Halley's Comet. Something that occurred once in a lifetime. Twice for those lucky to have been born at the right time and live long enough. Should she revel in her good fortune that fate had brought Mark into her life twice in only one week? Or should she let Halley's Comet pass her by?

Again.

Chapter 13

Focus on the positive.
-Author Unknown

As morning dew glistened the grass and thin fog hovered over Peterman Lake, Karma's dad rowed them toward their favorite fishing spot.

"You've been quiet this morning," her dad said.

Karma hadn't said much on the trip down and had spent the past ten minutes staring at the glassy water, watching the ripples from the boat roll over the surface.

She reached for her fishing pole. "Just tired."

Her dad didn't look convinced. "Tired? A morning person like you?"

She brushed a wavy strand of hair off her face and tucked it behind her ear. "Long week at work."

It wasn't a total lie. One week with Mark Strong would make any woman tired…from lack of sleep…because how could she sleep when she was fantasizing about such a magnificent man? And then there was last night and his proposal, the main reason for her silence. Her mind was still working over the pros and cons of getting involved with Mark outside the office.

On one hand was the potential for pleasure unlike anything she'd ever experienced, at the hands of the sexiest man she'd ever laid eyes on. God, but Mark did such erotic things to her body without even touching it. On the other hand was the danger of being caught, as well as the risk of engaging in taboo behavior. Getting involved with the company's consultant could be hazardous to her professional health if anyone found out.

"Don working you hard?"

She busied herself rummaging through her tackle box, re-familiarizing herself with her old lures. "No, not really." She tried to keep her voice even. "A consultant came down from Chicago on Monday. He's got everyone a bit on edge." *Some more than others.* "Everyone's wondering why he's here and expecting the worst."

Dad dropped the red brick they used as an anchor over the side of the boat. Rope was weaved through the holes and knotted around the outside to keep it secure. "Do you think they're going to lay people off?" He took her fishing rod and plucked a floating lure from her tackle box.

"I don't know." Her dad tied the lure to her line. "I hope not, but it's possible." In a way, thinking she was attracted to a man who held the power to lay off her coworkers was a bit morbid. As if she were a traitor. Then she remembered how Mark's lips had brushed lightly over hers last night and how her body lit up afterward. If being a traitor felt that good, then fine, consider her a turncoat. Let her coworkers fend for themselves.

"Well, whatever happens, it will all work out." Just like Lisa, her dad always searched for the silver lining.

"I guess." She took back her rod and cast her line.

After that, no more was said. Her dad was a serious fisherman. He had one rule: No talking. It scared away the *fitches,* as he called them.

And that was fine by her. No talking meant more fantasizing.

With the sun climbing higher into the sky, she wondered what Mark was doing? Was he thinking about her, too? Yeah, sure. If he was thinking about her right now, she was Miss America.

Chapter 14

Being there for a friend is one of the greatest gifts you can give. Another one is allowing them to be there for you, too.
-Doe Zantamata

Mark stood on the balcony of his Chicago apartment, overlooking Lakeshore Drive and Lake Michigan beyond. His bathrobe hung open, and he wore red flannel pajama bottoms over bare feet. A coffee mug warmed his hand. He had driven home after dinner with Karma last night and gotten in before midnight.

The sounds of Chris Botti and Sting drifted from inside the apartment, playing a slow jazz number that fit his pensive mood.

He sipped his coffee and smiled.

Karma. What an intriguing name. *What goes around comes around.* Isn't that what karma meant, generally speaking? *What you give is what you get. What you put out you receive. Fate. Kismet. One's lot in life. Destiny.* How had she been given such an interesting name? And was her name a sign that destiny had brought them together?

He grinned dubiously at the thought. He wasn't one to believe in fate, destiny, and all that. Especially not after what had happened with Carol. If fate existed as some kind of cosmic guiding system, why would it lead a person into a situation that inflicted that kind of pain?

He brushed the uncomfortable memories of his past aside before they could sour his mood. He would rather think about Karma.

She was such a delightful woman. He loved her hair. Longish but not too long, wavy, auburn—almost brown. And her eyes. Karma had luminous, hypnotic eyes, which popped against her flawless, pale skin. She was clearly a woman who didn't believe in tanning. Not even a spray tan.

In a way, she reminded him of Emma Stone from the nose up, but she had a pouty, heart-shaped mouth that was more like Scarlett Johansson's. A kissable mouth. Very kissable.

And she was so full of promise…shy and insecure, but willing to learn. He hadn't expected her to unbutton her blouse yesterday, but she had, which proved she wanted the excitement and the daring. Of course, she had rebuttoned it before dinner—a travesty he later corrected—but just the fact she had been willing to loosen her collar and show more skin at his suggestion in the first place indicated there was hope. Oh, the things he could teach her. He would lift her confidence, show her how to touch him, how to kiss him, as well as how to be touched and kissed in return. But most importantly, he would show her how to be the woman she wanted to be.

He imagined her clothes discarded on the floor in his bedroom, a very naked and gorgeous Karma lying supine on his bed as he massaged her incredible feet. With her expanse of pale skin against his darker complexion, wouldn't they look striking against one another?

He sighed, and body parts south of his waistline perked up, especially when he imagined her in only that very sexy pair of black heels he'd helped her pick out last night. Wow. Just wow. The image robbed him of breath. He inhaled sharply to keep the oxygen flowing.

Oh yes, the things he could teach her. But first she had to tell him yes. She seemed to be leaning in that direction, but there was always a chance she would tell him no when he returned to Indianapolis.

Sure, he could simply let her go, find someone else to date, or simply be single for a while. But he didn't want to let Karma go. For one, he didn't like not getting something he wanted. Second of all, Karma fascinated him. And third, something about Karma screamed that she needed him. He could free her.

Maybe it was a macho thing, but something about showing Karma the ways of pleasure he suspected she had only ever imagined brought out his inner caveman. He wanted to beat his chest and drag her back to his cave. Show all the other cavemen he was better than they were and could deliver in ways they couldn't.

Karma had become the project within the project…the prize in the Cracker Jack box he wanted to keep digging for…the rose whose petals he wanted to see unfold to reveal her as-yet-unseen depths.

Before his thoughts swept him further away, his phone rang.

Ducking inside, he smiled at his caller ID. "Hey, buddy. You ready to get your ass kicked?" He hadn't talked to Rob since the benefit last weekend.

Rob laughed. "You wish, old man. I've been practicing this week."

All the practice in the world wouldn't help Rob, even though he had been lucky a few times when Mark was having an off day. But today Mark was primed to release some pent-up energy. His game always excelled when he was keyed up, and Karma had him keyed *up!* As in, so far up that he would need a cinder block tied to his ankle to bring him back down.

"Old man, my ass. I'm younger than you are." Mark tossed his robe on the bed before snagging a T-shirt and a pair of shorts from the dresser.

"Only by a few months."

"So what? I'm still younger. And you'll be eating your words, pal. You don't know what you're in for. I might have a record-scoring day."

"Oh yeah? What's got *you* so worked up?"

As his best friend since junior high, Rob knew Mark well enough to know that if he was already gloating about a record day, something major had happened.

"Oh nothing." Mark sneered, dropped his change of clothes on the bathroom counter, and turned on the shower. He was going to need another one after a few games, but he didn't feel fully awake until he washed off the sleep and grime from the day before.

The line grew quiet. Then Rob started chuckling. "Oh shit. Don't tell me you met someone down there."

Mark laughed. "You know me too well, asshole." He didn't have to tell Rob right now that he'd actually met Karma at the benefit. He could announce that newsflash later.

"Jesus, Mark. Barely out of one relationship and into another. Hopefully you've told her up-front not to get her hopes up about anything serious."

"We're not dating. Not yet, anyway." Mark stripped out of his pajama bottoms.

"What? Are you telling me she can actually resist your charm?"

Mark checked the water's temperature. "Something like that. Look, I'll tell you about her later. I'll see you in a bit."

"Okay. Get ready to get your ass kicked."

"Fuck you. Not a chance." Mark disconnected and hopped in the shower.

Thirty minutes later, he pulled his BMW into the parking garage across the street from the gym. He met Rob on the court and clasped forearms with him.

"Hey, man. Lookin' good." Mark broke their man embrace and pulled the basketball from his bag.

Besides being his best friend, Rob was like a brother. Not only did he know all about Carol and the nightmare she had caused, Rob had lived through the hell of the aftermath, trying his best to pull Mark up by the bootstraps so he didn't do something stupid, like drink himself into an early grave. And there had been a couple of times death by alcohol poisoning had sounded appealing.

Those had been stupid times, and Mark never drank like that, anymore. But through the nightmare, Rob had been there every step of the way.

They hit the court and played three games before taking a break.

Grabbing a seat on one of the courtside benches, Mark reached inside his bag for water and a towel. The temperature had risen since morning, and he wiped the sweat off the back of his neck.

"Okay," Rob said, out of breath, "you were right. I surrender."

Mark laughed and downed a swig of water. "I warned you. Three games, man. I stomped your ass."

"Yeah, yeah." Rob wiped his face on his sleeve. "So, what's up with this girl? What's her name?" Rob plopped down beside him and grabbed his own water.

Mark lifted the water bottle from his mouth. "Her name's Karma."

Rob poured water in his hand then splashed it on his face. "I'm assuming things are progressing well, given how you just mangled me on the court."

"You could say that." Mark looked at Rob out of the corner of his eye, trying to hide the smile threatening to break over his face.

Rob's eyes narrowed. "Uh-oh. What's that look for?"

Mark sucked in a deep breath and grinned at the irony. "She's the executive assistant for the company I'm consulting with in Indianapolis."

Rob's mouth fell open. "Whoa. Are you serious? You could get in trouble for that shit."

Mark held up his hand. "Cool off. I'm not going to get in trouble. Mildly reprimanded at the worst. Besides, she hasn't agreed to go out with me, yet."

"Smart girl."

Mark scowled sideways at Rob's verbal jab. "She *is* smart, but I think she'll come around. This week we were just…you know…feeling each other out."

"Okay…" Rob looked like he was about to play devil's advocate. "Let's say she decides to go out with you. You wine her, you dine her…you do what you do." He gave Mark a hard glance. "And then she decides, 'Oh, wait, this isn't for me. I think I'll file a sexual harassment complaint.'" Rob's expression said it all. "Because, Mark, I know you have no intention of getting serious with her. And when you don't, what if she gets pissed off and retaliates?"

Mark took another drink, paced away, then turned back around. "She wouldn't do that."

"How do you know? You hardly know her, and—"

Holding up his hand, Mark cut Rob off. "I've gotten to know her pretty damn well, and she's not the type to play those kinds of games." He stretched his triceps. "I met her last Saturday, at the benefit."

"Come again?"

"She was there." He remembered when he first spotted her at the blackjack table. "Red dress, sexy shoes." He whistled. "I'm surprised you don't remember her. Every man in the place couldn't take his eyes off her."

"Where was I when she was around?" Rob poured more water on his face.

"Slackin', most likely."

"If she turns on you, you could be the one slackin'."

"Yeah, well, this may amount to nothing. I think she's worried we could get into trouble if anyone finds out we're seeing each other outside the office."

"She's right." Rob sounded like he was scolding Mark.

Rob and his conscience. He always considered all possible outcomes.

Still, Mark didn't need the gloom and doom right now. He wanted her, and she needed him.

"That won't happen." Mark wiped his towel over his face. The only person who could stop him from entering an affair with Karma was Karma herself.

"How do you know?"

"Has it ever?"

None of the women Mark dated had retaliated, and none had become upset enough to lash out. Mark treated the women he dated well. He didn't disrespect them, and even though he could have been more up-front about his intentions—and from now on, he would be—he wasn't an ass when he broke things off. In fact, a couple of the women he'd dated said he'd been the best breakup they'd ever experienced, and they had remained friends. He had even introduced one to the man she ended up marrying.

"No," Rob said reluctantly. "But there's a first time for everything."

"Are you *trying* to piss in my Wheaties, Rob?" Mark tossed his towel aside, irritated.

"No, but I don't want you to lose your job, either."

"I appreciate your concern, but I'm not going to lose my job. Seriously." He downed the last of his water and shoved the empty bottle back in his bag. "I like this one. She's different. And she needs me. So quit shitting on my parade." He paced away.

"Okay, okay." Rob joined him in a hamstring stretch at the chain link fence. "You like her. She needs you. That's good. It's a good fit. I won't shit on your parade, anymore. Just be careful."

Mark glanced sideways at his friend. Rob meant well. The guy was always looking out for Mark's back. "It'll be fine. And I'll be careful. I always am."

Rob straightened and patted his shoulder. "I know you are." He grinned. "But please tell me you don't think she'll be on the layoff list. For the love of God, don't let her be one that gets the can. That would so fucking suck."

Mark shook his head. "Not her. She's too good at what she does. She's more manager material than admin, in my opinion."

He thought about what Karma had said during dinner about her journalism degree. She had a passion for writing and didn't see herself at Solar forever, but she had been right about one thing. She was very good at her job. Karma had all the talent of a leader if she would just break free from whatever held her back, both sexually and professionally. Mark had a feeling the roadblock in both cases was one and the same.

"Oh, she is now? And you know this after…what? Only a week? Just how much do you like this girl, Mark? You seem to have given her a lot of thought."

Mark scowled and pushed off the fence. "Quit busting my balls. Are we here to talk about my lack of a love life or shoot hoops? Because I smell another ass-whoopin' comin' on." He snagged the ball from the bench, dribbled to the court, and went in for a layup.

Rob swept in under the basket and took the ball, then flipped it over his head and through the net. "I can multitask and do both, and since I'm destined to get my ass handed to me, anyway, why bother putting up a fight."

"You puss." Mark took the ball and dribbled out to the three-point line.

"So, have you got your in with her, yet?" Rob asked.

Mark sunk another basket then rushed in, tapped the rebound from Rob's hands, and went in for another layup. "Working on it."

"Yeah, I bet you are." Rob grinned. "I can see your wheels turning from here."

With a smile, Mark passed the ball back to Rob with more zip than necessary. "Come on, old man. Play ball."

"Old man? Fuck you, buddy. I'll show you old man." Rob drove hard.

Game on.

Discussion over.

For now.

Chapter 15

Embrace the change in your life.
-Author Unknown

After spending Sunday afternoon hashing and rehashing the pros and cons of taking Mark up on his offer with Daniel, Zach, and Lisa over lunch at Olive Garden, Karma was still waffling about what to do.

While Lisa had clung fast to her previous sentiments, insisting Karma throw caution to the wind and go for it, Daniel had taken a more philosophical approach.

"What do you *want* to do, Karma?" he had asked. "What does your gut tell you?"

At the time, she hadn't been able to answer, but his question had simmered on her mind all night.

Ultimately, what she wanted was a relationship like Daniel had with Zach. They were the quintessential happily married couple, totally devoted to one another. Once, Karma had asked Daniel why he had moved to Indianapolis instead of insisting Zach move to Chicago, which seemed like a better place to live for a gay couple. Daniel had said, "Love makes you do crazy things, Karma. Zach wants to live here, and I love him, so here is where I belong."

That's what she wanted. A man who was as crazy about her as Daniel was about Zach, and vice versa. For now, though, she just wanted more Mark. More of those wicked kisses and hushed whispers. More butterflies in her stomach. More fun. And her gut told her Mark was the perfect man to bring her out of her shell and show her that kind of fun. The kind that got a little sexy, a little sweaty, and all kinds of exciting.

Now, here it was Monday morning, and she was still struggling with her decision as she sifted through her closet, looking for something special to wear.

As he hadpromised in Chicago, Daniel had taken her shopping yesterday after lunch to liven up her wardrobe and had seemed thoroughly impressed she hadn't cowered at the prospect...and thrilled when she had picked out a classy, colorful outfit all on her own.

"This Mark fellow seems to be having a positive effect on you," Daniel had said as she paired a peach, floral print blouse with cropped skinny jeans and light brown gladiator sandals.

She had brushed off his comment with a breezy, "Maybe I just think it's time I add some color to my wardrobe, like you said."

"Whatever you say, honey." Daniel had fallen in step behind her, adding the top and jeans to the growing pile of clothes they had gathered for her to try on.

Karma touched the sleeve of the blouse, which now hung in her closet, along with a few hundred dollars of new clothes and shoes. She had even bought two necklaces and several new scarves, which Daniel had, of course, shown her how to tie and wear.

Today's importance loomed front and center in Karma's mind. Mark would return today, and he would expect an answer.

She had weighed all her options, and in some ways, she was no closer to having an answer now than she had been Friday night, but in others, she was already with him, whatever "with him" entailed. One thing she did know, though, was that she wanted to look nice today, but not too nice. Not like she was trying to catch his attention, and yet, that's exactly what she wanted.

She ended up dressing in cream-colored slacks, a pale-pink, scoop-necked blouse that tapered at her waist, and nude sandals with a wedged heel. She wrapped a long, gauzy, dark pink and cream scarf around her neck so that the ends hung down her front, and, for a change, she left her hair down and put on makeup.

When she got to work, Nancy hardly recognized her as she passed the reception desk.

"May I help you?—Karma? Is that you?" Nancy gaped as she took in Karma's new attire. "I thought you were a guest. My goodness, don't you look different. And so pretty. Did you get your hair done?"

Karma giggled, feeling almost as scandalous as she had in Chicago. "Yes, last weekend." She lifted a hand to her hair. "Daniel sort of gave me a makeover."

"That boy sure knows how to make a woman beautiful, doesn't he?" Nancy winked. She knew Daniel from all the times he'd come by for lunch. "Trying to catch Mark's eye, are we?" Nancy gave her a coy look.

"Oh…no." Karma's face heated as she vehemently shook her head. "No, no. Just, uh…updating my look. This is all Daniel, believe me. Well, I've gotta run." She hurried toward the stairs and up to her desk, afraid Nancy would see right through her. Nancy was second only to Jolene when it came to office gossip.

Mark arrived a few minutes past ten and strolled around the

corner down the hall wearing tan dress pants and a black, V-neck sweater. Damn. Just, *dayum*! He looked good in black.

Karma suddenly loved Monday mornings.

"Good morning, Karma," he said with a purr of innuendo.

"Good morning." She busied her hands with a pad of Post-It Notes.

Mark paused at her desk. "What an alluring color on you."

"Thank you," she said, playing along. "It's new."

"Of course it is." He smiled then stepped away from her counter. "I'm running late for a call." He pointed toward the conference room. "Would you mind grabbing me a cup of coffee?" He leaned in conspiratorially. "One sugar, please."

He certainly was in a good mood this morning, and asking her to get his coffee felt like code for him wanting to speak to her privately.

She scurried around the corner to the coffee station, poured him a mug, and grabbed a sugar packet and a stir stick. Wearing an eager grin, she practically floated to the conference room. Getting him coffee was becoming one of her favorite tasks, even though she'd only done so a few times.

She gently rapped her knuckles on the door as she entered.

He sat back and gestured for her to set his coffee down next to his tablet. "Thank you." He took the sugar packet and flicked it against his fingers. "And how are you this morning?"

She forced herself not to stare at his chest, outlined like a second skin by the thin cashmere. "Good. And you?"

"Good." He dipped his chin thoughtfully, watching her as he poured the sugar in his coffee. An uncomfortable, somewhat awkward silence followed. Then he looked past her, out the conference room door. "Are you busy tonight?" He spoke quietly as he met her gaze again.

"No." She whispered the single syllable on an exhale, feeling a hiccup of exhilaration rush through her.

He slid his hand inside his bag, which sat on the table beside him, and pulled out a nondescript, plain envelope. As he handed it to her, he said, "Open this when no one's around."

Karma tucked it against her stomach, feeling like they were plotting a coup. "Okay."

He smiled and nodded toward his mug. "Thanks again for the coffee. We'll talk later." He lifted the phone receiver, politely dismissing her.

With the envelope burning holes in her hand, she took her leave.

Once back at her desk, hidden by the high counter, she glanced around and unfastened the small metal clasp. Inside was another envelope marked *Personal and Highly Confidential.* This was like a treasure hunt or a game. She looked around again to make sure she was still alone before pulling the second envelope out of the first.

For Your Eyes Only, Karma was written in impeccable penmanship on the other side of the envelope, just below the flap. She almost giggled. She had the feeling Mark intentionally meant to play James Bond with his secret package.

Biting her bottom lip, she slid her finger under the flap and snapped the adhesive closure, then pulled out a folded, handwritten note on light blue, monogrammed stationery:

> *Dear Miss Mason,*
> *Care to take a "journey" with me? I'll pick you up at 6:00 sharp tonight.*
> *-M*
>
> *P.S. I would be delighted to see you in those black shoes you bought on Friday.*

His cell number was written in meticulous numerals along the bottom of the note with a request to RSVP her acceptance.

Take a "journey" with him? What was with the quotes? She looked back inside the envelope and saw a concert ticket. When she pulled it out, she giggled. The rock band, Journey, was playing at Deer Creek Music Center tonight. The show started at seven o'clock.

Her heart fluttered.

She grabbed her phone from her purse and typed out a text. *Yes. I'll take a "journey" with you.*

As soon as she hit send, she looked into the conference room.

Mark was still on his call, but his attention momentarily diverted toward his cell phone. He lifted it from the table, smiled, and then began typing with one thumb. Then he set his phone down. A second later, her phone pinged in her hand.

You honor me. Get ready for an adventure, Miss Mason.

An adventure? Now they had gone from a journey to an adventure? Karma's curiosity rose. He sure was going to flattering lengths to obtain her answer.

Karma thought five o'clock would never come.

After rushing home, she hurried up the stairs to her apartment, freshened up, then stood in her underwear, staring at the racks of clothes in her closet, completely lost over what to wear. She had all these new clothes and *still* felt out of her depth.

Deer Creek was an outdoor music center, which meant she could go casual if she wanted, but this was Mark she was talking about. And tonight was special, so she wanted to look nice.

She slipped into a new pair of dark denim trousers with flared legs, tugged on a lightly fitted, dark grey graphic tee Daniel had insisted she buy, wrapped a white scarf around her neck, and stepped into the peep-toe black pumps Mark had suggested she wear. Staring at her reflection in the full-length mirror, she conceded that she looked pretty damn good. Who would have thought she could put together an outfit like this? Heels with denim and a T-shirt? She actually looked chic.

At six o'clock sharp, Mark arrived with a firm knock.

She grabbed her purse and jacket then pulled open the door.

Oh. My. God.

He looked incredible. And here she thought he wore *suits* well. In a pair of dark blue, low-slung jeans and a navy Henley, Mark looked…well…sizzling.

"Hi." She felt her face heat, which it always did around him.

"Hi." He grinned and gave her the once-over, his gaze briefly falling to her feet as if he wanted to ensure she'd done as he asked. "You're a vision."

"Thank you," she said quietly, lowering her head and pulling in her shoulders.

"Are you ready?" He didn't seem to notice her sudden shyness.

She hung her jacket over her arm. "Yes."

"You've got your ticket?"

"In my purse." She glanced at her shoulder bag as she stepped into the outer hall and locked the door behind her.

"Have you eaten?" He followed her downstairs.

She shook her head. "I didn't have time."

"Me neither. I had to run a quick errand before coming over. You up for drive-thru?" He offered her an apologetic glance as he opened the car's passenger door. "Normally, I would take you someplace nice, but if I do that, we'll miss the concert."

"Drive-thru is fine." She knew they were on a timetable.

After zipping through a KFC for a pair of grilled chicken

sandwiches and coleslaw, they ate on the way to the music center and arrived with twenty minutes to spare.

"What a great night." Mark helped her out of the car.

"It's perfect." The sun still hadn't set, there wasn't a cloud in the sky, and while there was the hint of a chill in the air, it was warm enough she didn't have to put on her jacket.

Mark opened the trunk and pulled out a folded blanket. A price label was still stuck to the corner.

"Errand after work, huh?" She pulled off the sticker.

He smiled and shrugged. "Lawn seating," he said. "Everything else was sold out, but the lawn sounded more interesting, anyway."

She looked at her shoes with their three-inch heels.

When she peered back up at him, he seemed to be contemplating her shoes, too. "If I have to, I'll carry you."

She laughed. She couldn't help herself. The look on Mark's face was priceless. A mix of guilt and playfulness. He laughed with her, and she loved how, for just a few moments, his guard completely fell. His whole face laughed, not just his mouth. Cute crinkles broke at the outer corners of his eyes, and his perfectly straight teeth gleamed.

"I like you like this." She took the blanket from him.

He lifted a bag filled with bottles of water from the trunk.

"As opposed to…?" He slammed the lid shut and nodded toward the gate.

They turned and weaved their way around the other cars. "I don't know." She shrugged and spoke over her shoulder as he came up behind her. "You're usually so—"

"Charming? Debonair?"

She laughed. "Well, that too, but I was going to say mysterious and professional."

"Professional?" He said doubtfully, his tone more serious. "You make me sound so boring."

"Trust me, Mark, you're anything but boring." No way in a hundred lifetimes could Mark ever be boring.

She scanned the lawn seating filling quickly with concertgoers.

"Where do you want to sit?" He pointed to an open area in the back. "How about there?"

She wasn't sure how crowded the place would get by the time Journey actually took the stage. Right now, with the opening act performing, people were still milling around and settling in. "Sure. That looks good."

He took her hand and helped her up the slight incline of the lawn then set down the bag and took the blanket. After spreading it out, he sat down.

She settled in beside him.

She hadn't been here in years, but it still felt the same. There was something magical about this place. She didn't know if it was the fact that Deer Creek sat in the middle of nowhere, with nothing but cornfields surrounding it, or if it was because it *was* an outdoor venue, or if some other unexplainable force made the place so appealing, but Deer Creek was an almost mystical location.

"I haven't been here in years," she said, hugging her knees as she lifted her face toward the sun.

"Bring back memories?"

She smiled. "Maybe a little, but it's more than that."

"Like what?"

She turned toward him. "I don't know. It's just…different here. Relaxing." She recalled the last time she came here and grinned privately.

"What?" Mark elbowed her impishly. "Tell me."

She took a deep breath and bit her bottom lip. "The last time I came here was with a guy I didn't even like. At least not before that night."

Mark's eyes softened, but he watched her with the attention of a hawk eyeing a field mouse, hanging on every word.

"I was working at this little luggage store between my sophomore and junior years at Purdue, and this guy came in. He was nothing special and was kind of annoying, because I was trying to close out the register for the night. He kept asking me for my number." She rolled her eyes. "I gave it to him just to get him out of the store so I could close up, hoping he wouldn't call."

"But he did," Mark said.

She nodded. "Wouldn't you know?" She chuckled. "He asked me to come here and see Dave Matthews with him."

"He had good taste."

Karma bowed her head and cringed as she glanced at him out of the corner of her eye. "I never liked Dave Matthews."

"What?" Mark slumped his shoulders and dropped his head back. "How could you not like Dave Matthews? That's like saying you hate…oh, I don't know…homemade chocolate chip cookies. And who in their right mind hates homemade cookies?"

She held up her hand. "Hey, I was young and ignorant, okay? But…" she pointed her index finger. "By the end of the night, I was a convert."

His face softened again, and he scooted a little closer. "Why? What happened?"

She sighed wistfully. "I don't know. I can't explain it. I came here, not liking the guy—his name was Louis. I didn't like Dave Matthews. But by the end of the concert, everything changed. I saw Louis differently…attractive, you know? And maybe seeing Dave Matthews live was what I needed to like his music. Now, whenever I hear him on the radio or wherever, it makes my heart warm."

She melted a little from the way Mark smiled just then, as if he knew how special he was to have heard her story. Not many knew about that night.

"What happened to Louis?"

Her gaze dropped to the blanket, and she picked at imaginary lint. "He was only in town for a couple of weeks, doing some kind of training for his job. We went out a couple more times, but that was it. We stayed in touch for a few months and tried to get together again but never did." She had forgotten all about Louis until just now. Funny how certain places or images can bring back fond, long-forgotten memories.

But what had happened with Louis was the story of her life. The guys she met from around here only wanted to be her friend. But the one guy she had liked—who had liked her back and who she might have had a decent chance with—had ended up living five states away.

Mark wrapped his arms around his knees. "Damn. That would have been the perfect story if you two had ended up getting married."

Considering that for a moment, she nodded. "True, but then I wouldn't…" She drifted off and swallowed hard. She still wasn't entirely sure what was going on here. Between them.

"Yes?" He looked at her, his grey-green eyes glinting in the sunlight.

She held his gaze. "If he and I had gotten married, I wouldn't…" She looked away, the heat rising in her face as it always did when she was around him, and she shivered. Not from a chill in the air, but from nerves. "I wouldn't be here. Now." She cleared her throat. "With you." It was as far as she had gone to put herself out there since the night they had met.

He scooted closer, and his arm rubbed her back as he propped himself up and leaned in. Her fingers twisted together around her knees, and she kept her gaze averted as another shiver tensed her arms and made her teeth chatter.

"Are you cold?" His voice came from beside her ear, only inches away.

She shook her head and turned toward the sunlight. "No."

"And yet you're shivering."

"I'm not cold." Her mind raced and her thoughts ricocheted inside her brain like balls in a Ping-Pong tournament.

The muscles in her arms clenched. She was so nervous, but so excited. Goose bumps tickled up and down the skin on her back, legs, and arms. Her heart felt like it would beat out of her chest. When she spoke, her voice trembled. "Do you want my answer? Is that why you brought me—"

"Sshh." He placed his fingers lightly against her lips. "Later. You can tell me later." Mark nudged her ear with his nose, and his lips pressed gently against her neck.

That simple kiss sent a shockwave through her body, and it felt like the bottom fell out of her stomach.

"Thank you for telling me your story," he whispered. Then he slowly pulled away and settled beside her again.

Karma swallowed and glanced toward the stage where the opening act was finishing their set. But she couldn't focus. Her mind was scrambled, her body on high alert.

Taking a deep breath, the balance tipped inside her mind. She wanted this. She wanted what Mark offered. She wanted more kisses on her cheek, her neck…her lips. She wanted more dates like this one. More secretive James Bond notes passed covertly in the office. But more than anything, she wanted Mark to seduce her. She had never been seduced, and Mark seemed eager to do just that. And if being seduced was anything like what she had endured for the past week—especially the last twelve hours—Mark proved to be an exhilarating ride.

Karma was ready to leave the past where it belonged. In the past. She was sick and tired of being a "friend"…and of allowing her anguished childhood to dictate her present and her future. For the first time, with Mark, she felt she might have a chance to reset her course in life. One free of insecurity and inexperience. One where she could be who she truly wanted.

She turned toward the sunset, feeling something she hadn't felt in a long time.

Hope.

Chapter 16

Everything you want is on the other side of fear.
-Jack Garfield

Pleasant tension settled between them for the duration of the evening. Mark's magnetism lit Karma's awareness all night, and her body remained in a state of perpetual arousal just from his proximity.

After the last encore, the lights came up and, at close to ten thirty, it was time to go home. But to Karma, the night still felt young and full of magic.

She helped Mark fold the blanket, then they gathered their things, and without a word—only that delightful strain of expectancy—they ventured back to his car.

The drive home was quiet. Occasionally, one of them mentioned one of the songs from the concert, and a brief discussion ensued. Then they fell back into pregnant silence again.

Finally, Mark pulled into her apartment complex and drove around to her building. After parking, helping her out of the car, and walking her up to her apartment, he stood aside and waited for her to unlock the door.

"Do you want to come in?" They had yet to address the real reason for their date tonight, so it was now or never.

He smiled. "I was just about to ask if I could."

She pushed the door open. He slipped into her apartment…into her world. Everything was different between them now. With just that one small step of crossing from the outside into her personal space, everything changed. He was no longer Mr. Strong, a consultant working for her company. And he was no longer the prince in a fantasy world where she was Cinderella.

But what exactly were they?

Karma kept her gaze on him as she shut the door, took off her jacket, and placed it over the arm of the couch as he inspected her living room.

What did he think? And did he plan on kissing her? They were here. Inside her apartment. Surely, he intended to kiss her. Maybe she should eat a mint. She wanted to taste good if he kissed her.

"You seem apprehensive." He kept his back to her as he ran one hand over the spines of books in her bookcase.

Flustered, she uncrossed her arms, not even realizing she had crossed them. "No. I'm…it's just, I haven't had a man in my apartment in a long time." Come to think of it, she'd never had a man in her apartment. This was a first.

He flashed a disarming smile. "I know."

That's right. He had read her like an open book last Friday. She shook her head and looked at the floor. "Um…well…" She chuckled awkwardly. "I'm not so good with men."

"You're good with me."

"You're different."

"How so?"

She didn't know how to answer that. Her brain wasn't functioning properly with him perusing her things. "I don't know."

He pulled a book from the shelf and flipped open the cover so he could read the description inside the jacket. "Romance. Is that what you prefer to read?"

Her fingers twisted over one another. "Yes. And a little suspense."

"Mmm." He slid the book back onto the shelf. "And elephants?" He picked up a small elephant figurine, which sat among a dozen others.

"Yes." She gestured to another shelf where a larger collection of cat figurines sat on display. "And cats."

"Why elephants?"

"I started collecting them in junior high and it just sort of stuck."

"I see." He set the elephant down. "Do you have anything to drink?"

Where were her manners? "I'm sorry. Yes. I mean, no. I mean..." Her neck and chest blazed, and she was sure she had broken out in hives. With him in her apartment, investigating her private sanctuary, she could hardly think, let alone form coherent sentences. He probably thought she was a total dingbat.

Welcome back, inner dork.

Making like a scared mouse, she scurried off to the kitchen and pulled two glasses from the cabinet, filled them with ice, and poured them some tea.

When she returned to the living room, he was kneeling in front of her shelf of DVDs.

"Here you go." She held out his glass.

He stood and turned. "Thank you."

"Did you want to watch a movie?"

He sipped his tea and gently shook his head. "Maybe another time.

It's late."

She drummed her fingernails on the side of her glass and shifted her weight. He sure was taking his time getting to the point of the evening. "Would you like to see the rest of the apartment?"

Mark's penetrating stare weakened her knees. "Sure."

The place wasn't big, but she walked him through the dining room and kitchen, then back through the living room toward the hall. "Bathroom…" She flipped on the light to the hall bath. "Second bedroom…" She waved into the room she used as an office and storage space.

"No bed," Mark said.

"No. I use this room mostly for storage." She shut off the light and turned toward the partially opened door across the hall, where she paused, took a deep breath, and pushed it open. "This is my bedroom."

Mark stepped past her and looked around, immersing himself more fully into her personal domain. The full-sized bed was dressed with a yellow quilt her mom had made, and a pair of burnished orange throw pillows rested against the headboard. The scarf she had worn to work sat on the oak dresser beside her fishing hat. A large sunset seascape hung on the wall opposite the bed, between the doors for the closet and master bathroom.

"Nice picture," Mark said, admiring it.

"Sometimes I like lying in bed imagining I'm off on some tropical beach somewhere." Escapism had always fueled her fantasies. Maybe that had something to do with growing up without a lot of friends and wanting to be anywhere but where she was.

"You've got a nice apartment," he said, taking another drink of tea. "Cozy and quaint, but bigger than I expected."

For a long moment, they just stared at each other.

Karma's pulse quickened. Something about the way he looked at her suggested he was ready to talk about the topic they'd danced around all night, but why did she get the feeling it wouldn't be that simple?

"Did you have a good time tonight?" he finally said.

"Yes." She practically held her breath. "I had a wonderful time." *No sense lying.*

"So did I, and I'd like to have more wonderful times in the weeks ahead." He paused and strolled toward her dresser. "But it's up to you."

"I know." Her heart was racing. "Do you want my answer? Is that what tonight is about?" It had to be, but he kept dodging the subject.

He scanned the items on the top of her dresser then met her gaze. "I'd like you to give me your answer tomorrow."

"Tomorrow?" She hadn't expected that, but she was quickly learning that Mark liked the unexpected. "Why not tonight?"

"Where would be the fun in that?" Flirtatious amusement coated his expression as he flipped open her jewelry box and began sifting through the few trinkets she wore for special occasions. He pulled out a simple, circular gold brooch. It had been a Christmas gift from her dad years ago, but she hardly wore it anymore. Mark turned, holding up the brooch. "If your answer is yes, and you want to throw caution to the wind, then wear this to work tomorrow."

Karma took the gold brooch and folded it into her palm. "Okay?" The word lilted like a question.

"But there's a catch," Mark said.

"A catch?" An expectant buzz vibrated under her skin.

"Yes." Mark plucked her glass from her hand and set it on the dresser with his own. "A catch." He pulled her into his arms so that his face was only inches from hers.

She stiffened and held her breath as she looked into his eyes.

"If you wear that brooch tomorrow, then you'll be telling me you want more of this…" He barely brushed his lips against hers, making her suck in her breath as that bottom-falling-out-from-her-stomach sensation flip-flopped inside her belly again.

"And…?" she said breathlessly. If there was a catch, there surely had to be more to it than that. Kissing him wasn't going to be a problem.

"And it means you've agreed to see me outside the office." His lips skimmed hers again, barely making contact. "But what it doesn't mean is that I want a commitment. I'm not into long-term relationships." Their noses bumped as he teased her mouth, and she caught a glimmer of apology in his gaze. "I want to be up-front about that. I don't want to lead you on or make you think this is more than just two adults having a good time with each other."

Her lips tingled…as well as other parts of her body.

"If you wear that brooch, you want more of this…" He drew her bottom lip into his mouth, let his tongue play against her flesh, then nipped it with his teeth before releasing it. "But I need you to understand that's all I can give. I can give you pleasure, I can give you fun, but I can't give you forever. I can only give you the months I have while I'm here. I don't want there to be any misunderstanding about that. The last thing I want is to mislead or hurt you." He fell silent as if letting the weight of his words sink in.

She fell numb to everything but his arms around her and the way bolts of lightning zinged through her body. Mark delivered a kiss that not only sizzled but also scorched, short-circuiting her ability to reason.

With a blink, Karma's breath hitched as he closed his lips over hers again. She moaned into his mouth as the most incredible sensation of warmth spilled through her belly, into private places as yet undiscovered. Her thighs felt like hot lead. Damn, but Mark could turn up the heat.

She nodded against his mouth. She understood. She understood implicitly.

He broke away again, but stayed buried within her personal space, his arms around her, his forehead nudging hers. "I like you, Karma. You're sweet and innocent. I like that about you." He kissed her again. "But I also like that you seem to be a woman ready for more. A woman who wants to lose some of her innocence. I can give you that. I can teach you how to embrace your sensuality but maintain the innocence that makes you so alluring." He paused and stared at her mouth. "So damned alluring." He inhaled slowly then blew the breath out his nose on a contemplative moan. "I can help you discover what you like, what excites you, how to touch and be touched, and what turns you on.

What he was doing this very second was a good place to start, because she was definitely turned on.

He spoke quietly and more slowly than usual, as if each word held meaning. "I want to be the man who unleashes the sensual, sexual woman locked inside you. But only if you want me to. If it's too much and you're still worried about anyone finding out, I understand, and I won't ask again." He pressed his palm to his chest, right over his heart. "I promise. But I think we could have quite an adventure together. That's what I'm offering. An adventure. An opportunity for you to learn that you *are* good with men. You've just not been with the *right* men. What you need is a new perspective. I want to give you that."

She shivered, words escaping her. But then Mark had said enough to keep her mind busy the rest of the week.

He nodded toward her hand, still closed over the brooch. "That will be my answer. Wear that tomorrow, and I'll know you want to move forward. Don't wear it, and I'll never bring it up again." He paused. "But if you say yes, you need to know that I have rules."

"Rules?"

Kindness and understanding washed over his features. "Just a couple. Nothing crazy." He offered a tender smile. "Like I said, I'm not looking for forever, Karma. I'm not a forever kind of man. No commitments. Nothing serious. I want to make sure you know that up-front so there aren't any surprises." His gaze dropped to Karma's mouth then lifted to her eyes again. "But I *am* loyal. And if you say yes, you'll be the only woman in my life until after my work at Solar is done, and I'll want to be the only man in yours. Understood?"

No problem there. It wasn't like men were lining up to take her out. "Yes."

He brushed his thumb over the corner of her mouth. "I don't want to hurt you. I can't stress that enough. That's not my intent. I want to spend time with you, make you feel good, feel good in the process, have fun with you, but I can't commit to more than that."

"I understand." She had never expected him to marry her, and she appreciated knowing now where he stood rather than finding out later.

He held her a moment longer, and then he sighed, smiled, and let her go. "So think about it, and let me know tomorrow." He tapped her hand with his index finger. "And just so you know, there's no harm in saying no. If you really aren't comfortable with the idea of spending time together outside work, then I understand. So don't feel any pressure to say yes just because I want you to."

When had she grown so breathless?

Mark started for the door. "Sleep well, Karma, and good night. Thank you for a memorable evening." He stopped and smiled over his shoulder. "I'll see myself out."

Good, because right now her feet were rooted in place. Too stunned to move, her body warm and tingling all over, her knees weak, all she could do was watch him go.

A moment later, the front door opened and closed.

Except for the specter of his fiery kisses, which still lingered on her lips, she was alone.

She opened her fist and stared at the simple metal circle. If she wore it tomorrow, everything would change. But wasn't that what she wanted? The prospect was both exhilarating and terrifying. Breaking out of old comfort zones and habits was a daunting idea, but as her father always said, if you want to change some things in your life, you have to change some things in your life. You can't expect different results by continuing to do the same old things.

Maybe it was time to follow Dad's advice, because she definitely wanted to change some things in her life.

"Good night," she whispered.

Chapter 17

In the end, we only regret the chances we didn't take, relationships we are afraid to have, and the decisions we waited too long to make.
-Author Unknown

The next morning, Karma steeled herself, stepped out of her car, and marched toward Solar's entrance. Mark was already there. His BMW was parked in his usual spot.

With a confident yank, she pulled open the door, sashayed past the deserted reception desk, and took the stairs to her quiet space outside Don's office. Mark's voice came from the conference room, deep and full. He was already on the phone, even though it was only seven thirty.

After setting down her purse and draping her jacket over the back of her chair, she strolled around the corner to the coffee station, poured a mug, added one packet of sugar, stirred it, and carried the hot mug into the conference room.

Mark faced away from the door, leaning back in his chair with one hand behind his head and his phone to his ear. "Yes, I know, Pat, but here's the thing…"

She clunked the mug down on the table beside a sheet of paper filled with doodles of faces. Looked like Mark was a doodler, and a good one at that. Some of his doodles were of celebrities.

Startled, Mark sat forward and spun around. As soon as his eyes landed on her, his eyebrows lifted with appreciation, and his gaze swiftly dragged down her body, all the way to her black platform heels, then slid back up her legs, the black pencil skirt, red V-neck short-sleeved sweater, all the way to the gold brooch pinned to the red scarf tied in a cowl around her neck. After staring at the brooch for a full two seconds, his delighted gaze lifted to hers.

Jutting out her chin, she nodded once, spun on the ball of her foot, and marched back to her desk.

Sure, she had misgivings and insecurities about whatever *this* was between them. But if she said no, she would regret it for the rest of her life. She would feel like a coward, and she didn't want to be a coward, anymore.

So, as with the deep end of the pool, she was jumping in without a life preserver. She could learn to swim later.

"Uh, no. I'm sorry, Pat. I was momentarily…distracted," he said. "Could you repeat that?"

She grinned at making him lose his train of thought, but her knees still went weak. She tittered with excitement, anxiety, the thrill of things to come, and a healthy dose of oh-my-God-did-I-just-do-that? Adrenaline raced through her veins, making her heart rate spike and her breath come in tight, short bursts.

Reaching her desk, she collapsed on wobbly legs. Her hands shook as she tried to type in her log-in. Three attempts later, she unlocked her computer.

Damn it! She needed to calm down. Mark was just a guy. He put his pants on the same way everybody did. He ate, drank, slept, and got sick just like the next guy. So then why was he so friggin' special? Why did he hold the power to make her legs weak, her hands tremble, and her heart race with nervous anticipation?

She tucked her hair behind her ear and looked up. Mark faced her, phone still to his ear, his other hand behind his head. That satisfied grin was still plastered on his face. After a long moment, he brought his hand around, placed it over his heart, closed his eyes, and slowly nodded his head in silent gratitude.

She nodded back, albeit more covertly, her eyes shifting to the side then down to her desk.

She turned away, took a steadying breath, and willed her fingers to stop shaking as she started weeding through her e-mail.

Let the adventure begin.

Chapter 18

Your struggles develop your strengths. When you go through hardships and decide not to surrender, that is strength.
-Author Unknown

Tuesday night, Karma sat on her couch, finishing a plate of homemade lasagna. The TV was turned to some random movie she was neither interested in nor paying attention to. She simply wanted noise to drown out the barrage of voices that echoed through her head. So many questions, so much confusion. And no answers.

Mark had left the office with Don at ten o'clock this morning to attend two off-site meetings and a client business dinner. She hadn't heard from him all day, and now that they had entered into what felt like a covert affair, she was antsy to see him.

At eight thirty, her phone dinged with a text. Snatching it from the coffee table, her heart skipped. The message was from Mark.

Are you busy?

She typed out her response. *No.*

Less than thirty seconds later, her phone chimed again. *Can I come over?*

Her mind screamed, *Yes! God yes!* Instead, she typed, *Sure.*

She stared at the blank screen, biting her lip, eyes wide. Something about the fact that he was texting her gave her a perverse thrill.

She actually jumped when her phone dinged again.

Be there in fifteen.

She hopped up, quickly cleaned her dishes, put away the leftover lasagna, rushed to check her hair, took a few deep breaths, and returned to the living room.

A few minutes later, he arrived with a quiet knock.

Butterflies took flight, angels sang, and rainbows and unicorns danced around her heart.

"Hi," she said, holding the door open.

"Hi." He had changed into loose jeans and a faded-blue T-shirt, and he held a small, gift-wrapped box in his hands.

She waved him in and gestured toward the couch. "I wasn't sure I would hear from you tonight."

"I would have called sooner, but dinner ran late, and I wanted to pick something up before coming over." He held out the box as he settled into the couch.

"What's this?" He was already buying her gifts? She had never received a gift from a man before.

"Just a little something I thought might be fun to help us get to know one another." His devilish smile told her this wasn't just any ordinary gift. "Go ahead, open it."

"Is this going to embarrass me?" She removed the bow on top.

"I guarantee it."

"Oh God." She hid her face in her hand, making him laugh.

"Oh, come on. It's not *that* bad."

She ripped off the paper, pulled out a four by five box, and read the front. *Cosmo's Truth or Dare: Our Naughtiest Game Ever!* Dumbfounded and speechless, her mouth flapped open, closed, and then opened again as she lifted her gaze to Mark's. Was he serious?

"Here, let me open that for you." Mark took the box from her and lifted the side, which closed magnetically. The top opened like a book, and inside was a deck of cards.

"What exactly did you have planned tonight?" She gulped and eyed the cards as if they were scary intruders. It didn't take a genius to figure out by the cover of the box that this was a game for two consenting adults. And, yes, while she had agreed to move forward with Mark, consenting to whatever the *dare* portion of this game likely entailed wasn't what she had in mind this soon in their relationship…or whatever this was between them.

Mark thumbed through the deck—there had to be at least two hundred cards—then set them on the coffee table.

"Don't worry. I don't plan on *daring* you to do anything. I just thought we could go through some of the truths and learn a little more about one another, and maybe have a little fun and a few laughs."

"Why do I get the feeling you just want to make me as uncomfortable as possible?" She had felt the color drain from her face the moment she read the game's title.

"That's precisely why I bought the game."

"Huh?" Was Mark sadistic?

"What I mean is that, sometimes it takes uncomfortable circumstances for us to find ourselves. The more uncomfortable the better if change is what you want." He took her hand. "And I think you want change, or you wouldn't have worn that brooch today. Am I right?"

He made a good point. "Well…yes."

"Trust me. I just want to get to know you. That's all. So I can take better care of you." He searched her eyes for understanding.

She liked his choice of words. *So I can take better care of you.* How many women could say that the men in their lives held such attitudes?

"Okay," she said, feeling her nerves ease.

He let go of her hand and sat back. "So let's just play *Truth or Truth* with our game. No dares tonight." He nodded toward the cards on the table. "Just pick up a card, and ask me the question. I'll answer then do the same. How's that sound?"

Karma took a deep breath and eyed the cards. "Okay. But if I die from embarrassment, tell my family I loved them."

His deep, throaty laughter tickled her ears. She loved his laugh.

"I promise," he said, crossing his heart. "Now, go on. Take a card and ask me a question."

She picked up the top card. Just reading the question to herself made her face burn.

"Okay," she said, sighing, "Do you like your hair pulled during sex?" She couldn't even read it aloud with a straight face, let alone make eye contact.

"Hmm, I guess that depends on the situation, but yes, generally speaking, I like when a woman pulls my hair during sex."

Curious now, Karma looked up. "Really? Why?" She figured it would hurt if someone pulled her hair, whether during sex or otherwise.

He shrugged, and his left eyebrow shot up. "I guess I like it because it shows me the woman is really enjoying herself. That she's completely lost to her passion." He paused. "I take it you've never had your hair pulled like that." It wasn't a question.

Karma briskly shook her head and set the card down like it was a hot potato. "No."

"Didn't think so." Mark reached for the deck and pulled off the next card. A crooked grin spread over his mouth as he read the question. "Who was the first person you ever kissed? Was it good or bad?"

Well, that wasn't too bad. A question like that wasn't likely to send her into a queasy fit. She reluctantly told him about kissing Tony in high school and how she froze up, which made him laugh.

"Okay then, how about the second guy you kissed?"

"Hey, that's two questions."

He crossed his hands in his lap. "Just getting to you know you."

"Fine, play by your rules." She took a deep breath and blew it out. "The second guy I kissed was named Brian, and…" She cringed. "That kiss was kind of bad, too."

"How so?"

Of course Mark would want specifics.

"He and I were both…um…virgins, and I kind of froze up with him, too. Just like with Tony."

"How did you and Brian meet?"

"At a movie theater where we both worked during senior year. Brian attended a different school than I did, but we got to be pretty good friends at work."

"Did you end up having sex with Brian?" Mark's eyes never wavered from hers.

Flames shot through Karma's face and down her neck, and she dropped her gaze to her hands, which rested in her lap. "Yes. Eventually."

"Was it good?"

She shook her head. "Not really."

"Tell me about it."

She knew what Mark was trying to do. He was trying to get her to open up and become more comfortable talking about this kind of thing—trying to enforce *change*. But right now, this had to be the most awkward, difficult conversation she'd ever had. Even worse than the time she got called to the principal's office in junior high for calling a classmate who was bullying her a skanky bitch. Not her finest hour.

She lifted her gaze to his and found warmth and safety staring back. Mark really did have her best intentions at heart, and he clearly wanted their time together—as little as they had—to mean something and make a difference.

She gathered the courage and moved forward. "Brian and I were virgins. We met at work." Each sentence felt labored, but as she forced herself to continue, it grew easier. "He was an usher, and I worked in the concession stand. After work, we often hung out together, and now that I think about it, he probably liked me more than I liked him." Brian had been a nice boy, and, at the time, she had felt like he was as good a guy as any to lose her virginity to. Now she wished she hadn't, but at the time, all she wanted was to get her first time over with in hopes it would make her feel more grown-up and help put her past behind her.

As she relayed the story, the memories of that night six years ago rushed into her mind, and they felt just as fresh, just as raw.

Brian's mom had been out for the evening, and he had stolen a condom from her bedside table before rushing back into the living room where Karma waited for him, half naked, on the floor.

He began to put on the condom, and then, "Damn it!"

"What?" Karma frowned as Brian scampered bare-assed out of the living room and down the hall toward his mom's room again. The only light came from the TV, which was fine by her. The less light, the better.

"Condom broke," he called back.

Karma sat up in the shadow-strewn room and straightened her work shirt, which smelled like buttered popcorn, then pulled her jeans over her lap, waiting for him to return. The only way she could do this was if she could keep on some of her clothes. No one had seen her naked before. Brian didn't seem to mind her shyness, though. Then again, he was an eighteen-year-old virgin, too. He was probably just happy he was finally getting laid.

She tucked her long, mousy brown hair behind her ears and looked around. Some B-rate monster flick was on TV, and the smell of two-hour-old pizza wafted from the open box on the nearby coffee table. This wasn't how Karma imagined she would lose her virginity. On a hard living room floor, which was covered with carpet that looked like dirt and felt like fuzzy tree bark, but at least tomorrow she could wake up and know she had finally done it.

She eyed the afghan tossed over the back of the couch. A blanket was a good idea. This carpet didn't exactly look sanitary on her bare bottom. She pulled the afghan to the floor and spread it out, sitting back down and covering up with her jeans again just as Brian returned from his mom's bedroom. He held two more condoms in his hand.

"Just in case I break another one," he said breathlessly, dropping to the floor in front of her as he tore one open.

Unlike her, Brian was naked, and his erection strained toward her. It looked a little too big to fit.

She gulped and took a nervous breath as he put the condom on.

"There," he said with a smile and wiped his hand on the blanket. "Did it right this time." He laughed nervously. "I tried to put the last one on backward."

"Oh, okay." Karma nibbled her lip. She hadn't known there was a right or wrong way to put on a condom, but now that she thought about it, it made sense. "So…now what?"

Brian clumsily lurched forward and kissed her, pushing her to the floor. She bonked her head.

"Sorry," he said, wriggling around on top of her.

"No, it's okay. Just..." Her leg was pinned, and she worked it out from under him. "There." She bent her knees on either side of his hips as he fumbled around, pushing against her like an excited bull charging a matador.

"Am I in the right place?" Brian grunted and shifted, and his erection bumped and pushed against her.

"I don't know...ow!"

"Sorry."

"That's okay. I don't think that's—ow!"

What were they doing wrong?

"Here, maybe if I..." Brian reached down, grabbed his penis, and began shoving it against her private parts as if it were one of those round blocks in a children's game and he was trying to jimmy the thing inside a square hole. "Can I move these?" He let go of his erection and tugged on her jeans, which still lay over her hips.

"Um...I don't..." She didn't want to lose her security blanket, but it was dark...and he wasn't looking at her down there...and she was more concerned with keeping her top half covered than her lower half, anyway...and maybe it would be easier for him to get inside her if her jeans weren't in the way. "Okay, sure."

He yanked them out from between their bodies and tossed them under the coffee table.

"That's better," he said, taking hold of his penis again.

He pushed, he prodded, and then, with a sigh of relief, he unceremoniously found where he had been trying to go for five minutes.

"Ow!" Karma winced and dug her nails into Brian's shoulders as he gained entry. *Ow, ow, ow!* Damn! Was it supposed to hurt this much? She'd read somewhere that a girl's first time could hurt, but she hadn't expected this kind of pain. In the movies, women usually looked like they were enjoying this, but there was nothing enjoyable about what Brian was doing to her. At all.

Brian bucked and looked like he was having a seizure as he began hammering away, and it felt like it, too. Her poor vagina. Would she even be able to walk tomorrow? God, what was he doing?

"Oh, uh-huh. Good...yes...is it good for you?" Brian was like an overly excited jackrabbit, and he spouted words in a way that sounded foreign on his tongue, as if he'd heard them in a movie—maybe the same ones she'd seen where the women actually *enjoyed* having sex—and thought he was *supposed* to say them.

Karma held on to his spasming body and tried to nod. "Yes." It wouldn't help to tell him the truth that this was the worst kind of pain she had ever felt, except for that time when she fell and cut her leg on a jagged rock poking out of the ground. But even that had lasted only a few seconds. This pain had gone on for almost a minute already, and it was getting worse.

Brian's eyes were closed, so he couldn't see the distress on Karma's face as he continued bruising her tender flesh with his penis of death. "Yes, so good…I can't stop…Karma…oh…oh…uh-huh…there…" Brian huffed, puffed, and made like a giant jumping bean as he pounded her fragile flesh even harder.

OOOOWWWW!

Her back and hip bones ground against the floor, and white-hot pain seared her insides. She wanted it to be over. Just hurry up already and be done. This shit hurt.

In less than two minutes from start to finish, Brian's body began to jerk. His breathing intensified and his animalistic grunts rose on a crescendo. Then he slammed his hips into her and fell into epileptic shudders. A long, ragged exhale poured from his open mouth. Then he collapsed on top of her. Done.

Thank God.

Afterward, Karma had stared at the water spot on the ceiling, numb, with flames licking the inside of her vagina as Brian remained on top of her, gasping for air. But the pain had been a small price to pay for achieving a rite of passage.

"I'd begun to think I would never have sex," she said, coming to the end of the story. "But there, on Brian's living room, with *Godzilla* roaring from the TV and cold pizza on the coffee table, I finally did it. I lost my virginity." When she finished, she glanced at Mark, who had grown so quiet it was almost as if he weren't there.

"That was your first time?"

She nodded and looked down at her hands, but not before she saw a flash of emotion pass through his eyes.

"Did the two of you have sex again after that?"

"A few more times."

"Did it get better?"

"No, not really. It didn't hurt as much, but it was always rapid-fire fast, like he didn't want to get caught or something."

"And you never had an orgasm?" Mark watched her closely, as if he were taking each of her answers and building a file in his head.

"No."

"And how many lovers have you had since Brian?"

She knew Mark already understood there hadn't been many, and now was the moment of truth.

"I'd like to say none, but there was one more, but I don't really count him."

Mark's eyes narrowed briefly, and he tilted his head slightly to one side. "Why not?"

"Because we only did it once."

"Only once? Was that your choice or his?"

"His, but after I found out why, it was mine, too."

Concern etched the lines of Mark's face as he shifted on the couch. He appeared both worried and concerned, as if he wanted to know what happened but wasn't sure he should ask.

"Richard was an ass," she said, making the decision for him. "He only wanted one thing, and I was too gullible at the time to know that. He seduced me, and I use that term lightly, because all he wanted was sex."

"How did you know him?"

"He was part of the crowd Daniel and I hung out with in college for a while. He got to know me, and after a couple of 'dates'..." she made air quotes with her fingers, "we had sex."

Mark sat forward. "Did you want to?"

"At the time, I thought I did, because, like I said, he seduced me. He told me how much he liked me, and how alike we were, and how he knew from the moment we met that I was special. Blah, blah, blah."

Mark chuffed. "He didn't seduce you. He lied so he could use you." He sounded disgusted, and didn't that just make him seem like her knight in shining armor.

"Yes, I figured that out the hard way." Silence stretched between them for several seconds. "A few weeks later, I learned that was Richard's MO. He moved in, targeted girls who were shy and quiet, then did his thing."

Mark pressed his lips together and his face grew tight, but he didn't voice whatever frustration she could tell sat on the tip of his tongue. A moment later, he said, "I'm sorry."

"It's not your fault," she said.

"I made you think about it."

She smiled. "I'm pretty tough. I can handle it."

He gestured toward the cards. "If you want to stop playing, we can—"

"No, I want to continue."

"You're sure?"

"Positive." Talking about all this was strangely freeing. She felt like she was molting, shedding old layers of herself to reveal more of the woman within.

He sighed and sat back. "Okay then, it's your turn. Pick a card and ask me a question."

She could tell that, at some point, Richard would come up again, even if only in passing or indirectly.

"Okay," she said, picking up a card. She snickered when she read it. "This is a good one. What's the most flexible sex move you can do? Tell me why it's *awesome*?" She emphasized *awesome* even though it wasn't emphasized on the card.

Mark burst into laughter. "What? Seriously?" He grabbed the card and read it to himself.

Karma laughed, which was a nice change from the oh-so-serious line of questioning she had just endured. And maybe channeling all that seriousness was why she and Mark both continued laughing a little too hard for several seconds.

"I can't say that I have any flexible sex moves," he said, flicking the card toward the table. It fluttered and spun on the air before gliding to the floor. "Unlike you, I don't do yoga. I think I'd break something if I tried to get flexible. Ask me another," he said. "I didn't like that one and can't answer it, anyway. Besides, I owe you after that last round of questioning."

She snagged the next card on the stack. "Would you rather be lightly spanked in bed or have a feather run softly over your whole body?"

"Mmm." Mark sank into the cushions and looked up at the ceiling. "Definitely the feather. Or maybe hair." He turned his eyes on her. "I like a woman's hair to glide down my chest and stomach."

There was only one time a woman's hair would glide down his chest and stomach, and that was if she was taking her mouth *down there*. So, yeah, this game had just taken an interesting turn.

"Has anyone ever used a feather on you?"

He licked his lips. "Once or twice."

Her mind took the next logical step. "Have you ever used a feather on anyone?"

His single dimple dug into his right cheek. "Once or twice."

"And…?"

"It can be very pleasurable," he said. "Perhaps I'll show you sometime." Before she could say anything further, he grabbed the next card on the deck. "My turn." He read it to himself first. "What's the first thing that pops into your head when I say oral?" He lowered the card and gave her a slightly wicked smile. There was no doubt where his mind had gone.

And considering where her thoughts had just been a minute ago with the whole hair-on-his-body idea, her mind had gone there, too, because her first thought was of giving Mark a blow job. But no way was she going to say that, especially when she had never given one. There had to be a law that stated if you'd never given a blow job, you couldn't use the term.

"Hygiene!" she said a little too forcefully.

His left eyebrow rose as he narrowed his eyes. "Why don't I believe you?"

She shrugged and quickly picked up another card, trying to hurry ahead before he could entrap her into another long line of questioning that was sure to embarrass her. "Have you ever been aroused at work? Give me details."

"Yes," he said. "I have been aroused at work. Very recently in fact." He sat forward and leveled her with a look that held enough steam to hard boil an egg. "Friday, when I suggested that you unbutton your blouse, and when you did…?" His gaze swept her face, and a wistful smile played over his mouth. "That really turned me on."

Oh wow, okay, so…uh-huh. The game was definitely getting more interesting.

He held her gaze for a long moment then picked up the next card as he cleared his throat. His smile brightened as he read the question to himself. "I like this one," he said. "I can't wait to hear your answer." He looked up, eyes twinkling. "What physical trait of mine first caught your eye?"

Way to put her on the spot. She pressed her lips together, thought about it for a second, and tried to envision him sitting beside her at the blackjack table. She had turned toward him, and a split second before she looked at his face, she saw his hands. He had rugged, sure hands. The kind that when they held you made you feel like you were really being held. She hadn't known that at the time, but she'd found out soon enough.

"Your hands," she said definitively.

"My hands." He glanced at them.

"Yes. Then your eyes, then your mouth, and then your chest when we were dancing."

A glimmer of recollection crossed his face. "Ah, yes, I remember." He grinned, making her blush as she recalled feeling him up. "You did seem a little *taken* with my chest at one point."

Looking down, she forced herself not to laugh. "I guess you caught that."

"Mm-hm. It was cute how you reacted when I caught you, too."

She sighed. "Okay, you can stop embarrassing me now."

He laughed and settled into the cushions again. "Are you a chest woman?"

"A chest woman?" She frowned in confusion. "What's a chest woman?"

"You know how some men are leg men, some are boob men, stuff like that. Are you a woman who likes men's chests? Do they turn you on?"

"I never thought about it that way, but yes, I guess so. I also seem to notice a man's arms and his hands, too." She gestured toward his. "Obviously, since that was the first part of you I noticed. Hmm…chests, arms, hands, shoulders. I guess I'm more of an overall upper body kind of gal."

"I see." The file he was building on her sounded like it had just grown a bit more interesting, much like the conversation.

She snagged the next card before she could dork out any more than she already had then almost choked as she read the question. "Do you think toe sucking is totally hot or really gross?" She started laughing. Toe sucking? Really? Who came up with these questions?

"Totally hot, for sure," he said without hesitation, cutting off her thoughts.

Karma's mouth fell open. "What? Really?"

He nodded emphatically. "Oh God, yes." He glanced down at her sneakered feet. "I'm what is called a *foot* man." As evidence, he lifted hers and unlaced her sneakers without pulling them off, even though it looked as though it took all his willpower not to as he caressed her ankles. "I thought you would have figured that out already. I haven't done a very good job hiding my interest in your feet."

She remembered how he'd looked at them last Friday at the department store, how he'd moaned just a little, and how he'd seemed so affected when he'd told her she had beautiful feet, but the thought had never occurred to her that there were men in the world who got turned on by feet or that he was one of them. Discovering this little nugget about Mark was like finding a chunk of gold in her carpet, and his reasoning for asking her to wear the black peep-toe pumps to the concert suddenly made more sense. Finally, this game had given her something she could slip into her mental Mark file.

"You mean, if I took off my shoes right now…" She gently pushed her toe against the heel of one sneaker so that it pushed halfway off her foot. His eyes instantly flared as he dropped his gaze. "Does this distract you?" She grinned daringly as the vixen side of her personality shoved her conservative persona into the shadows.

He moaned and laid his head back, taking a heavy breath. Then he cast her a warning glance. "Yes, that distracts me."

"Oh, I'm sorry," she said as innocently as she could muster as she began to tuck her foot back into her shoe. "I'll just put my shoe back on and—"

He grabbed her foot and pulled off her sneaker. "No. Don't." His heated gaze raked her face. "Please." He dropped her sneaker to the floor, pulled off the other, and dropped it as well. "If you don't mind, I'd like you to keep your shoes off." His breathing sounded labored, as if he was forcing himself to calm down, and his eyelids drooped, giving him a sexy, drowsy appeal.

His expression lit something primitive and debased in the pit of her stomach. "My feet really turn you on that much?"

He blinked heavily, and as if he were holding a sacred gift, he lifted her right leg by the ankle, opened his legs, and nestled the sole of her foot against his crotch. He was hard. Very hard. An airy moan broke in his throat. "Yes. Your feet really turn me on that much." He took a heavy breath and blew it out like he was trying to meditate. Then he swallowed and, holding her sole against him, leaned over and picked up a card. "Your turn." He took a moment to compose himself then read the question. "Which do you think is hotter: sex standing against a wall or bent over a table?"

Karma had never done either, so how could she answer honestly? "I don't know."

"Let me guess, you have no experience with either way, right?" He still sounded sexually bent but a bit calmer.

She bit her lip and nodded.

"Does one sound more interesting than the other?"

She thought about it for a moment then shook her head. "Not really."

Mark grinned as if making a mental note. "Well, we'll just have to help you figure that out, won't we?"

Gulp.

"I guess." She grabbed the next card. It certainly was getting warm in here, especially with her foot still pressed to his erection. After reading the card to herself, this next question wasn't going to cool things off, either. "On a scale of one to ten, how sensitive are your…uh…your nipples?" The words caught in her throat, and she coughed before reading the second half of the question. "How would you like me to…um…touch them?" She slowly lifted her gaze.

He looked like a wolf ready to devour her.

"My nipples are pretty sensitive, so I'll say about an eight or nine." His voice had grown deeper. "I like when a woman touches them or licks them. Or *bites* them." He cleared his throat and shifted on the couch, making her foot rub down the hard length of him. "And you have sexy teeth."

"Sexy teeth?"

He nodded. "Oh yes. Very sexy. I want you to do naughty things to me with your teeth. No drawing blood or anything like that, but…"

She felt light-headed. "No, of course not."

"It's just that…" He licked his lips. "I like the idea of your mouth on me, Karma."

And she liked the idea of his on her.

Mark waited a moment before grabbing the next card from the deck. The corner of his mouth ticked upward. Oh boy, this was going to be a good one. She could just tell.

"Describe exactly what it feels like when you orgasm."

Thud!

"Um, well…" She exhaled heavily through pursed lips, making her cheeks puff out.

Mark set down the card and casually sat back, waiting for her answer, a patient smile on his face.

"Okay, so…" Her fingers twisted in her lap. "You already know I've never had an orgasm during…um…sex."

"From what you've told me, I assumed that was the case. But you have had an orgasm, haven't you?"

If she said yes, she would be admitting to masturbation, and something about that felt too personal.

"Karma," he said, his voice lilting as he rocked himself against her foot. "Do you give yourself pleasure?"

"Oh hell," she said, huffing as she rolled her eyes. "Fine. Yes. Yes I do. God, this is so embarrassing."

"And…what does it feel like?"

She set her jaw and slapped her hands on her thighs. "Good, okay?

It feels good."

He threw his head back and laughed so hard his whole body shook. "Fine, I'll take that. But…" He held up his index finger as if making a point. "An orgasm you give yourself rarely feels as good as one someone else gives you, and almost never as good as one you have during sex."

"Oh, and you know this how?" She plucked the next card off the pile. "Oh wait, let me guess. Lots of practice, right?"

His single dimple creased his cheek. "Something like that, yes. But I've also read a lot on the subject." His eyebrows shot up as if he'd had a Eureka moment. "As a matter of fact, I'm going to build you a reading list. I have a few books in mind that I think you'll enjoy."

She lowered her face into her left hand and groaned. "I feel like Luke Skywalker being trained in how to use The Force."

Mark burst into laughter again. "Are you calling me Yoda?"

She had to admit, it was pretty funny. "No. You're better looking than Yoda."

"I certainly hope so." He pointed to her card. "Okay, ask me."

She read the card. Her heart performed another perfect swan dive into the pit of her stomach, and she glanced warily at him.

"Go ahead," he said. "I can already tell this one's good."

He had no idea.

"Okay, um…" She looked back down. *Here goes.* "Take me to a place in the house where we haven't had sex." Her gaze flicked nervously to his before she continued. "Kiss me…and then whisper what you would do to me if we were to…get it on there." She lowered the card to her lap and kept her head down.

Mark waited a moment then lifted her foot from between his legs, leaned toward her, and reached for her hand. Without looking at him, she took it. As he moved into the middle of the couch, he tugged her onto his lap and situated her so that she faced him. Her legs straddled his thighs.

Her heart beat like a wild drum in her chest.

"Come here," he whispered, caressing her cheek in such a way that drew her face to his. His lips found hers and held them in a static kiss. He didn't move, and neither did she. All that mattered was the simple, chaste connection and the way a thousand tiny starbursts exploded throughout her body. His kiss seemed so innocent, and yet it sent shards of erotic desire into her blood.

He broke away, but held her close. "Since we haven't had sex, yet, I choose here." He patted the couch. "And as for what I would do to you here, I would make you stand in front of me, where I would slip my hands up your skirt and pull off your panties. I would invite you onto my lap and whisper how sexy you are…" He bent around and kissed her earlobe. "You're *very* sexy."

A shiver raced down her spine.

His lips skimmed down her jaw to her chin. "I would kiss your neck." And he did, letting his tongue sneak out to lick a fiery trail from one side to the other.

Karma felt like she was in a vicious state of sensory overload. She was practically panting.

"And I wouldn't stop making love to you until you came." His breath washed over the skin of her neck, and his lips closed over her shoulder as he licked her. "Your first orgasm with a man inside you," he said a moment later when he met her gaze again.

As badly as she needed oxygen, she could hardly breathe.

"Oh," she whispered breathlessly. Apparently she could barely speak, too.

His gaze dropped to her mouth, and a heartbeat later, their lips meshed again, this time with more force. A quiet groan broke from deep in his chest.

She wrapped her arms around his neck and shoulders. No way was she letting this moment go. All night, they had talked about sex. Visions of him in various states of undress had taunted her throughout their game, and she had felt his magnificence against the sole of her foot for at least ten minutes. They had fallen under the very spell the game was designed to cast, because they were unraveling into lust faster than a stripper takes off her clothes.

"Bite my lip," he muttered against her mouth. "Let yourself go."

She thought she *had been* letting go, but clearly he knew her better than she knew herself, because the moment he told her to let go, she found a fifth gear she hadn't thought possible. Her tongue danced with his, and he groaned low and loud, and when she did as he asked and took his bottom lip between her teeth, he practically growled, and his fingers curled into claws on her back, pulling her closer.

"That's my girl," he said when she released his lip. Then he assaulted her mouth again, nipping her lip as if to show her the pleasure she had just given him. And it *was* pleasurable. Being bitten, even if only lightly, knocked her good side clear out of the picture, leaving only the vixen she had discovered in Chicago.

Passion rose in her blood, turning her into someone else. She was no longer sweet, shy, good Karma. She was lusty, sultry, bad Karma.

A woman lost to her desires, driven by erotic need, who wanted to experience pleasure only a man could give. That only *Mark* could give.

He pulled away, and she opened her eyes to find him grinning at her, his gaze hooded.

"What?" she said, breathless.

His left eyebrow twitched. "You're pulling my hair."

She glanced up and found that her hands had curled into fists, and tufts of his dark brown hair poked out between her fingers. She quickly opened her hands and let go.

Of course, this made Mark laugh. "I wasn't complaining. Remember, I like when a woman pulls my hair."

"Uh, yes…" She sheepishly looked away. "I got a bit carried away."

He pulled her down so that her forehead rested against his. "I know. And I liked it. A lot."

For a long moment, nothing was said as Mark ran his palms slowly up and down her back. "I want to be the first man to show you what you've been missing, Karma," he said softly. "I want to succeed where others have failed."

Her bashful side made a subtle reappearance, and she curled in on herself. "Why?"

He caressed her cheek. "For one, I think you deserve to know what a really good orgasm feels like, don't you?"

When he put it that way, how could she say no?

His fingertips brushed back her hair. "Second of all, I'm a man. And, like most men, I'm proud and have a big ego. I'm not afraid to admit it. And when I make a woman feel good…when I give her such intense pleasure that she screams my name as she's falling into the most unbelievable orgasm she's ever had, I take great pride in that." He hesitated and narrowed his eyes. "Especially when I know she's never felt anything like that before." He paused to let his words sink in.

Karma's entire body heated. They had most definitely sunk in.

Who says egomania is a bad thing?

Mark shifted against the couch, and she felt his erection press against her. "To know that I awakened that part of a woman gives me tremendous satisfaction, Karma. It's the best ego boost in the world." His gaze danced back and forth between her eyes. "So, the most direct answer to your question is that I want to feel you fall apart and come undone under my touch." He took a shaky breath and closed his palm over her cheek. "My God, but just the thought of that…to see you, head thrown back, that heart-shaped mouth open as you cry out…" He rubbed his thumb over her bottom lip. "Let's just say the idea turns me on very much."

The idea turned her on, too, as in way on.

"There's something undeniably sexy about you, Karma," he said. "You intrigue me, and I want the pleasure of discovering you, and of helping you discover yourself if you'll let me. Will you? Let me?"

As the air in the room froze and her heart beat in a wild rhythm, hope and anxious anticipation broke over Mark's expression. His intense stare never wavered.

The most lascivious aspect of their pending affair pressed solidly against the apex of her body, and she had to force herself not to rotate her hips. How would he feel inside her? What would it feel like to finally have an orgasm—a *real* orgasm—during intercourse? Mark promised to answer all those questions and more.

What he was offering was more than she ever could have imagined. He was handsome, charming, intelligent, and confident in his abilities. He was the kind of man women dream of. And he wanted to be with her. *Her!*

If you want to change some things in your life, you need to change some things in your life.

"Yes," she whispered. "Yes, I'll let you."

She bit her lip and a shudder danced up her spine as he smiled.

Mark had to be a magician, because only a magician could have made her behave the way she had tonight.

This was going to be good. So very, very good. She didn't regret her decision to wear that gold brooch to work today one bit. Not one damn bit.

Chapter 19

Talking to your best friend is sometimes all the therapy you need.
-Author Unknown

On Wednesday, Mark flew with Don to Pennsylvania to meet with a couple of leasing companies about warehouse space. At lunchtime, Lisa cornered Karma, and there had been no way she could keep all the wonderful, sexy details of the night before to herself.

"Oh girl, I am so jealous," Lisa said over their bowls of lobster bisque. "You are going to have so much fun, and when he's through with you," Lisa snapped her fingers, "you will be a whole new woman. I just know it."

"We'll see." Karma couldn't deny that Mark made her feel things she had never felt and do things she'd never done. But would that really translate to a whole new her? Or would she fall back into her old ways once Mark was gone?

"This isn't a permanent relationship, you know."

"What do you mean?" Lisa scraped the last bite of soup from her bowl.

"Well, when his work here is done and he goes back to Chicago, that's it. No more relationship."

"He told you that?"

"He said he's not a long-term kind of guy." She raised her shoulders in a small, quick motion as she dipped a chunk of bread in her bowl. "But," she held up an index finger, "he said that while we're together, there won't be anyone else. Even though he's not into long-term relationships, he's very committed. He won't see anyone else and doesn't want me to, either."

"Well, that's good," Lisa said. "At least you know he won't screw you over."

"Exactly." Karma liked that everything was laid out up-front. There was no pressure to behave a certain way so she didn't chase him away. No wondering whether or not he was seeing someone on the side, no fear of being hurt. She knew what this was and what it wasn't, which alleviated a lot of oppressive mental weight.

She pushed her empty bowl aside.

"So, the two of you will have a good time while he's here." Lisa sipped her drink. "You'll have a good time, he'll show you what you've been missing…" A mischievous smile played over her mouth. "And he'll give you the best four to six sexual months of your *life*."

"Lisa! Sshh!" Karma gasped and quickly looked around to make sure no one had overheard.

Lisa giggled. "Oh, hush. Nobody heard me." She leaned over the table and whispered excitedly, "But, oh my God, Karma! Mark is *the* hottest guy *ever*, and he wants *you*. And not only does he *want* you, but he wants to make you feel things you've never *felt* before." She giggled again. "This is so freaking *awesome*!"

Lisa sounded almost as excited as Karma felt. "I know. Maybe you should pinch me to make sure I'm not actually dreaming."

"Oh, you're not dreaming, sister. But you'd better make sure you don't forget your best friend here. I expect all the juicy details, so don't even think about holding out on me." She hunched against the table and snickered.

After spilling the rest of the details of her Tuesday night, she and Lisa returned to the office. To the bleak dreariness that was her world with Mark out of town.

Thursday wasn't much better. Uneventful, if not slightly torturous. She had gotten used to Mark's presence, and the space felt a little empty without him there.

After returning on a late flight Thursday, he was back in the office on Friday morning.

As she worked on Don's expense report, she glanced toward the closed conference room. Mark was in another meeting. This time with Don and the director of sales. But then, that came with his job. He had a lot of meetings and sat in on a lot of conference calls.

"How's your boyfriend today?"

Karma's head snapped around, and a cold chill swept down her spine as Jolene slinked up to her desk. "W-what?"

"Your *boyfriend*? Mark?" Jo sneered and gestured toward the closed conference room.

For a second, Karma thought Jolene had found out about her and Mark, and that sinking feeling of pure terror—the one you get after watching the original *Amityville Horror* and hear a noise like footsteps but it's really your heart beating in fear—doused her gut.

Then she saw the snarky, cat-claw look in Jolene's eyes. Ever since Mark had shunned Jolene last Friday when she invited him for drinks, Jo had become downright mean. Not only had she begun making snide comments to her in passing, but she also stopped by Karma's desk and snapped about one sales report or another on a regular basis.

Same ol' Jo. Just like in school, only older.

The best thing Karma could do was play Jo off, even though her bullying was mentally exhausting. "Ha ha," she said flatly. "Funny, Jo."

"You know you like him." Jo's perfectly shaped eyebrow spiked over her eye, as if she was daring her to deny her feelings.

"No, I don't." Karma didn't like lying and instantly cringed on the inside. It felt like Jo could see right through her, just like back in junior high.

"Sure you don't. But you *are* his little coffee fetcher." Jo's taunting knew no bounds. She leaned forward and rested her arms on Karma's counter. The gesture mashed her boobs together and showed off cleavage ample enough to make a Kardashian jealous. It was as if Jolene was purposely flaunting her impressive bust in a show of supremacy over Karma's smaller one. As if bust size translated to seniority. "I see how you get his coffee every morning. You're trying to get his attention, aren't you?" Her words uncoiled like a scorpion's tail, full of sting.

Karma shriveled under the onslaught. "No, I'm not. I'm just—"

"Don't waste your time." Jo's crystal blue gaze snaked over her. "He would never be interested in someone like you, anyway. You're too...*plain*." She smiled sweetly as if what she'd said was meant to be a compliment instead of a slap in the face. "Someone like Troy is more your speed. You should set your sights on him. I hear he's available."

Troy worked in IT and wore what looked like seventies retro plaid button downs every day, and his hair always looked like it needed to be washed. He was a nice guy, but awkwardly quiet and not at all attractive. Jolene's comments were meant to be cruel—to both her *and* Troy—and Karma felt bad for him.

"That's not nice, Jo," Karma said meekly, looking away.

"Whatever." Jolene pushed off the counter, tossed her hair off her shoulders, and crossed both arms over her chest. She huffed and turned up her nose. "I really don't care." She waved her manicured hand dismissively. "But that's not why I'm here."

That's exactly why you're here.

"I need the reports from last quarter." She refolded her arms and tapped her index finger impatiently against her skinny biceps. No "please." No "when you have a minute." Just, "I need them." As if she expected Karma to stop everything this instant and get them.

"Right now?" Karma said, glancing toward the conference room. "I was right in the middle of—"

"Gawd!" Jolene sighed and rolled her eyes as if Karma were the stupidest person on the planet. "I thought you could multitask, Karma. But if it's too much for your little brain to handle, I'll just tell Jake—"

"No. Just give me a second." Karma minimized the expense report application and opened the folder of quarterlies.

Old memories of Jolene picking on her at school crept into her mind, along with all the old feelings of inadequacy, failure, and shame. Karma may have gotten a haircut, she might be wearing new clothes, and for the first time in her life a hot man wanted to go out with her, but that didn't mean that everything had changed just-like-that. She couldn't expect to snap her fingers and let go of the past as easily as she'd let go of six inches of hair and a bad wardrobe. Some pains ran too deep to dismiss without a fight, and right now, Karma's miserable childhood memories were definitely fighting back. As if no matter what she did, she couldn't shed the past, or the sinking feelings of inadequacy. Her younger self cowered in her mind against Jolene's vicious onslaught. Would Karma ever be able to let go of the past and set her bruised, younger ego free?

"Today would be nice," Jolene quipped then huffed out an exasperated sigh.

Karma dug up the soft copies of the last batch of quarterly reports then pulled a hard copy from her files. "Here." She handed the spiral-bound booklet to Jo without looking at her. If she did, Jo would see the tears stinging the backs of her eyes and tease her even more. "I'll e-mail you the soft copies."

"Good." Jo snatched the booklet out of Karma's hand and strutted away.

After Jo was gone, Karma pushed away from her desk and darted to the bathroom, where she spent the next five minutes huddled in the handicapped stall crying. Damn it! Just…DAMN IT! She knocked the side of her fist against the wall. Why did she let Jolene get to her? If Jolene would do her own damn work, she wouldn't need to come and interrupt Karma's day and turn her inside out. That's what Karma should have said to Jo. She should have gotten in Jo's face and told her that from now on, she could do those damn quarterly reports herself. Who did Jo think she was, getting snarky with Karma when running quarterlies wasn't technically Karma's job? If anyone had a right to be angry, it was Karma. She did her job and she did Jo's, but did she get any thanks for saving Jo's ass on an almost daily basis. Hell no.

God, when was she going to put her foot down and tell Jo to do her own damn job if she wasn't grateful for the help?

Karma frowned and batted the tears off her cheeks.

And what business was it of Jolene's whether or not she got Mark's coffee? Why did Jo even care? It wasn't like Mark was asking *Jo* to get his coffee. No, he asked her to do that. And she was fine doing so, especially since it gave her a chance to flirt. So, Jo could go screw her—

The bathroom door squeaked open, and the lava flow of thoughts shut off in Karma's head as if someone had closed a spigot.

"Karma?" It was Lisa. "You in here?"

Karma sighed. "Yes." Before she could stop herself, she sniffled then immediately closed her eyes and cringed. Great. Lisa would know something was wrong.

"You okay?"

The jig was up. No sense lying. "No." She reluctantly opened the stall door and stepped out, certain that her face was blotchy from crying.

"What happened?" Concern washed over Lisa's face.

"Jolene happened." She whipped a paper towel out of the dispenser and blotted away her tears before looking in the mirror. Her eyes and nose were red, and she had cried away some of her mascara and under-eye concealer. "How did you know I was in here, anyway?" She ran cold water over the towel, wrung it out, and pressed it under her puffy eyes.

"I've been trying to get ahold of you for ten minutes," Lisa said. "Mark called me and asked if I knew where you were."

How long had she been in the bathroom? She checked her watch. Oh God. She had been in here for almost twenty minutes. "Mark called you?" Mark knew she and Lisa were friends and that she had told Lisa what was going on. He'd been a little concerned at first, but then Karma reassured him Lisa wouldn't rat them out.

Lisa nodded. "I figured if he was calling me, something was wrong, so I came looking for you."

Great. Not only was she a big crying baby, but now Mark would ask her where she'd disappeared to the next time he had a chance. And she wouldn't be able to lie. Karma turned and plopped her butt against the counter.

Lisa touched Karma's arm and nodded toward the door. "Come on. Let's go to lunch, and you can tell me what happened with Jo."

Karma cringed and shook her head. "I don't want him to see me like this."

"He and Don left for lunch about five minutes ago." Lisa gestured toward the door. "So come on. I'll take you to Olive Garden and feed you garlic bread and salad and get you good and happy again. He'll never know. We can chalk it up to feminine mystique." She smiled cautiously.

Thank God for Lisa and her glass-half-full mentality, because Karma really needed to talk. Lisa had always been her sounding board, and between what was happening with Mark and how Jolene had taken to bullying her again, Karma's ends were frayed.

Karma smiled tightly and followed Lisa out of the bathroom.

On the drive to Olive Garden, Karma relayed what had happened with Jolene. By the time they were seated at a table, Lisa was cussing Jolene's name.

"As a member of Human Resources," Lisa said, "I want to tell you to file a complaint against that bitch." She nabbed a warm breadstick from the basket. "But as your friend, I know it's not that simple. I know you don't want to do that."

"No, I don't." Karma picked off a piece of her breadstick and popped it in her mouth. "I don't want to cause any more problems than there are already, and filing a complaint will just make Jo more crafty."

"And this all started the day you said she asked Mark to drinks and he said no? And paid you more attention than he paid her, I might add." As an afterthought, Lisa added, "Good for him." Then she held her hands up innocently. "I mean, at least from what you've told me, that's how it sounded."

"Yeah. So?"

"It sounds like Jolene's jealous."

Karma let that sink in for a moment. "Jealous? Of what?"

"Not what," Lisa said. "*Who.*"

The waiter brought their salad and two bowls of Pasta e Fagioli. He grated Parmesan over the top of Karma's then departed.

Karma leaned forward. "Are you saying that Jolene is *jealous*? Of *me*?"

Lisa dipped her head to one side as if the answer was obvious. "That's exactly what I'm saying."

"Oh come on. Look at me. What does Jolene have to be jealous of?"

Lisa set her spoon down and frowned. "Seriously, Karma?" With a huff, she wiped her hands and sat forward. "Yes, let's look at you for a second. Have you looked in a mirror lately? You're stunning. Ever since you got your hair cut and started wearing makeup and girl clothes, you've been turning heads all over the office. You haven't just caught Mark's eye. You've caught the eye of every available man in the office…as well as the eye of a few of the unavailable ones. Haven't you noticed?"

Dumbfounded, Karma could only shake her head.

Lisa smiled patiently. "Karma, Karma, Karma. Sweet little innocent Karma. You need to open your eyes and look around."

"I don't get it. I— "

"There's nothing to 'get,' Karma. You're finally embracing your sexuality, and men are taking notice. That's why Jolene is jealous. She's no longer the hottest commodity on the market, so of course she feels threatened by you. You're disrupting the natural order of things, and she'll do whatever she has to do to put you back in your place. At least, in the place where *she* thinks you belong. Are you going to let her do that to you? If you want this new you that you've discovered, you have to *own* it, and you have to let Jolene know you're owning it." Lisa snapped her fingers.

Karma had never been in the spotlight or considered a "hot commodity," so she couldn't wrap her mind around what Lisa was telling her. "I *do* want to own it," she said with a nod. "I don't want to let Jo bring me down, but I don't know how to stop her."

"Stand up to her." Lisa whooshed her hand into the air then dropped it back to the table. "Don't let her push you around. Tell her to do her own damn job if she doesn't like having to ask you for those stupid quarterlies. She's only asking you for them to get under your skin. Ten to one she doesn't even need them and only uses them as an excuse to harass you." Lisa lifted her spoon and pointed it at Karma to add emphasis. "Mark my words, she's just going to keep being a bitch until *you* put *her* in *her* place."

Karma stirred her soup with a breadstick. "This just sucks. Why does life have to be so hard?"

"Hey, nobody said changing was going to be easy. In fact, it never is." She stabbed her fork into a black olive on her salad plate and briefly pointed it at Karma before popping it in her mouth. "Any time you try to change, forces push back. They don't call them growing pains for nothing. As you grow and change, it hurts more, because you're putting out a new message that those around you aren't used to. They've grown accustomed to seeing you a certain way, and now you're trying to show them something else. Some will embrace it, and others, like Jo, will fight it. She doesn't want you getting stronger. She doesn't want you to break out of the mold she's put you in, because then that means she'll have to face the fact that she's still the same bitch she's always been and that she no longer has control over you, which will shine a spotlight on how incredibly lonely and inadequate she is." Lisa bobbed her head. "Think of it that way and you kind of feel sorry for her."

Karma thought about what Lisa had said for a second then shook her head. "Nah. I still don't feel sorry for her."

Lisa laughed. "That's the spirit. Now you're coming around."

What Lisa said had merit. Jolene was one big spotlight hog. If Karma was, in fact, taking that spotlight away, Jolene's recent behavior made a lot more sense.

"I didn't ask for this," Karma said. "I didn't ask for the guys in the office to notice me more than her." That still baffled Karma, but if Lisa said it was true, then who was Karma to question her. Lisa had her finger on the pulse of the office better than Karma did. If something was going on, Lisa knew about it.

"Of course you didn't," Lisa said. "You're too busy being a good employee. Karma, the 'worker bee.'" Lisa tucked the handle of her spoon into the palm of her hand and made air quotes with her fingers. "But that doesn't change the facts. You've turned heads, and now you're a threat. You're pretty. You're smart. And you've got Mark's attention, which Jo wants. True, she may not know exactly how much you've got Mark's attention, but in the office, you're with him all day. Jo would kill to get that kind of time with him, and you're the one who has it. So, not only are you stealing the spotlight, but you're also the 'lucky bitch'—Jo's words, not mine—who gets to be around Mark."

"Wait. What? Are you saying she said that?" Karma scowled at what sounded like evidence that Jo had been talking about her around the office.

Lisa held up her hand. "Not to me, but I overheard her talking to Nancy earlier this week."

"And you didn't tell me?"

"I didn't want to upset you. I'm sorry. Maybe I should have told you sooner, but I didn't want to ruin how happy you've been."

A weak smile played over Karma's mouth as she thought about Mark, the source of all her happiness. "It's just hard to hear, that's all. I don't like being talked about."

"Who does? But take it as a good sign she's treating you like this, Karma. It means she sees you as a threat. And if she sees you as a threat, then you're moving in the right direction. You're moving forward. But like I said, change isn't easy, and the way Jo's acting is proof of that. You just have to ignore her as best as you can, stand up to her when given the opportunity, and understand that her behavior is more about *her,* not you. It's about *her* insecurities, *her* feelings of inadequacy. Isn't that the truth of all bullies?"

Karma nodded and smiled. "You always know how to make me feel better."

"That's because I'm awesome," Lisa joked, finishing the last bite of her soup. "And because I'm your friend," she said more seriously.

"And I love you for it."

"And I love you." Lisa reached across the table and patted her hand. "I love seeing you finally spreading your wings, Karma. You deserve to be happy more than anyone I know."

Karma blushed and looked away, never good with compliments.

Lisa snagged the last breadstick. "And I'm glad you decided to see Mark outside the office. He's really good for you." She bit off the end before aiming the rest at Karma like a wand. "But don't forget, you have to tell me *everything*."

With a laugh, Karma shook her head. "How can I forget? You won't let me."

At four thirty, Mark's last meeting of the day finished as Karma was putting the final touches on a presentation for Don. Thankfully, Mark hadn't asked where she had been earlier. She really wanted to get through the rest of the day without thinking about what happened with Jolene.

Her phone vibrated on the desk, and she checked the screen.

Mark. *You and me? Dinner tonight?*

Five simple words, but the impact they had was similar to receiving notice that she had just won the Publisher's Clearing House sweepstakes. Her heart rate ramped up, a tingle zipped down her back, and an uncontrollable urge to send a fist pump into the air splattered her self-control against the wall like it had been shot with a bazooka. She barely contained the squeal that rose from the pit of her stomach. Barely. Instead, she cleared her throat and typed a reply.

I have yoga until 6:30 with Lisa, but will be home after.

Yoga? At the gym we share?

After reading his text, her eyes narrowed. Why did she get the feeling he had something up his sleeve? She texted back. *You got a membership there?*

Yes. So maybe I'll bump into you tonight.

She glanced into the conference room. Mark's face was buried in his tablet, his phone in his left hand, a grin on his face. She typed out another text. *You're going to the gym tonight?*

She looked up in time to see him lift his phone as it vibrated. He read, and without acknowledging her, he started typing.

I will now. Maybe I'll even be in your yoga class.

Goose bumps instantly sprang up all over her body. How could she perform Downward-Facing Dog, Extended Puppy, and Happy Baby Pose if he was watching her? Heaven forbid he would set his mat behind hers.

I thought you only used the weights, she sent back.

Afraid for me to see you in your yoga attire performing a sun salutation that will make your perky breasts the center of my attention?

She gasped, and when she looked up, he was grinning wider than before, but he still wasn't looking at her. Were her breasts perky? She wasn't entirely sure how to handle the flattery.

I was more worried about my bare feet now that I know of your foot fetish. She fought back a giggle.

Ah, yes. There is that, isn't there? I'm definitely going to be in your yoga class now.

Well, if he wanted to play, she would play. *Fine. I hope you're an advanced student, because I'm not carrying you out when you pull a muscle.*

He actually chuckled as he read her message.

So little faith in me, but you're right. I don't do yoga. You win. I'll stay safe in the free weights.

Good idea. She stole a glance at him as he typed.

I think you just don't want me staring at your assets – and your bare feet – in class.

That stinker. *Damn right. I knew you had ulterior motives.*

Guilty. Did I mention that I'm a hot-blooded man? ;) Now go home. It's 5:00. I'll see you and your assets around 6:30.

You're bad. I'll see you then.

She gathered her things, cast another glance into the conference room at Mr. Sexy, then headed out.

As far as she was concerned, the day had just started.

At six thirty, Karma rolled up her yoga mat, put her gym shoes back on, said good night to a couple of her classmates then headed into the bowels of the gym's fitness area with Lisa, Daniel, and Zach.

Machines, treadmills, stair climbers, and ellipticals crowded the floor, and the place was busy. Looked like all of Clover had decided to get in a workout before their Friday night dates. All the equipment and people made it hard to find Mark.

"Do you see him?" she said to Lisa while she stretched. As if she hadn't already done enough stretching in yoga class.

"No, but I'm not surprised. God, what happened? Was there a weight lifting convention here we didn't hear about or what?" Lisa joined her in a stretch.

"I am dying to meet this guy," Daniel said beside her. "Just so I can see what all the fuss is about. You two make him sound like Adonis."

Zach snickered as he finished putting his yoga gear in his duffel bag. Then he glanced up and arched one brow as he slowly stood. "Hello. Who is *that*?"

Karma turned and looked into Mark's intoxicating eyes as he joined them.

"Hello." He appraised her in your yoga pants and tank top.

"Hi." And there was the heat in her cheeks again, right on schedule. She turned toward Daniel and Zach and introduced them. "Daniel, Zach, this is Mark."

Mark seemed to have the same effect on men as he did on women, because both Daniel and Zach looked a little starstruck. They took turns shaking hands.

"I'm glad to finally meet you, Daniel," Mark said. "Karma's told me a lot about you, and it seems I have you to thank for allowing me to meet her in the first place."

"Well, it wasn't all my doing." Daniel wrapped his arm around Zach's waist. The gesture seemed as much a reassurance to Zach as it was a way of bringing him into the discussion. "If Zach hadn't gotten sick, I never would have taken Karma to the benefit."

Mark bowed his head toward Zach. "Well, thank you for being sick…I guess." He laughed and flashed Karma a glance before turning his attention back to Zach. "I hope it wasn't too serious, though. You look fine now."

Zach practically swooned. "Oh yes, I'm fine. Thank you. It was just a touch of food poisoning."

Mark frowned. "Oh, I'm sorry. That's never fun."

The three men talked among themselves a moment, and Lisa caught Karma's eye with a smile so wide she was beaming. It was clear how much Lisa liked Mark.

The five of them chatted a couple more minutes, and then Karma turned toward Mark and said playfully, "So, what are you doing here?"

"Admiring the view." He winked, and Karma's face burned.

The devil.

"And that's our cue to leave," Lisa said, glancing between Daniel and Zach. "Now that we know Karma's in good hands, our work here is done." She patted Karma on the shoulder. "Go forth and have fun, my child."

"I'll call you later," Karma said.

Lisa looked from Karma to Mark. "Make sure she does *not* call me later, okay? The girl needs to get her priorities straight." She gave Karma a pointed look.

"I'll see what I can do." Mark met Karma's gaze. "You heard the lady. No calling her tonight. You're stuck with me *all* evening."

She liked how that sounded.

"Care to take a walk with me to cool down?" he said once her friends were gone.

"Sure." She followed him out, dropped her bag in her car, and met him at the entrance to the trail that surrounded the property, which, at one time, had been a combination of farmland and wooded terrain. Now it served as a large recreational park.

It was almost seven o'clock, but the sun was still hanging on, well above the horizon.

A spring storm had rumbled through after lunch, leaving cool, crisp air in its wake, and now a breeze flowed out of the northwest as the remaining clouds cleared. Karma zipped up her hoodie against the slight chill in the air. Thin banks of high clouds striped the sky to the north and west, creating the start of what promised to be an impressive sunset, and moisture glistened the blades of fresh, young foliage that painted the landscape bright green. Puddles of water dotted the pavement.

In spring, Clover lived up to its namesake. With its dense foliage and the conservation of green space, the city of Clover transformed into an emerald paradise every May.

"I call this the perfect night," she said. A gentle gust lifted the tendrils of hair that had fallen out of her ponytail.

"What makes it perfect?"

She held out her hands. "It's the perfect temperature. Not too cold, not too hot. Cool enough for a jacket, but not cold. And there's a nice breeze that makes everything feel alive. Makes me feel like I'm on the beach or something…just without the water, except after it rains, of course." She gestured toward a puddle. "But that doesn't count. And who doesn't love a sky that gorgeous." She pointed toward the peach-colored clouds that would eventually turn deep orange as the sun crept lower. "Perfect." As if she had just described the definition of the word.

"I see what you mean." He walked alongside her, both of them silent for a bit, enjoying the evening. Then he said, "What happened to you today? At work? You disappeared for a while."

Karma's gaze dropped to the pavement. She had hoped what had happened with Jolene wouldn't come up tonight, but no such luck. "It was nothing." She sighed. "I just had a little run-in with Jolene that upset me, but I'm better now." She darted a cautious glance at him. "Jo and I go way back. I knew her in school, and we haven't had the smoothest history."

Mark gave a slow, single nod. "I see. But everything got worked out?" He lifted his eyebrows questioningly.

"I wouldn't necessarily say that." She smiled sheepishly. "But Lisa took me to lunch and helped give me some perspective."

"Well, I'm glad." He slid his hand into hers, weaving their fingers around one another. The gesture made Karma's heart do a little flip. "Lisa seems like a good friend."

"She is. The best."

About a quarter mile into their walk, they came to the ornate terra-cotta bridge that was the highlight of the trail around the property. It bowed above a gurgling creek, which had been fed by the earlier rain.

Mark stopped and looked over the railing at the rushing water below. "I haven't had a chance to talk to you since Tuesday. How have you been?"

"Good." She shyly averted her gaze, worried he would see in her eyes all the torrid thoughts she'd had about him the past few days, or that she had read every single Truth or Dare card from their game and pondered how she would have answered the questions that hadn't been asked. Of course, the dares from the game had fed her fantasies. There were quite a few she hoped they could try someday.

"I know I laid a lot on you," he said, "and we haven't seen each other for a couple of days. Do you have any more questions?"

She looked at him and realized she did. "Just one."

"Okay."

"Why me?"

They began walking again, leaving the romantic bridge behind.

"Why not you?" His voice massaged the syllables the way his fingers took that moment to twine more securely between hers.

She thought about that for a second then laughed when she couldn't come up with an answer. "I don't know. I guess I'm just not used to attractive men asking me out. I'm more the girl guys like to hang out with, be friends with, but not date."

He squeezed her hand. "Being friends with a man is the perfect stepping-stone toward something more meaningful."

She laughed. "So far, that hasn't happened."

"Why do you think that is?"

Mark seemed to like asking her questions that made her think, even when it sounded like he already knew the answer. She got the impression he would make an excellent teacher, because he had a way of making you figure things out without coming right out and telling you what the answers were.

She considered his question then said, "Because until a couple of weeks ago, I didn't look or act like I wanted more?" She inflected as if asking a question instead of answering one. Just the way she'd done in school when she was called on in class. Maybe Mark really was a teacher.

He smiled but didn't speak.

"I wasn't putting out the right signals," she said, elaborating. "I've enabled men to think that being friends was enough. That I would always be there…as a friend. I put my personal feelings aside to make *them* comfortable. Aaaannd...I didn't take into consideration that men are visual creatures. I thought that if they really liked me I wouldn't have to change my appearance. But…"

"Yes?"

"Men *are* visual. They see the wrapping paper before they see what's in the package."

He barked out a laugh. "That's a great analogy."

"Is it true?"

After a short pause in which he seemed to think about it, he said, "More or less. You're right. Men are very visual. Even I noticed your dress and how you looked before I noticed the little nuances of your character. And I like to think of myself as someone who looks past appearances at the person inside." He shrugged. "I guess I'm not as unique as I'd like to think."

"Oh, you're unique," Karma said with a giggle.

He glanced at her. "So are you." He spoke with such conviction that she stopped laughing.

She bit her bottom lip and averted her gaze. "I guess I've always just seen myself as average." Lisa's words at lunch still echoed in her thoughts, about how men saw her differently now. She still couldn't wrap her mind around the idea that maybe she wasn't so average after all.

"Average is underrated."

"Most men would disagree with you."

"I'm not like most men." He squeezed her hand. "And I happen to think you're not average at all. In fact, I think you're pretty extraordinary."

The trail led them into a grove of tall, full trees.

Karma gazed up at the bright-green canopy. "Before I met you, I would never have considered myself your type."

"And what do you think is 'my type'?"

"Oh, modelesque, tall, blond, beautiful—"

Mark stopped so suddenly that what she was about to say caught in her throat. He backed her against the trunk of a silver maple hidden in the shadows and took her face in his hands, gazing intently into her eyes. "Karma, you are all those things…and more."

"But—"

"Ssshh." He let go of her face, took her hand, and settled it between his legs.

Her eyes popped open and she sucked in her breath. He was hard. Not fully erect, but definitely hard. Because of her? Did simply being with her arouse him that much?

"I can assure you, you *are* my type." He held her hand against him for several seconds, revealing nothing in his expression except the gravitas of sincerity. Dignified and intense, his eyes searched hers for any doubt she didn't believe him. His gaze dropped to her mouth. "You…are…my…type. Are we clear on that?" He arched one brow as the corner of his mouth lifted seductively.

Awareness connected him to her like a tether. This was real. In that moment, all her doubts vanished. "Yes," she said quietly.

He gently pushed her hand away, curled his fingers around hers once more, cleared his throat, and moved as easily as the breeze as he pulled her back onto the trail.

He seemed to know her scrambled mind needed a minute to collect itself, because they walked in silence for a while. His hand felt good around hers. His fingers were thick and strong, with smooth callouses at the bases. Probably from lifting weights. She liked his warm, firm hands. They made her feel secure.

What kind of life had Mark led? What of his love life? He had hinted at his past, but they had never discussed it. At least not beyond the superficial, surface stuff.

Mark's phone buzzed in his pocket, and he retrieved it with his free hand then smiled at the screen.

"What?"

He shoved his phone back in his pocket. "Oh, just a little surprise."

The way he said it implied it was a surprise for her. "What kind of surprise?"

He laughed. "One that will definitely turn your face red." He glanced at her out of the corner of his eyes. "Which I love, by the way. You're such an obedient blusher." He tugged her toward the parking lot and picked up his pace. "Come on. Let's go."

"Where?"

He paused, looking much too pleased with himself. "When you get home, you're going to have a couple of packages waiting for you."

"Packages? For me?"

He nodded. "Yes, but don't open them until I get there. Promise?" The wicked glint in his eye made her wonder what exactly she had waiting on her doorstep.

After parking her car, Karma rushed inside and up the stairs to her apartment. Just as Mark had promised, two boxes sat outside her door. One from Amazon and one from a company called Cārvāka.

Cārvāka? She had never heard of it.

She unlocked her door, carried the boxes inside, and set them on the dining room table, where she studied them as if doing so would somehow reveal their contents.

Amazon could be anything, but Cārvāka?

She tugged her tablet from her bag and set out to see if she could get any hints from their website.

A chill zipped down her spine and her eyes flew wide as soon as Cārvāka's page loaded.

Sex toys. Mostly glass dildos. But they sold other items, too.

What the hell was inside that box? Being that she couldn't open it until Mark arrived, all she could do was stare. And not just stare, but S-T-A-R-E. As if the top would fly open and an army of Chuckie dolls would burst out wielding tiny sex toys instead of knives.

But then the fascination crept in, and she turned back to the website. She had never played with sex toys, never owned a vibrator or a dildo or…*anal beads*? She blinked at the strand of beads that popped up on the rotating window on the site's home page.

Did Mark use this stuff? Better yet, did he want *her* to use it?

With a rushed check of the time, she realized she needed to get cleaned up. After taking a lightning-fast shower, she briskly dried her hair and pulled it into a damp ponytail before brushing on a bit of face powder and blush. She was just whipping on a touch of mascara when a knock came at her door. She shut off the bathroom light and dashed into the living room with a furtive glance toward the mystery boxes.

"Hi," she said, standing aside so he could come in.

"Hi." Mark kissed her cheek, catching her off guard, and carried in a bag from Café Nine. His dark hair was still damp, and he smelled faintly of Irish Spring, the same soap her dad used. "Ah, there they are." He spied the boxes. "You didn't peek?"

"No." Technically, she hadn't peeked. Just investigated. But now she was more curious than ever about what he had bought her. "Can you give me a hint?"

"Nope," he said, sounding a little smug.

"You're evil."

"But it's a good kind of evil, right?"

"I'll tell you after you show me what's in the boxes."

"You say that as if you already have some idea." He set the bag on the kitchen counter. Then he spied her tablet and grinned. "Have you been researching?"

She picked at the groove in the molding surrounding the entrance to the kitchen. "Maybe a little."

"I'm not surprised. You're resourceful. I've noticed that about you." He began unloading the food. "So, what did you find out?"

"Not much." She busied herself grabbing glasses from the cabinet.

"You visited Cārvāka's website, didn't you?" He laughed softly.

"Maybe." She shrugged and grabbed the iced tea from the fridge.

"So you know what they sell."

"Maybe."

The empty bag crinkled as he set it aside. "Ah, but do you know what Cārvāka stands for?"

Other than being the name for an online sex shop? "No."

"Cārvāka was an Indian hedonistic school of thought. According to the Cārvākas, there was nothing wrong with pleasure and sensual indulgence. They didn't believe in an afterlife and believed that pleasure should be the aim of living."

Well, that explained it.

"I see." She poured their tea and avoided making eye contact as she set the glasses on the counter beside their food.

"Thank you," he said, taking his glass and sitting down before continuing. "Cārvāka is what I would refer to as a provider of classy, high-end intimate items created specifically for pleasure in all its pursuits. Some are even custom made to order."

She sat down next to him, her mind reeling. She'd seen a documentary once about the sex industry. There were companies that could mold a man's erect penis and create a dildo that replicated his member. Was Cārvāka one of those companies? Was there a replica of Mark's penis sitting on her dining room table right now? Was that what he meant by "custom made to order"?

Not six feet away, God only knew what was inside that box, waiting for her, ready to give her Cārvākian pleasure. About a dozen competing thoughts splintered inside her mind, making it hard to think and separate one from another.

Then she noticed that he'd brought her a turkey artichoke panini and tomato bisque—her favorite—and all other thoughts ceased. "How did you know I like this?" She turned toward him as he was about to take a bite of his own sandwich.

Pausing, he lowered his panini and looked at her. "I saw you eating it for lunch one day last week. Actually, I had to make my best guess about the sandwich, but the soup was pretty obvious."

"You noticed? And remembered?" Once more, he had surprised her. The men she knew didn't notice such things, and if they did, they certainly didn't remember them.

"Of course I did." He gave her one of his patented crooked smiles, one that showed his single dimple. "A man who is genuinely interested in a woman remembers what she likes. He notices what she eats, what she reads, how she wears her hair." He smoothed his fingers over her hair. "He takes care of her. That's his job. Well, maybe not his job, but certainly his responsibility." He gestured toward her food. "Now eat."

He takes care of her. That's his job. What an unusual yet refreshing perspective.

"Yes, sir," she said dramatically, digging in. "So bossy."

"Sir?" His browed twitched. "We'll see if you're still calling me that after you see what I got you."

The boxes on the table practically flashed like a beacon. *Blink…blink…blink.* It was a tad unnerving…and yet utterly, undeniably exhilarating.

After eating, he helped her clean up then gestured for her to have a seat at the table. "Do you have a knife?"

She pointed to a small drawer under the dish rack. "There's a utility knife in there."

He retrieved it and joined her. "Are you ready?"

Her wide-eyed gaze swept from his face to the boxes and back. With a nervous nod, she said, "As ready as I'll ever be."

He sliced through the tape on both boxes and flipped open the flaps. From Karma's vantage point, she couldn't see the contents, and when she tried to sit up and peer inside, Mark slid the boxes farther away.

"No peeking."

Defeated, she dropped back into her chair with a perturbed sigh.

He fished around, knocked what sounded like books and smaller packages against the insides of the boxes, smiled, made a contemplative noise or two, and then looked at her. "Okay, before I begin, let me explain why I bought you these things."

Of course there was a reason. This was Mark, and it was becoming clear that he had a reason for everything he did.

"Talking to you over the past couple of weeks, I've learned quite a bit about you."

She nodded, remembering their encounter in the parking garage and everything else they had discussed. "Yes."

"We don't need to go into all of that, but my concern is that...well...it's been a while since you've been with a man. I, uh..." He glanced down and pursed his lips as if choosing his words carefully. "I don't want to hurt you." He met her gaze again. "Do you understand?"

It took her a few seconds to catch his drift, but then she drew in her breath. "Ooohh...uumm..." And there went her blush response again.

He cleared his throat and glanced back inside the box, his face red. This was only the second time she had seen him blush, and goose bumps prickled her skin at the reminder that Mark was only human and could be affected by what was happening between them as much as she could. And she certainly received the message he was sending without him having to spell it out. Some men took pride and bragged about the size of their manly parts, but Mark seemed more self-conscious—or maybe self-aware was a better term—as if he knew that size could be a detriment. Too big and, as he'd warned her, it could hurt.

She didn't want it to hurt with Mark.

"Should I be scared?" She had felt him with the sole of her foot and the palm of her hand, but only through his clothes. She had never actually seen how big he was, so she didn't exactly know his full length and girth.

He grinned. "No, but we should be careful. And you should prepare." He lifted a brown leather case from the Cārvāka box and set it on the table. It looked like an oversized jewelry box, like the kind that holds expensive necklaces. "Have you ever heard of dildo training?"

"No."

He smoothed his palm over the top of the case. "Well, it's when a woman uses progressively larger dildos to prepare for intercourse. That way, when she finally has sex, it doesn't hurt. Do you understand?"

"Uh-huh." With that explanation, she had a pretty good idea what was inside the case.

He reverently opened it as if he were unveiling a sacred artifact. Inside, nestled in a black, satin-lined pillow, were four glass dildos in graduating sizes. The first was simple and slender, with a small tapered protrusion on one end, a slight bulge about two-thirds down, and with a round handle on the other end. The next was a thicker version of the first, with two bulges and a heart-shaped handle. The third, which was rose colored, was thicker still, with a large egg-shaped tip, a shaft with rounded nodules along the exterior, and two large knobs at the end to use as a handle. The fourth, a deeper shade of rose than the third, was shaped like a penis, slightly curved, with a bulbous head, a thick shaft, and ridges swirled candy cane style at the other end.

"That's about how big I am," he said, pointing to the fourth. He gave her an impish smile.

She could see his concern. Brian the wonder stud had been nowhere near that big, and it had still hurt like hell.

He closed the box and placed his hand over hers. "You'll start with the smallest and work your way up. I'll help you."

Exactly what kind of help would he be?

The question must have shown in her expression, because he smiled and held out his hand. She took it and stood.

His arm immediately encircled her waist and pulled her close as his lips brushed over hers.

Heat instantly bloomed between her legs.

He caressed her hips with both hands as he kissed his way down to her neck.

She didn't know what point he was trying to make, but he could make it all night if he wanted to. He was damn near melting her.

After several more seconds of his persuasive lips on her skin, his tongue peeked out and licked a fiery trail up to her ear. "Are you wet?" he whispered.

She could feel the slippery sensation in her panties. "Y-Yes."

"*That's* how I plan on helping you." He pressed his lips against the tender place just under her ear. "When you're aroused, it's easier to slide the dildos inside you. The same way it makes it easier for a man to slide inside you." He paused, and his cheek rose as if he were grinning. "I plan on making you very wet."

"Oh." Now she understood. She liked his definition of help.

Pulling away, he guided her back into her chair then reached back inside the box. The evidence of his own arousal pressed against the seam of his jeans, and now Karma was even more curious. If his penis was anything like that largest dildo, it had to be pretty damn impressive.

When he pulled his hand out of the box, he held another case, similar to the first, only much smaller. Small enough to hold a bracelet.

"These are Ben Wa balls." He popped open the lid. The hinges crackled.

Inside were two metallic black balls that looked like large marbles. He lifted one and let it roll in his palm. Soft, musical chiming rang from inside.

"What do I do with those?"

He handed the ball to her. It was cold and shiny and just a little on the heavy side for its size. "There are a lot of uses for Ben Wa balls. Pleasure, feminine health, that sort of thing. Many women use them to increase the strength of their vaginal muscles, and that's how I want you to use them." He grinned. "Well, at least at first. We can explore their pleasurable side later."

Her face heated, and she placed the ball back in its indent on the satin pillow. "Okay, so how do I use them to 'increase the strength' of my muscles?"

Mark reached into the Amazon box and pulled out a book. *A Woman's Guide to Pelvic Health*. He handed it to her. "By doing Kegels. This book explains how."

"Kegels?"

"Yes, you'll thank me later."

"What do you mean?"

"You'll see." His wry expression sent a thrill through her body.

Mark lifted more books out of the box. One had a papaya on the front. Another a red chili pepper. Another was a massive, yellow tome that looked like a softcover encyclopedia on all things sexual.

"What's all this?" she said.

"An education." He sat down again. "Remember how I said I was going to build you a reading list? Well, this is just the beginning. If you read these, you'll know more about sex than at least seventy-five percent of the population."

Karma looked at her pile of booty, feeling a little overwhelmed but excited nonetheless.

"How do you know so much about..." she waved her hand at her gifts. "All this."

He sat back in his chair. "Are you asking how it is that I know so much about sex? Or about a woman's body...her needs? Or how I knew where to buy all these things?" He glanced at her stash.

"Take your pick."

With a contemplative dip of his head, he said, "I was once in your shoes."

"What do you mean?"

He sat forward and crossed his forearms on the table. "I didn't know what I was doing. I thought I did, but it became clear I was pretty clueless. I thought I was Casanova, but I was just a bumbling fool."

"You? Bumbling?" Karma found it hard to believe that Mark could ever have "bumbled" when it came to sex. The guy looked like he knew his way around a woman's body the way a running back knew his way around a football field.

A beguiled expression crossed Mark's face. "Is that so hard to believe?"

"Well, yeah."

"Why do you think that?" Ulterior motives laced his tone.

She gestured toward him. "Well, I don't know. I guess you just don't strike me as the bumbling type." Her mind replayed their moments together. "You seem like a man who knows what he's doing." A nervous spat of air burst through her lips. "And the way you kiss..." Heat flushed her face. "You just...you're definitely not a bumbler."

He reached for her hand. "And how do you think I got this way?" He played his fingers over hers.

She shrugged. "I don't know. Experience maybe?" *And lots of it.* She couldn't meet his eyes.

"No." He shook his head. "Experience only takes a person so far. If experience was all it took for a man to know what a woman wants and to become an expert lover, then all those idiots out there who've slept with scores of one-night stands wouldn't be idiots, but fabulous lovers."

He had a point. "Okay…?"

"Remember when you told me how awful your first time was?"

Of course she did. But what did that have to do with him? "Yes."

"My first time wasn't quite that bad, but it was pretty damn close. I was an idiot, but I got better as I went along. Not great, and certainly with a lot to learn, but better." He hesitated, and a ghost of dark emotion flitted across his face. "Then I got into a serious relationship. By then, I thought I knew what I was doing, but I was still so ignorant. It took losing her to realize I needed to change. If I was going to become the kind of man women felt could take care of them, I needed to learn what they wanted, and I needed to learn what *I* wanted, too." Shadows passed over his face as if he was remembering a time from his past. "I couldn't continue being ignorant about women, and I couldn't continue being selfish in the bedroom." His face marginally brightened as if he had cast aside whatever memory had briefly haunted him. "So, I started reading. A lot. I devoured every book I could find on the subject. I even began reading women's magazines."

The mystery that was Mark began to unfold. So, this was how he was so attuned to her.

"I don't like being a failure. At *anything*." He met her gaze. "I refuse to be a failure, and that's what's driven me." A moment of silence passed between them before he continued. "You're changing like I did. This very moment, you're changing. I can see it in your eyes. I've seen the change since the benefit in Chicago. You're not the same woman you were two weeks ago."

Karma's mouth went dry. Once again, he pegged her, because she had felt the change, too. And not just with her clothes. She felt the change on the inside. "I know. I've felt it."

"And the more you learn, the more changes you'll make."

Meeting Mark felt almost preordained. How else could she describe it? He had entered her life at the exact moment she had needed him to—at the very point in time when she had realized there was more to life than she was living—and now he was becoming her personal guide to the sexual universe.

"Now," he said, "I have one more gift to give you, but you're not allowed to use it until I say so, which should be about the time you've gotten comfortable with the second dildo."

She leaned forward, trying to sneak a peek.

He lifted a velvet drawstring bag from the box, opened it, and pulled out a purple contraption that looked like some high-tech, phallic tool from *Star Trek.*

She ricocheted backward. This was not a glass dildo, but something else entirely. The thing had a bulbous head and ridges down the side like a real penis, and it had this protrusion that curved up and away from the main unit with what looked like little ears on the end. And there were all sorts of bumps along the exterior, with silver beads inside

"It's just a vibrator." He held it toward her.

At first, she shook her head. That was not "just a vibrator." And how do you hold something like that? The thought of wrapping her hand around the shaft was pure humiliation, even after the conversation they'd just had.

"Oh come on, take it." He laughed at her bashfulness.

Tentatively, she wrapped her fingers around the base and pulled it out of his grasp.

"I take it you've never used a vibrator?" Mark sounded amused.

She shook her head, staring at the purple gadget in her hand. "No."

"Okay, well this is called a G-spot Rabbit vibrator." He pointed to the little ear things. "That stimulates your clitoris, and when you turn it on…" He switched the power on and the whole thing began vibrating in her hand, and the penis head began rotating.

"Oh God!" She dropped it on the table. "What the hell! What's wrong with it?"

Mark nearly fell over laughing as he picked up the squirming, churning, appendage of death. "It's supposed to do that."

"What? Turn into Linda Blair from *The Exorcist*?"

He laughed harder and shook his head. "No, but yes. It stimulates your G-spot when it rotates."

"G-spot?"

This conversation was getting beyond out of control. What the hell was a G-spot?

Appearing bewildered, Mark stopped laughing. "You don't know about your G-spot?"

Had she missed something? The way he continued staring at her like she had something between her teeth made it clear she had.

Mark's stare intensified, morphing into concern. "Haven't you ever learned about your G-spot?"

"Um..." She searched for words. Obviously, he knew something she didn't, and it was important, or he wouldn't be looking at her as if she had just told him she didn't know how to drive a car. "I don't...well..."

Mark set down the vibrator and leveled her with a look so full of compassion it nearly took her breath away. "And I receive yet another piece of the curious puzzle that is you." He glanced down briefly before looking at her again. "Let me try and explain what your G-spot is." He took a breath. "Inside your vagina, along the front wall, is where you'll find your G-spot. It's part of your clitoris. Or rather, your clitoris is part of your G-spot. When stimulated, it gets hard and a little rough. Like it has ridges on the surface. Once it's stimulated, it provides a woman with a great deal of pleasure, and it creates a more intense orgasm than with just clitoral stimulation. Women who experience G-spot orgasms say they're incredible." He looked at her expectantly, as if prompting her to fill in a blank.

All she could do was frown. Clitoral orgasms and G-spot orgasms. Wasn't an orgasm just an orgasm? She had always thought so, but now here comes Mark Strong—Mr. Sex Ed—and he turns her sexual universe on its head. Was he saying that there was more than one type of orgasm and that clitoral orgasms were only the beginning? That G-spot orgasms were the crème de la crème? Hell's bells! The only way she had come before was by playing with her clit, and those orgasms were fabulous.

She gave him a frustrated glance. "Are you saying they're stronger?" This was so much to take in.

He frowned and tilted his head curiously to the side. "Haven't you ever had a vaginal orgasm? Haven't you ever given yourself one?"

Vaginal orgasm? Was this a third type of orgasm? She had to be the most pathetic, inexperienced, naïve woman on the planet.

He sat down and scooted closer. "A vaginal orgasm is another name for a G-spot orgasm," he said. "See, there are two types of female orgasm." He spoke matter-of-factly, as a teacher would to his students. "Clitoral and vaginal, or as some call it, a G-spot orgasm." He lifted his hands as if they were scales and he was presenting each to her. "Obviously, both feel good, but a vaginal, or G-spot, orgasm is much more intense. Deeper." He lifted one of his hands higher than the other as if to show that one held the vaginal orgasm. Then he dropped both hands into his lap as he sat forward. "Let me put it this way: A vaginal orgasm is to a clitoral orgasm the way a fresh-from-the-oven, chocolate chunk brownie drizzled in warm caramel and vanilla bean cream is to a piece of Dove milk chocolate. Both are good, but one makes you moan while the other just makes you smile."

Chocolate chunk brownie versus a square of Dove milk chocolate? There was an analogy she understood. Yes, she would definitely enjoy the brownie the way he described it much more than the milk chocolate, but that didn't mean she wouldn't devour a whole bowl of Dove squares if given the chance.

"Have you ever had a chocolate chunk brownie drizzled in warm caramel and vanilla bean sauce, Karma?" Mark took her hand.

She thought about it for a moment, still flushed and feeling deer-in-the-headlights. "I don't know."

"You don't know?"

She hadn't even known what a G-spot was. How would she know if the thing had given her a chocolate chunk brownie?

"How would I be able to tell?" She self-consciously dropped her gaze.

When she glanced back up, his wicked grin stirred the warmth between her legs back to life. "Trust me. You'd know if you had."

His thumb caressed the backs of her knuckles.

She took a deep breath. "Obviously, my love life has been pretty pathetic. I think you know that because of what I've told you."

Tender strokes of his fingers lent silent encouragement. "I wouldn't say pathetic. You've just had poor lovers. They didn't know how to make love to you. I'm going to change that."

"You've got your work cut out for you." She felt so small.

"Do I look intimidated?" His gaze locked to hers like a promise.

"No," she said.

"That's because I'm not. I like a challenge. And I know what you're capable of." He looked at the items on the table then pulled her onto his lap and locked his fingers at the small of her back. "I'm so glad your friend's husband was sick the night of the benefit."

It was an odd thing to be happy about, but she understood how he felt. Grinning, she bit her lip and covered her face with her hands as she shook her head. Was this really happening? She still couldn't believe it. She dropped her hands to his shoulders. "So am I."

He inhaled then exhaled slowly, gazing at her mouth. "We're

going to have so much fun together, Karma." His gaze lifted to hers. "I'm going to teach you things about your body you never knew…show you things you've only ever imagined." His hands glided up and down her back. He leaned forward and pressed a tender kiss to the corner of her mouth then one on her cheek, and several more as he drew a line to her ear. "I *will* take care of you," he whispered. "You can count on that."

And for the third time that night, heat fired low in her belly. Every moment with Mark, every breath she took, and every secret glance led her one step closer to the woman she wanted to become. And further away from the uncertain, naïve girl she wanted to leave behind.

Chapter 20

If you can make a girl laugh, you can make her do anything.
-Marilyn Monroe

Back at his condo, Mark packed a duffel for his trip back to Chicago tomorrow morning then peeled off his shirt and jeans and slipped into a pair of flannel pajama pants.

He was still semi-erect from his evening with Karma.

She was quite the character. He chuckled as he went to the bathroom to brush his teeth, recalling the look on her face when he had pulled out the vibrator. Priceless. In an instant, he had known she'd never used one before.

That was going to change. If he had his way and enough time, she would get very familiar with toys in the bedroom. She was about to experience a lot of firsts, and Mark wanted to be there to experience every single one. Screw that. He wanted to *give* them to her.

He rinsed off his toothbrush, shut off the bathroom light, and situated himself against the full, firm pillows propped against the bed's headboard as he snagged the remote from the nightstand and turned on the flat screen across the room, trying to ignore the ache between his legs.

Karma's reaction to the vibrator was exactly why he had given it to her in the first place. She needed to get more familiar with her body and lose her inhibition about taking pleasure for herself.

He liked the thought that he would be her first. Not her *first* first, but he would be the first to give her an orgasm she didn't have to give herself. And he *would* give her an orgasm. No doubt about it. That little angel was going to fall apart under his touch if it was the last thing he did.

He took his phone off the nightstand and typed out a text. *You're not trying out your new toy, are you?*

A minute later, she sent him a reply. *What if I am?*

Oh, she wanted to play, huh? *Then you're breaking the rules and I'll have to punish you.*

Punish me?

Yes. Punish you.

It took a few minutes to get a reply. *Are you being serious?*

He laughed. She was adorably gullible. How could he not play with her just a little? *I'm very serious.*

It took her a while to reply, as if she were trying to decipher just how serious he was. *I'm not playing. Just reading. I turned on the vibrator, but that's all. I swear.*

He could almost see her in a tizzy. In time, she would learn when he was joking and when he was serious, and that he would never punish her. Not like that. If he ever played those kinds of games, that's all they would be. Games.

LOL. I'm only kidding. I wouldn't punish you.

You're mean.

He chuckled. *And you're adorable.*

You're forgiven.

She could be so cute. *Thank you. But I seriously do want you to refrain from using your new toy for the time being. Methods, Miss Mason. I have methods.*

Yes, yes. Methods. Why do I get the impression your methods are going to be the death of me?

He grinned. *If they work, they WILL be the death of you, my adorable protégé. The death of the old you and the birth of someone new.*

I'm sorry, but I don't have time for anything philosophical right now. I'm too busy reading about my clitoris, the little engine that could.

Mark's eyes shot wide. *Excuse me? Come again?*

I can't "come again." You won't allow me to come at all right now, Mr. Strong.

Oh now, who was this little vixen texting him, because she surely wasn't sweet, innocent Karma. *I never said you couldn't come, just that you can't use your favorite new toy. But more importantly, who are you? And what did you do with sweet, innocent Miss Mason?*

LOL. She's right here and if you could see her face, you'd see she's very embarrassed.

And why would she be embarrassed?

Because she's not used to saying such things.

A-ha. Well, we'll just have to work that out of her, won't we? I like her potty mouth. A woman who looked innocent yet engaged in dirty talk was so sexy.

You would.

I'm hurt.

No you're not.

Yes I am. I'm a very sensitive guy.

Sensitive my ass, Mr. Strong.

He threw his head back and laughed. So feisty. *Fine. Call my bluff.*

But I want you to tell me more about your reading material. Would you care to elaborate on what you're reading this evening?

Not at the moment.

Do I have to go back to your apartment? If I do, I might have to rethink that whole punishment thing.

Ugh. You are relentless. Stinker. >:(

Who would have thought texting could be this much fun. *Yes, I am. :)*

Fine. I'm reading one of the books you got me. The papaya book. Second chapter: Her Clitoris: The Little Engine That Could. I'm assuming you know what I'm talking about since you told me you've read this book.

Yes. I did. And yes, I do. He had read parts of that book several times, in fact. That book had left the women he had dated very satisfied…and occasionally speechless. It was a book every man should read and study.

So, you understand just how important the little engine is, right? she texted.

His grin grew wider. *Yes. I'm very aware of its importance.*

Okay. Good. Just so we have that clear.

He waited a moment before replying. *Just wait till you see what my tongue can make your little engine do when my finger pays a visit to your Kegel-enhanced G-spot, Miss Mason. (Damn, I wish I could see your face right now)*

It took longer for her next text to arrive. *If you could, you'd laugh at how red it is. And then there's that whole deer-in-the-headlights look I'm working. It's quite sexy. I can't believe you said that, btw.*

Oh, believe it, Miss Mason. I said it, and I mean it. I can't wait to take you and your little engine to all sorts of wonderful places.

You keep saying things like that and I'll have to break your rule.

Don't you dare. I want you saving that for me.

Selfish much?

Damn straight. Your new vibrator doesn't get a taste until I do. And once more I wish I could see your face. He could text her all night.

MR. STRONG! Stop that!

LOL. You're so cute when you text angry.

Grrrr.

Mark relented with a sigh. *I'm only teasing. I plan on taking my time with you. Alas, but Mr. Vibrator will have you before I do, but don't think that means he'll be better.*

Wow. That's some ego.

Confidence, Miss Mason. It's confidence.

If that's what makes you sleep at night, she shot back.

I do sleep rather well. Speaking of which. It's late. I should let you get back to your…ahem…reading.

Yes, it is late, and I do have a lot of reading to do. My teacher loaded me up. Thanks for the chat. Good night, Mark.

Good night, Karma. He waited a few seconds then sent one more message. *Sweet dreams of my tongue on your little engine.*

MARK!

I love when you scream my name.

Grrr. I'm looking for Mr. Vibrator.

Don't you dare.

Then quit sexing me up.

The air froze. *You're sexed up?*

Are you?

He glanced down at the tent in the sheets. *Maybe. Are you?*

Extra long pause. *Maybe.*

Hmm. Nice. Very nice. He tapped out his reply. *Well then…hurry with your reading, Miss Mason. And get started on your Kegels. And I can see I'll have to get right on helping you with your dildo training, won't I? Because the faster you work, the sooner we can turn those maybes into something much more affirmative. And much more hands-on.*

He couldn't wait to touch her in that way the first time. Feel her body react to his. Would she quiver? Moan?

He loved this part. The thrill of the chase. The hunt. He lived for it.

Karma's next message came through. *Well, if you would stop distracting me, I could read a lot faster, you know. Not that I really mind all that much. Just sayin'.*

LOL. Well, I won't keep you any longer then. Good night, Karma. Here's to little engines and all that goes with them.

LOL. Good night, Mr. Tease. Have a safe trip back to Chicago.

Chuckling to himself, he set his phone back on the nightstand then shut off the light. What a surprising exchange. If he wasn't mistaken, Karma might have just started coming out of her shell.

Chapter 21

If you change the way you look at things, the things you look at change.
-Wayne Dyer

On Saturday, Karma went to her parents' house and watched the playoff game with her dad then stopped by the store on the way home to pick up milk. Leaving the dairy section, she decided that, while she was at it, she might as well check out the health and beauty department, where she could find such items as…oh…condoms.

It couldn't hurt to have some on hand, just in case. Mark had made it clear that sex was part of the plan. It would be irresponsible not to be prepared.

At least, that's what she kept telling herself as she slinked off and came at health and beauty the back way, stealth-like, as if that made a difference. For crying out loud, she was just going after condoms, not meth or bomb-making materials. Just condoms. Simple, innocent, latex—

She halted as she came out from behind a shelving unit full of hair care products.

Jolene and her boss, Jake, were huddled together. He had his arm around her, his hand on her butt. Her breasts were pressed seductively against his chest, and she was working the same look on Jake that she had on Mark that day she had asked him to drinks.

Karma quickly ducked back behind the shelf and peeked out in time to see Jo nip the side of Jake's neck as he chuckled nervously and said something Karma couldn't quite hear, but which sounded something like, "Jolene, we're in public."

"I don't care," Jo said. "I'd fuck you right here if I could. You've got me so horny. And it's your fault for forgetting to bring them." She pressed in close and nibbled his neck, grinning as if she was doing something wicked.

"Jo. Stop."

She giggled, and Jake squirmed like she had a hold of his penis.

"At least wait till we get to the car," he said.

"Oh, I'm going to ride you so hard tonight," Jo said. "Just grab a box. Hurry up."

Jake snatched a box of condoms off the shelf and followed Jo toward the registers like a puppy.

Well now. Wasn't this interesting. Jo and Jake.

Karma didn't want to get Jake in trouble, but this was a major ace in her pocket. Jake was married, and not just married, but married to the daughter of Solar's president and CEO, who was also the founder's son. Jake was in a position to lose everything if his affair with Jolene became public knowledge. Why would he risk it?

It was Jolene, that's why. Her sway over men—except for Mark, of course—was almost mystical. She could make Tim Tebow give it up if she wanted to, and that man had serious convictions about his virtue.

Karma waited until Jo and Jake paid and scampered out the exit, off to do God knew what to each other, then proceeded into the aisle they had just vacated. There were so many condom options. Ribbed. Extra large. Colored. Plain. And about a hundred different brands. But she couldn't stop thinking about Jo and Jake long enough to focus on selecting one.

How long had their affair been going on? The two certainly looked comfortable with each other. She filed through her mental database of all the times she had seen the two together in the office. The way they looked at each other. The way they hushed any time anyone was near. The closed-door meetings he had with her every week.

Holy crap! This had been going on for a while. How had she never noticed?

Because she was little Miss Naïve, that's why. She simply didn't notice such things. But surely someone had. Then again, maybe not. Or maybe they had and didn't care or didn't want to get involved.

Abandoning the condoms, Karma made her way to the checkout and paid for the milk, her mind swimming with the knowledge that had fallen into her lap. She hoped she would never have to use it, but it was a nice safety net.

Aside from her eye-opening Saturday night, Karma spent most of the weekend gobbling up the books Mark had given her. It was fascinating reading. She had learned more about her body and his than she had in a whole semester of sex ed, and with a little self-exploration with her finger, she had discovered her G-spot. She had even given herself her first G-spot orgasm. Mark was right. It was stronger than a clitoral orgasm, but she had a feeling a G-spot orgasm the Mark Strong way would be even better. A perverse thrill shot through her private places at the thought.

She had also started her Kegel exercises. In a way, her yoga training assisted with those, and she was beginning to understand what Mark had meant by how she would thank him for introducing her to them. As she did the exercises, she actually got turned on. Enough so that afterward, she was aroused enough to masturbate and explore her G-spot again. And just wow. After Kegels, that little dynamo was especially sensitive and packed an even bigger punch.

Monday night, after a day that saw Mark go from one meeting to the next, Karma sat on the couch, watching a weather update for an approaching storm, waiting for Mark to arrive. He had texted earlier that he was finishing up his last meeting and would be over as soon as he grabbed a quick bite and a shower. He had offered to bring her dinner, but she had already eaten.

A little before eight o'clock, he announced himself with a quiet knock.

"Hi, stranger," he said, all charming smile and dazzling eyes. He leaned in and kissed her cheek.

"Hi." She blushed and looked away.

After a few days apart, some of her bravado from Friday's text session had dissipated.

She closed the door behind him. The man sure could work a pair of jeans. And royal blue? He looked good in blue. And red. And black. And…hell, Mark could make 70s polyester plaid and a Fu Manchu look good.

"I brought dessert," he said. He lifted a plain white bag.

"Dessert?" She followed him to the kitchen.

He motioned for her to have a seat at the bar. "No peeking."

"You like surprises, don't you?" She sat down on a bar stool and leaned on her elbows.

"Don't you?" He glanced mischievously over his shoulder as he set the bag on the counter.

"Surprises are good. Yes."

Keeping his back to her and shielding the bag, Mark grabbed a plate from the cabinet and began pulling out items and set them on the counter.

"They're saying a bad storm is on the way." She gazed at the way the muscles of his back and shoulders flexed and bunched under his shirt as he went about his business. What if she walked up behind him and slid her hands under his shirt so she could feel all that strength roll against her palms? Mmm, that was a nice thought.

He had such thick arms, too. In a suit or long-sleeved shirt, you didn't really notice how big they were, but in a short-sleeved shirt like he was wearing tonight, you couldn't miss them. Arms, hands, chests. That's what turned Karma on, and Mark had each in spades.

"Yes, I saw that on the news while I was getting ready to come over," he said. "Are you afraid of storms?" He scooped something out of one of the containers and placed it on the plate, but Karma couldn't see anything but the wall of his impressive body.

"No. I love storms."

He looked over his shoulder. "Me, too. We get some good ones in Chicago." He turned back around.

"So, what have you got there?" She lifted off her seat and craned her neck to see around his arm. All she saw was something that looked like chocolate.

That was a good sign. Chocolate was good.

"Just wait," he said. "No peeking." He stepped to the side to block her prying eyes.

She huffed and flopped back down on the bar stool. "You know, making a woman wait for dessert is grounds for getting the cold shoulder." As if she could ever give him the cold shoulder.

"We'll see." He sounded so self-assured.

She drummed her fingers impatiently as he worked far too slowly. "Are you plating for Gordon Ramsey over there?" she said.

He threw her a fake glare over his shoulder. "Hush, or you won't get any chocolate chunk brownie." He turned, and in his hands, he held a plate with the most incredible piece of culinary artistry ever created.

Her mouth gaped as he crossed the kitchen and set the masterpiece on the counter in front of her.

The brownie was a double stack of chocolaty goodness, one square settled on top of another at a diagonal. Large chunks of dark chocolate nestled within each perfectly baked morsel, and what looked like dollops of fudge oozed like heaven from the sides down to the plate. Golden caramel zigzagged over the top and down the edges, and what looked like vanilla cream was drizzled perpendicularly to the caramel and pooled around the base of the bottom brownie.

Mark returned to the bag, pulled out one last container with two cherries inside, and situated them just-so on the top of the mountain of decadence.

"Here's to chocolate chunk brownies and all they entail," he said with a smile, cutting off a gooey bite with a fork and holding it toward her.

"Oh, you're good," she said, leaning forward.

"I know." He winked playfully as she took the forkful into her mouth. "How is it?" His eyes twinkled and one corner of his mouth curved upward as he watched her eat.

Flavors crashed together and exploded against her taste buds. This had to be the best damn brownie she had ever eaten. *Ever!* Angels should have been in her kitchen, singing and rejoicing, or weeping with overwhelming ecstasy, it was so good.

"Oh my God," she mumbled through brownie. "Mmmm." She closed her eyes and relished the taste and exquisite, melt-in-your-mouth texture. She moaned again, chewing slowly. Flavors burst one over the other, chocolate upon chocolate with a hint of vanilla and caramel, which coated her tongue like ribbons of buttery goodness.

"Good?" he said, crossing his arms and resting them on the counter.

She nodded, swallowed, and then took another bite. Mark grinned, straightened, and returned to the bag on the opposite counter, where he pulled out a small blue square, returned, and set it in front of her. It was a piece of Dove milk chocolate.

Covering her mouth, she laughed. "I see your point," she said, looking at the brownie then the Dove square.

If a G-spot orgasm the Mark Strong way was indeed like this brownie, which should have had a spotlight on it, then she was definitely in store for a lot of moans instead of smiles. But she would take the smiles, too.

He leaned on the counter. "And what's my point, Miss Mason?"

With a coy smile, she eyed her plate then looked back at him. "Let's just say I hope you give me lots of brownies if they're going to be this good."

A devious smile lit his face as the mood shifted slightly toward sexual. "I can manage that."

She picked up the fork and grabbed another bite. "My God, this is good."

"Can I have a taste?"

"Can a man experience chocolate chunk brownies?" She smirked and licked caramel off her fork.

"No, but I can choose to withhold them."

"Awe, you're no fun." Giving in, she nodded toward the silverware drawer. "Grab a fork there, teacher, and dig in and help me eat this incredible thing."

As he joined her, she stared at the planes of his face, his Grecian nose, his strong chin with the small dimple in the center, the sharp slope of his jaw, and the way the muscles of his cheek and jaw bunched and flexed as he chewed. Seriously, the guy was gorgeous.

And he was here, with her, giving her chocolate chunk brownies…or preparing to, however you wanted to look at it.

He swirled the last piece of brownie in the vanilla sauce on the plate, and her gaze dropped to his hand.

"I like your hands." She set down her fork, reached across the counter, and caressed the backs of his fingers. His skin was warm. "They're man's hands."

"Oh?" He sounded intrigued. "And what exactly are man's hands?"

"The kind you have," she said evasively. The atmosphere around them heightened with sensuality, and her pulse quickened.

Mark set his fork on the empty plate and came around the counter. "You can do better than that." His voice purred from his throat, low and seductive.

"Haven't we discussed this already," she said as he spun her around on the bar stool and stepped between her knees.

"Only that you're a woman who likes hands, but not what makes mine 'man's hands.' I'm eager to hear your definition." His sexy smirk sent a quiver of heat down her spine. Before she could utter another word, he gripped her hips and tugged her sharply toward him.

She gasped at his aggressiveness. "That. What you just did. That's what makes them man's hands."

"Does it now?" He encroached more fully into her personal space and licked his lips. "Duly noted." His palms flowed down the tops of her thighs. "But I'm glad you like my hands."

Her breath hitched. "Why's that?" He was so close she could feel his body heat.

"Because my hands like touching you." For emphasis, his palms slid back up the outside of her thighs to her hips, where he took hold of her again. He leaned in. "By the way, you look nice tonight," he whispered, drawing his tongue down to her bare shoulder. He let go of her hip and brushed back her hair.

She was wearing a demure, baby-doll halter that fit more securely around the bodice but draped like the skirt of a flowing gown below her breasts. She almost hadn't put it on because of how much skin it showed, but now she was glad she had. "Thank you."

His lips brushed over her skin. "How's your reading coming along?" He sounded distracted.

Breathless, Karma's pulse quickened. "Good."

"Learning anything about yourself?" He softly kissed the side of her neck.

She nodded, and her eyelids drifted shut. "Mm-hm."

"And your Kegels? You've been doing them?" His lips eased up the side of her neck to her ear.

"Mm-hm." She tried not to melt.

"And your training?" His voice was a hot whisper.

It took her a moment to understand he was referring to the glass dildos. "You haven't been here to help me," she whispered back, sounding like she'd just dove into a pool of chilled water from the way her breath hitched.

"I'm here now."

Yes, he was. Very much so.

He dotted tiny kisses back down her neck and along her jaw, and then paused only a second before taking her bottom lip between both of his.

That falling sensation she was beginning to associate with Mark's kisses swirled inside her stomach the moment their mouths touched, and when his tongue flicked along the seam of her lips in a tender invasion, the weightless sensation flared again like hummingbird wings in flight.

He tasted like chocolate and vanilla, and his lips were smooth and warm. Strong. Demanding, but in a subtle way that hinted at forced restraint.

Not long ago, Karma would have tensed in his arms. Her inexperienced, self-conscious side would have forced her to anxiously withdraw, but those days were quickly fading into the past. Mark was gently leading her down a new path, guiding her smoothly into a new existence. One where she relaxed more, enjoyed the experience of being in a man's arms, and felt more comfortable seeking what gave her pleasure.

When had she ever felt beautiful and desirable before Mark came along? Never. Gratitude blossomed for these gifts he was giving her, and for once, she let herself go. She gave in to the ravenous yearning that begged her to explore what he offered. Surging against him, her arms drove around his shoulders, and her legs locked at the ankles around his hips.

In unison, they both moaned, and his mouth crashed hard and deep against hers, bending her backward against the force of his arousal. The backs of her shoulders dug into the counter behind her, and his grip tightened as he tugged her lower body forward on the stool until the juncture between her legs met the hardness beneath the zipper of his jeans. Lust bulleted down her thighs and up her spine, making her groan and grind herself against him. A guttural rumble stirred from his throat at the increased contact, and he thrust himself against her as his teeth latched onto her bottom lip.

They'd gone from playful teasing to full-on fuck-me mode in less than five seconds. Their chemistry with one another was off the charts and undeniable…breathtaking and mind-blowing.

Gasping into his mouth, Karma shoved her fingers into his thick hair and gripped a handful as she would the mane of a stallion if she were riding bareback. If she didn't hold on tight, she would tumble off, and she didn't want to fall. She wanted the ride to keep going. He growled as she reinforced her grip with both hands and let her tongue dance with his. She was lost to unbridled passion, consumed by desire.

Then she was being lifted off the stool. And not just lifted, but hoisted like a maiden being rescued from a dragon's lair into her savior's arms. Without breaking the urgent kisses shattering her mental barriers, Mark carried her through the living room, down the hall, and to the bedroom. Somewhere in her conscious mind, she knew where they were going…knew the intimacy her bedroom implied…but she couldn't stop him. The last thing she wanted was to put an end to the incredible, lip-searing way his mouth took hers over and over…the way his tongue stroked hers as if he couldn't get far enough inside her. He kicked the bedroom door open, hustled her inside, and crashed over her as they fell onto the bed.

Mark was like ocean surf quickly building in strength and power, rolling against her, consuming her, relentlessly spiraling her up, up, and still further until she was riding on the crest of his wave.

She had been starving, famished for pleasure. Now Mark was giving it to her.

The voice in the back of her mind told her she needed to stop, but her body was too far gone to listen, too caught up in its gluttonous binge.

Mark's mouth, his lips, his tongue…they ravished her, stole her breath, further weakened whatever thread of resolve she had left. It was like he was just as hungry as she was. As if he, too, was overwhelmed with the need to take all he could before it was too late. They were soaring out of control, and he didn't seem capable of stopping any more than she was.

Then one of his hands pushed under her blouse, speeding toward her breast.

That's when Karma shot back to reality the same way she had in his hotel room the night they met.

"No!" She jumped and slammed her hand down on his before she could stop herself.

Mark jerked away and yanked his hand out from under her shirt, eyes wide and confused, as if he, too, had just come back to his senses.

The sexually intoxicating mood vaporized. Gone. Destroyed again by Karma's childhood memories.

"I'm sorry." Karma immediately felt the need to apologize. "I just—"

"Sshh." He cupped her face and shook his head. He appeared dazed. His brow crinkled. "I shouldn't have…" He trailed off as if he wasn't sure what he shouldn't have done.

They were both breathing hard, strained to their physical limits.

Old memories rushed back from Karma's childhood. This wasn't his fault. It wasn't him, it was her. And how cliché was that? *It's not you, it's me.* Blech! She didn't want to say something so pathetic at a moment like this.

"Mark—"

"No. I'm sorry." He rolled onto his back. He seemed disoriented and stared up at the ceiling.

Awkward silence filled the open space, murdering the intense chemistry that only moments ago had connected them. Would she ever rid herself of the damage of her childhood?

"Mark…" Karma sighed, hating the cool air that replaced the warmth of his body. "You don't understand." She closed her eyes, said a silent prayer for courage, and sighed as she glanced at him again. "Look, I need to tell you something. Something about my past. Something important." She needed to be honest with him. Didn't he deserve that much? Didn't *she*? Perhaps it was time to face the past once and for all. "Maybe if I explain, you'll understand." And maybe if she explained, she could finally banish the shame. She rolled onto her side, facing him.

His eyes were closed, and his chest rose and fell heavily.

After this, there wouldn't be any secrets left. Mark would know more about her than anyone else, except for maybe Lisa and Daniel.

As Mark opened his eyes and rolled his head to look at her, she felt an odd sense of relief. She hadn't even begun but already felt better. Just the thought of telling him the painful truth was enough to alleviate the strain that had been on her nerves since she'd met him.

Mark's mind was still in all kinds of improper places. He couldn't believe he had almost made love to her. Here. Right now. Tonight. Before she was even ready. But he had careened out of control once Karma wrapped her legs around him and kissed him in earnest. She had felt so good, and her mouth felt so right on his.

He had never wanted to make love to a woman as badly as he had wanted to make love to Karma. Even now, his body throbbed to join with hers. God, what was wrong with him? He needed to focus, calm down, listen to what Karma had to say. From the way her eyes glistened with unshed tears and her fingers worried over themselves, whatever was on her mind was important.

Taking a deep breath to rinse the lusty cobwebs from his thoughts, he rolled onto his side to face her. "I'm listening." He still felt awful for pushing her the way he had. He had promised to take care of her, and yet he had rushed her like a bull. What had he been thinking?

Outside, distant lightning flashed, and a low rumble of thunder announced the coming storm. Inside, Karma seemed to have a storm of her own brewing, her eyes filling with shadows.

"When I was a kid, I was a bit of a tomboy," she said. "I was kind of geeky and scrawny with long hair and glasses." She rolled her eyes. "A real looker, you know." A forced smile that showed she was trying to be funny dashed across her face then disappeared. "My dad was still working his way up the corporate ladder, and we weren't the richest family in town. We did well, but in Clover?" She blew out a derisive puff of air. "Unless you're a one-percenter here, you're bait. And for a kid in school, it's even worse." She grew quiet as evidence of hard memories shadowed her face.

"What happened?" Memories of his own harsh childhood bubbled into his mind. He had been teased ruthlessly for dancing. Surely, Karma hadn't been made fun of like that. The idea that she had endured something so ugly hurt his heart. He reached out to brush a strand of hair away from her face.

Her gaze flicked to his hand, and she smiled. "I was a late bloomer," she said. "Really late."

"What do you mean?" Was she talking physically or something else?

She hid her face behind her hand. "This is so embarrassing…"

"If you don't want to talk about it, I'll understand."

"No," she said immediately, drawing her hand away from her face. "I want to tell you. I need to get this out once and for all. It's just hard."

He brushed his fingers over her cheek as more thunder, closer this time, rumbled outside. "Take your time. I'm not going anywhere."

She had the loveliest face. Smooth skin. Cute, slightly upturned nose that sort of reminded him of a rabbit's. And her pretty lips were swollen and pouty after their bruising make-out session.

After a moment, she breathed in and forced herself to continue. "So, okay…I was a late bloomer. When most of the other girls in school started to develop breasts in sixth or seventh grade, I was still flat as a pancake. And the fact that I wasn't part of the affluent, popular crowd singled me out even more. Add to that my younger brother loved torturing me, and you might see where this is going."

Yes, he was beginning to get some idea, and a mix of despair, sympathy, and anger roiled in his veins.

"Well," Karma said, continuing, "things didn't get better as I got into high school. The other girls kept developing, and I kept *not* developing." She sighed. "It wasn't until late my freshman year that anything began to grow on me at all…other than my stupid hair, of course. By then, the names I was called had already become engrained with my classmates, fueled, of course, by my brother and Jolene." She slouched. "Yes, Jo was part of the crowd who made fun of me, along with the girl my brother ended up marrying, Estelle. But they weren't the only ones. I was teased everywhere. In the girls' locker room. Between classes. After school. On the bus. It was awful. This went on for years."

Mark shifted closer and rested his hand on her waist. It wasn't much, but it was a small gesture of how he wished he could protect her. Everything he learned about Karma, including this, made his picture of her that much clearer. He had suspected something tragic had occurred in her past, but he hadn't imagined anything like this. No wonder she had reacted the way she did when he shoved his hand up her blouse. And no wonder she had fled his room the night of the benefit. Hadn't she frozen up then the same way she had tonight…right after he touched her breast? He would have to be more careful from now on. Slow down and be more patient.

"I was called Mosquito Bite and Pancake…and other more *offensive* names." Her voice grew quiet. "People told me that I was so flat that even the walls got jealous. When I was in eighth grade, someone taped a training bra to the outside of my locker. I was mortified when I got to school and saw it. Everyone laughed as I tried to take it down, but they had used a lot of tape. The hall was full of kids laughing and pointing, and I was desperately trying to rip off all the tape. Another time it was a jock strap and a note that said, 'Maybe you're better equipped to wear one of these instead of a bra.' After that, kids teased me that I was really a boy dressed like a girl." Tears welled in her eyes, and Mark could hear in her choked voice that she was forcing herself not to cry. It took every ounce of restraint not to pull her against him and hold her, but he sensed she needed to get this out.

"The humiliation was endless." She sniffled. "Another time in eighth grade, I liked this boy named Dave. Dave Warren. We shared a lunch period. And I always carried my journal with me. I was always writing in it. Between classes, during class, on the bus. I wrote about Dave a lot."

Her thoughts seemed to be tumbling out in random order.

"I was always too shy to talk to Dave, even though his lunch table was next to mine and he sat behind me in history class." She took a deep, shaky breath. "So, there I was, in the cafeteria. I set my books on my table, went up to get my lunch, and when I came back, my journal was gone."

Mark tensed. This story couldn't have a happy ending and he wished he could go back in time and right the wrong that had been done to her that day.

"I freaked," she said. "I looked everywhere. Then I heard the laughter." She cringed and briefly covered her face. "I turned around, and there was my brother, Jo, and Estelle, reading my journal. My *diary*. All my private thoughts, all the poems I'd written…all of it about Dave." She visibly sagged. "Dave was right there. Right beside them. And Johnny began reading out loud. 'Dave is so cute. I wish he would ask me out. Does he even know I exist?' God, it was humiliating. Dave looked at me like I was a hideous monster, and Johnny kept taunting me. *'Karma's got a cru-ush, Karma's got a cru-ush. Mosquito Bite's in loooooove.'* It was awful. I can still hear his stupid voice teasing me." She shook her head against her palms. "Everyone laughed…the whole cafeteria. I just wanted to crawl into a cave. I gathered my books, pried my journal from Johnny's hands, and ran out of the cafeteria as Johnny and his friends yelled after me, calling me all those horrible names and laughing."

She began to cry, and that did it. Unable to hold back any longer, Mark wrapped her in his arms and pulled her against him. "It's okay. Ssshhh." He rocked her.

She buried her face against his chest and let out a tight, quiet sob.

For a couple of minutes, he simply held her as rain began to fall outside and the lightning and thunder grew closer. He knew firsthand what Karma had experienced, because he had, too.

"The worst part," she said, "is that Jolene ended up getting with Dave after that. They were a couple for the rest of the school year." She sniffled. "Jo's been adding insult to injury all my life."

He stroked her hair as she continued to cry.

A few minutes later, she pulled away and took a deep breath. "Anyway, that's why I reacted the way I did when you…you know…touched me. I've just never quite gotten over the stigma." She sighed and shrugged almost apologetically.

"I think I figured that out." He wiped his thumb over her tear-moistened cheek.

With a sad smile, she pointed her finger at him and put on a brave face. "That's what I like about you, Mark. You're quick." She was obviously trying to lighten the mood.

He kissed the tip of her nose. "If I was really that quick, I would have known sooner not to do what I did."

She shook her head. "No, no. I was into it. God, I mean, no one's ever…" She trailed off and ducked her head. When she spoke again, her voice was low, whispery. "No one's ever kissed me or touched me the way you do."

Mark's heart beat a little harder for her. Karma was so damned innocent, and she'd had such a traumatic childhood. He never would have imagined her past had been so bad. "I like it," he said quietly, brushing his fingers through her hair. "I like kissing you." What an understatement. He fucking *loved* kissing her. So much so that his normally patient libido had risen like a cobra ready to strike.

"Me, too." She tipped the crown of her head against his chest, and her delicate fingers curled against his stomach.

The bashful yet imploring gesture pulled at Mark's soul, and he smiled as he kissed the top of her head. "You know," he said, "those kids were wrong about you, Karma. If they could see you now…see the beautiful woman you've become…you could make them all eat their words."

Her body burrowed into his. "I guess in some ways I still see myself the way they saw me back then. You know, ugly and gangly. Flat."

Mark frowned at her confession. Was she saying that she was ashamed of her body? That she thought her breasts weren't big enough? "Karma, you're a beautiful woman. *All* of you." When she didn't immediately respond, he pulled away. "Look at me."

Trepidation and uncertainty shone from her eyes as she raised her face to his. He had to show her how perfect she was. How beautiful. Because clearly, remnants from the past still haunted her self-image. She truly didn't realize how perfect she was.

"Come here." He got up and bobbed his head toward the full-length mirror hanging on the wall by the bathroom. "I want you to see something." He held out his hand.

Karma's gaze darted to the mirror. "Mark..."

He waved his fingers and nodded toward the mirror. "Come on. You need to see this."

Dreading what was about to happen, Karma gingerly sat up, swung her legs around, and took his hand. She followed him across the room as another flash of lightning lit the shadows.

Stopping in front of the mirror, Mark turned on the bathroom light then stepped behind her. "What do you see?" He nodded toward her reflection in the mirror.

What she saw was a scared little girl cowering inside a woman's body. "Me," she said noncommittally. She knew what he was after, but she couldn't say it.

"But what do you *see*?" He pulled back her hair.

"I don't know." She dropped her gaze to the floor. She didn't want to look at herself right now.

"Do you want to know what *I* see?" He placed his hands on the sides of her face and lifted so she was looking in the mirror again. Her eyes met his in the reflection. "Look at yourself," he said. She forced herself to do as he asked. "Here's what I see when I look at you." He wrapped one arm around her waist and caressed his other hand over her cheek. "I see perfect, clear skin. Smooth, youthful, and healthy. I know women who would kill to have your skin."

She'd never noticed that before, but looking closely at her face, he was right. Her skin was pretty damn flawless.

"And your eyes," he said. "They're big and bright and the most extraordinary shade of green. I've never seen eyes quite that color, and, to be honest, they're mesmerizing."

Once again, she had never paid attention to her eyes before, but now she stared at them as if seeing them for the first time.

Mark continued ticking down her features. Her heart-shaped lips, her flat stomach, her supple hips, her delicate hands, even her button nose and her "sexy" ears, which he nibbled on as he whispered how attractive they were. Finally, he drew back and pulled her blouse tight from behind so that the fabric stretched over her breasts.

She sucked in her breath, suddenly self-conscious.

"And your breasts, Karma," he said softly, leaning down so that his chin almost rested on her shoulder. "Are you worried they're too small?"

Licking her lips nervously, she gave a tight, shaky nod. Couldn't he loosen his hold on her shirt?

"Well, I'll let you in on a little secret." He drew even closer and whispered, "I think they're perfect. Absolutely perfect."

Perfect? He thought those slight mounds under her shirt were perfect?

"That's right, Karma. They're perfect. A nice handful, a bit perky. Did you know that when you walk just so that they actually bounce a little?"

She shook her head, unable to speak. Did she actually have ample enough breasts that they bounced? Really?

"Well, they do. And it drives me wild." He slowly released her shirt. "Do you trust me?"

Seeing herself through fresh eyes, in a way she never had before, she swallowed, briefly pressed her lips together, then whispered, "Yes."

His hands slid around to her stomach, on the outside of her blouse, and she watched the reflection as they slowly crept upward as he kissed the side of her neck. With racing heart and quickened breath, she blinked drowsily as his thumbs pressed against the underside of her breasts. Pausing, he seemed to be gauging whether or not she was going to let him continue. When she didn't resist, he drew his palms up and over her breasts.

"They're supple and sexy," he whispered in her ear. "The perfect handful. And anything more than a handful is a waste, if you ask me."

She had never thought of her breasts as sexy or supple. Least of all perfect.

He squeezed gently, and her nipples hardened. "Still trust me?" he said quietly.

Thunder rolled outside.

He had just made her see herself with new eyes. Hadn't he proven himself over and over by now. "Yes." She had never trusted anyone more.

Keeping his left hand where it was, Mark dipped his right hand under the hem of her blouse. She knew what was coming, but unlike before, she was ready. His fingers brushed like feathers up the side of her stomach, his hand pushing the shirt away. The sultry caress left a tingling trail up her abdomen. In the mirror, the outline of his fingers approached her breast. Then his hand cupped her, and the warmth of his palm pressed against her. And then his left hand joined the right, and both hands held her breasts, skin to skin, heat to heat.

"Put your hands on mine," he said, pressing more firmly against her from behind. She could feel his erection against her bottom, and a torrid fantasy of being bent forward and forced to watch him take her in the mirror broke unbidden inside her thoughts.

She did as he said and covered his hands with hers. If she thought kissing him had been exciting, watching in the mirror as his hands shifted under her blouse, and feeling his fingers curl around her flesh, was damn near the most erotic thing she'd ever experienced.

"Now do you understand?" he said against her ear. His deep, gravelly whisper reached down and cupped her between the legs.

Panting, she nodded and rested the back of her head against his shoulder. Between Mark's erection on her backside and his hands on her breasts, she was in sensory overload.

"Better?" he said.

She nodded. This was much better. Much, much better. "Yes."

"Every day," he said, "I want you to look in this mirror and imagine me behind you. I want you to touch your breasts like I am..." He squeezed, softly raked his blunt nails in as he made loose fists, and then circled them around as he spread his fingers once more. "I want you to touch yourself and realize how beautiful you are...how perfect your breasts are...how sexy you are."

Blind to everything but his palms massaging under her shirt, she nodded, eyelids drooping. Right about now, she would do anything he asked. She was putty in his hands.

"Will you do that? Every day?"

Again, she nodded. "Yes." She would if only to relive this moment again and again in her mind.

Just then, a bolt of lightning struck right outside her building. Under the Mark Strong onslaught, Karma hadn't even realized how close the storm had come, but as her eyes darted to the window, she could see how violent the wind was. Trees swayed as lightning flashed again. The power blinked then cut off and blinked back on. The instant explosion of thunder was so powerful it shook the walls. Karma yelped.

"Holy shit!" Mark jerked behind her, his hands clamping down on her breasts, and then he burst into nervous laughter as he let go and pulled his arms from under her shirt.

She looked over her shoulder, laughing with him. "Scared?"

"Goddamn, that was loud." He continued to laugh as he looked toward the window then scrubbed his hands up and down his face.

The thunder had jarred them both out of their erotic interlude, which was probably a good thing. If they'd kept on the way they were, they would have ended up back in bed, and while the idea of making love with Mark sent a shard of *yes-please* through her blood, she kind of liked the slow seduction happening between them. Besides, if he was as big as he alluded, she really did need to prepare. It had been far too long since she'd been with a man.

"Don't worry. I'll protect you," she said, glancing back toward the mirror.

"Oh you will, will you?" He met her gaze in the reflection and smiled.

"Sure." She grew more serious. "Especially since you've taken such good care of me."

He blinked, bent forward, and kissed her shoulder. "My pleasure."

She smiled. "Mine, too, because, once again, that was pretty, uh…pretty nice…what we just did." She paused and looked at her reflection. Mark had opened her eyes. She cocked her head to the side as she studied herself in the light from the bathroom. She no longer saw the little girl. She saw the woman. "Thank you."

He hugged her from behind. "You're welcome." He said it as if he knew exactly why she was thanking him.

But that was Mark. He always seemed to know what she was thinking and almost knew her better than she knew herself. And maybe, in some ways, he did.

Chapter 22

When genuine passion moves you, say what you've got to say, and say it hot.
-D.H. Lawrence

After holding her a while longer and listening to the storm rumble past, Mark left Karma's place around eleven o'clock and returned to his condo. Upstairs, he changed into sweats and lay down, only to reach for his phone less than a minute later. He simply couldn't let the night go. It didn't feel complete.

"Hello?" He heard the smile in Karma's voice as she answered.

"Hi." An easy quiet came over his body as he settled more comfortably into the mattress.

"Did you forget something?"

That was a loaded question, because he felt like he'd forgotten to bring her home with him. She should be here, beside him, in his arms, dozing. What did she look like when she slept?

"Just one thing." He shut off the bedside light, bathing the room in darkness except for the faint glow coming through the windows from the street lamps. "I was supposed to have helped you tonight...with the first step of your training."

"You did help."

He frowned into the darkness. "What do you mean?"

She giggled. "Ummm...I'm...uh..."

Then it occurred to him. "You are? Right now?"

There was a short pause. Then, her voice soft, airy, and graced with self-conscious guilt, she said, "Yes."

"Mmm, well then I'm glad I called. I was going to ask if you'd like me to help you over the phone."

"How?"

"Have you ever had phone sex?"

"No." Curiosity and anticipation infused her voice.

"Do you want to?"

After another short pause, she whispered, "Yes."

He was hard. So damn hard for her. He pushed the waist of his sweats down to release his erection. "Are you in your bedroom?"

"Yes."

"On the bed?"

"Uh-huh."

"Is the light off?"

"No."

"Turn it off."

There was a rustling sound, then a soft click, and then she came back. "It's off."

"What are you doing?" He still hadn't touched himself, but his erection ached for contact. "Do you have the smallest dildo with you?"

"Yes."

"And…do you have it inside you?"

"I did a few minutes ago, but not now."

Oh Jesus, the thought almost made him moan. "Did it hurt?"

"Not much. Are you okay?"

"Yes. Why?"

"You sound different."

"I'm turned on." He blew out a heavy breath. "*Really* turned on. Aren't you?"

She hesitated. "Yes." But she sounded shy, too, which only made him want to hear her come that much more.

"Slide it up and down for me," he said. "Up and down your clit…tease yourself."

"I am."

Oh, God. "Are you wet?"

"Yes."

"How wet?"

She moaned and sighed. "Very wet." After a silent moment, she whispered, "I'm always wet around you."

Fuck. It was a good thing he wasn't with her. He wasn't sure if he could merely be a bystander. "That's good, because you make me hard. I feel like I'm always hard lately, and it's because of you."

She moaned again.

"Is your clit swollen?"

"Mm-hm."

"Rub the tip of the dildo over your clit for me, Karma." He reached down and wrapped his hand around his cock. "Rub it in small, slow circles. Imagine it's me…my cock on you."

She sighed into the phone.

"You like the idea of that, don't you?"

"Uh-huh."

"Me, too. Are you rubbing yourself?" He began stroking in long, easy pulls, palming the head before stroking back down.

"Y-Yes." He heard her shudder.

"You feel so good," he whispered.

"You can feel me?"

"Yes. Very much." He really almost could. "Tell me how I feel against you, rubbing the head of my cock on your clit?"

Another shuddering breath, followed by a muffled sound, as if she'd shifted on the bed. "You feel…good."

"Just good?"

"Hard. You feel…hard."

"I *am* hard." His breathing deepened and he gripped himself more firmly. "Put me inside you, Karma. Slide me in."

She panted lightly into the phone before she uttered a long, soft groan.

He closed his eyes and imagined himself above her. How would she feel? "You're tight. Am I hurting you?"

"No."

"Does it feel good?"

"Yes." She drew the word out on a breath.

"That's because you're very wet and very ready for me." And he was ready for her, too. He didn't want to use his hand. He wanted her touching him right now.

"Are you…touching yourself?" she said.

"Yes."

"Omigod," she whispered quickly, almost unintelligibly.

He grinned. "You like that I'm touching myself?"

"Yes." She whimpered.

"It turns you on that I'm here, stroking myself, wishing it was you touching me instead."

"Mark…"

"Hold the dildo inside you, Karma, and use your thumb. Rub your clit. Make yourself come for me. I want to hear you."

"I am…"

"That's good." He couldn't stand it and stroked himself in earnest now.

"Mark…?"

"Yes?"

"I'm close."

"Me, too."

She grew extremely quiet, almost too quiet. Then, after several seconds as his orgasm flamed to life at the base of his spine, she gasped. Once. Twice. And again, her pitch rising with each breath.

"Come, baby." He almost growled the words as his own orgasm tightened his scrotum, making his shaft swell.

She cried out, and it sounded like she dropped the phone, because everything grew muffled, but he could still hear her in the background, gasping and moaning.

Hearing her like that, lost to lust and depravity, sent him over, and with a grunt, his release shot out onto his stomach. Every muscle in his body clenched again and again through each throb, until finally he growled out a long, heady exhale and sank into the mattress.

A moment passed then Karma spoke into his ear, as if she were really there beside him. "That was sexy."

Breathless, he managed a weak, sated chuckle. "Back atcha. I wish I could have seen that."

"Me, too."

He smiled and blinked his eyes open. "Soon enough."

"I can't believe I just did that." The smile was back in her voice.

"Believe it. You've made quite a mess of me." He glanced down at the glistening splatter on his stomach.

"I'm sorry."

"Don't be. It was worth it." He took another breath and blew it out as he reached for a Kleenex. "I'm glad I called."

She giggled. "Me, too."

He wiped himself down and tossed the tissue aside. "I want you to use that dildo every day, even if you don't masturbate. Okay? You can even slip it in and leave it there while you watch TV or something, or as part of your Kegels. Do that for a few days, then switch to the next one."

"And you'll help me?"

"If you want me to, yes." He would gladly assist. "You sounded like you were already doing a fine job on your own, though, but I can always offer my services, if necessary."

"I'll keep that in mind."

"I'd like that." Mark pulled up his sweats, rolled off the bed, and started for the bathroom. "I'll let you get to bed, but thank you for a lovely evening. It was…" He thought about all she had revealed earlier and how touched he'd been that she'd shared something so personal. Then he recalled standing behind her at the mirror, holding her from behind, staring at her beautiful reflection. "Enchanting."

"Enchanting. I like that."

"Me, too. I'll see you tomorrow."

"Good night," she said. "Thanks for the call."

He smiled as he turned on the faucet. "Good night, Karma. Sleep well."

He hung up, set the phone down, cleaned up for bed, and then brushed his teeth. When he lifted his gaze to his reflection before shutting off the bathroom light, he was still smiling.

Now, the evening was complete.

Chapter 23

In order to know virtue, we must first acquaint ourselves with vice.
-Marquis de Sade

For the next few days, Karma did as Mark told her. She stood in front of the mirror every morning and every night, staring at her naked reflection with a new sense of self-respect, telling herself she was beautiful. She and Mark talked or texted every night, and she graduated to the next size in her dildo kit. On Friday, they got together for dinner and what ended up being another intensely smoldering make-out session that ended with a lot of groping and forced abstinence on both their parts. At this rate, Karma wasn't sure how much longer she could hold out. It was becoming clear that she and Mark had incredible chemistry and that when the time came, he would definitely deliver all he had promised and then some.

One good thing came from their lusty Friday night, though. Mark gave her permission to start experimenting with her purple vibrator. So, after he left, she pulled it out of her panty drawer. It just made sense to store it near her underwear.

The vibrator was a little bigger than dildo number two. The latex wasn't as friendly to her womanly parts as the glass, but she finally reached success without too much discomfort after calling up the fantasy she'd had about Mark behind her at the mirror. That was all it took for Mr. Vibrator to do his magic.

And damn! What magic! That little rabbit ear thing that vibrated over her clitoris? Holy wow! And the way the shaft rotated and hit her G-spot—yes, she was getting well-acquainted with the G—nearly blew off her toes. She came so hard and so fast that it was practically over before it began. So, she did it again. And then once more just because she wanted to.

Exhausted and smiling, she fell asleep around midnight and was still smiling when she popped awake Saturday morning. She simply could not wipe the smile off her face. She was walking around in a state of perpetual arousal. What had Mark done to her? She was turning into a nymphomaniac.

Karma was still smiling as she returned home from her nine o'clock Pilates class when her phone rang. She set down her bag and glanced at the ID.

Mark. He had driven back to Chicago this morning for Mother's Day weekend.

"Good morning," she said.

"Good morning. You sound cheerful. Sleep well?"

"Very well. You?" She practically skipped to the kitchen.

"Mmm." He chuckled, but it was the quiet laugh of naughty things remembered. "Eventually, yes."

A grin broke over her mouth. "What exactly are you saying?" She opened the refrigerator.

He laughed again. "Let's just say I'm very happy this morning."

Her hand stopped halfway to the cup of yogurt she was about to fish from the fridge. "Mark!"

"What? I'm a mature, warm-blooded man."

More like *hot*-blooded.

"Did you…? After you left my…?" Complete sentences seemed in short supply all of a sudden. But why was she so surprised? Hadn't she done the same thing? Three times, in fact?

"Yes I… And yes, after I left your…"

She giggled at the way he mocked her. "Stop it."

"You're so cute when you're flustered."

"I'm glad you're amused." She grabbed her blueberry Yoplait and shut the fridge.

"I'm glad you amuse me. But, yes, I did take certain liberties with myself upon returning to my place last night. Are you really so surprised? We have been getting quite *familiar* with one another—and after what we did on the phone earlier in the week, is it so hard to believe I do that sort of thing when I'm alone? And, I might add, there was no way I was going to get any sleep whatsoever if I didn't relieve some pressure."

The man just couldn't come right out and say "I masturbated." He had to make even that simple, seemingly perverse act sound perfectly normal and justified…and artistic.

"What about you?" he said. "Did you…? After I left your…?"

What an incorrigible man. But to be mocked by Mark—so playfully and personally—was very all right. He gave good mocking. Not like Johnny's. Her brother's brand of mocking was another beast. One that should be shot, killed, and dismembered. Mark's mocking should get its ears scratched and a reward. Maybe she would give it a treat next time she saw him.

She pulled a spoon from her utensil drawer. "I'm a good student, Mr. Strong."

"And…?"

She pulled the foil lid off her yogurt. "And…that means I do as my teacher tells me." By now, they'd joked about being teacher and student so much that the nicknames had become terms of endearment.

"Okay. So…?"

She giggled and took a bite of yogurt. "Let's just say you've got your work cut out for you. Hank is very good in bed." Calling it Mr. Vibrator just felt strange. Giving it a name was much better.

"Hank?"

She laughed. "That's what I named him."

"Good God, why?"

"Because…I don't know. It's just easy. And Mark was already taken."

They laughed together.

A moment later, Mark continued, "And you're calling it a *him?*"

"Oh yes, after what we did last night, he is most definitely a he and not an it."

More laughter. Three weeks ago, she would never have had this conversation. But despite the fact that she still got shy enough around Mark in person that she couldn't *fully* relax, she was getting way more comfortable talking to him on the phone about subjects that, at one time, would have gotten stuck in her throat. Something about the fact that he couldn't see her face made her bolder, and she said things during their long-distance conversations and texts she probably would have choked on in person.

"So, I take it you completed your homework assignment?"

"Yes. And I went for extra credit, too," she said proudly.

"Really now?" He suddenly sounded a bit more intrigued.

"Mm-hm." She sucked another portion of yogurt off her spoon.

"And just how much extra credit did you go for?"

She tried and failed to hold back a giggle. "Ummm…"

"Karma?" His voice held a warning, and she imagined he had one brow arched and a playful smirk on his face. "Do I have to confiscate Hank?"

She laughed again. "Don't you dare!"

He sighed. "I've created a monster."

"A more liberated monster," she corrected.

"Mmm, I guess I can live with that. But don't get too used to…*Hank.*"

"Why's that?"

"Have I mentioned that I have an ego?"

She bit her bottom lip. "I think you did mention that once or twice."

"Okay. Well, I refuse to let a power tool perform better than I do. So, you have your fun with *Hank* while you can, because when I get hold of you, you'll wonder what you ever saw in him."

"Those are mighty strong words, Mr. Strong. Some would say fightin' words."

"Damn straight. I do like a challenge. And you've just given me one. *Another* one."

"Another one?"

"Yes. Another one."

"What do you mean?"

He chuffed softly. "My dear Karma, if you only knew just how upside down you've turned my world. You've been nothing but challenges and surprises—pleasant ones, I might add—since the moment I met you. One long, complex, and unbelievably irresistible list of challenges and surprises." He paused. "And I am absolutely drawn in. Hook, line, and sinker. You have my attention, Karma. All of it. And I do *not* intend to disappoint."

Her spoon hung like an abandoned thought over her yogurt cup.

After a moment's silence, Mark said, "You remember that next time you and *Hank* spend time together." She heard the smile in his voice. He knew he had just blown her mind. Again. "I'll let you go. See you Monday, Miss Mason. Enjoy your weekend."

Before she could say another word, Mark ended the call, but not before she heard him chuckle.

Oh, he was bad. So very bad...but so very good.

Was it Monday, yet?

Chapter 24

I am trying to find myself. Sometimes that's not easy.
-Marilyn Monroe

"I am beautiful."

Dressed in underwear and a T-shirt, Karma stared at herself in the mirror as she repeated the affirmation, just as she had yesterday morning before Pilates, and just as she would tomorrow before work, and the next day, and the next, just as Mark had told her to do.

She had heard Daniel discuss the concept of mind over matter before. Of repeating affirmations to change your mind-set in a karmic practice of putting out good energy to receive good energy back, but she had never tried it. She didn't know why, though. Maybe she had become complacent. People had a way of becoming complacent and accepting the status quo instead of searching for ways to change and improve.

Karma didn't want to be part of the status quo, anymore. Complacency would no longer do. Not now that she had met Mark and he had opened a whole new world of possibilities.

If she was being honest, though, the change had begun before she met Mark, even before she put on that red dress and envisioned herself inside a fantasy where she could be anyone she wanted. Her transformation had begun her freshman year of college, when she had abandoned her father's dream to become an engineer and embraced her own desire to become a writer. It had only been a baby step at the time, and one she hadn't recognized until recently as being the real her trying to break free. That one small change had been her first effort to discover her true self.

In hindsight, she realized she had always done what everyone else had expected. She had studied academics in school even though she wanted to pursue more artistic endeavors. Dad had compromised and allowed her to take piano lessons when she was a kid, and she later taught herself how to play guitar, but her class schedule had been packed with math and science. If not for English, homework would have been a drag. At least she had managed to convince her parents to let her join the basketball and cross-country teams in high school. Back then, she had loved distance running.

She hadn't run in years. Not since sophomore year in college. She missed it. For her, running had been almost meditative. Maybe she would go for a short run later in the day. Perhaps start training for a 5k. The thought was surprisingly empowering.

In the mirror, her gaze dropped to her chest. Mark had called her breasts perfect.

"I am beautiful." She smiled at her reflection, believing the words. Mark had made her feel beautiful.

She pulled off her T-shirt. *Were* they perfect? Instead of seeing the definition of small in her reflection, was she really seeing the definition of perfection?

Gentle swells pushed upward from the confines of her bra. Her skin was smooth and flawless, and for the first time, she looked—really looked—at her breasts. Always before, she had averted her gaze, too insecure to face the perceived flatness.

But her breasts weren't flat. She did have hills on her chest instead of valleys. Screw those stupid kids who had bullied her.

Taking a deep breath, she reached around and unclasped her bra. She held it in place for a moment, and then, with eyes closed, she let it drop to the floor. Slowly, as if unwrapping a gift, she opened her eyes again.

"I am beautiful." Her words were a mere whisper now, but a feeling comprised of equal parts relief, happiness, and revelation hugged her heart.

Her pale nipples puckered against the air, forming tiny round nubs the size of baby peas. She had small, pert nipples that capped smaller-than-average breasts. But her breasts weren't flat, and they weren't ugly. In fact, now that she was giving them a hard look, they looked perfectly proportioned to her body. She was naturally lean, like her father, with hips that looked more athletic than curvy. When she turned to the side, her bottom curved in a way that balanced perfectly with the small stature of her breasts. She was no Jennifer Lopez, but her bottom was…well…nice.

Hmm. How about that? Amazing what an objective assessment—and one very hot man—could do to change how she viewed her body.

"I *am* beautiful."

It would take time for her to fully adjust her perspective, but this felt like another breakthrough moment, similar to the one she had experienced when she made the decision, despite her dad's protests, to change majors. She had felt such a burden lift off her soul that day, just as she felt one lifting now. For the first time, she saw herself the way Mark saw her.

Screw her stupid brother and his wife, Estelle. Screw Jolene, too. Screw all her stupid childhood classmates.

The past was the past, and she was moving forward.

She retrieved her bra from the floor and put it back on. As she pulled her T-shirt over her head, she crossed the room and sat on the bed. The case that contained the pair of black Ben Wa balls sat on her bedside table. So far, she'd done her Kegels without them. For some reason, the idea of putting them in her vagina had intimidated her. Well, no more of that. She was a grown woman, for crying out loud, not a baby. It was time to grow a pair and woman-up.

She took the balls out and rolled them in her palm. They were heavier than they looked, but not too heavy.

She lay upon the bed, lifted the waistbands of her shorts and panties, and then slid the first ball around until she found her entrance. Before Mark had taught her about her G-spot, she hadn't been accustomed to putting her fingers inside herself, so it took a while to get the ball in place, and then, just like that, it slipped inside.

She actually gasped. Hooray! Success.

In went the second, more easily than the first.

Recoiling into the mattress and squeezing her eyes shut, she slowly poked her finger more deeply and pushed the balls in as the instructions said to.

She withdrew her finger and took a deep breath. She'd done it. She'd accomplished another first. Then she did her Kegels before taking care of her housework. Dishes, laundry, vacuuming. Mark had said she could leave the balls in for a while, which would help strengthen her inner muscles, so she didn't take them out.

As she worked, she worried the balls would slide out on their own, but despite a slight heaviness, she hardly felt them as she went about her business. After a while, she didn't feel them at all. She finished the laundry, cleaned the kitchen, made a pot of chili, and read more from the books Mark had given her. She was learning so much, such as how to give a whole variety of hand jobs and the joys of anal sex. Yeah, anal wasn't something she would try any time soon.

By the time she finished the books, she would know enough to be truly dangerous in the bedroom. But reading and doing were two different things, and while all her new knowledge sounded great in print, when it came to the rubber meeting the road, would she be able to perform?

At nine o'clock, she figured it was time for the Ben Wa balls to come out before she got ready for bed.

She went to her bedroom, put on a pale blue, oversized nightshirt, and lay down.

The instructions had said she could maneuver them out with her fingers or stand up, crouch, and cough. The idea of doing a crouch and cough reminded her of a man's prostate exam, so she opted for getting squeamish with her finger instead.

Deep breath. Insert finger. Dig a little. Ah! There was ball one. After a couple of tries, she hooked her finger around it and pulled it out. Nothing to it. Now for round two. In she went. Where was it? The tip of her finger grazed it. Gotcha. Oops, no. Slippery little sucker. Visions of Julia Roberts shooting a snail across the restaurant in *Pretty Woman* made her smile. Okay, try again. Oops. Slipped away again. This wasn't funny, anymore. Come here you little bastard.

After five minutes, panic began to set in. She couldn't get ball number two to cooperate. Another five minutes later, and she was crouching and coughing as if she had pneumonia, but still no ball. Number two wasn't budging.

What if the ball got inside her uterus? Could that happen? What if she couldn't get it out? Would she need surgery? Oh God! How embarrassing would that be?

She rushed to her laptop and pulled up everything she could find about Ben Wa balls, how to get them out, and whether or not they were safe for prolonged use.

The good news was, they couldn't get into her uterus. That was a relief. There were a few other tips about how to remove a stubborn ball, and it was apparently pretty common for one to dig in its heels and not come out. She eventually found a thread on a message board—a whole friggin' thread hundreds of comments long—devoted to posts from women who had suffered the same fate. Most of them posted they'd had to get their husbands or boyfriends to fish the stubborn thing out.

Great. Just great. She could hear that conversation with Mark now. "Hey, could you come over and pull out my Ben Wa ball?" As if it were the same as asking him to come and clear a clog in her kitchen sink or help her move the refrigerator.

No, she would do this herself. She tried a couple of other suggestions, such as jumping up and down, as well as bearing down like she was giving birth, and still the tiny, seemingly innocent ball remained rooted firmly in place. Great. Women could squeeze something the size of a small watermelon from their vagina every time they gave birth, but she couldn't even pop out a marble-sized ball. Maybe she just needed labor pains and someone standing over her telling her to breathe and push, and the little sucker would shoot out like a torpedo. As it was, that wasn't happening.

She lay down on the floor and tried using her finger again, but after another five minutes with the same results, she gave up.

There was nothing more she could tonight. Her insides were sore and irritated after so much prodding, so she would give it a rest and try again in the morning.

And if that didn't work…?

"Ugh." She flopped her arms down on the carpet and stared up at the ceiling as a heavy chill settled inside her gut.

If she couldn't get Ben Wa number two out on her own, she would have to…

"Please, God, don't embarrass me like that."

But that's what it might come to.

Mark just might have to ride in on his white steed, his silver armor gleaming in the sunlight, and save her from the curse of the evil Ben Wa ball.

Chapter 25

Life is a shipwreck but we must not forget to sing in the lifeboats.
-Voltaire

After struggling with the ball again before work the next morning, without success, Karma dreaded the moment when Mark would arrive back from Chicago. As soon as he saw her face, he would know something was wrong.

It was almost ten o'clock, and all she had done the entire morning was obsess over what she would say. How do you start a conversation that would end with something along the lines of, "I have a ball in my vagina and need your help to get it out"?

Smooth. Really. Mark would die laughing.

"You look like you're trying to figure out how to tell someone you're pregnant," Jolene said, sliding up to her counter like a viper. Her eyes even looked like snake's eyes, slit and menacing, as if she were preparing to strike. All she needed was the forked tongue. On second thought, she already had a forked tongue. What she really needed were the fangs.

Jo tossed her blond hair off her shoulder and set down her coffee mug. "Is Mark the daddy?" she said, her voice a jealous hiss.

Only if you count a Ben Wa ball as a fetus, you snarky bitch.

Karma was beyond over Jo's pissy attitude. Jo had been nothing but a venomous scourge for over two weeks. And now that Karma knew Jo's special secret about her relationship with Jake, she wasn't about to be intimidated.

"Can it, Jo. I don't need your shit this morning."

Okay, where had that come from? Surely the "I am beautiful" mantra she had been repeating every morning hadn't turned her into a bitch, not unless beautiful meant bitchy.

I am bitchy, I am bitchy, I am bitchy.

Jo's face wrinkled into a sour smile that didn't reach her eyes. "You're just upset because Mark isn't here, yet, and you can't *fetch his coffee.*"

Enough was enough. If this wasn't one of those times Lisa had been referring to when she told Karma she needed to put Jolene in her place, Karma didn't know what was. "What is your problem, Jo? I don't mind getting his coffee, and if it helps him get his work done faster, then who gives a flip if I get his coffee or not? That's my *job*, Jo. And while most executives get their own coffee nowadays, some still like their admin to get it for them."

Jo rolled her eyes. "But you're not his *admin*, Karma."

Karma leaned back in her chair and crossed her arms. "I am while he's here. And that's a directive from Don. So, if he wants me to get his coffee, I get his coffee. What do you care, anyway? He's not asking *you* to do it. Oh, but that's the problem, isn't it? He asks me to do it and not you."

Let the gauntlet be thrown.

"You're just a little brown-noser, Karma." Her words took on a more desperate tone, as if she knew she was losing this battle.

"That's pretty funny coming from you, being that your nose is so far up Jake's ass that you can tell what he ate last night and check for cavities." Now wasn't the time to reveal what she knew about Jo and her boss, but damn, did she ever want to throw that ace on the table and throttle Jo's world.

Jolene gasped. "How dare you—"

Karma got to her feet. "How dare *you*! Don't you have enough work to do without bogging down your time harassing me? Oh, that's right. You're so busy spreading gossip around the office and causing trouble that *I* have to do your job."

Where this piss and vinegar was coming from, Karma had no idea, but after over a decade of keeping her mouth shut, she was done taking Jo's shit—and everyone else's. Maybe this outpouring was just her soul's way of putting out the trash.

Pure rage rose in Jo's eyes, and her face colored deep red as if she were an old-school thermometer about to reach maximum temperature.

But Karma was beyond caring. She'd endured enough. For the first time in her life, she actually looked in the mirror and saw someone who wasn't flawed. Someone she liked. She felt empowered, more confident…maybe even a bit angry—no, furious—that she had wasted so many years as a victim. Over a decade of resentment and pent-up frustration needed an outlet, and lucky Jo, she was in the right place at the right time to catch the mental fallout.

And goddamn it! She had a tiny fucking ball stuck in her vagina! This was not the day to fuck with her!

"How dare you," Jo said again, apparently too stymied to come up with something original. She picked up her coffee and took a step back. "You have no idea what—"

"Oh, just stop it, Jo." Karma leaned forward. "You're lazy. I know it. You know it. Everyone knows it. If you worked as hard doing your job as you do at getting out of it, you'd be employee of the year."

Jo gaped, but Karma wasn't finished. She was digging the hole now. She might as well shovel down to the requisite six feet to make a grave.

"You're a gossip, a troublemaker, and a liar, Jo. And you dump your work off on everybody else, especially me. Everyone sees it, and I can't believe I've put up with it for so long. You're the most unbelievably lazy person I know. How you've survived this long without getting fired is beyond me." Well, not anymore. Now that she knew about her and Jake, Karma had a pretty good idea how Jo still had a job at Solar. She speared eye daggers at Jolene, only barely keeping a lid on her knowledge of Jo and Jake's affair. "Now, get out of my face before you really piss me off."

Speechless and blowing steam out her ears, Jo spun and marched off, disappearing around the corner in a flurry.

The tongue-lashing had been long overdue. Karma had stood up for herself. She had finally had enough and unloaded.

And then reality hit.

What had she done?

She had just pissed off the office gossip. And even though she had major ammo on Jolene, Jo could still cause *big* problems with her *big* mouth.

Mark wouldn't be pleased with her behavior.

Shit just got real.

As if she didn't have enough to worry about with the black Ben Wa ball from the fires of hell stuck in her vagina, had she just kicked a sleeping dog?

It was thirty minutes later when Mark appeared at the end of the hall. He turned the corner, smiled, then frowned when he saw Karma's face.

"Good morning, Karma." He gave her a hard look as he passed.

"Good morning."

He was going to kill her for how she had behaved with Jo.

As soon as he sat down at the conference room table, he took out his phone.

An instant later, her phone vibrated with a text.

What's wrong?

She typed out a quick response. *I need to talk to you.*

A couple of minutes later, Mark poked his head out the door. "Karma, could you join me, please." He turned and headed back to his chair.

She grabbed her notebook and a pen and hurried into the conference room.

"I need your assistance on a confidential project, if you don't mind," he said, not looking at her. "Could you shut the door?"

She closed the door then joined him at the table.

With their cover in place for anyone who might have overheard, he looked up and smiled. "That's a lovely outfit. Green is a good color on you."

"Thank you." His compliment didn't do anything to ease her mind.

He sat back. "Okay. I see this is serious. What's wrong? Are you okay?"

The Ben Wa ball had become the least of her worries after her exchange with Jo.

"I'm fine. Sort of." She sat down and sighed. "But something happened."

"Okay?" Mark said cautiously. "Tell me."

"It's Jolene."

Mark's left brow arched as if he knew all about Jolene already. "Let me guess. She's stirring up rumors about you."

Karma nodded. "Not just me. You, too."

Mark cocked his head. "I already know. I was hoping it wouldn't get to you, though."

"You know?" Of course he knew. Mark was all but a mind reader, wasn't he? The guy had serious skills of perception that bordered on the supernatural. Look at how easily he'd figured Karma out that night they went to St. Elmo's.

He nodded. "Not much gets past me, Karma. And it wouldn't be the first time someone tried spreading rumors about me." He studied her. "What happened?"

Karma took a deep breath. "Ever since you turned her down for drinks, she's been trying to stir up trouble, and she's making inappropriate comments about how you're my boyfriend, and then today she got…well…she made a comment that caused me to snap."

"Snap how?"

Karma hung her head and let it all go in a string of anxious babbling. "I sort of blew up. I'd just had enough of her crap, and, as you know, she's been antagonizing me since we were kids, and I was done, just over it, and I told her she's lazy and how she's lucky to still have a job. I'm so sorry. I just blew up. I don't know what came over me. I've never done anything like that before and it's so unlike me but now she's probably out there spreading horrible gossip about you and me and what if someone believes her and you get in trouble and..." She paused long enough to breathe and looked up.

Mark had leaned back in his chair, a half-suppressed grin plastered on his face.

"What?" she said.

"Are you finished?" he said benevolently.

"Aren't you angry?"

The patient look on his face, along with the small shake of his head, surprised her. "No. Should I be?"

"I thought...I just..."

"You thought I'd be mad at you for putting a notorious, lazy gossip in her place?"

She nodded. "Well, yes."

Mark leaned forward, elbows on knees. "If I didn't think it would draw attention, I'd applaud you."

She was so lost.

He got up and walked to the window, turned, and crossed his arms as if he was putting on his professional persona. "I've known about Jolene since day one. I've met with and talked with almost everyone who works here. In my own way, I've asked them lots of questions about job functions, personnel, performance, who they think goes above and beyond, who doesn't, and who causes trouble." He returned to his chair and put his hands on the back. "I can assure you, those who matter, and even more who don't, know Jolene causes trouble and dumps her work on you. And I can assure you, those same people hold you in much higher esteem—and value—than they hold Jolene. If Jolene tries to spread rumors about you and me to tarnish your name, you've got some serious allies here who will put a stop to it. She's created a lot of enemies with her gossip, because she's targeted everybody. Like you, I'm surprised she's still here, and, between you and me, if I get my way—and I've no reason to think I won't—she won't be here after I'm gone. But that stays between us."

Had he just confirmed that one of the functions he was performing was to recommend layoffs?

"I won't say anything. But Mark, what if *she* does? All it takes is one person to cast doubt."

Mark sat back down. "Don't worry about Jolene. I'll deal with her. Leave her to me. I know things about her that could get her into serious trouble."

"So do I."

He cocked his head to the side. "Like what?"

"Like…" She glanced at her feet. "Well, um…"

"Do you know about her and Jake?"

Karma looked up. "How do you know about that?"

"I'm good at what I do," he said slyly. "I am very perceptive, and I listen to what people say, as well as what they don't. I knew about them within my first week here. If she wants to cause problems, I won't play around with her. Or him. They'll both be gone so fast it will be like they were never here. I've been given carte blanche regarding personnel and who stays and who goes, and while I don't abuse my power, I'm not afraid to wield it."

Well, then. How was that for having an army behind her?

"So, you're not angry?"

"Not at all."

"And you don't think I should apologize for what I said? You know, to try and smooth things over?"

"Only if you want to. That's your call. But I wouldn't if it were me. She had it coming."

Whew. This convo had gone better than she thought it would, but now she had to figure out how to tell him about her other problem.

"Do you feel better?" he said, giving her that winning smile she'd come to love.

"A little, yes. But…"

His brow furrowed. "There's more?"

She squeezed her eyes closed and covered her face as she bent over in an attempt to hide. This was so embarrassing.

"Miss Mason? What else have you done?"

"I need your help." She spoke against her palms.

"You need my help? With what?"

She slapped her hands into her lap and looked up. "I-did-what-you-told-me-and-used-those-little-Ben-Wa-ball-things-and-now-one-is-stuck." The words tumbled out so fast they all sounded like one long word mashed together.

"It's what?" He blinked hard, his eyebrows shooting high into his forehead.

"It's. Stuck." She hissed through clenched teeth.

"How long has it been stuck?"

"Since last night."

He threw his head back and laughed.

"Thank you. I'm glad you're so amused by my situation." She crossed her arms and tapped her foot.

"I'm sorry." He composed himself. "Okay. So let me see if I have this straight. You need me to help you get the ball out? Is that what you're saying?"

Flames shot up her neck and into her cheeks. "Yes, that's what I'm saying. I can't get it out. I've tried everything."

He licked his lips and fought back a smile. "You do realize what this will entail?"

She blew out a heavy breath and closed her eyes. "Yes."

"Are you ready for that?"

She opened her eyes to find him staring, one brow arched and eyes wide as if he wanted to convey just how familiar he would have to get with her anatomy to do what she was asking.

She nodded. "I don't have a choice. I'm desperate. Believe me, if I could get it out on my own, I would."

He smiled and nodded. "Don't worry. I'll be very professional." He winked. "This won't be the first time I've had to assist a damsel in distress in removing a Ben Wa ball. They can be a little tricky. However, I have a feeling this will be the most fun I've had with the task."

She groaned and hung her head. "I'm so mortified."

"Don't be. You don't see me complaining, do you?"

"Of course not. You're too busy having fun at my expense."

"Okay, okay. I'll stop teasing." He paused, and it looked like he wanted to take her hands in his, but he didn't. That would be too risky. Even their discussion was risky, although they spoke in hushed voices. "So, okay. I'll pick up dinner—it's the least I can do, right? I mean, if I'm going to put my fingers inside you, I should at least feed you."

"Ha ha." She sighed. "You're funny."

He chuckled. "I'll be over around seven. I'll take care of everything. Promise." He held up his right hand as if taking a Boy Scout oath. Would he want a badge after he removed the ball?

"Thank you."

He gazed at her for a long moment, and she got the distinct impression that he wanted to kiss her. Right there. Just take her in his arms and kiss her. Then he cleared his throat and nodded. "Okay. You'd better get back to work. We'll talk later."

She stood, picked up her notebook, and went to the door.

As she opened it, he said, "Thank you, Miss Mason. The end of the day is fine on that. No rush."

She glanced over her shoulder. "It won't take long. I should have it finished within the hour."

No one was around, and Don was traveling today, but the cover-your-ass was necessary, just in case.

As she sat back down at her desk, her phone vibrated with a text.

I'm looking forward to searching for your lost ball.

That stinker. *It's not lost, Mr. Strong. It's just being difficult. Like someone I know.*

He chuckled, but didn't reply. Enough had been said already. But at least her dreaded conversation was over. Now she could focus on more important things. Such as trying to figure out what to wear tonight.

A basket over her head would be perfect.

Chapter 26

That which does not kill us makes us stronger.
-Friedrich Nietzsche

A few minutes before seven, Mark arrived with corned beef sandwiches and vegetable soup he'd picked up at "this great little deli" he discovered, as he'd said on the phone when he called to take her order. He also brought a six-pack of Heineken.

God love him.

He set his gym bag by the door. Why he had it with him, Karma had no idea. Maybe he'd brought forceps and a pair of pliers to fetch Ben Wa. Or a large magnet. That would do the trick.

After eating, he grabbed his duffel bag and nodded toward the hall. "And now…we have a procedure to perform."

Incredulous and embarrassed, she groaned and shook her head. "You are taking way too much delight in this."

"I just love seeing you squirm."

"Well then, you'll really love me in just a little bit, because squirming is about all I'll be doing." She lifted her beer and drained the bottle. "Let's do this." Might as well get it over with. She was ready for the little black ball from Ben Wa Land to end its sequester inside her body.

Mark followed her to her room.

"How do you want to do this?" she said.

He tried not to smile but failed. Yes, he was having way too good a time at her expense.

"Well, I'll step into the bathroom and get ready, and you…" He glanced at her jeans. "You need to take everything off below the waist and lie down on the bed."

Take everything off below the waist?

"Do I really need to take off all my clothes?" She wasn't ready for him to see her naked. "Can't you get it out some other way?" As if he could *think* the ball out of her or perform a Criss Angel Mindfreak magic trick.

He set his bag on the floor and took her hands. "I *do* need full access to do this." He was trying to lighten the mood with humor, but he must have seen the raw humiliation in her eyes, because he sighed and grew deadly serious. "I'll be professional. I promise. You can turn off all the lights and get under the covers. Will that help?"

"I suppose."

He let go of her hands and gestured toward her bed. "You get ready. I'll step into the bathroom." He winked and picked up his bag. "You tell me when I can come out."

He disappeared into her bathroom and closed the door, leaving her alone.

"I can do this," she whispered to herself. She hurried out of her jeans and underwear, glancing over her shoulder at the closed bathroom door. "Really, I can."

She hastened to turn off the light, close the blinds, and get under the covers.

Deep breath.

She clasped her hands over her sternum. Her palms were sweaty. She quickly wiped them on her comforter and re-clasped them on her stomach.

"I'm ready," she called.

A moment later, the bathroom door opened.

She looked over.

What the heck?

Mark was wearing goggles, a surgical mask, a shower cap, and latex gloves. He lifted his hands in front of him like a surgeon.

In an instant, the ice broke, and she burst into laughter at the same moment he did. He pulled off the shower cap and goggles, tossed them on the bathroom counter, shut off the light, and strolled to the bed. Once he sat down beside her, he pulled down the mask.

"I was hoping that would loosen you up," he said, leaning over her.

She giggled and wiped a tear from her eye. "It did. Thank you."

"I've always wanted to play doctor." He pulled the mask over his head, snapped off the gloves, reached around, and pulled a small bottle of lube from his back pocket. Then he set it on the nightstand.

"Gynecologist?"

"Something like that." He looked down at her discarded panties on the floor, then back at her. "I see you're ready for me."

"Is that a double entendre?"

"Would you like it to be?"

She bit her lip and felt a shiver in her abdomen from the way he looked at her. His gaze burned into hers as if he was suddenly as intent on what he was about to do as she was. As if reading her mind, he grabbed the bottle of lube, got up, and went around to the other side of the bed, where he lifted the blankets just enough to slip under and join her.

"Relax," he said, propping himself on one elbow. "Relax and open your legs."

"You'd think after what we did on the phone, this would be easier," she said nervously, easing her knees apart.

When she felt his hand take hold of her leg and lift it over his thighs, she inhaled sharply then slowly exhaled.

"Everything's more personal in person," he said. "Anonymity makes us brave. When you can't see me, you're more able to connect with what you want, because you're not thinking about how I'll react or what I think. When I'm with you…" his hand skimmed along the inside of her calf to her foot, "you become more self-conscious. You're wondering if I like what I see, what I'm feeling." His fingers tickled their way back up her leg. He paused a moment and closed his hand over her knee. "Just so you're not worrying about all that…yes, I like what I see, as well as what I feel."

She trembled at his words and the warmth of his hand on her leg.

"Just relax," he said softly. "Let me do the work." His fingertips trailed back down to her bare foot. "Mmm." He grinned. "No socks."

"Should I have put them on?"

"You should always wear socks around me unless you want me excited." He grinned and smoothed his fingers over the top of her foot and up to her ankle.

"I'll remember that."

"Mmm, I'd rather you not."

"Is this what you consider professional doctor behavior?" she said quietly as his fingers lightly tickled their way up her leg.

He smiled. "Just getting you used to my touch." His voice was quiet but deep.

He spent another few seconds caressing her legs, sending sizzles into her abdomen and down to her toes, and then shifted his hand higher. He pulled his hand out from under the covers, popped open the cap of the lube, and drizzled a little on his fingers. She wanted to tell him she was already nicely lubricated.

"You ready?" he said.

She nodded, and he slipped his hand under the blankets again.

"I'm going to touch you now, okay?" he whispered.

He had already been touching her, and didn't her tingling body know it, but she knew what he meant. She met his gaze and waited, holding her breath. It was as much of an acknowledgement as she could muster.

His sure fingers slid between her outer labia, pressed in, parted her inner labia, dove farther down as if searching, and then stopped.

"Take a deep breath," Mark said.

She inhaled, and as she exhaled, his middle finger forged inside.

This was the first time a man had put his finger inside her. The sensation was foreign but pleasurable. Similar to how it felt when she put her finger inside herself, but Mark had big hands and wider fingers than she did, and even though it was just a finger, she felt full. He probed farther, stroking her G-spot. The contact was enough to make her suck in her breath.

"I feel it," he said, concentrating.

"I feel it, too." She spoke breathlessly.

His finger halted, and the corners of his mouth lifted. "Are we talking about the same thing?"

She licked her lips and stared, feeling like she was floating. "I don't know. What are you talking about?"

"The ball." His grin grew wider. "What were *you* talking about?"

"*Not* the ball." The words breathed out on a dreamy sigh. Her nervousness began to evaporate, and for the first time she felt...sexy. Sexual. The way she imagined a woman was supposed to feel in bed with a handsome, virile man like Mark.

His finger gently hooked inside her and stroked her pleasure zone again. "Is that what you feel?"

She closed her eyes and let out a long, quiet sigh. "Yes."

"Well, we'll come back to that later." His thumb smoothed up to her swollen clit and drew a single firm circle around it. "For now, tilt your pelvis for me." She did as he asked. "That's good. Hold on."

His finger wiggled back and forth, and the pressure inside grew more and more pleasurable. The rest of his fingers cupped her crotch. Her breaths grew more shallow the longer he played fetch with the ball.

"You sure went to a great deal of trouble to get me to put my finger inside you," he said, grinning. His finger strained deeper.

She huffed in protest, too distracted by her rising arousal to respond verbally.

"Are you sure you didn't do this on purpose? I mean, I can think of better, easier ways to get me to do this without risking life and limb to retrieve a little metal ball."

Trying to hold back her smile, she nudged his free arm. "Stop making fun of me. Just do your job and get that thing out."

"You make it sound like an alien."

"It feels like one."

"Did you even *see Alien*?"

Now they were talking about aliens and movies about aliens? Really?

"Yes, I did."

He frowned, concentrated, and hooked his finger inside her. His face scrunched as if he was working hard. A moment later, his face relaxed, and he smiled. He slowly pulled his finger out of her, and then held up the little ball between his thumb and forefinger. "Got it. Now, does this look like a molting, evil, acid-bleeding creature to you?"

The most wonderful ache between her legs protested the removal of his finger, but she managed to laugh and give him a playful shove. "Stop teasing me."

He laughed with her. "Is that any way to thank me for saving you?"

The man was incorrigible. "My hero," she drawled sarcastically.

"That's more like it." He tossed the ball to the floor.

She began to pull her leg from over his, but he quickly gripped her knee and held it back. "No, no. I'm not finished with you."

"What are you doing?" But she already knew. At least her subconscious did, because sparks erupted inside her belly.

The look in his eyes confirmed her suspicions.

He released her knee and skimmed his palm up her leg as his torso pressed against hers. "Trust me?" he whispered against her lips.

With flames licking their way into the place his finger had just vacated, and molten arousal flowing into her limbs, she would agree to anything he asked. "Yes," she said breathlessly.

Moments ago, they had been laughing and joking, but now the air crackled with rising hunger. She wanted more. She was ready for more.

His fingers danced up and down her inner thighs, sending shocks of sensation into her labia, up through her vagina, to her clitoris.

If he could make her feel this way with just his hand, she could only imagine what he could do with his mouth. After all, he had read the papaya book, which meant he knew what it took to give mind-blowing oral sex. Just what kinds of magic tricks had Mark picked up from his studies?

His hand drew near center again, but this time, he didn't pass over to her other leg. This time, the very tippy-tips of his fingers barely touched her as he brushed them over her lips.

Arousal spiked in her core, and wave after wave of tingles lapped at her vulva with each pass of his fingers.

She squirmed and moaned, turning her pleading gaze to his. His intent, hooded eyes seemed to drink her in as if he had never seen anything more captivating.

He let his fingers caress her more directly, brushing the length of his fingers against her privates. A minute later, he altered the pressure again, using his fingers like a paintbrush, heavily stroking them up and down.

Sensations unlike any she'd ever felt surged through her, and she found it hard to lie still. More. She wanted more.

But Mark progressed at his own pace, slowly drawing his fingers up, then driving them back down. He spread her both ways, teased her clit, and sent her heart rate into the stratosphere.

Until finally, he planted his palm fully against her and slowly plunged his middle finger back into her depths.

She gasped and thrust her hips to meet him.

"Will you take your shirt off for me?" he said quietly. It was a request, not a demand.

Her heart rate spiked. "I'm not sure…"

"You don't have to," he whispered, "but I think you'll like it. I know I will."

Her gaze danced around the room. It was a little darker now. The sun was creeping toward sunset. Her eyes met his again. Down below, his thumb drew slow, persuasive circles around her clit, and his finger stroked the front wall of her vagina. Why not do as he asked? She was beautiful, right? Even so, she wanted something from him if he wanted her to do this.

"You first," she said.

"Ah, a negotiator." He grinned, removed his finger, and yanked his shirt off in one smooth motion.

If Mark was hot with his shirt on, he was even hotter with it off. Karma stared. Yes, stared. Dark but short, sparse hair swept toward his sternum, down the ridge in the middle of his chest, and pointed toward the center of his stomach, which was impressively ribbed with muscle. Mark was a man who took care of his appearance.

God bless sit-ups and whatever else he did to keep that six-pack.

"Your turn," he said. The expression on his face showed that he enjoyed the way she was staring at him.

She swallowed. He had fulfilled his end of the bargain. Now she needed to. Slowly, she grabbed the hem of her shirt and lifted it up her torso. For so long, she hadn't wanted anyone to see her naked, but Mark was beginning to change all that. He had told her she was beautiful. He had said her breasts were perfect. And he had made her start believing it.

Mark's eyes held fast on her body as she peeled the shirt over her head. Then she held her breath and, with trembling fingers, she unfastened her bra. A part of her couldn't believe she was doing this, but the other part reveled in the fact that she was. It felt like she was about to pass some kind of milestone…complete a rite of passage.

Their eyes met, and she inched her bra off her chest. Little by little, she revealed herself to him, and his gaze lowered in a way that suggested he didn't want to miss a moment, until finally, she pulled the bra away altogether and set it aside.

His hand slid back under the covers and between her legs. "You're beautiful." He spoke softly, his gaze ranging left to right, from one side of her chest to the other.

"I'm nervous," she whispered in the growing darkness.

"Don't be." He eased his finger back inside her.

A moment later, he rolled down beside her, and his skin met hers. So warm, so electric. So incredibly *hot*.

I am beautiful.

When his mouth closed over her nipple, all rational thought screeched to a halt. He drew the tight, puckered bud against his tongue and laved her with the patient lust of a man who knew what he was doing. Then he drew his tongue up her breast, to the side of her neck, and finally to her ear.

"You're driving me crazy," he whispered, just as he began massaging his thumb over her clit.

She was driving *him* crazy? What did he think he was doing to her?

"Put your arms around me," he said, lifting his body so he could scoot closer.

She did as he asked. He felt so big, so powerful. The muscles of his back rolled against her palms. God, he was majestic.

She closed her eyes and moaned as his finger found her sweet spot again. His thumb and middle finger worked in perfect harmony, finding a rhythm, working in tandem to drive her insane with need.

"You're close," he said, dropping his mouth to her breast again. "I can feel your clit getting harder." He groaned and laved her nipple.

Nipple and clit connected on some invisible fuse, and the first telltale sensation of pending orgasm burned through her.

She sucked in her breath. "I think I'm…oh God…yes."

He replaced his thumb with the heel of his hand and gripped her like a bowling ball, rubbing her clit and that incredible inner spot more aggressively, increasing the pressure. At the same time, he sucked her nipple against his tongue and gently flicked it. A bolt of electricity zinged from her breast into her vagina, and she gasped as her orgasm reared.

She could hardly breathe. Her orgasm built and built…and built. For what felt like an eternity, it threatened to consume her. It rose like a slow burn, creeping closer to the edge.

"Yes…yes…yes." Each whispered syllable rose in pitch and intensity, taking her closer to boiling over.

My God, she had never felt anything like this.

She ground her hips against him, gripped the back of his head to hold his mouth against her breast. The more he teased her nipple, the better it felt between her legs. What sorcerer's trick was he playing on her anatomy?

"Yes, *yes,* YES! Mark!" She threw her head back, the wave cresting.

"Bear down," he said.

She did and held her breath. The pleasure! My God, the pleasure! What was happening to her?

Like an explosive blast, her orgasm skyrocketed into orbit, and then crashed into her with the force of a bomb. Was this a side effect of the Ben Wa ball being inside her for so long? Or of the Kegels she had been doing faithfully every day? Or was it just…Mark? Whatever the cause, she wanted more.

Her entire body convulsed. She lost all control over her muscles. It was as if a hundred doctors were tapping their tiny triangular hammers against all her reflex points at once. Her arms and legs jerked endlessly, her stomach twitched in violent spasms, and the only sound she could make was a garbled moan as her climax completely destroyed her.

It wasn't until about a minute later that she stopped twitching and finally opened her eyes. Echoes of her orgasm still hummed through her muscles, but at least she had regained control.

The expression on Mark's face was one of awe. "My God, that was…breathtaking." In an instant, his mouth was on hers, his tongue seeking to connect. Still breathless, she breathed him in drunken gasps. She was totally open, as if the intense intimacy of such a powerful release had shattered all inhibition, as well as the walls that normally concealed her. Gratitude beamed from her soul, uniting them.

"I've never seen a more beautiful orgasm," he said against her mouth. His hand was still in place, his finger still inside.

"I've never felt anything like that before," she whispered back.

He grinned, and his teeth pressed against her top lip as his eyes searched hers in the growing shadows. "Now *that* was a chocolate chunk brownie," he said.

His finger began rocking inside her. Slowly. Very slowly. Waves of warmth blasted through her, mere ghosts of what she had just experienced, but pleasurable nonetheless.

"I'm beginning to understand." She wrapped her arms around his shoulders, finding comfort under his body in the dark room. The brownie, the Kegels, the Ben Wa balls, the reading, all the preparation. Mark's methods clearly held merit. He really did know what he was doing. As if she had ever doubted.

"I told you you'd thank me later."

"Yes, you did." She sighed as his finger continued to coax pleasant sensations from her body.

"Shall I try for a double serving?" He nudged his forehead against her temple, his eyes closed.

Just the thought made her insides turn to mush.

"Yes, please. I'm still hungry." As his finger stroked that special place inside her, she could already feel another orgasm building.

"Mmm. Me, too."

Thank God for stuck Ben Wa balls and chocolate chunk brownies.

And G-spots. She couldn't forget those.

Chapter 27

Turn your face to the sun and the shadows fall behind you.
-Maori Proverb

Karma awoke the next morning with a spring in her step and a smile on her face. A deep ache that had nothing to do with too much Pilates core work pulsed in her belly.

The things Mark had done to her last night! With just his hand. There had to be laws against experiencing that much pleasure.

As she got ready for work, an odd sensation pulsed between her legs, making her breathless. It sort of felt like driving really fast over a small dip in the road, making her stomach flutter for an exhilarating split second. Only, in this case, it wasn't her stomach that fluttered. It was her girl parts. And the quivering, blossoming feeling didn't diminish. It simmered and rolled constantly, stealing her breath, and she could barely think of anything other than Mark. His hand. His fingers touching her, probing, stimulating her G-spot. And—oh!—there she went again, her body flying as butterflies took flight in her core.

She had never experienced such acute erotic awareness. She felt like a sexual Christopher Columbus, discovering her body and the pleasure it could give.

Stepping onto the stoop outside her apartment building, she took a moment to stop, close her eyes, listen to the morning birdsong, and absorb the first rays of sun on her face. When she opened her eyes again, the sky seemed brighter, the grass greener, the air more crisp. And she had yet to stop smiling.

She'd had her first official orgasm…*with a man.*

Maybe she was silly for getting so excited about what had happened last night, but she didn't care. To her, this was huge. Her first touchdown, her first home run, her first half-court buzzer beater. A major achievement in not only her sexual growth, but also in her growth as a woman. She felt like even though she had lost her virginity six years ago, she had still been a virgin last night, and now Mark had taken her flower, even though he had yet to pluck her petals with more than just his fingers.

But that day would come, and when it did, what came before would be nothing. After last night, she was convinced Mark would deliver in spades on all his promises.

Her phone dinged inside her purse and she pulled it out. She smiled more brightly when she saw Mark's text.

Truth or truth?

She giggled and replied, *Um, let me think. Truth.*

He replied a few moments later. *If you had to choose between $10,000 and being able to easily have multiple orgasms for the rest of your life, which would you pick?*

Karma laughed. *After last night, I think I'm sold on multiple orgasms.*

Me, too. Last night WAS rather impressive. I can still feel you quivering against me.

So can I. Now stop talking like that. I have to be at work soon, and you're turning me on.

She got inside her car just as her phone dinged again.

See you at work. PS You're turning me on, too.

How was she going to make it through her day with him just a glance away? It was only seven thirty, and she was already aroused.

Once at work, she practically skipped up the stairs then nonchalantly peeked into the conference room.

Disappointment deflated her. Mark wasn't in, yet. That was a first. He was almost always there before her. She assumed he had texted from the office.

She set about logging in to her computer and checking her e-mail, but her mind remained distracted, and she squirmed against the ache between her legs.

This was going to be a long day.

"Good morning."

Karma spun around to see the Adonis named Mark Strong stroll up the hall. He was dressed in charcoal grey slacks and a sleek, burgundy pullover. His hair was still damp. The beguiled smirk on his face told her he was still thinking about last night.

"Good morning." She pulled herself together.

He stopped at her desk. "Nice blouse." His chin dipped as he dropped his gaze to her navy blue top.

"Thank you. It's new."

Heat passed between them.

"You had a pleasant evening, I assume?" He made no motion to depart.

Her cheeks flushed. "Yes. Very. You?" These platonic games they played were so fun.

Mark's grin widened. One thick, dark brow lifted, and he lowered his voice. "I'm never late for work, Miss Mason. Never. But for some reason, I just couldn't seem to get out of bed this morning."

She checked the clock on her computer. It was ten minutes after eight. She glanced at him. Her lips parted, but no words came out.

He leaned closer. "I had a *very* good night." His voice lowered further. "And a very good morning, as well."

Could the heat around her desk have been any more tropical? Lust burned her, and she wanted to follow him into the conference room and climb onto his lap.

Good thing no one was around to see them, because they would have witnessed sparks flying in all directions. If Mark wasn't careful, she would throw aside propriety, shove him into the conference room, lock the door, and ride him like a cowgirl for the next hour.

Yeah, right. In her fantasies maybe. Brazenly having sex in the office was not something she could do. Not even close. She was too conservative. Maybe she had entered the land of the sexually affluent last night, but that didn't mean she was totally reformed.

"Would you mind getting my coffee, Miss Mason?" Mark said, standing up straight. "I've got to make up some time this morning. Besides, it always tastes just a little bit better when you add the sugar." With a wink, he spun on his heel and walked to the conference room.

The rest of the day was pure torture. Karma could barely concentrate, and more than once she found herself staring off in a daze, her thoughts replaying last night over and over. His talented finger, finding her G-spot, the way he effortlessly unfurled its power, the way his tongue danced over her nipples, and the press of his body in the darkness.

Mark had her downright hypnotized. Entranced. Mentally enchanted and so heavily aroused that she had to slip away midmorning for a quick release in the ladies room. And then again in the afternoon. She had never pleasured herself at work before, but in one day, Mark had so enraptured her that once wasn't enough.

She was turning into a damn nympho. And you know what? Fine with her.

Chapter 28

Our deeds determine us as much as we determine our needs.
-George Eliot

Mark ended up going out of town with Don Tuesday afternoon to visit the company's subsidiary offices, and the two didn't return until late Friday night. Mark had called her a couple of times from the road, but the conversations had been short because he and Don were entertaining vendors, customers, or potential business partners well into the evening.

Apparently, that was the life of a business consultant. At least, that's what it seemed like from Karma's perspective. How did he maintain such a high level of social buzz? Karma would have been exhausted.

On Friday night, after going to yoga with Lisa and Daniel, Karma returned home late with takeout from Greek Tony's.

She ate, changed into a pair of peach Capris and a white graphic tee, and crashed on the couch around eight o'clock to watch a movie.

When her phone rang a few minutes later, she was disappointed when the caller ID said it was her dad.

"Hi, Dad. What's up?"

"Hi, honey. I wanted to make sure you're still coming over on Monday."

Where had the time gone. Was it Memorial Day already?

"Absolutely. Are you grilling Cuban-glazed chicken?" Her favorite.

"You know it."

"Then count me in for a couple pieces and leftovers."

"I'm making extra just for you."

Her dad knew her too well. She would end up munching on leftover chicken for days.

"Johnny and Estelle won't be there, will they?" Those two ruined every event they attended at her parents' house. Johnny argued incessantly with Dad when he wasn't hassling her, and Estelle played Johnny's cheerleader.

"No. Not this year," Dad said. "Your brother said he and Estelle are having a small gathering at his place."

"Good."

Dad laughed. He knew the score between her and Johnny. And he related. Johnny bugged the crap out of him, too, with his pompous, holier-than-thou attitude.

"How's everything else?" her dad said.

She wanted to tell him she had met someone, but she didn't think her dad would understand that she was involved in a relationship that was going nowhere but promised to turn her into an orgasmic dynamo.

"I'm good, Dad. How about you and Mom?"

"Your mom and I are going to see the latest Marvel movie tonight. You want to come?"

Spending the evening with her parents was tempting, but all she really wanted to do was chill out at home. It had been a long, busy week at work, even without Mark there. "I'd love to, but I'm already down for the night. Thanks for asking, though. But…Marvel? Really? Mom wants to see that?"

Dad made a breathy, impatient noise. "It has that guy, what's his name? The guy who played Thor."

"Chris Hemsworth," her mom yelled from the background, as if she was impatiently standing by the door.

"Right, *Chris Hemsworth,*" Dad said. "So, of course your mom wants to see it. It was *her* idea."

"I see." Her mom had fallen in lust with Chris Hemsworth after seeing *Thor* and had since bought every movie he'd been in, even the ones in which he'd played only minor roles.

"Should I be jealous?" Dad said.

In the background, her mom laughed. "Don't be silly. You're the one who benefits from my Thor addiction, anyway."

Karma cringed. "Okay, I sooo didn't need to hear that." The thought of her parents making out like horny teenagers in the backseat of their car in the movie theater parking lot was like acid on her brain.

Her dad laughed. "I've still got it, honey."

"Dad!"

"Don't *'Dad!'* me, Karma." He chuckled. "How do you think you were made?"

She slammed her eyes shut. "Okay, I'm hanging up now."

More laughter from Dad. "One of these days, you'll find a good, strong boy who will show you what I'm talking about."

"DAD!" What would he say if he knew she already had a "good, strong boy"? Right now. Who wanted to show her all of what her dad

was talking about...and that he had already given her a taste...and would probably give her a whole lot more before summer was over?

"Bye, honey. See you Monday. Your mom is pulling me out the door."

"Ugh. Whatever. Bye. Have fun at the movies."

"Oh, I *will.*"

In the background, her mom squealed. "JOHN!"

Karma grimaced. "Get a room. Bye."

Her dad was still laughing as she hung up. Her parents were something else. Still together after, what was it now? Over thirty years? They had waited a long time after getting married to have her and Johnny, so they were older than the parents of most people Karma's age.

Johnny was already married with child number one on the way, and he was only twenty-two. But then, Johnny had always known he would marry Estelle, even when they were kids, and he already earned six figures a year as the founder of a social media marketing company. Two years at technical college, and he already had his life neatly put together and figured out. Lucky him. And he didn't let anyone forget it, either. He was ultra-competitive, just like Dad, which was probably why they didn't get along. Not the way Dad got along with her. She was *Daddy's girl.* Johnny was *his son.* The differentiation didn't sound like much, but she and Johnny were fully aware what the distinction meant in her family.

Get-togethers usually turned into contests, and sometimes Johnny threw her in the middle as bait to lure Dad into a game of verbal sparring, pointing out her flaws. Of course, Dad always stepped in to defend her.

This year's favorite taunt was how, at twenty-four, Karma still had no prospects of getting married, and that if she waited much longer, her biological clock would expire and she would pass her prime to have kids. Johnny could be such an ass. He had been one when they were kids, and he was still one now. But he was her brother, and occasionally—rarely—he was a good guy. But the constant nit-picking and jeers that had gone on since they were kids were getting old. If he wasn't careful, he could be next on Karma's hit list now that she'd already given Jolene a serious kick in the ass.

All the more reason why it was best that Johnny skip the cookout at their parents' house.

A few minutes later, her phone rang again. If this was her dad, she was *not* going to answer. Not after the image of him and mom getting it on had scorched her brain.

She checked the caller ID and smiled. Mark.

"Hey," she said.

"Hey you." It sounded like he was driving.

"Where are you?"

"On my way back to Chicago."

Karma's heart fell. He hadn't even stopped by to say good-bye. She had hoped against hope to see him before he left, because he was out all next week on vacation.

"Oh, okay."

"You sound disappointed."

"No, just..." She forced herself to sound more cheerful. "I'm just tired. But I'm glad you called."

At least that much was true. She shouldn't have been so disappointed that he had left without stopping by first. After all, he had made it clear right from the beginning what this was between them and what it wasn't. And what they weren't was boyfriend-girlfriend.

"I've got something I want you to work on next week," he said.

"An assignment?"

"Something like that."

"Do I need to write this down?"

He laughed. "Only if you want to, but it's pretty simple."

"Okay, shoot. What would the teacher like his student to do while he's out of town?"

"Well, besides the obvious *training* that he is very eager for you to complete, he would like for you to start talking to men. You know, flirting with them. That sort of thing."

She stiffened. "I thought you said you didn't want me to see other men while we're together."

"That's right."

"I don't understand."

He made a quiet noise like a soft laugh. "I just want you to talk to them, not go out with them."

Okay, she could see the difference, but she was still confused. "Why?"

"Because you need to learn how to talk to men...and preferably not tell them you're a model."

She covered her face with her free hand and forced herself not to laugh. "You're never going to let me forget that, are you?"

"Nope."

"Okay, so I'm supposed to flirt with men for the next week. You do know what you're asking, right?" Of course he did. Hadn't Mark proven time and again that he knew her better than she knew herself?

"I most certainly do."

"So you know how hard it is for me to talk to men and not stick my foot in my mouth, the night we met notwithstanding."

"Yes, which is precisely why I want you to do it."

She sighed, not feeling comfortable with this assignment. She knew how to talk to men when she was just hanging out with them, but she hadn't the first idea how to actually flirt. In the past, her meager attempts at flirting had been geek-worthy disasters. She had come off more like Rain Man than an intelligent, fully functioning adult.

"Karma? You've gotten quiet on me."

"Yes. I'm just…"

"This assignment bothers you, doesn't it?"

"Yes." She bowed her head.

"Why?"

"I've just never been good at talking to men."

"You talk to me just fine."

"You're different."

"How so?"

"Because I know you."

"You didn't know me when we met."

Mark had her there.

"Look," he said. "Just talk to them. Be yourself. Smile and say hi. If you're at the store, ask a guy if he can help you get something off the top shelf. Stuff like that."

"You make it sound so easy."

"Because it is."

She tucked her hair behind her ear. "Why is this so important?"

He paused. It was just a tiny hesitation, but Karma caught it. "Because when I leave in a few months, I want to make sure you'll be okay."

A tiny knot of sadness broke inside her heart.

When he left.

In only a few months, Mark would be gone, and she would be alone. Of course he would want her to find someone else. This was his way of teaching her how.

"I see," she said.

Another pause. "But I'm not gone, yet." He almost sounded a little sad himself, as well as a touch possessive.

She had to keep reminding herself not to get too attached. Mark didn't plan on staying. He couldn't have made himself any clearer on that point than he had.

What would happen to her when he left? Would she revert to her old ways, or would she remain the woman Mark was bringing out from her shell? Thinking about the near future made her sad. She didn't want to be reminded that he wouldn't stay in Clover forever.

Meeting Mark had been the most incredible wake-up call. He had a way of unraveling her defenses and making her feel safe with just a glance, with only a word or a touch. He was whimsical and playful, but overflowed with grace, dignity, and power. She felt comfortable around him, which wasn't something she could say about other men she had been attracted to. She and Mark clicked. He got her, and she felt like she got him…that they understood one another. How would she find that connection in another man after he was gone? She was beginning to think she wouldn't be able to.

"Karma? Are you there?" he said quietly.

She hadn't said anything for several seconds. "Yes, I'm here." She settled her head on the back cushion of the couch.

"Are you okay?"

"Just…I don't know. I guess I just wish you were here."

He paused. "Open the door."

"Huh?"

"You heard me. Open the door."

She glanced over her shoulder at the door, then, suddenly hopeful, sprang off the couch. When she pulled the door open, Mark stood on the other side, his phone against his ear.

"You didn't really think I was going to leave without saying good-bye, did you?"

A smile crept over her face, and she lowered her phone as he stepped inside.

He took her phone and set it next to his on the arm of the couch, then cupped her face in both hands. "Hi."

"Hi," she whispered, a split second before his lips came down over hers.

As he swept her away on a sea of warmth and bliss, all her worries and fears dissipated. This was what he did to her. Every time they were together, there wasn't room for sadness and worry.

There was just Mark and her. Kissing.

And once more, everything was perfect.

Mark kissed the crown of Karma's head as he wrapped his arms around her shoulders on the couch. She snuggled into the crook of his body.

He really had planned to leave for Chicago tonight, but the flight had gotten in late, and he was just too tired to make the drive. So, he had rescheduled tomorrow's lunch meeting with his boss to one o'clock instead of eleven so he could drive to Chicago in the morning. Tonight, he would spend a little time with Karma. He'd begun to miss her and really didn't think he could go a whole week without seeing her.

There was something about Karma that called to him. When he was with her, he felt safe. She warmed him in all the right places, and he found that he smiled more than usual around her.

Honestly, his suggestion that she start talking to other men was his way of putting a little distance between them, because he was growing too close. He couldn't afford to fall for her, because he had meant it when he'd told her that when his assignment at Solar was finished, so was their relationship. Falling for Karma wasn't an option, and he couldn't let her lose sight of the inevitability of his departure.

Even so, now that he'd told her to talk to other men, he wanted to take it back. He didn't like how it felt when he thought about her flirting with others while he was gone. Maybe she would find a man more to her liking and end their affair early.

The idea of that happening should have filled him with relief, because then he wouldn't have to be the one to end it later. Instead, thinking she would break things off with him first rattled his heart.

He pulled her a little closer and kissed the top of her head again.

"You're touchy-feely tonight," she said, wrapping her arms more securely around his waist. He liked how she held him as though she would never let go.

"I…" The words *missed you* caught in his throat. Thinking them and saying them were two different things. One was okay, while the other was a path he couldn't go down. "I just, uh…I just want you to know that I know how hard it is to talk to strangers. I know this makes you uncomfortable, because when I did the same thing, it was uncomfortable for me, too." His excuse sounded silly, but it was a decent save from going down the path of the emotionally involved.

"You?" She sat up and faced him.

"Yes. I know it might seem hard to believe, but at one time, I was pretty shy, just like you. He tapped her nose with the tip of his finger. "But trust me, it gets easier to talk to the opposite sex the more you do it."

"My dad always taught me to never talk to strangers."

"In which case, you and I never would have met, and I wouldn't be here now." He swept his palm over her silky hair. He couldn't stop touching her. "And that would be a crying shame, wouldn't it?"

She laughed. "Touché."

He plucked her hand from her lap and twined his fingers around hers. "Exactly. And I like being here with you."

"Me, too, but I simply can't imagine you being shy."

"Why not?" He laid his cheek on the cushion and gazed into her luminous eyes. Being with her was so damn easy. He didn't have to force anything and could just be himself.

She slid down and placed her head on the cushion beside him, mirroring him. They were like lovers in bed, staring at each other after making love. "You just don't strike me as the shy type."

"Well, I was." He tucked his leg between both of hers as she curled toward him. "I've never told you about my childhood, have I?"

"Not much." Her gaze filled with curiosity, as if she knew he was about to invite her in to his secret world. One not many were privy to.

"Well, I was brutally teased." He sighed. "You know how you told me about how the kids teased you?"

She nodded, growing more serious.

"I had a similar experience."

"I'm sorry," she whispered. "What happened?"

"Remember when I told you that my parents are dancers, and that my mom taught me how to sew?"

"Yes."

"Well, she also made me take dance lessons."

Fond adoration shone from Karma's eyes. "Dance?"

"Yes. Mostly Latin style, but ballet, too." He remembered the endless hours he spent in the studio during summer vacations and how, when school resumed in the fall, so did the teasing. "That didn't go over well at school," he said.

"Did you have to wear a leotard?" she joked.

"Yes. The slippers, too."

She giggled. "I bet you looked adorable."

"I looked gay."

Karma laughed.

"I have nothing against gay people," he said with a chuckle. "But when you're not gay and people think you are, it can be a problem."

"I can imagine." Her amused expression was a fraction short of comical.

"You're not helping."

"I'm sorry." She pursed her lips and snuggled closer. "Please, go on."

"By the time I was in junior high," he said, "the other kids teased me on a daily basis. And in Chicago, kids can be rough. I got beat up a lot, but my parents just told me to tough it out. That they would stop giving me a hard time if I ignored them. I wanted to take karate classes or something to teach me how to fight back, but they wouldn't let me. So, I went to school, got called a faggot or a fruitcake or worse, got pushed and shoved in the halls between classes. I was miserable."

Those had been rough years.

Karma offered a compassionate smile. "I'm sorry." She kissed his cheek. His skin warmed where her lips touched him. If anyone could understand what he had gone through, it was Karma.

He brushed her hair affectionately off her face then continued. "When Rob and I became friends, we both got teased. The other kids called us lovers and taunted us. They called us all kinds of names. Why Rob put himself through that just to be friends with me always baffled me. I know now it's because he got teased, too. He was a pudgy kid." Funny how the passage of time could change so much. Mark was now a successful businessman and Rob had leaned out and lost his baby fat in high school. "Rob saw how badly I was teased and could relate. Nobody else wanted to be our friends, so we became friends with one another. Like attracts like, right?"

"I never thought of it like that, but that makes sense."

"Anyway, except for Rob, I hated everything about going to school. Every day was hell. I didn't talk to anyone before I met Rob, and even after I met him, he was the *only* person I talked to. Even when I became a big basketball star in high school I didn't talk to anyone. Some of my teammates still thought I was gay and kept their distance, but they respected my skills on the court enough not to make fun of me anymore."

Karma's fingers squeezed his. This was a side of him he had never let her see…his vulnerable side with the painful past. But he wanted her to know she wasn't alone, and that she wasn't the only one who had demons to face.

"Anyway, I couldn't talk to girls." He chuffed. "I remember this one girl, Cassie. God, I had such a crush on her in seventh grade. I tried asking her to the spring dance with me. What a disaster."

"What happened?"

"She laughed. And not just laughed, but told all her friends so that they could laugh, too. It was pretty traumatizing. I'd put myself out there to this girl who I was crazy about, and she turned my life into a living hell. It took until my junior year to try again."

"Kids can be mean."

"For a guy, it can be pretty deflating. So, yeah, if I hadn't been scared enough about talking to girls before, Cassie made it terrifying. I was afraid of the rejection and of looking stupid…being laughed at." He met her gaze. The pain of old memories haunted him. "I was seventeen before I kissed a girl and eighteen before I had sex. And *that* was a joke. I mentioned that before. I was awful. Like your Brian, fumbling around like an idiot. She knew more than I did, and I spent myself in less than five minutes." He paused, not wanting to remember the dark times but unable to avoid them. "I really liked that girl, too, but she ended up dumping me during prom."

"*During?*"

"Yes. Can you believe that? I'd bought the tux—because, well, my mom refused to let me rent one—and I'd bought the corsage, paid for dinner at the nicest restaurant in Chicago, rented a limousine, paid for the tickets, and when we got to the prom she spent the entire evening with some other guy. I ended up riding home in the limo by myself."

In hindsight, it was like the prom had been a warm-up for what Carol would do to him later. Was he destined forever to have such awful luck with the opposite sex? Nothing good had ever come from any significant relationship he'd been in, which confirmed his decision never to fall in love or become seriously entangled again.

Karma remained quiet, her gaze sharp, almost penetrating, as if she was putting the pieces together about his inability to commit.

"It took me a while to figure things out when it came to women." He looked at her hand on his chest. It felt good there. Like it belonged.

"What happened? How did you do it?" Hope and curiosity sparked in her gaze.

"I met a dancer at my parents' studio. Her name was Carol. We dated for almost two years. I was her fill-in dance partner at first, but it became clear she had major talent, so my parents found her a partner she could grow and compete with at the international level since I was set to attend business school." His mind drifted to Antonio. "Things didn't work out between Carol and me after that, and we broke up." Bitterness edged his voice, and it was clear from

Karma's expression that she heard it.

"Was it a bad breakup?" she said softly.

Bad didn't even begin to describe the nightmare he had endured at Carol's hands. "You could say that." He looked away. "But it was my own fault. I was young and stupid. I still didn't know anything about what women wanted or needed. I was inexperienced, fumbling my way around, maybe even a little selfish. I didn't treat Carol well enough. I chased her away. I didn't put her needs before my own. I didn't talk to her enough. I thought I knew what she needed, but after she left, it became clear that I didn't." He couldn't bring himself to tell Karma what had really happened. If he started down that road, he would end up in the bathroom with his head over the toilet. Some things were better left unsaid. "But by leaving me, she made me see I needed to change. That's when I began reading…studying, like I mentioned before."

"Studying women?"

"Yes. I knew I had to make myself a better man. I thought I could win her back, but…"

"You didn't." Karma met his gaze.

She had to see the pain haunting the depths of his eyes…memories best forgotten.

"I failed with Carol," he said. "And, like I said before, I don't like to fail." He took a deep breath as the shortcomings of his past pushed front and center.

"Is Carol why you're not a long-term kind of guy?" she asked tentatively.

Even though he couldn't tell her exactly what had happened with Carol, he could at least acknowledge the truth. "Yes, something like that." He forced a smile. "But my point is I never wanted to be that man again. A man who couldn't please a woman or be what she wanted or needed." He caressed her cheek. "I didn't want my past to affect my present or my future anymore. But I had to force myself out of my comfort zone to do it. I had to learn how to talk to women, and not just talk, but listen. Just like you need to learn how to talk and listen to *men*. So that you're ready when the right one comes along. So you can talk to him instead of letting him pass you by."

He cupped her face and stroked her eyebrow with his thumb. Once more, the thought of Karma talking to another man sent ice through his veins, but what could he do? His course was set. His path was laid out before him. Eventually, he would leave and Karma would move on, whether he liked it or not.

Karma got it now. And the power of her understanding was borne of a past not unlike her own. Mark understood her. Why? Because he had also dealt with childhood bullying. Who better to understand the torment she had endured and vice versa? Like attracts like. Isn't that what he had said a few minutes ago? But unlike her, he had overcome. Now he wanted to help her do the same.

She thought of all he'd told her. About the teasing and Carol. Especially about Carol. He couldn't commit to anyone because of how he had failed with her. So, maybe seducing women and succeeding with them helped him atone for whatever guilt he still felt over what had happened with his ex. In his way, he was proving to himself over and over again that he wasn't a failure. Only, he never allowed himself to fully reach the pinnacle of success, because he never allowed a relationship to reach the level of commitment.

Was he scared? Was that why Mark insisted on keeping relationships short term? Because whatever had happened between him and the women of his past had been so traumatic he never wanted to risk being hurt again? He had a history of giving away his heart only to have it crushed. Maybe that was why he couldn't commit, because doing so felt like he was setting himself up for failure.

He said he had changed so his past didn't affect his future, anymore, which was all well and good. Karma was all for finding ways to release what held you back. Wasn't that why she had embarked on this journey in the first place? Only, with Mark she got the impression that whatever had happened in *his* past *was* affecting his future. If what had happened with Carol was his reason for maintaining emotional distance, wasn't it obvious that he still wasn't past it and that it was, in fact, impacting his decisions for now and tomorrow?

What if Mark was so caught up in the past that he was unable to see what appeared so plainly visible to her? He was so intent on helping her find the right man, but what if that was him? What if he was so keen on guarding his heart that he let happiness pass him by?

She wanted to point that out, but instinct held her tongue. She didn't think pushing him would help. It might even cause him to retreat further into his self-imposed emotional prison. No, this was something he would have to figure out on his own, without her interference. He was here to help her, not the other way around.

They gazed at each other for another long moment, then Mark said, "I should probably go. I just wanted to come over and tell you good-bye before I left."

"Are you still going to drive up tonight?"

"No. I'll leave in the morning."

"Good. I don't like the idea of you driving this late. You look tired."

"Not *too* tired."

"What do you mean?"

"Just this." He drew her to him and kissed her. Passion erupted as he persuaded her mouth open with his tongue and sought out hers.

This was a good-bye kiss to end all good-bye kisses…and one to fill her mind with all sorts of ideas to keep her warm while he was gone.

When he broke away moments later, he breathed in heavily through his nose as he eyed her mouth. "I'll definitely call you."

"I hope so."

He began to pull away then stopped. "By the way, how's your training coming along?"

She grinned, understanding exactly what he was asking. "I'm on the third one."

"Mmm, then by the time I get back, you'll be ready?"

"Ready? For…?" Arousal hummed through her body. She could think of a hundred things she was ready for right this second, and all of them involved Mark.

"For me."

"You?" Her heartbeat kicked up a notch.

He pulled her close and drew his mouth around to her ear. "Yes. Ready for me to make love to you."

"Oh."

"Yes." He kissed her cheek then helped her up as he stood and tucked his phone inside his pocket. Then he placed his thumb and forefinger under her chin, tipped her face to his, and settled a chaste kiss on her lips. His thumb brushed back and forth on her chin as he pulled away. "Have a good holiday."

She let him out then locked up. A minute later, she watched out her window as he drove away.

Nine days. Nine days without him.

It already felt like an eternity…and he'd only just left.

Chapter 29

The state of your life is nothing more than a reflection of your state of mind.
-Wayne Dyer

"Hey, buddy. Long time no see." Mark clasped Rob's hand as he joined him on the basketball court.

"How's life in Indy?" Rob dropped his bag on the pavement. "Getting anywhere with that girl of yours?"

Mark picked up the basketball he'd brought along. "As a matter of fact, things are going well."

Rob looked surprised. "Oh really now."

Mark frowned. "What's that smirk for?" Mark shot from the free throw line. The ball bounced off the front of the rim. That wasn't normal. Mark and free throws went hand-in-hand like milk and cookies. He couldn't remember the last time he missed a free throw.

Rob chuckled and snagged the ball. "Now I know there's something special about this girl. First, the goofy-assed smile on your face and now you miss a money shot? This might be my lucky day."

"What goofy-assed smile?"

"The one you had on your face when I asked about your girl." Rob sank a layup then tossed the ball back.

Mark scowled. "Screw you."

"Screw *you*!" Rob made a face as if he was imitating Mark then laughed. "You like this one. And not just a little. You like her a lot. I can tell."

"Fuck you, Rob." He pulled up, shot a jumper…and missed…again. Shit. What was wrong with his game today?

Rob smirked and grabbed the rebound. "So, what gives? You getting soft in your old age?" He dribbled around the court, and Mark followed, falling into guard.

"Hell no. You know I don't want a relationship."

Rob shot a jumper that bounced off the front of the rim. Mark caught the rebound and made an easy layup. Finally! A basket.

"I didn't say anything about you wanting a relationship," Rob said. "I just suggested you're getting soft." Rob gave him a don't-shit-me look. "But since you brought it up…"

Mark's face tightened, and he pressed his lips together as he waved Rob off. "It's nothing. I'm not going soft. Now shoot the damn ball."

Rob squinted at him, and Mark knew he wasn't buying the brush-off. And rightfully so. Mark was conflicted about Karma. Ever since their last conversation, he had been thinking about her a lot. Not an hour went by when his mind didn't drift to thoughts of her at least once, and every time, fond warmth wrapped around his heart.

Something had clicked between them Friday night. Revealing his childhood had built a bridge from his soul to hers. They understood each other. He'd never had that before—a woman who could relate and knew firsthand what it was like to be bullied as a child, as well as the mental and emotional scars that carried over into adulthood.

It had felt nice being able to talk to her about his past. Karma didn't judge him. She listened and related. That wasn't something Mark took lightly. But he didn't want to discuss it with Rob.

Thankfully, Rob dropped the subject and, after a few more practice shots, they played two games of one-on-one before taking a break.

Out of breath, Rob carried the ball to the bench and sat down. He plopped the ball on the pavement beside him. "Okay, level with me." He shot Mark a look while wiping the sleeve of his shirt across his forehead.

Mark glanced into his bag. "What are you talking about?" But he had a feeling. The tension between them on the court had been thick.

"I know your ass too well." Rob cracked open a bottle of water. "You sucked out there." He gestured toward the court. "It was hardly a contest. I never beat you, and I *kicked your ass*."

Mark started to protest, but Rob cut him off.

"No, Mark. Something's up. You only play like that when something's bugging you, and even then, you don't play *that* bad. You only play like that when you've been..." Rob trailed off, but Mark knew what was coming. "When you've been thinking about *her*, okay? Sorry. I hate bringing her up, but it's true. You only play like shit when you've been thinking about Carol. And today's the worst. And now you're smiling like a lovesick kid when you talk about Karma." Rob shook his head and waved his arms. Water sloshed out of his bottle and onto the ground, but he didn't seem to notice. "So, level with me. What's going on?"

This was why he both loved and hated Rob. He saw everything and never held back.

During the Carol fallout, Rob had been the one to pick Mark up and put him back together. He had seen Mark at his best and his worst, and he was still around. The guy was like Velcro. He'd attached himself to Mark and would never leave him. He was the one person Mark would always be able to trust and count on.

Then Mark thought of Karma. He was beginning to think he could trust and count on her, too. Especially after their last conversation.

He cleared his throat and took a drink of water. "I told Karma about Carol."

"You what?" Rob's eyes shot open.

"Just cool it." Mark scowled and held up his hand. "I didn't tell her *everything*. Just enough." He swallowed a drink of water. "She's different, okay? She's not like the others."

Rob grumbled and bent over, elbows on knees. "You're fucking up a good thing, man."

"Fucking up a good thing?"

"Yeah." Rob shot him a foul look. "Unless you're falling for her."

Mark only stared.

"Are you?" Rob's gaze burned into Mark's.

Mark snapped out of his mental turmoil and guzzled another chug of water then wiped his mouth. "Hell no. You know how this works for me. No commitments. No emotional attachments. Nothing long term. Remember?"

"Yeah, I remember." Rob sat back and leaned against the chain link fence. "Do you?"

Mark blew out a frustrated breath. "Fuck you, man. I haven't forgotten what this is about."

"Whatever."

"What's that supposed to mean?"

"It means that you've grown cozy enough with your new leading lady to tell her about the one woman who started this whole long list of affairs and who cut you down so viciously you drowned yourself in vodka for months before getting your shit together." Rob groaned. "Are you kidding me, man? You don't tell any of them about Carol, and you told *her*? You're walking a slippery slope, buddy. I hope you know that."

Mark shoved his water bottle into his bag. "I'm not walking a slippery slope. I told Karma this isn't a forever thing. I know what I'm doing. She's just…different." Mark wiped his towel over the back of his neck. "She comes from the same place you and I did. She's like us."

Rob's narrowed eyes studied him. "What do you mean, 'she's like us'?"

Mark picked up the ball and squeezed it between his palms.

"When she was a kid, she was bullied in school like we were. She was teased and called names. She went through hell. Just like we did."

Rob relaxed a little. "Okay. So?"

"So…I trust her. That's all. She understands. She can relate to what I went through. It's a…" *connection*. He wanted to say he and Karma had connected, but that would set Rob off again, and, to be honest, Mark wasn't ready to admit that out loud. "It's just nice to be able to talk to someone who comes from a similar background. Is that a crime?"

Rob shrugged and shook his head but didn't say anything.

Mark got up and dribbled the ball a couple times. "So, maybe it *was* stupid to tell her about Carol. Maybe I *did* open up too much. My mistake. But at the time, I was trying to get *her* to open up, so I used my past with Carol to convince her she could talk to me and work with me. It was necessary to get the job done. That's all."

That was a lie. Mark had told Karma about Carol because he wanted to. In the moment he had let his guard down and spilled more than he should have. But that didn't mean their relationship was turning into anything more than just another affair.

It was another lie, because it did feel like his relationship with Karma was way more than just an affair.

But it wasn't like he owed Rob an explanation. Hell, he didn't need to justify his actions to anyone.

Shit. That was a lie, too. With Karma, he was so far out of his league, seemingly rewriting the terms of engagement as he went, that he felt like he had to justify himself *to himself* for breaking his own rules. Damn it. He liked Karma more than he wanted to. Rob was right. He was walking a slippery slope.

Mark paced away then turned back, determined to regain control. "Well, like I said, I didn't tell her everything."

Rob stood and stretched his arms. "What? Like you didn't tell her about how Carol jilted you? Left you at the altar. How she ran off and fucked—"

Mark winced and threw out his hand to cut Rob off. "I don't need a recap, Rob. Okay? Shit!" The mental image of finding Carol with Antonio nearly made him gag. Even after all this time, the memory still affected him. Why? Because he had failed. He hadn't been enough. Never again would he let that happen.

Rob hitched his hands on his hips and looked down. "I'm sorry. I shouldn't have said that."

How could he be angry with Rob? The guy had come as close to sharing blood with him as two people could get. Rob had earned the right to get in Mark's face and give him a piece of his mind…and to lay shit out unfiltered.

"Look. Let's just play, all right?" Mark dribbled out to the court and shot a three-pointer.

And sank it.

Whoosh!

Thank God.

Rob nodded. "Okay, but don't mess shit up. Leave Carol in the past where she belongs, and get yourself straight about this Karma girl. I don't want to see you getting so fucked up I have to drag your sorry ass out of the bottom of a vat of vodka again. You got it?"

"It wasn't *that* bad." Thickness settled in his throat, and he avoided Rob's gaze. Those months after Carol devastated him had been rough, and vodka had been his go-to companion.

"It was bad enough." Rob took a shot and ran in for his own rebound.

"Well, I'm not that person, anymore." He caught a pass from Rob. "That pity party ended five-and-a-half years ago, okay?"

Rob shot him a dubious glance. "Fine. Just keep it that way."

"Don't worry about me. I've got it under control. I always do." As he faked and drove toward the basket, he thought he heard Rob murmur, "Yeah, that's what I'm worried about," but he didn't pursue it. This conversation was over.

Mark was done talking about Carol and bad memories. He wanted to think forward.

What was Karma doing right now? Was she thinking about him?

Because, damn him, he couldn't stop thinking about her.

Chapter 30

Experience is what you get while looking for something else.
-Federico Fellini

Karma surreptitiously scanned the titles on the Relationships and Sexuality shelves at Barnes & Noble. Who would have thought there would be a whole rack for everything from the Kama Sutra to Tantric Sex to how to perform a quickie or go down on a man…or a woman? Not to mention all the anthologies of erotica and several surprisingly thick volumes of *Letters to Penthouse*. Word porn was alive and well.

As she browsed, she recognized a couple of the books Mark had given her. The papaya book was here, as was the *War and Peace* of sexual manuals she was still working her way through. That monster book had to be at least a thousand pages long and covered everything. No topic was off limits. Toys, lubes, penis types (apparently there were many different types of penises…and each type could stimulate a woman differently), S&M, different kinds of condoms, vibrators, cock rings, and so much more. She was becoming quite the expert.

Mark would be proud.

As for her progress in Flirt Quest, however, that was another story.

Her first foray into the realm of Flirt Quest hadn't gone well. Saturday night, after Pilates class, she had gone to the supermarket with the sole intent of striking up a conversation with a man. She ended up knocking over a display of Kraft Macaroni and Cheese.

Smooth.

Too embarrassed and nervous to try again, she had skipped out on Flirt Quest yesterday. She had made a personal goal with herself to talk to a new man every day so now she was a day behind. Thankfully, Mark hadn't called or texted to check on her progress, but that wouldn't last forever. He was bound to contact her soon, which meant she would stay out all day if she had to, to get caught up and impress him with her efforts.

But first…books.

Her eyes lit on a book titled, *Blow Him Away: How to Give Him Mind-Blowing Oral Sex.* Oh, she had to give this one a peek. She had always sucked at sucking. Or was that blowing? Ugh. See? She sucked at the blow. She wasn't even sure of the lingo.

The contents looked promising. There was a chapter on how to use her tongue, another on the anatomy of the penis, another titled "Becoming a Fellatrix." Hmm. Interesting. She flipped through and saw a few diagrams. Okay, this was a keeper, especially since it looked like she and Mark were ramping toward the big moment. She needed to be ready.

After spending almost a half-hour flipping through several of the other books, she ended up choosing one of the volumes of *Penthouse* letters, an anthology of erotica, *The Joy of Sex,* a book of 365 sexual positions (were there really that many?), a book that dove into the sexual lives of people in America, and a second book on giving blow jobs—she needed all the help she could get giving head if she was going to impress Mark with her virgin lips.

Mission one accomplished. She had the next month's reading material.

Now she needed to find today's Flirt Quest man, as well as one makeup assignment.

With her books cradled in the crook of her arm, she ventured off. An artsy type browsed through the reference books, and a guy who looked like he would be more comfortable under a car than in a bookstore was working his way through the magazines. He stopped and, yep, picked up *Road & Track.* The prospects didn't look good.

Then she turned and saw a not-unattractive, mid-to-late-thirtyish, salt-and-peppered man scouting out the Science Fiction. He wore dark denim, a tan button-down, and those dark brown shoes that looked like a cross between gym trainers and hiking boots. He didn't look as buff as Mark, but he looked healthy and in shape. In short, he was a good prospect.

Glancing around, she took a deep breath and made her approach. Maybe she could avoid making a fool out of herself this time.

Pretending to be looking at book titles, she scooted closer…and a little closer.

He glanced her way, and she smiled.

"Excuse me." She reached in front of him for a random book.

He stepped back. "Sure."

She blushed and backed away, averting her gaze, but not before she saw him smile again.

For a moment, she didn't say anything, just nervously flipped through the pages of the book she'd picked up. Okay, she needed to make conversation. What should she ask him? Maybe a book recommendation? No, that was stupid.

"Have you ever read this author?" she asked, and held the book up.

He nodded. "Actually, yes. I love his work. You've never read Neil Gaiman?"

"No."

"Do you like science fiction? Horror?" The man had a nice smile and kind, brown eyes. If she hadn't been involved with Mark, she might have been interested.

"I'm more a romance reader," she said. "But I'm trying to branch out and read something new." Wow, this was already much better than Saturday night's mac and cheese incident.

He smiled down at her. He was taller than Mark, but not by much. "He's one of my favorite authors. His books are amazing. He may not be Stephen King, but he's got a huge following."

"Oh?" She looked at the book she'd picked up. "Sounds like just the *something new* I'm looking for then."

The man's gaze shifted to the stack of books in her arm. His smile quirked, and he quickly averted his gaze and chuckled. "Uh…um…." He chuckled again and fidgeted as if he had an itch on his butt, and then glanced back at her books.

She looked down. The blow job book was on the top of her stack. The words "Blow Him" in large, red letters jumped off the cover.

"Oh God. Oh, these…" She quickly turned the book over, her face in flames. "This is just, ah…a um…a special project." She slammed her eyes closed. Special project? What? Was she on a blow job crusade? "That came out wrong. I meant I'm doing some research…" Research? In how to give a good blow job? Okay, so that wasn't any better. She sighed and looked up. "Would you believe these are a gag gift for a friend?"

He was trying not to smile, but failing. "Is that what you *want* me to believe?"

Feeling like a piece of toilet paper stuck to the bottom of a shoe, she nodded. "Sure, uh-huh. That would be great." She waved the Neil Gaiman book in the air. "Thanks for the book recommendation." She placed it on top of her stack, turned, and escaped Science Fiction faster than the U.S.S. Enterprise entered warp speed.

She figured she could hide in Nonfiction for a while, at least until she recovered.

Flirt Quest was officially a nightmare. She was two for two. Two complete crash-and-burns out of two attempts. And this one included an embarrassing penis reference. Great. Smooth. Maybe Mark would take pity on her when she told him how miserably she was failing and cancel this assignment before it killed her. Cause of death: humiliation.

With her eyes buried in the spines of all the new releases in nonfiction, she saw another shopper approach out her peripheral vision. She began to get out of the way.

"We just keep bumping into each other."

She turned and looked up. It was the man from the science fiction aisle.

"Oh, um. Yes. I guess we are." She checked to make sure Mr. Gaiman was still covering her *Blow Him* book. He was.

The man cleared his throat and pretended to be interested in the books on the shelf, but she could tell he wasn't. Had he come looking for her? Was he hoping she would give *him* a blow job?

"My name's Brad, by the way." His gaze flickered to hers.

"I'm Karma."

"Nice to meet you, Karma." He cleared his throat again and pulled a book off the shelf and opened the cover.

"You, too, Brad." She looked away, fidgeting. She couldn't take any more humiliation today. "Well, I should be going." She pointed to the registers.

"Yeah. Yeah. Me, too." Brad set the book back on the shelf, smiled, and lifted the two Sci-Fi books he'd grabbed earlier.

She began to walk away, but Brad stopped her. "Um, wait. I was wondering…"

She turned. "Yes?"

"Would you like to have a cup of coffee or dinner sometime?"

Shut the front door! He was asking her out? Was this for real?

"Oh, um…wow." She didn't have a lot of experience in the getting-asked-out department. What should she say? Yes? No? Maybe?

Then she remembered Mark's rule. She wasn't allowed to be with anyone while she was with him.

"What do you say?" Hope twinkled in his eyes.

He seemed so nice.

She looked down. "I'm very flattered you asked," she said. "And I would say yes, but I'm sort of involved with someone already."

Brad smiled but was clearly disappointed.

Disappointed. Over being told no by her? No man had ever been disappointed by a rejection from her. Probably because she'd never been asked out before. Brian had been a spur-of-the-moment thing, and Richard had been…well, a colossal mistake. No man had ever stopped her in a bookstore or anywhere else to ask her to dinner.

Thank you, Mark.

"That's too bad," Brad said.

"I'm so sorry. You seem like a great guy, too." And he did. "And attractive, if that makes you feel better." Was this the kind of thing a woman was supposed to say when turning a guy down? She had no idea. All she could do was wing it.

His cheeks colored. "Thank you. You're sweet to say so." He pulled out a business card and handed it to her with a subtle wave of his hand. "If you're ever not *sort of involved* with someone…" He paused and smiled. "Or if you just need advice on books or want to talk about Neil Gaiman…" he chuffed good-naturedly, "I'd love to hear from you."

She took his card and tucked it into her pocket without looking at it. "Okay. I'll remember that."

Brad hesitated a moment then pointed to her stack of books. "He's a lucky guy."

Her voice caught in her throat, and she blushed. "Oh…uh—"

He held up his hand. "I'm only kidding. Gag gift. I know." He winked. "Pleasure meeting you, Karma."

"Same here."

She watched him leave then pulled his card out of her pocket. Brad Anderson. He was a partner and the office director for a local engineering firm.

Nice.

She had faced her fear, struck up a conversation with a strange man, and even though she had severely embarrassed herself, she had caught his attention, and he had asked her out.

And the guy wasn't a loser. He was a smart, successful man. One who looked and acted mentally and emotionally older than fifteen.

So, that was how this flirting thing was supposed to work, huh? Even when she failed miserably at the task, she succeeded.

Talk about empowered. Maybe there was hope yet.

She tucked his card in her pocket and scanned the store for her next target.

Chapter 31

Lust's passion will be served. It demands, it militates, it tyrannizes.
-Marquis de Sade

Mark sat on the couch in the living room of his Chicago apartment, his socked feet propped on a round, leather ottoman. His tablet lay in his lap, and he flipped through another of Solar's project manuals as he sipped coffee. He was supposed to be on vacation, but he couldn't stop working.

Lightning flashed from the dark clouds overhead, and he glanced at the open sliding glass doors that led to his balcony. Thunder rolled, and the first raindrops pattered onto his deck chairs and table.

He closed his eyes and settled against the cushions. Not long ago, he had been with Karma during a thunderstorm. That had been the night he'd almost gotten carried away and made love to her before she was ready.

So much had happened since then.

Warmth spiraled inside his chest, and things got serious inside his sweats as a case of the stiffs paid him a visit for what felt like the hundredth time since Friday night.

Setting his tablet aside, he grabbed his phone from the coffee table. He needed to talk to her. *Hey. You busy?*

A minute later, she replied. *Hey you. Not really. Just reading. ;)*

He grinned at the wink face.

And just what are you reading?

I'm not sure I should tell you.

Mark arched one eyebrow. *You're reading something naughty, aren't you?*

Maybe.

Tell me.

I think I'd rather show you.

Show me? Now his curiosity was definitely piqued.

Yes. When the time is right.

I can be back tomorrow.

LOL. No, Mr. Impatient.

How about a hint?

A couple of minutes passed before she replied. *Okay. Here are a few names of chapters in the book. Serious Sexercises, Advanced Techniques, and Understanding Your Man: Using His Fantasies to Your Advantage.*

She was reading about how to please a man. Nice.

That sounds like fascinating reading. Learning anything new?

Yes.

Such as?

Not gonna say.

He laughed. *You're such a tease.*

What can I say? I'm learning.

That you are. What about your other lessons? How are they going?

Great.

Are you still doing your Kegels?

Yes.

And using your Kegel weights? He had purchased a pair of glass eggs for her to use in place of the Ben Wa balls. They were easier to remove.

I have one in now.

His breath hitched. *Will I have to help you remove it?*

I wish. I think I like when you help me remove my Kegel weights.

She was getting him worked up. As if he needed help in that department. *I like it, too. Very much.*

Then I'll see what I can do about getting another ball stuck.

He cleared his throat and shifted to make more room for his thickening erection. Maybe he should change the subject before things got out of hand. Or in hand, as the case may be. *You do that and I will be happy to assist. What about your other assignments?*

I'm progressing to #4 tonight.

Aw, hell. This was excruciating. Talk about your bad weeks to take a vacation.

And men? Are you talking to men like I asked?

He pursed his lips and clenched his teeth. Why had he given her that damn assignment? Because she needed it, that's why. He wasn't going to be around forever, and Karma needed to get comfortable talking to men. Period.

Flirt Quest is improving. I failed miserably Saturday, was too mortified from Saturday's failure to try yesterday, but made up for it today by talking to two men. One at the bookstore and one at the gas station. The bookstore guy actually asked me out.

His grip tightened on his phone, and he scowled as he re-read her words. She had gotten asked out? As in to dinner? Who was this guy? Was he good for her? Would he treat her right? Adrenaline surged in his blood, making it hard to type.

He did?

Yes. Handsome, older guy. Not a loser.

This was unexpected. If there had been any doubt before, there wasn't now. He never should have given her this assignment. What if she said yes? What if she wanted to go out with this guy instead of him? Was he about to lose another woman he was in—

Whoa! He was not in love. She was not Cassie or Carol or the girl who dumped him at the prom.

What did you tell him?

His breath came in short bursts as he waited for her reply. He felt panicked. If she said yes…if she had agreed to a date with this guy…. He blinked and shook his head. He wasn't ready to lose her. He wasn't ready for another woman he cared about to leave him.

And yet she was just an affair. He had no intention of staying. Theirs wasn't a relationship like the one he'd had with Carol.

In fact, Karma being asked out was a good thing. Right? Wasn't that what he wanted for her? In the end, wasn't that what this affair was all about? Helping her get out there and find the guy who would treat her like a queen and marry her? What if this guy who'd asked her out was *that guy*? Maybe Mark should step aside and—

His phone vibrated, and his gaze shot to the screen.

I told him no. I don't really think he was my type. Nice guy, though.

Mark breathed a sigh of relief. She had said no. Thank God. He pressed the dial button and brought the phone to his ear.

"Hello?" she said, the smile evident in her voice.

"So, what is your type?" He felt more relaxed now that he heard her voice.

She didn't answer right away, as if collecting her thoughts. "Well, I'd say my type is about six-one, maybe six-two, with dark hair, amazing greenish-grey eyes, unbelievably sexy arms, and an uncanny ability to remove small round objects from tight places."

"I see," he said, grinning the smile of a man who'd just had his ego majorly stroked.

"Yes, my type is very sexy." She chuckled. "So, how did I do?"

"What? With describing your type?"

"Uh-huh."

"I'd say you've got good taste."

She laughed. "I do, huh?"

"Most definitely."

"Did I mention my type apparently has a very big ego, as well?"

"No."

"Or that he commands every eye in a room when he enters it?"

He leaned back. "You're not doing anything to make that ego any smaller, you know."

"I know," she said. "But oh well."

He reached over and turned off the lamp beside him. "You know, it's storming here right now."

"It is?"

"Yes. It reminds me of that night at your apartment. You know, when I got a little carried away and you stopped me." What was he doing? This was dangerous. He was dipping his toe into emotionally involved territory again. Even so, he didn't want to stop.

"I remember," she said.

"I figured you would." It wasn't like that night had been that long ago. Two weeks maybe?

"Just what does it remind you of, I wonder?"

Phone Karma was flirtier and racier than In-Person Karma, but the distinction between the two was beginning to blur. What would he find when he returned to Indianapolis? Just how far would she have come in the nine days he was away?

"It reminds me of how you felt under me," he said. "How enticing you looked."

"Anything else?"

"Yes. Such as how soft your lips were and how good your skin tasted."

"You tasted pretty good yourself."

"Did I?" He settled deeper into the couch and pushed the waist of his sweats down to release his erection. "You know, you're different on the phone. Have I ever told you that?"

"No."

"You are. Phone Karma is more daring than In-Person Karma." He grinned at the nicknames. "At least for the moment."

"I'll have to work on that."

"Mmm. I wish you were here." He said it before he could stop himself, the words tumbling out unbidden. But he didn't want to take them back. He *did* wish she were there. With him. So he could invite her onto his lap and feel the warmth of her body on his.

"Me, too."

"If only you didn't have to work this week, you could come to Chicago, and I could take you out."

"I could call in sick."

"Tempting, but no. You shouldn't. I'll see you soon enough. And it will be better after waiting so long."

"You know," she said. "You're different on the phone, too."

"Oh? How so?" He smiled and wrapped his hand around his shaft, stroking slowly.

"You're more open, too. Different. *Phone Mark.*"

He chuckled. "Well, maybe *Phone Mark* is feeling amorous this afternoon. Maybe a little lonely. A little sexually frustrated…"

"So is Phone Karma." She spoke quietly, almost hesitantly.

He stroked himself a couple more times and palmed his sensitive head, neither of them saying a word for a long moment.

"So, how would Phone Karma feel about phone sex?" He kept his voice low and soft to match hers.

"She's open to the idea."

"Would she like to? Now? With me?"

Pause. "Yes."

"Mmm." He sighed and closed his eyes. "You're already touching yourself aren't you?"

"Yes. Are you?"

"Uh-huh." He stroked more heavily. Long, twisting strokes. "Are you wet?" He wanted her wet, swollen, and ready.

She panted into the phone. "Yes. This weight thing inside of me…? Just…mmm…it feels…"

"Good?" That's right. She had a Kegel weight inside her. Applying pressure just like his cock would when he made love to her.

"Yes," she breathed.

"Does it make you hot?" It was making him hot just thinking about it.

"Yes."

"How are you touching yourself. Tell me."

She paused then said, "I'm using my middle finger."

"More. Tell me more. Are you rubbing side-to-side? In circles? Is it all external, or do you let your finger slide inside?"

A heavy breath broke through the phone, following by a soft moan. "External, at least for now. I'm using my index and ring fingers to hold my…" She hesitated for a heartbeat. "They're holding my lips apart, and I'm using the tip of my middle finger to draw small circles around my clit."

"The way my tongue would if I were with you right now."

She moaned again. "Yes."

"Would you like to know how I'd lick you?"

"Yes," she whispered hotly.

"I'd lick all around you, up one lip then the other, avoiding your clit, getting you hot, making you want me that much more. You want me now, don't you?"

"Y-Yes."

"Mmm. Then I'd use my thumbs to draw your lips open, fully exposing your swollen clit. Very slowly, torturously, I would run the tip of my tongue in a circle all the way around it, never touching it, making you squirm until you were begging me to finish you."

He stroked faster as he built the fantasy.

"I would ease my finger inside you, find your G-spot, and as I stroked it, I would gently flick your clit."

"Oh God." He heard the mental image hit her, and she shuddered through the phone.

"Put your fingers inside yourself, Karma. Find your G-spot. Stroke it."

"Mark…" Her voice was filled with urgency.

"You like my tongue, don't you?"

"Yes."

"You want me to suck you."

"Yes."

Stroke-stroke.

"Has a man ever gone down on you?"

"No."

"What a shame." He licked his lips. "Because I want to taste you."

She moaned quietly. "I want to know what that feels like."

"And I want to watch you squirm. I want to hear you sigh and feel your fingers in my hair as I flick the tip of my tongue against you."

Her breath trembled.

"You're going to come, aren't you? You're going to come against my mouth." And he was going to come, too. Any second, he was going to go.

"Yes."

She grew quiet…almost deathly so. But he could hear her tiny gasping breaths.

"Come for me, Karma. Come on my tongue."

"Oh God, oh God!" A heartbeat of silence followed, and then. "YES!"

He heard the way her body jerked. Muffled, shaky noises broke through the phone. It was enough to toss him over.

"I'm coming." His eyes slammed shut and his abdomen convulsed, and jets of semen spurted across his shirt as he groaned long, low, and deep.

After several seconds of ecstasy, he drew in a heavy breath and blew it out. "Fuck." That had been fast…and intense.

For several long, euphoric moments, nothing was said. Just hard breathing and tiny moans.

Finally, she uttered a breathless laugh. "That was sexy as hell, Phone Mark."

"Thank you, Phone Karma. You sounded pretty hot yourself." He could almost see her blush through the phone.

"I've had a very good tutor."

"I don't think he can take all the credit." He still fought to catch his breath and glanced down at the mess on his shirt. A mess well worth the effort to clean up.

"Maybe not, but he can take most of it."

"You're sweet." He pulled his sweats back up.

"And you're…"

"I'm what, Karma?"

"You're…very sexy."

"Right back atcha." He lingered, not wanting the call to end, but he had to finish going through Solar's project manuals, and he needed to take a shower and grab a change of clothes. "I should probably get going. I need to clean up."

"Me, too." She giggled. "I have to leave for my parents' house soon. And I need to get back to my reading."

"Aaahh, that's right. The mysterious reading about how to please a man."

"Something like that."

"Well, I won't keep you from *that* then. Especially if I get to be the benefactor of whatever it is you might be learning."

More laughter. "I certainly hope so. But don't get your hopes up too high. I'm still a novice."

He shook his head. "Don't underestimate yourself, Karma. Just the sound of your voice is enough to get me hard."

She gasped.

He laughed. "And with that, I think it's time I let you go."

"You stinker."

"I am that. Enjoy the rest of your Memorial Day."

"You, too. Bye, Mark."

He set his phone down and smiled as another bolt of lightning lit the sky.

He had always liked storms, but now he was beginning to like them even more.

Chapter 32

I will not let anyone walk through my mind with their dirty feet.
-Mahatma Gandhi

Karma sighed and looked up at the white ceiling of her bedroom. What a nice phone call that had been. Surprising. She'd heard Mark come twice, but had never seen him. Did he look as sexy as he sounded? Did he close his eyes? Leave them open. Clench his jaw? How did he feel? Would the muscles of his back bunch under her hands? Would his body stiffen and shudder?

She tried to imagine him on top of her, under her, behind her. These books she had been reading—and especially the pictures in the Kama Sutra book—had given her a lot of ideas to play with, each of them more exciting than the last.

Doggy style, for instance. She had never done that. But something about the pictures of couples where the man was behind the woman excited her more than all the others. Would Mark do that?

A check of the time showed Karma was running late, so she removed the glass egg, hopped up, changed, pulled her hair into a ponytail, and hustled out the door. She could fantasize about Mark doing her doggy style tonight after she got home.

Less than fifteen minutes later, she pulled onto her parents' street and nearly stopped the car. Johnny's big fat Audi was in the driveway. Shit. He wasn't supposed to be here. That's what Dad had told her...that Johnny was having a small Memorial Day get-together at his house. So, what the hell was he doing here?

A dark cloud formed over Karma's head, and it had nothing to do with the storms they were supposed to get later tonight. The same ones hitting Mark right now, as a matter of fact. But if Johnny and Estelle had decided to crash Dad's cookout, tonight was going to suck balls.

She opened the door and was greeted by her cat, Spookie, who lived with her parents because her apartment complex didn't allow pets. She really needed to look for a new place so she could have her cat with her twenty-four-seven. Spookie wasn't Mark, but she did give good snuggle.

Spookie purred and crisscrossed between and around her ankles.

"Hey, pumpkin," Karma said, lifting the all-black bundle of fur-

and-purr into her arms. Spookie settled against her chest, her paws making biscuits on her shoulder, and nuzzled her cheek. "I've missed you, too, love bug." She carried Spookie to the kitchen, where her mom was already in conversation with Estelle…and Jolene. Great. The day just got better and better.

"I wish he would learn not to antagonize him," Mom said, glancing out the window.

Estelle stood at the sliding glass door beside Jolene, both of them gazing out into the backyard.

"Hi, Mom," Karma said, entering the kitchen.

Jolene flashed her an evil glare then glanced out the door again. If only she knew that Karma was aware of her fling with Jake, she might have been less cocksure.

"Hi, sweetheart," Mom said. She kissed Karma's cheek and appeared relieved she didn't have to deal with the terrible twosome by herself anymore. Mom was just as uncomfortable around Estelle as she and Dad were. It seemed the only one who got along with the pointy-nosed woman was Johnny. Well, and Jolene. "I see you found Spookie." Mom rubbed the cat's ear.

"More like she found me as soon as I walked in the door."

Mom smiled. "She misses you."

"Well, I miss her." Karma stroked the cat's silky fur and nodded toward the backyard, where Dad and Johnny appeared to be in a heated discussion in the back corner. "What's going on out there?"

Normally, Karma tried to avoid Johnny and Dad together whenever possible, because when those two got around each other, they were like roosters in a cockfight, and she was usually the one who ended up losing feathers and bleeding. Not to mention, Johnny still felt the need to constantly torture her, just like when they were kids.

Mom waved her hand dismissively and returned to the stove. "Oh, Johnny's just being Johnny. You know how he is."

Yes, Karma knew all-too-well how Johnny was.

Estelle shook her head. The gesture almost looked like pride. Estelle and Johnny were like vinegar and oil, separate, but in a good-for-each-other kind of way that usually left everyone else with a sour face. To make matters worse, her raging pregnant-woman hormones made her even less tolerable, if that was even possible.

"Well, that's my Johnny," Estelle said. "He never backs down from anyone. You know that."

Karma struggled to bite her tongue. *Yeah, Mom knows that. She raised him. He was hers before he was yours, dummy.*

"What are they talking about?" Karma strolled to the door, avoiding eye contact with el prego Estelle-o and her sidekick Not-so-Jolly Jo.

"Mm-hi, Karma," Estelle said, her greeting coming out like a snobbish, nasally slur.

"Hi," Karma said blandly. "What are they talking about?" It would be nice if someone could answer that question.

Mom huffed and threw the kitchen towel she was holding over her shoulder as she checked on the guava glaze for the chicken. "They're arguing over the best method to seed the bare patch in the backyard."

Estelle rested her arms over her swollen belly. "We had the same problem when we bought our house last year." She waved her long fingers and kept her gaze out the back door. "Hopefully your dad will take his advice. Our yard looks *fabulous* now."

Karma exchanged glances with her mom and forced herself not to say something snarky. "Well, I'm sure Dad has it under control." She opened the fridge and pulled out a beer with the hand not cradling Spookie's rump. She rarely drank, but the niggling on her nerves told her this was a good day to partake.

"Oh, I'm sure he does." Estelle offered a dramatic conciliatory glance toward her and Mom, as if they were toddlers in need of a grown-up. "I'm just saying Johnny knows what he's talking about."

"Johnny *always* knows what he's talking about. That's the problem." Karma managed to twist off the bottle cap and took a healthy swig.

Estelle huffed, opened the door, and stepped out onto the patio. Jo followed, flashing Karma an eat-shit glance, and slid the door closed again.

Karma shot her mom a hard look. "Dad told me they weren't going to be here today?"

Chagrined, her mother stopped stirring the glaze. "They had a change of plans. Something about running out of propane for the grill."

"And he couldn't go get more?"

Mom gave her a look that confirmed what she was already thinking. Johnny had come over to stir up trouble. Most likely with her. Well, to hell with that. If he tried, he would get a dose of the new and improved Karma. Either she had finally grown a spine, or all those affirmations she was telling herself were now paying off, but one thing was certain, she was done taking Johnny's—and everyone else's—shit.

"And then he had to go and bring Jolene," Mom said. "When he knows you two don't get along."

"I'm sure that's *why* he brought her." Karma took another drink and looked outside at her jealous coworker with permanent PMS and a case of verbal diarrhea. And the horns and forked tail she had started growing didn't help.

"Your dad doesn't like her, either. To be honest, I think your dad appreciates you being here. The day will be more tolerable with you here."

"He could have at least warned me."

"I know, honey. But they just showed up. He probably didn't even think about calling." She smiled in that way that all mothers must have to master before becoming parents. It was a mix of compassion, humor, and apology. "Why don't you go out there and give your dad some moral support." She patted Karma on the back of the shoulder.

"Why can't Johnny just cool it and stop being a jerk?"

Mom shrugged. "Think of it this way. Your brother teaches us patience."

She lowered Spookie to the floor. "No. He teaches us that he's a Grade A asshole." With Bud in hand, she reluctantly went outside and joined Estelle and Jo on the patio. Dad and Johnny's bickering seemed out of control.

"Hi, Dad!" She waved to get her dad's attention.

While Johnny was in midsentence, her dad waved back and began to walk away. "Hi, honey. You made it."

Johnny scowled after him and threw his hands in the air. "I wasn't finished."

"I was," Dad said over his shoulder.

Good for Dad.

Estelle sucked her teeth. When Karma looked at her, she was pursing her lips and scowling, which made Karma want to slug her. But she was sure there was some law against hitting a pregnant woman.

Dad hugged her. "Hi, sweetie."

She squeezed him back.

"Hi, *Carmine*." Johnny brushed past her, making no secret that he loathed her intrusion on whatever lesson he'd been trying to teach Dad.

Jolene snickered at the masculine nickname Johnny had teased her with when they were kids.

"I see you still haven't outgrown your junior high insults," Karma said as her dad turned his attention to the grill. Mom brought out the glaze and handed him the pan.

The nickname had been a dig to imply Karma was a boy instead of a girl. Well, now she was a woman…with claws…and big woman balls. Thanks to Mark. So Johnny needed to watch out.

Johnny was holding a bottle of beer and laced the fingers of his free hand between Estelle's. "Only because they still piss you off, sis."

What a little shit. This was why she avoided Johnny like he was a Norovirus. A few hours with him left her in need of intense therapy, partly because his insults cut with the precision of a neurosurgeon. Johnny magnified her faults, dissected them, and splayed and gutted her in public like she was no more than shark bait.

But Johnny's lapses of judgment didn't just begin and end with Karma. He was naturally a cocky little cuss with the ego of Zeus and the god-like attitude to go with it. The fact that Karma worked as a "lowly" executive assistant when he was the owner of a successful business at such a young age only added fuel to his irritating spew of insults.

As if reading her mind, Johnny said, "How's *work*?"

He emphasized the word like it was profane, but Karma knew he simply wanted to point out that he considered her job *work*, while his was a *career*. In his opinion, there was a big difference.

She parked at the table by her dad, who was paying eagle-eyed attention to the conversation, ready to jump in to rescue her at a moment's notice. Which, of course, was what Johnny wanted him to do and what Karma wanted to prevent.

"Work's fine," she said casually.

"I hear a consultant has come in to restructure the company and lay people off." Johnny exchanged glances with Jolene, who sneered.

Of course Johnny would have heard about that. But what bothered Karma even more was to hear Johnny talking about Mark with that self-righteous tone. "I suppose our esteemed Jolene told you that, huh?" Karma pointed her beer bottle Jo's way. Karma was no longer the quiet one who kept her mouth shut. A couple months ago, Karma wouldn't have been confrontational. She would have taken their shit and let Johnny cut her to the quick. But that was old Karma. Johnny had yet to meet Karma, version two-point-oh.

"Is it a secret?" Estelle said innocently. Too innocently, which was confirmation that Jo *had* been talking about Mark. And probably her, too.

"If I were you, I'd get my résumé ready and start looking for a new job," Johnny said. "We recently let go two of our administrative staff. They're simply not needed, anymore. Unemployment statistics show that administrative employees are on the endangered species list. Their jobs are becoming obsolete, with management taking on more of the tasks typically done by administrators. This consultant guy is probably going to axe your job, sis."

"That's enough, Johnny," her dad said, jumping to her defense.

But Karma could fight her own battles now. "No, Dad. It's okay." She placed her hand on his arm.

Estelle leaned forward and tapped her bony, cold fingers on the back of Karma's hand. "Don't worry. If you lose your job, I know the Director of Human Resources at the University Hospital Downtown. I helped decorate her new home. I'm sure I can get you in for an interview."

"First of all," Karma said to Johnny, "shut up." Then she turned on Estelle. "And *don't worry*, Estelle, I'm not going to lose my job. I don't know the first thing about working in a hospital, anyway, and wouldn't want to."

"Look, Karma," Estelle said in that quiet, fake-concerned tone of hers, "Jo told us all about the consultant you're working with." She nodded between Jo and Johnny then looked back at Karma. "We're just trying to help." The way Estelle said the word *help* made it clear that Jo had gossiped about how she thought Karma and Mark were an item.

She wasn't going to give them any more fuel for that fire, but she could sure turn on the fire hose.

"You know," she said, looking at Jo. "Johnny's right. Administrative staff *is* becoming obsolete, and one or two of Solar's admin staff just might get the axe before Mark's job here is done. So, Jo, has Johnny suggested that you get *your* résumé in order and start looking for a new job, too? The way I see it, I outrank you, and since I already do half your job while keeping up with my own, I figure that if I go, you go. What do you think? Wouldn't that make sense to you?" She glared at Jo, then Estelle, and then Johnny.

All three looked a bit stunned. She had never doused them with their own vitriol before. Always in the past, she had taken their crap in near silence.

But this was the new her, and she was ready to unleash a little payback.

"Uumm…" Jo's yap opened and shut, but no words came out.

Johnny started to say something, but Karma cut him off.

"No. You shut up for once, you self-righteous little shit." She got up and shoved her finger into his chest. "I've had enough of your crap, *little brother*. Emphasis on little." She dropped her gaze to his crotch and let it rest there long enough to let everyone know what she was referring to. She had grown up with the weasel and seen him in his birthday suit a time or two—after which she had wanted to burn out her eyes. But he wasn't exactly packing heat in the meat department the same way she wasn't packing it up top. She suddenly wanted to kick herself for not realizing that sooner. Using that against him when they were kids might have shut him up. Better late than never, because he was certainly quiet now, with a red face to boot.

Karma pointed at Jo then glared at Johnny again. "I suppose she's tried to tell you that the consultant and I have a thing going on, too. Am I right? She's trying to pass that shit around the office, too."

Estelle averted her gaze. Johnny set his jaw uncomfortably.

"And you believed her, didn't you? Even though you know she lies and gossips about everything. Everyone knows it. She's a big, fat, lazy liar, and you both think she would be telling you the truth about…what? An affair? That I'm sleeping with some guy that could 'axe my job'?" She made air quotes at Johnny. "Really? You think I'm that stupid? You're such an ass!"

Technically, she wasn't lying. She and Mark hadn't slept together. Not yet, anyway, in either the literal or figurative meaning of the phrase.

But so what if she was? She hated lying, but if lying was the only way to put Johnny and Estelle in their place and get Jo off her trail, she would lie her ass off. She wasn't going to let Mark get in trouble for what they were doing with one another. He was the best thing that had ever happened to her, and she would do whatever it took to protect his job and his reputation.

By now, Mom had rejoined them on the patio. She held a plate of corn on the cob wrapped in foil, and Dad was standing behind her like a sentry.

"I've had it with all three of you," Karma said. "I don't want to hear one more word from any of you about my job, my personal life, or anything else. Got it?" She looked at Jo. "And if I hear any more rumors or gossip you've spread that I'm being inappropriate with Mark, I'm going to HR and filing a report, and I don't think you'll like what I put in it." She thought about Jo's affair with Jake. "You hear me, Jo? I'm finished with your shit." She turned toward Johnny. "And as for you, pencil dick, my name is Karma. From now on, you call me by my given name or risk this being the only child you'll ever have." She pointed to Estelle's belly. "Because your nuts will be too far up your ass to give you a second. I'm done being your punching bag."

The Three Stooges remained speechless.

After several long, awkward moments, Dad stepped forward. "I think the three of you should go." Dad squared his shoulders and gestured toward the door. "You weren't invited today for a reason, Johnny, and until you can behave like a part of this family, maybe you should keep your distance."

Mom nodded, even if the look on her face showed she was still trying to process Karma's smackdown.

"Fine." Johnny gestured toward the sliding door and followed Jo and Estelle as they disappeared inside. He stopped and glared at Karma. "We're leaving, *Karma.* Enjoy your dinner."

"Oh, we will." Her own glare never wavered, and she held Johnny's gaze like her eyes had claws. Johnny finally broke the contact and left.

"Okay, where did *that* come from?" Dad said, sitting down at the table.

Karma turned and looked at her parents. "I'm just done, Dad. I'm done being the victim. Especially Johnny's victim."

This was the new her. The empowered, strong, confident Karma. Okay, so she had a way to go before she was totally transformed, but standing up to Johnny, Jo, and Estelle was a major first step.

Mom hugged her. "I'm proud of you, honey. I mean, he's my son, and I love him, too, but I understand where you're coming from. He's made your life pretty miserable for a long time now."

Why couldn't she and Johnny have the kind of relationship other people had with their siblings? At one time, she had tried everything to get along with Johnny. All she'd done was tear herself into emotional shreds. Until Johnny grew up and took his head out of his ass, she couldn't be around him.

She headed inside to the bathroom.

The door opened and Jo stepped out, her face flushed. When she saw Karma, fire rose in her eyes. "That was a nice show out there," she hissed, crossing her arms.

"Are you finished? I have to pee." Karma was so done with this bitch.

Jo grabbed her arm, refusing to let her pass. "You might have your parents and everyone else fooled, but I know the truth."

"Let go of me and get out of my way. I'm not playing your games, anymore." She tore her arm from Jo's grasp.

A smug grin plastered over Jo's face. "I saw Mark pulling into your apartment complex the other night."

Karma's heart nearly stopped. "So? Big deal." Jo could have been bluffing. Doubtful but possible. Karma began to shove past her only for Jo to block the hall.

"I couldn't believe it was him, of course. I couldn't imagine why he would be pulling into *your* apartment complex unless he was going to see you." Jo looked way too imperious. "So I turned around. I had to know for sure, because, I mean…" Her gaze strolled down Karma's body then back to her face. "Look at you." She curled her upper lip. "You're so…plain." She said the word like it was another name for the plague.

Karma cocked her head to the side, her heart hammering. "You're not going to get to me, Jo. You're just trying to cause trouble. I'm not the only one who lives in those apartments. If it was Mark, he could have been there to see someone else."

Jo's smile turned sickly sweet with a hint of poison. "Oh no, he was there to see you." She paused as if she wanted to prolong the suspense.

Despite the panic awakening her fight or flight response, Karma held herself together. It wasn't as if she was completely uninsured if Jo had seen her with Mark. She still had a powerful ace in her pocket. If she had to play it to keep Jo's mouth shut, she was ready. "Do you think you might get to the point sometime today, Jo. I really do have to pee."

Jo puffed out a derisive breath. "I pulled around to your apartment and saw Mark's car outside your building. Then I looked up to your window and saw you open the door and let him in. He kissed you." Jo's blue eyes burned with jealousy and arrogance. "So deny it all you want, Karma. You're fucking him. You're fucking our consultant." A venomous half-smile widened her mouth. "He must be pretty hard up if you're the best he can get." She chuffed. "Just wait until I file a complaint with human resources about this. He'll be gone like that." She snapped her fingers. "And you won't be the little do-gooder, anymore."

Jo began to walk past, but Karma caught her arm and yanked her back, spinning on her.

"Well, if you do, make sure to tell them about how you're fucking your boss while you're at it," she said.

Jo's face drained of color, and the air in the hall plunged into ice.

"Oops. I guess I wasn't supposed to know that, huh?" Karma offered a sugary grin. "Oh well, surprise!"

"You have no proof."

"I have all the proof I need. I saw you with him. The same way you saw Mark with me." She let that sink in. "You were at the store. In the condom aisle. I think you told him—and this is a quote—'I'm going to ride you so hard.' And I think you might have also said you would fuck him right there if you could." She paused to let Jo mentally catch up. "I was there, hiding behind the hair brushes, you unbelievable idiot." She shook her head. "Jake. What are you thinking, Jo? *Jake*. He's *married*. To the *owner's daughter*. Talk about colossal fails. This takes the cake." She offered Jo a half-shrug. "I wonder what would happen to you and Jake if someone were to let HR know you two are fucking each other? In the office, no less. Don't think I haven't figured that out, and I'm sure plenty of others have, too, and would vouch for my story if I came forward with what I know. I mean…" Karma sucked her teeth. "I'm not known to be a gossip like you are. I haven't pissed off half the office with my backstabbing lies like you have. So, when I open my mouth about something this scandalous, I think I'll have a lot more ears than you will. People might actually pay attention to what I have to say and not brush me under the rug as a frivolous troublemaker. Regardless, if this gets out, I don't think it would be good for either of you, Jo. Jake would lose his job. Probably lose his wife. And you'd be shunned if not fired."

"You bitch."

Karma smiled. "Well, I've been called worse. By you, no less."

Jo continued to seethe, but she seemed lost for words. Apparently, she hadn't expected a rebuttal to her threat.

"So, you go ahead and turn Mark and me in, Jo, and I'll be sure to do the same to you." She crossed her arms. "Now, are you *sure* you saw Mark at my apartment, or do you think it might've-could've-been someone else?"

The color had returned to Jo's face, and it was the deepest shade of crimson Karma had ever seen. The defiant-but-defeated look in Jo's eyes made it clear she knew Karma had her by the throat. Her hands were tied. If she even whispered a hint of what she knew about her and Mark, Karma would have her job within the hour. And not just her job, but Jake's, too. As well as Jake's marriage. Karma would only get a slap on the hand, because at least she wasn't involved with a married man—the owner's son-in-law, no less. Jo's crime was far worse than Karma's, and Jo knew it. She stood to lose a lot more than Karma did.

"Fine. It was someone else." Jo spun and marched away.

A moment later, the front door slammed shut.

Karma ducked into the bathroom, her hands shaking. She had revealed her ace. But at least now she had secured an unlikely ally in keeping her secret. And she had finally silenced Jo once and for all. Not to mention her brother. It was sort of exhilarating seeing the two of them finally get what they deserved. For so long, they had dished a nasty spew of insults at her, but today, in one empowered moment, she had turned the tables and shut them both down.

Johnny might still try to cause trouble, but her gut told her Jolene would no longer be a problem. There had been something in Jo's eyes—something Karma could only describe as fearful awareness—that indicated Jo had come to the realization that she'd finally met her match. That she had pushed Karma one step too far and the jig was up. There would be no more picking on her. No more bullying. No more threats. It was clear that Jo now realized Karma had the upper hand and was beyond her reach, immune to her petty games.

For Jo, that meant the fun was over.

Karma smiled at her reflection. She had achieved another pivotal moment. No more would she allow herself to be a victim. From now on, she called the shots. No one would take away her happiness.

She took a minute to let the adrenaline rush of facing off with Jolene subside. Then she found Spookie and carried her back out to the patio, where the bundle of black fur promptly made a bed in her lap.

If she couldn't share her revelatory accomplishment with Mark, she would share it with the next best thing: the coolest cat in the world.

Chapter 33

Passion is energy. Feel the power that comes from focusing on what excites you.
-Oprah Winfrey

"How about that one?" Daniel said, pointing to a picture of a woman wearing a lacy red chemise.

Karma shook her head and made a stink face. "I don't want red. It's too cliché."

Daniel arched a dubious brow. "And yet red is the color you were wearing the night the two of you met."

"All the more reason to choose a different color," she said with a decisive nod. "To mix things up."

"Well, men love red," Daniel scanned the rest of the pictures on the page. "But if you don't want red, we'll find something else."

Daniel and Lisa had come over to help her look at lingerie. If she and Mark were moving forward, she wanted to be ready, and boxer shorts and a tank top as sexy bedtime attire just didn't seem grand enough to impress a guy like him. And now that she had squashed the pesky bugs that were Johnny and Jolene, she was eager to shed all her old skins, including the sexually modest one. This required lingerie. Classy, sexy, make-him-stare lingerie.

Lisa had suggested a website called Yandy, where she had bought a few pieces of lingerie in the past, and while Karma had seen a few passable items, so far nothing had jumped out as *the one* that would turn her first time with Mark into something eternally unforgettable.

Lisa returned from the kitchen with a bowl of freshly popped popcorn. "Any luck?"

Daniel shook his head. "She's shot down anything red or black, so I'm running out of ideas."

Lisa set the bowl of popcorn on the coffee table. "Well, what about that one?" She pointed to a slinky garment that looked like purple Band-Aids connected by a whole lot of string.

Karma wrinkled her nose. "The thong I'm wearing has more material in it than that."

"You're wearing a thong?" Lisa said.

Daniel leaned forward and lightly smacked her butt. "Since when do you wear thongs?"

"Since a few weeks ago." Karma buried her nose back into the website, wishing she hadn't brought it up. "And hands off the merchandise, Danny, or I'll tell Zach you're going straight on him."

"He'll never believe you." Daniel nonchalantly munched on a handful of popcorn.

She stuck her tongue out at him.

"My little Karma is finally growing up," Lisa said, pretending to wipe a tear off her cheek.

Karma slapped Lisa's leg. "Cut it out. Focus. I need to find lingerie for this guy. Something not sleazy. Something demure. Something—"

"What about that?" Daniel shoved his index finger toward the screen, pointing at a sheer, antique-white baby-doll with a lace and satin bodice. He tapped the screen and pulled up the details. Delicate lace decorated the hem, and a satin sash circled the high waist, which fell just under the model's breasts.

"It's *innocent,*" Lisa said.

"It's perfect!" No doubt. This was the one.

Daniel clapped once and pumped his fist. "That will drive your man crazy."

The frilly baby-doll wasn't overtly sexy in an in-your-face kind of way. It was sexy in an I'm-still-innocent-so-be-gentle-with-me-but-not-too-gentle kind of way that fit her perfectly. Daniel was right. This would drive Mark crazy.

She scowled at the price. Almost sixty dollars. Why was lingerie so damn expensive? This was for a special occasion, though, so her credit card balance be damned.

"I'm getting it." She added the baby-doll to her cart.

Lisa pointed. "Make sure to buy the white thong, too. It'll look good underneath."

"Good call." Karma added it to the cart. "Can you guys think of anything else I need?"

Daniel sat back with a sigh. "Candle wax, whips, chains, handcuffs."

"Danny!" She smacked his arm, making him laugh.

Lisa giggled. "You're going to give him a night he won't forget, Karma." She grabbed a handful of popcorn. "I can't believe you two haven't already done the deed. I figured that would have been old news by now."

Karma pulled out her credit card and started filling in the order information. "I wasn't ready. And besides, he wanted to take his time."

"I guess."

Daniel gave Lisa a playful shove. "Leave her alone. Our little Karma is about to become a woman." The two snickered.

"Fine, laugh it up." Karma double-checked all her info on the screen, making sure to add two-day shipping, then tapped the icon to place the order before smiling at them over her shoulder. "Done."

"Mark has been so good for you, girl," Lisa said, smiling like a proud momma.

Daniel nodded in agreement. "Before long, we'll be going to your wedding."

Karma held up her hand and shook her head. "No, that's not what this is about. Remember, I told you that this is just a temporary thing."

"Temporary, my ass." Daniel snagged some popcorn. "I hear the way you talk about him. You're falling in love with him, Karma. And from the way it sounds, he's falling in love with you, too. At least from what you've said."

"You're reading too much into things. Mark doesn't want that. He made that clear from the get-go."

"He might have made it clear from the get-go, but sometimes things change, honey. And it sounds like your beau and you are changing, if you get my drift." Daniel's eyebrows rose as he gave her a meaningful look.

Lisa remained quiet, but Karma could tell by her expression she agreed with Daniel.

"Well, you're wrong. This is just about having fun. That's all." Karma set her tablet aside, dug her hand into the popcorn, and tried not to acknowledge that Daniel was right. She *was* falling in love with Mark. But that was *her* problem. Mark wouldn't stick around and be her boyfriend after his assignment at Solar was finished, let alone be her fiancé or her husband. She refused to entertain the idea that their relationship would ever be more than two people sharing a mutual attraction for one another. No strings attached.

And if her heart got splattered to hell and back later? Well, that would be her own damn fault for wanting something Mark had warned her he would never give.

Chapter 34

Three things cannot be long hidden: the sun, the moon, and the truth.
-Buddha

The following Saturday, Mark returned to Clover a day earlier than planned. It had been eight days since he had seen Karma. Well, eight-and-a-half, but who was counting?

Apparently, he was.

And he wasn't going to let another day pass without seeing her.

He parked outside her apartment, picked up the bouquet of periwinkle hydrangeas and lilacs interspersed with white calla lilies, took the stairs to her apartment two at a time, and knocked as he hid the flowers behind his back.

He heard the deadbolt unlock. "Dad, you're earl—Mark?"

"Hey you." It took all his self-control not to pick her up, kick the door closed behind him, and carry her to the bedroom.

"You're back early." Her exuberant smile wrapped around his heart and squeezed.

"I thought I would take an extra day to get settled before Monday." It was a lie. He had come back a day early because he couldn't stop thinking about her and wanted to see her.

"I'm glad. I was starting to miss you." She stepped aside to let him in.

He pulled the flowers from behind his back. "For you."

She beamed and dove her nose into one of the lilies.

The way she closed her eyes and inhaled, all angelic innocence, made him stand a little taller.

"Roses seemed too ordinary for you," he said, pulling a card from his pocket. On the envelope was a doodle of their faces, side-by-side, on the flap. He had been doodling her face a lot.

She opened her eyes and rewarded him with the most beautiful smile he'd seen in over a week. "That's sweet. They're gorgeous."

He leaned in and kissed her, letting his lips linger on hers as he slid the card into her free hand. "So are you."

She took the card then buried her nose inside the bouquet again before turning for a vase on one of her shelves. "I'll just put them in some water."

In the kitchen, she set the flowers and vase on the counter and grinned at the caricature of her face on the envelope. "This is pretty good." She turned it toward him. "I've noticed you doodle a lot, mostly faces. What's up with that?"

Leaning against the counter, he shrugged. "Just something I've done since I was a kid. I used to sit in my parents' studio and draw pictures of the dancers. As I got older, I got better. Now, it's a habit. I don't even realize I'm doing it most of the time. I'll be sitting in a meeting or on some conference call, and then I'll look down and have a sheet full of faces."

She laughed, opened the envelope, and pulled out the card he had gotten her. It was nothing fancy, just a sentiment of how much he enjoyed spending time with her. After reading it, she smiled and slipped the card back inside the envelope. "Thank you."

"You're welcome."

She turned for the sink and grabbed the vase.

"So, it sounds like you're expecting your dad. Should I leave?" He noted the silken, wavy spill of her hair over her shoulders, as well as the way her loose-fitting jeans hugged her rump. He might have been a man with a major foot fetish, but he liked asses, too, and hers was damn near perfect.

Speaking of feet, she wasn't wearing any shoes. What was she trying to do? Drive him crazy?

As the vase filled with water, she looked over her shoulder. "Dad shouldn't be here for a while. If you had been him, I would've been surprised. This is way early. He's coming over to watch the game later."

Mark was a little disappointed. He had hoped to spend time with her tonight. But then, he had stopped by without calling first.

"I won't stay long then," he said. "I just wanted to check in and see how your lessons are coming along."

"They're going well." She flashed her eyebrows to hint at just how well. "The new books I bought have been educational."

"Maybe you'll let me take a peek before I leave." He stepped a little closer.

"Maybe. If you're good." She turned back to the sink.

A hundred fantasies flashed through his mind about just where he wanted those feet and how he would worship that fine, firm rear view. He nearly panted as he gazed down at her bare toes poking out from under the ragged hem of her jeans.

She giggled, and he snapped his attention to her face. She shook her head, her cheeks rosy.

"Caught you," she said.

He cleared his throat and grinned crookedly. "Guilty, but it's not my fault. You've been warned."

She laughed and set the half-filled vase on the counter. "Yes, I have, and had I known you were coming over, I would have put on my fuzzy slippers."

"Fuzzy slippers?"

"Uh-huh. Little bunnies."

Joining her, he helped her arrange the flowers, casting her a shameless grin. "No bunnies. I like your feet just as they are."

She gave him a wary glance. "Will my feet be safe for the evening? Maybe I should put on shoes." She picked up the vase and moved it to the dining room table. She bent over slightly and pushed it toward the center.

The opportunity was too good to resist, and he moved behind her. As he wrapped his arms around her waist and pulled her ass against his groin, she shot upright and gasped. The sound bolted a spear of warmth—not lust—down his spine. Lust he could have understood, but warmth? The kind of warmth that comes with something more intimate than lust. That was unexpected.

He quickly shook off his dismay and bent his head so his mouth rested beside her ear. "I'm also an ass man, and I do like yours in these jeans." He chuckled low, with quiet confidence. "So, you can put on shoes if you like, but I think it's your backside that needs to be worried this evening." With that, he stepped away and gave her a gentle swat on the right cheek.

She squealed and spun around, her hand going to where he'd slapped her rump, her face alight with surprise. Even though she tried to look appalled, her eyes danced with excitement.

"You spanked me!"

"You have a very spankable ass."

"Mark!"

He laughed. "Hey, I couldn't help myself."

"Couldn't help yourself, my ass."

He laughed harder. "Exactly. *Your* ass. That's my point."

She turned bright red and groaned before falling into a fit of giggles. "Oh God." She dropped her face into her hand.

He pulled her toward him and rested his hands on her hips. "You set yourself up for that one, babe."

"And, as usual, you took full advantage."

"But you're so cute when you're embarrassed." He pulled her a little closer.

She buried her face against his chest, as if trying to hide herself.

"Make that ultra-cute. Maybe I should try to embarrass you more often if this is your reaction. I kind of like this." He snuggled her more firmly against him.

She pulled her face back and blinked up at him. "Don't you dare. You're supposed to be helping me come *out* of my shell, not pushing me further inside it."

"Oh, that's right. I guess I am. Damn." He snapped his fingers as if he had momentarily forgotten what it was he was doing there. "But isn't this much more fun?"

After so long apart, being with Karma again felt right in about a hundred different ways.

Something about Mark was different, but Karma couldn't put her finger on it. He was more touchy-feely, more approachable. And he looked at her differently, which had nothing to do with her feet.

"So, I've been thinking about…" His fingers edged down to the waist of her jeans so that his fingertips slipped underneath and rested on the upper curve of her butt.

"Yes?"

He took a deep breath and pulled her a little closer. "I've been thinking about you a lot."

"You have?"

"Yes."

"And what have you been thinking about?" Karma tried to sound unaffected even though she was anything but.

"How I'm not sure I can go much longer without making love to you."

Her eyes drifted closed and she leaned into him. She had been thinking a lot about that, too.

They remained like that, standing together, for several long moments. Nothing was said, but the weight of his words tightened something inside her. Something needy and wanting.

He tugged his fingers from inside the waist of her jeans. "Do you have time to show me your new books before your dad gets here?" Mark's deep, sexy voice cut into her like a hot knife through butter. She practically melted. But this was Mark. He could make *I have this strange rash* sound sexy.

"Sure." She slowly inched herself out of the warmth of his arms, took his hand, and led him to her bedroom.

Her new books were stacked on the dresser. She had even returned to Barnes & Noble a couple of days ago to buy more, as well as a couple of books on affirmations and the power of positive thinking. She was in a total transformation of mind and body, and the more she read, the more she wanted to learn and change.

Mark rifled through her growing pile of books. He paused over one, made an appreciative noise, then picked up another and nodded his approval.

"I've read this one," he said of one of the how-to-have-hot-sex books. "And this one." He showed her the 365 sexual positions book. "And these." He pointed to the books on the Kama Sutra and Tantric sex. "I'm glad you're reading them."

Of course he would have read some of these books. And probably a whole lot more.

He stopped and smiled when he came to the two books on how to give a man mind-blowing oral sex. His gaze slid to hers.

"Now, I'm sure *this* is interesting reading."

She blushed. "It is."

"Learning anything new?"

"Yes." She refused to look away. Old Karma would have. New Karma was stronger than that.

"And you plan on using your new knowledge sometime soon, I assume?"

"Maybe."

"Mmm." He turned his attention back to her stack of books and picked up the *Letters to Penthouse* and one of the books on sexual fantasies. "These can be fun."

She had already read most of those two books. "Yes. I enjoyed them."

He set the books down and pulled her back into his arms. "You did, did you?" His eyes twinkled as his mouth curved into a crooked grin.

"Yes."

"And just how much did you enjoy them, I wonder?" He drew his lips down her neck. "Did they give you any ideas?"

"A few." She gripped his shoulders.

His tongue slid back up to her ear. "Were there any favorites?"

Good God, Mark was a force of nature tonight. He was like a rising flood that encroached so slowly you didn't realize the danger until it was too late. And it was definitely too late for her to seek cover. All she could do was fight to stay afloat. "A couple, yes." She dug her nails into the backs of his shoulders.

"Tell me." His lips dropped fiery kisses down her jaw to her chin, and then hovered over her mouth as his gaze burned into hers.

She nibbled the inside of her bottom lip, staring up at him. "There was one story of a woman at a party. She wandered through the house to get away from the noise and the crowd."

Mark remained silent as she recounted one of the more erotic fantasies she had read.

"It was a large house, and the woman found her way to a darkened room filled with exercise equipment. A moment later, a handsome stranger joined her. He had followed her."

"She had caught his eye?" Mark spoke against her lips. "Is that it?"

Karma nodded. "Yes. He thought she was attractive."

Mark kissed his way to her ear and whispered, "And what did he do to her in that room with all the exercise equipment?"

The air between them steamed, and Mark gently nudged her toward her bed.

Karma's breath came in quiet, tight bursts. "She was nervous at first, but he was sexy. Even though she didn't know him, he excited her. She wanted to get to know him better. She wanted more."

"And he gave it to her?"

"Yes." As the backs of her legs made contact with the side of the bed, Mark guided her down. She scooted back, and he parted her legs and nestled between them.

"What did he do to her?" He dropped his mouth to the hollow of her throat and softly nibbled her tender skin.

Karma moaned and involuntarily arched her neck, pushing her throat against his lips. "He made love to her on one of the weight benches."

"Mmm." Mark pushed himself up and looked into her eyes. "Did he make love to her?" He paused then said, "Or did he fuck her?"

Oh wow. She suddenly understood why people liked intimate dirty talk. That one, four-letter profanity sent a jolt of electricity straight between her legs.

"He fucked her," she whispered. Her voice trembled.

Mark shuddered and closed his eyes as he lowered himself against her.

So, Mark liked dirty talk, too. Good to know.

For at least a minute, Mark seemed to be at war. He didn't speak, barely moved. The tension in his body and the way he inhaled and exhaled, as well as the quiet, pained moans that broke inside his throat as his lips tapped lightly against her skin as if he were marking time, made it clear he was in the depths of a fierce battle.

"Are you okay?" she said, running both hands down his back.

Her touch—or maybe her voice—seemed to soothe him, and he relaxed a little as he buried his arms under her and tucked his face against the side of her neck and nodded.

"I just need a minute." His gruff voice massaged her senses.

Karma gently combed her fingers into his thick hair and lightly kissed his temple. "You feel good." Very good. Too good to let go of. "I'm glad you're here."

Mark lifted his head from her shoulder. His glazed eyes met hers, and in a split second, something primal passed between them. Something dark and full of desire that refused to be denied.

Air rushed into the cocoon that surrounded them, and Mark surged like a vicious wall of fire as his mouth crashed down on hers.

His hands dove into her hair. She wrapped her legs around him. *More, now!* Whatever this was between them needed to come out now!

He rolled to his back and took her with him, holding her close.

"I missed you," he said.

"I missed you, too." She tugged on the hem of his shirt and had just pushed her hands underneath when a noise from the living room startled her.

The front door.

"Honey?" her dad called.

"Shit!" she whispered, meeting Mark's stunned gaze as they froze. She hopped off and immediately began straightening her clothes.

Mark rolled off the bed and pulled down his shirt before hastily running his fingers through his hair.

"Karma?" her dad called again. She heard the door close and the jangle of her dad's keys.

"Hi, Dad!" she yelled. "Gimme a second. I'll be right there." She looked at Mark, feeling like a horny teenager caught getting it on in the backseat of her parents' car.

"I'm sorry," Mark whispered. Guilt haunted his eyes.

She waved off his apology. "Are you okay with him seeing you?"

"Are you?"

She didn't have much choice. "I'll figure it out."

He checked himself over and smiled. "This is your fault, you know."

"How is this *my* fault," she whispered.

Mark quietly swatted her butt. "Because you're too damn sexy for your own good, that's why."

"You say the sweetest things," she said sarcastically, fidgeting with her hair some more. "Do I look okay?

"That depends? How do you want to look?" He smirked and pulled her against him.

"Quit that." Karma pushed away and smacked his arm.

With a playful wince, he pulled back. "You look fine. How do I look?"

Karma really didn't want to answer that, because he looked good enough to lick. "As good as you're gonna. Come on." She led him out of the bedroom and into the dining room.

Her dad was in the kitchen unloading takeout from Olive Garden.

"Hey, Dad," she said. "You're a little early."

"Well, I thought we could eat and—" He stopped midsentence when he turned and saw Mark standing beside her.

One hell of an awkward silence followed.

Mark finally cleared his throat and stepped forward. "Hi, Mr. Mason. I'm Mark."

"Mark?" Dad warily shook his hand, but his gaze slid questioningly to Karma, then to the flowers on the table, then back to Karma.

"Mark's a friend of mine," she said.

"A friend," Dad said dubiously.

"Yes," Mark said in the stretch of silence that followed. "I came by to say hi, but was just on my way out."

"Uh-huh." Dad turned back toward the Olive Garden bags.

"I'll walk you to the door." Karma pushed against Mark's arm.

"It was nice to meet you," Mark said to her dad's back.

"Hmph." Dad didn't turn around.

She followed Mark to the door and into the outer hall. "This should be fun," she said quietly.

Mark took a deep breath and blew it out. "I'm so sorry. I should have left when you said he was coming over."

She held up her hand. "No. It's okay. I'll handle it."

He looked concerned. "Well, you can call me later if you need to."

"I might just do that." Karma nodded toward her apartment. "He doesn't look happy."

"You sure you don't need me to stay?"

"No. It'll be fine."

"Okay. I'll talk to you later." He kissed her cheek. "Good night."

"Night." She waved as he started down the stairs, and then went back inside to see her dad in the dining room, staring at her like she was a stripper.

Uh-oh. It looked like she had some explaining to do.

Dad frowned and disappeared into the kitchen again.

"Dad." Karma joined him and grabbed plates from the cupboard. "It's not what you think."

"Who is he?" Her dad wouldn't look at her.

"He's a friend, Dad."

"Sure he is, and I'm your mom." He scowled at her out of the corners of his eyes. "Now, who is he?"

She blew out a frustrated breath. "Dad, he's—"

"Mark," Dad said. "His name is Mark." He frowned. "That consultant you're working with at Solar is named Mark."

She could see her dad's wheels turning and putting everything together. "Yes, that's right." *Shit.*

He pointed an accusing finger toward the door. "Karma, are you dating the consultant?"

She couldn't really call it dating but didn't know how else to explain. Dating would imply they were in a relationship that could actually go somewhere. "I'm not actually dating him, Dad."

"Well, are you *sleeping* with him, then?" Her dad raised his voice and slammed the foil pack of garlic bread on the counter.

"No!" His reaction chilled her bones. She hadn't seen her dad this angry in a long time.

"Well then, what were the two of you doing in your bedroom when I got here? I knocked on the door, and when you didn't answer, I used my key." He raised his hands in a gesture of surrender. "At least now I know why you didn't hear me knock." He grumbled unintelligibly under his breath and turned for the fridge.

"Dad, it's not like that. It's—" She didn't want to lie, especially to her dad. "I like him, Dad. And he likes me."

He spun around. "And you're willing to throw away your career on that?" He huffed and stood akimbo. "This won't end well, Karma! You work with him! What are you thinking?"

Karma's mouth fell open. Her dad hadn't take such an aggressive tone with her since she'd switched majors at Purdue.

"What am I thinking?" She slapped her hands on her hips. "Well, for starters, maybe for once I'm thinking that I'd like to go out with a nice looking man who's interested in me."

"For God's sake, Karma, there are plenty of nice looking men out there. You don't need to risk your job on..." He waved toward the door. "*THAT*."

She pointed an angry finger in the same direction. "*THAT* happens to be the best man I've ever gone out with, Dad!"

"You can do better." He spun toward their food, giving her his back.

"Where? Where, Dad? I've tried to 'do better' and it's gotten me nowhere. Every guy I've gone out with—and there haven't been that many, I might add—has turned out to be a major loser. Would you like to hear how awful they were?" She had used an online dating service last summer, which had been horrific. She began ticking off the list of dating nightmares scrolling through her mind from those two awful months. "Okay, let's see, there was the guy who 'channeled the moon's energy' to try and look down my blouse, a guy who defined taking me to a car dealership as a date, a guy who invoiced me for my half of dinner when I didn't put out. Shall I continue, Dad? Because that's just some of what I've had to put up with from men." She didn't want to mention Richard or Brian. "There are a lot of serious assholes out there, and I think I've met them all, but Mark isn't one of them. He isn't like that. He's a gentleman. He's nice. He treats me well. And he's made me feel as if I'm actually desirable for the first time in my life. Yes, Dad. *Desirable*." She slapped her palm in the center of her chest. "*ME!* Mark thinks I'm perfect. And for once, I'm starting to believe it. All my life I've felt lost and inferior and imperfect, like I didn't know who I was. But now, because of Mark, I don't feel that way, anymore. He's given me my confidence. He's helped me find my voice. So, fine. He and I work together. So what? I'm seeing Solar's consultant. But you know what? I'm glad. I refuse to regret it, no matter what happens." She didn't realize she had tears in her eyes until she came up for air.

Her dad stood across the kitchen from her, staring. "I didn't know it was so bad for you, honey."

She swiped her palms across her cheeks to wipe away the tears. "Well, it has been. But it's not anymore. And it's because of *that man* who just walked out the door." She pointed toward the living room.

Her dad sighed. "I know it seems that way now, honey, but he's not good for you."

"How can you say that? You don't even know him."

"I know that he works with you, and that's not right, Karma. He's taken advantage of his situation to get close to you."

"He didn't take advantage of the situation, Dad. I met him before I even knew he was going to be working at Solar. I met him in Chicago when I went to that benefit with Daniel."

Her dad frowned and turned away. "I don't care." He continued unpacking food. "Once he found out the two of you would be working together, he should have ended it. It's not right." He stopped and leaned his arms on the counter, keeping his head down. "And you lied about it." His accusing glare skewered her heart. "On Memorial Day, you lied and told everybody you weren't seeing him."

He had nailed her.

"I'm sorry, Dad. But I couldn't let him get in trouble."

"*Him?*" Dad pushed against the counter and gritted his teeth. "What about *you*, Karma? Aren't you worried about yourself?"

"Sure I am." She huffed and crossed her arms. "That's why I lied. To protect both of us." It was a lame excuse.

Her dad exhaled heavily. "Karma, what do you think is going to happen here?" His heated gaze pierced hers again. "Do you think this *boy* is going to stay with you? Do you?"

Karma couldn't find her voice to respond. She let her gaze drop to the floor.

"I'll tell you what's going to happen," her dad said, his voice calmer. "That boy is going to have his fun with you and you with him, and along the way, you're going to fall in love—hell, you probably already have. Then, when his job here is done, he's going to pack up, go back to Chicago, and leave you here. Alone and broken-hearted. Is that what you want? To be used like that?"

"Dad…" Karma's voice sounded small. Her dad had no idea how right he was about so many things.

"Is it? Because I thought I did a better job raising you than that."

"You did, Dad." Karma willed herself not to cry. "Mark isn't *using* me. It's not like that with him. I know what I'm doing."

"Do you know what *he's* doing?"

"Yes, Dad. Okay? I know what this is and what it isn't. I know he's going to go back to Chicago."

"And you think he's going to take you with him. Is that it?"

"Of course not. That's not going to happen."

"And you're okay with that?"

"Yes."

Her dad's narrowed eyes and clenched jaw said he wasn't buying it, but he didn't push further. "Fine, but I hope you're right about knowing what you're doing, Karma. I don't want to see you get hurt by that boy." *Boy.* Not man. Calling him a boy was like an exclamation point. It was the judge's gavel falling. No matter what happened from here on out, Mark's fate was forever sealed in Dad's eyes.

"He won't hurt me," she said. "Now, can we drop it and eat?" She dug the serving spoon into the lasagna as if she were digging through rock.

Dad spooned fettuccine onto his plate then speared it with a fork, turned, and walked out.

Great. Father-daughter night had just been reduced to an awkward, speechless cesspool.

Chapter 35

Not all of the puzzle pieces of life seem to fit together at first. But, in time, you'll find they do so, perfectly.
-Doe Zantamata

Mark shut the door that led from the garage to the kitchen and flipped on the light.

Things had almost gotten out of hand tonight. Again. If not for Karma's dad, Mark didn't think he could have stopped from taking things all the way, which wasn't how he had planned their first time. But she had looked so sweet, and he had missed her more than he thought. Then he'd seen the books on her dresser, and his mind ran away with him. By the time she started telling him about the fantasy from the Penthouse book, he had already been losing his restraint.

He had almost gotten himself under control, though, but then she scratched her fingernails against his scalp and kissed the side of his forehead. After that, the animal inside him had reared up and struck, refusing to be collared. In that instant, he had wanted her in a way he had never wanted a woman.

What was it about Karma that excited him beyond his ability to maintain control? That overrode every shred of reasoning he possessed? The moment he saw her, logic fled and passion ruled. In only a month, he had grown unbelievably addicted to her, and he was in no hurry to give her up.

He pulled off his shirt as he climbed the stairs to his loft bedroom, where his home office took up half the spacious room. Maybe it was time to invite her over. She had yet to visit him at the condo, and maybe on his own turf he could regain control and not let his mind wander down paths that could never be.

Tonight, for instance. He had wanted to make love to her. Not because it was part of some timetable and he felt she was ready, but because…well…it had felt *right*. So incredibly right. With Karma, he didn't have to hide. She made him feel secure, which was strange, because he was supposed to be the one making *her* feel safe. And yet, he couldn't deny what he felt. Karma made him forget about the pain of his past, which was something no other woman had ever done. In her way, she was helping him as much as he was helping her, which was something he hadn't expected.

He stuffed his shirt into his laundry bag and changed out of his jeans into a pair of sweats. He was still hard. He had been since the moment he saw her bare, pink-tipped toes.

Kicking back on the bed, he ignored the reports lying beside him and turned on the news. But his mind wasn't focused on the rising price of gasoline, or the shooting that had taken place on the South Side, or even on the approaching cold front. His gaze was fixed on the ceiling, his thoughts still on the unbelievable, enigmatic, ever surprising bundle of sweetness and sizzle named Karma Mason.

What had happened after he left her apartment. Had she told her father who he was? If so, had he read her the riot act? Probably so. Any good father wouldn't want his daughter in such a relationship.

Mark could have stayed to lend support, but leaving had been the right thing to do. He didn't need to meddle in her family life, especially since he would return to Chicago when this was all over. Standing beside her in an argument with her dad would have only created confusion.

More confusion.

He couldn't let himself lose sight of how this would end. No matter how much he liked her or how eager he was to have her, he had to keep his head about him. This was not the time to let his emotions take over.

"What are you doing, Strong?" he said quietly, chastising himself. "You're blowing it." He rubbed his palms over his face. *Get your head on straight and quit thinking she's different than the others. She's not. She's just another woman. That's it. And she, more than all the others, holds the power to hurt you the most. Don't let that happen. Do what you said you'd do and leave it at that. By winter, you'll be back in Chicago, and she'll still be here. That's the plan. That's what you told her. And that's how it's going to be.*

He decided to forego the reports until morning, went to the bathroom, hopped in the shower, and gave himself what his body had wanted for the last hour.

As he came, it was the fantasy of Karma kissing his temple, scratching her nails against his scalp and shuddering through her own orgasm that he replayed through his mind.

So much for his pep talk.

Chapter 36

Passion makes idiots of the cleverest men, and makes the biggest idiots clever.
-Francois de La Rochefoucauld

Sunday afternoon, Mark set aside his work and sent Karma a text. *How did it go last night after I left?*

A couple of minutes later, she replied. *Dad kind of freaked, but so did I.*

How so?

Before she could reply, he dialed her number.

"How did I know you would call?" she said.

"Because you're getting to know how I operate."

"Ah, that must be it."

He leaned back in his chair. "So, what happened?"

She relayed the details of the conversation with her father while he doodled her face on his notepad. Twice. When she finished, Mark set down his pen and ran his palm down his face. "I didn't mean to cause a problem between you and your dad."

"You didn't, Mark. I love my dad more than anything, but he's always been difficult when it comes to men…or boys, as he calls them. To be honest, I don't think he would have liked you even if you weren't working at Solar. You could have gone to Harvard or Yale and dined with the Queen of England, and he still wouldn't have liked you."

"Actually, I came close to going to Harvard."

"Really?"

"Yes. It's not all it's cracked up to be. The business school in Chicago was more to my liking."

"Well, even if you'd gone, Dad still wouldn't like you. He thinks you're using me."

"I *am* using you," he said jokingly.

"Shut up." She laughed.

"Oh wait. *You're* using *me*. That's right. I got confused."

"Mark."

He chuckled. "I don't mind being used."

"I'm not using you."

He settled back in his chair, getting serious again. "I know."

"We're two consenting adults enjoying each other's company," she said with finality.

"That we are." The fact that her dad knew they worked together posed another problem, though. "Do you think he'll tell anyone at Solar about us?" Her dad knew some of her coworkers and was friends with Don.

"I doubt it, but it's possible."

"Karma, if this has become too much for you, I'll understand if you want to end it. I don't want you and your dad—"

"No," she said. "I don't want this to end. It's too late now, anyway. He already knows. If he's going to tell anyone, he's going to tell them whether we continue seeing each other or not. If I'm going to get in trouble, I may as well make it worthwhile, right?"

He smiled. "Who are you? You're definitely not the same woman I met in Chicago."

She giggled. "Yes, I am. I'm just a new and improved version of that woman, thanks to you."

"You're a lot more ballsy."

"Is that bad?"

"Absolutely not. I like seeing you sticking up for what you want."

"Well, I want you."

Gratitude and humility sliced down his spine. Her words briefly rendered him speechless. He liked being wanted by her…wanted badly enough that she was willing to risk getting in trouble to keep seeing him. What a strange feeling this knowledge gave him. He couldn't promise her forever. He couldn't love her. She knew this. He hadn't given her one good reason to put herself, her job, her reputation, or her relationship with her father on the line, but she was willing to jeopardize all those things to be with him.

He suddenly felt so small. He wasn't worthy of such devotion, and yet he was more grateful than words could express.

"Karma, you risk too much for me."

"It's worth it." The words sounded familiar. "Remember when you told me that? That night in the parking garage when I asked why you would risk getting in trouble just so we could see each other, you told me it was worth it. Now I get it. I understand now what you meant."

That night felt like so long ago and yet like only yesterday. He had been in control then. He had known what he was doing, and the course with Karma had seemed so simple. So cut and dry. In those first couple of weeks, he had guided her as he'd wanted, leading her, teaching her, molding her. Their conversations had been almost clinical at times, so one-sided and bleached of intimacy. Now, he didn't want to mold her. He liked her just the way she was.

What had started out as two adults simply seeking pleasure from one another—one the teacher, the other the student—had transformed into something much more complicated. What had once been impersonal was now *deeply* personal. His emotions were involved in a way he hadn't bargained for.

She was in control now. Every day, he felt his authority slip further out of his grasp, right along with his heart, and he couldn't walk away if he wanted to. His discipline waned. Before he met Karma—and after Carol—he had been a stalwart, emotionless vacuum, able to turn on and off at will. Women liked that about him, because it made him a challenge. Now, he was switched on all the time. Thoughts of Karma invaded every moment, and for the first time in years, he struggled to contain himself. He wanted Karma. This was no longer about helping her come out of her shell or about teaching her what she'd been missing. Their relationship was about sharing. About being together. About the smile she gave him every time they talked or texted. About how her cheeks reddened every morning when she saw him walk around the corner at the office. About the way her arms felt around him and the way his felt around her. It was about so many tiny little things that felt so incredibly monumental.

The teacher had become the student. He was changing, and it was because of her. But he didn't want to change. Change scared him. One day, she would leave him if he didn't leave her first, so he had to keep things in perspective. He couldn't let her steal his heart. She already possessed too much of it. If she took the whole thing, it would only hurt more later when she gave it back.

"You're good for me, Mark," she said, snapping him from his thoughts. He had absently doodled her face a third time. "Like I told my dad, I'm different now, and you're the reason why. Not because you're my boyfriend, but because you've made me see myself differently. I don't want to lose that when I feel like there's so much more to learn."

He didn't feel he could teach her anything else. She was perfect as is.

"What if your dad does tell Don? What then?" The irony that he was now the one voicing concern was further proof of how far the control had slipped from his grasp.

"I don't think Dad will tell him, but if he does, he does. As you said before we got involved, 'we'll deal with it.'"

It would be easier if she ended it now, because then he wouldn't have to later. The thought of leaving her at some unknown but foreseeable point by year's end wasn't something he relished. That was like looking forward to his next bout with a stomach bug. He knew it was looming out there somewhere, and he knew when it hit it would be the most miserable few days of his life, but there wasn't much he could do to stop it.

"I don't want you to end it, either," he said honestly. Would it be easier if she did? Yes. Did he want her to? No.

"Well then…good." She sounded pleased.

Mark stood and strolled across the room to the window, eager to regain at least some of the control he had relinquished. "Speaking of Don, he and I have to fly out east tomorrow morning to talk to the leasing company about warehouses. We'll be gone until late Thursday." He drew the curtain aside and looked out over the courtyard behind his condo. "So, I was hoping you and I could spend some time together next weekend."

All. In.

The brief silence that came through the connection before she answered was enough to indicate she knew exactly what spending time together next weekend entailed. He wanted more, and it was clear she was ready.

"I'd like that," she said.

"It's a date then." He let the curtain drop and made his way back to his desk, where he picked up his pen and began doodling again. "I'll call you later in the week to make plans." Taking the lead put him back in the driver's seat.

"Okay. I'll…um…keep reading my books."

The tip of his pin swirled and drew a pair of heart-shaped lips. "That would be a good idea, but don't worry," he smiled as Karma's face began to take shape on the scrap of paper a fourth time, "if you miss something in your reading, I'll be more than happy to give you hands-on instruction."

"Such a devoted teacher you are."

"I just want you to get your money's worth." He drew a button nose on his caricature.

"But I'm not paying you."

"Oh, yes. That's right." A pair of large, luminous eyes came next. "Well then, I suppose I can only claim perfectionism as my motivation. I am nothing if not thorough in my teaching methods, Miss Mason." Even as he said the words, his heart wasn't in them. He was no longer the teacher, even if she didn't realized it.

"And I am nothing if not your eager apprentice, Mr. Strong."

"Why do you always make me sound like Yoda?"

She laughed. "I don't know."

"Does that make you Luke Skywalker?"

She giggled coyly. "No. I'm Princess Leia. You can show me your *Force*."

"Mmm," The tip of his pen slashed color into the irises. "In that case, do you think I can get you to wear that sexy outfit from Jabba's palace next time I see you?"

She laughed again then said, "If that's what it takes for you to bring out your best, Master, then I suppose I can."

When had Karma grown so overtly sexual? He liked this side of her. She pushed his buttons in all the right ways. "You know, if I wasn't so set on waiting, I'd stop by tonight and explore your new, bolder side. What's gotten into you, anyway? You don't normally talk with such…" He searched for the right word. "Sexual *innuendo*."

"I don't know." She paused for a moment as if thinking. "Maybe it's that I haven't really seen you in a week—last night notwithstanding. And about that, maybe I'm still a little…oh, I don't know…*rattled* by what we did right before my dad showed up."

"Rattled?"

"Yes, rattled."

He pressed his lips together and smirked. "You liked it?"

When Karma answered, her voice was light and airy, almost wistful. "Yes."

"So did I." And if her dad hadn't shown up, Mark would have seen that blazing kiss through until Karma cried in pleasure, her body shuddering beneath his as he took her to the heights he so badly wanted to show her…and which she obviously and so eagerly wanted to experience.

She lightly cleared her throat. "And maybe I'm growing bolder because I've been learning so much from my books. They say that with knowledge comes power, and I believe it. I never knew there was so much to learn about all this sex stuff."

He rocked forward in his chair. "Sex stuff. Now there's a scientific term for you."

Her breezy laughter lifted his heart. "Stop making fun of me, Master Mark."

"Dream of it not, I will," he said in his best Yoda impersonation, which was pretty bad.

Karma laughed harder.

Mark leaned his arm on his desk, admiring the four caricatures of Karma's face staring up at him from the paper. "Well, all the 'sex stuff' is going to wait until next weekend, so you'd better get your rest this week while I'm gone."

"Oh? Why's that? Do you plan on keeping me awake for two straight days?"

Mark's voice dropped, and he grew deadly serious. "I just might. By this weekend, I'll have been away almost two weeks, with last night's very pleasant, sexy, and *unfinished* kiss still haunting me. I might not be able to control myself once I get my hands on you again."

His words had the effect he was after. Numb silence answered him through the phone. A moment later, Karma practically whispered, "I see your point."

"I thought you might." He drew in a breath and slowly blew it out, so aroused that he knew he'd need a shower if he was going to get any more work done today. "And with that, I should be getting off here. I have a lot of work to do before I meet Don in the morning, and I'm not going to get any of it done listening to your sexy voice."

"Awe, you do say the sweetest things." He heard the smile in her tone.

"So do you. Now, get back to your reading and your Kegels and all your other wonderful lessons, but leave Hank alone. I don't want you touching him. You're mine now. The next time you come, I want it to be with me. So…no playing."

"None?"

"None. Nada. Zilch."

"No fair."

He chuckled. "You'll understand next weekend why I want you to wait. Trust me on this. Now, promise me you won't play."

She hesitated.

"Karma? Promise me."

"Fine. I promise," she said with obvious reluctance. "I trust you."

"Good. That's what I want to hear." He checked the time. "Okay, sweetheart, I've got to go. I'll call you later this week."

They said their good-byes, and Mark set his phone on his desk, ready to address the raging hard-on putting pressure on the seam of his jeans. He didn't want Karma to play with herself, but if he didn't, he wouldn't be able to hold himself back long enough to perform next weekend. So, for him, the more he masturbated in the next six days, the better. For her, abstinence was key. She would understand why soon enough.

Okay, so maybe there were still a *few* things he could teach her.

Chapter 37

I am good, but not an angel. I do sin, but I am not the devil. I am just a small girl in a big world trying to find someone to love.
-Marilyn Monroe

Karma didn't think Friday would ever arrive. As busy as she was all week, time should have flown faster, but as is usually the case when there's something to look forward to, time crawled.

Six weeks ago—hell, even five weeks ago—she would have been a nervous wreck about what was to come this weekend. Mark planned on making love to her. This was *it*. The old Karma would have been queasy with nerves, but new Karma was excited. She trusted Mark. Like an expert gardener, Mark had cultivated the delicate, vulnerable seedling of her newfound sexuality. He hadn't forced her to grow faster than she was capable of. More like he had coaxed and prepared her to blossom at her own pace. His words of encouragement and his guidance were fertilizer, and his kisses and gentle touch were water. He was attentive and patient, and in him, Karma had found a lover worth giving herself to. One who waited until she was ready, and only then would he pluck her fruit.

And it was harvest time. He had gently pulled her along, showed her how beautiful she was, urged her to realize her own beauty, and now waited for her to give herself to him.

Was she still nervous? Hell, yes. But was she so nervous as to be crippled? No. These were good nerves. The kind of nerves a speaker channeled into a kick-ass speech, not the kind that caused a breakdown.

So, when Friday morning finally dawned, Karma eagerly awoke. After getting ready for work, she smiled as she picked up the gold brooch that had been the catalyst for the official start of their affair. Mark would understand its meaning when he saw it pinned to her scarf. The brooch was her way of telling him that she was ready for this weekend. Ready for whatever their time together brought. That her answer was yes to whatever he wanted to do, because she knew he would care for her body as well as he cared for her mind.

She arrived at work before he did. Not surprising since it was seven thirty and his return flight yesterday had been delayed due to weather. He and Don hadn't returned to Indianapolis until almost midnight.

At nine thirty, Mark appeared at the end of the hall, wearing the navy, pin-striped suit that made him look like the sexiest executive on the planet. There were power suits, and then there were *power* suits. This was the latter. Why did she get the impression he had worn it for her?

"Good morning, Karma." His gaze dropped to the red scarf secured around her neck. "That's a pretty brooch."

She lifted her hand and fondled the gold circle. "Thank you. I wear it on special occasions."

His eyes narrowed with understanding as one side of his mouth lifted. "And that special occasion today would be…?"

"Oh, it's just special." She waved her hand dismissively.

"That it is." He winked and turned for the conference room, grinning as he walked away.

The devil. He was going to make today unbearable. She got up, went to the coffee station, and prepared him a mug.

"Thank you," he said as she set the coffee on a Solar coaster beside his tablet.

"You're welcome."

"And…" He stopped her before she could leave. "Thank you for the brooch."

She smiled. "You're welcome for that, too."

He spun his chair toward her, looked behind her to make sure no one was listening, then whispered in a voice so hot she practically melted, "If we were alone, I'd bend you over this table right now."

Her mouth fell open, and heat exploded between her legs.

He leaned closer. "I'd lift that pretty skirt, peel off your panties, and bury myself inside you until you cried my name and quivered around my cock."

Karma closed her mouth and swallowed, feeling the heat between her legs intensify, but she couldn't utter a single word in reply. He had never talked to her like that. Maybe he should do so more often.

With a grin, he turned back toward his computer. "Thank you for the coffee, Karma."

She was dismissed. But clearly, he was pleased with her reaction. Otherwise, he wouldn't be wearing such a Cheshire cat smile.

Fighting the slippery sensation between her legs, she returned to her desk, sat down, and glanced into the conference room. Mark's smoldering gaze was the sexiest I'm-going-to-fuck-you-so-hard look she had ever seen. As in anywhere. Not even in the movies had she seen a more salacious expression.

Yes, Mark was going to make today unbearable…but in the most incredible, stimulating way. But two could play at that game.

Right before leaving for lunch with Don, Mark's phone vibrated on the table next to his tablet. With a nonchalant glance, he read the message.

I'm not wearing any panties.

WHAT?

His head snapped around. Karma wasn't looking at him, but her coquettish grin told him she knew he was watching her. Was she serious? Just the thought that she wasn't wearing underwear caused his cock to bob to life.

Are you pulling my leg? he texted back.

No. Want me to prove it?

When he glanced back, her face was beet red.

Don't tempt me. Damn, he was already stiff.

Now we're both worked up, aren't we?

Woman, I get worked up just looking at you, but now I'm worried for your safety tonight.

Tonight?

Yes, tonight. My place. 7:00. Bring an overnight bag with enough clothes to make it to Sunday. I'm keeping you for a while. Especially now that you've shown me you're more than ready to take the heat.

I have?

Karma, if you've really taken off your panties, I think we both know the answer to that.

She smiled when he glanced at her. She looked at her phone, thumb-typed a reply, and a moment later, his phone vibrated.

I really have taken them off, and oh my God, I can't believe I did.

Does it feel sexy?

Yes.

You're something else, you know that?

It's your fault.

Mine?

Yes. You've turned me into a nympho.

He chuckled. *That could be a good thing. With the right man, of course.*

And you're the right man?

Absolutely. But you kept your promise this week, right? No playing?

Yes, I kept my promise. Which is probably why I did something as foolish as take off my underwear. I'm horny.

This time he laughed. *Karma! I can't believe you said that. Such a potty mouth.*

He heard her giggle. A few seconds later, he received another text. *I can't help it. You wouldn't let me play with Hank this week.*

You need to break up with Hank. You need a real man.

But I don't want to hurt his feelings.

You need to be more worried about hurting mine. I'm a sensitive guy. Who has an ego. Remember? I refuse to let a power tool be better than I am.

Something tells me you have nothing to worry about in that department.

He grinned. *Well, I'll give it my best.*

Deal.

Good. Now, quit sexing me up. I have to have lunch with your boss in a few minutes and I don't want him to get the wrong idea.

LOL. Okay, I'll stop, but only because I don't want Don stealing you away.

Such wit.

You don't have to worry about that, he texted. *You're a lot cuter than Don.*

When he looked at her, she wore one of her signature angelic smiles. The ones that caused his heart to beat a little harder and his skin to warm. He hoped to see many more of those smiles this weekend.

And in the weeks to come.

Chapter 38

The real lover is the man who can thrill you just by touching your head or smiling into your eyes – or just by staring into space.
-Marilyn Monroe

Karma pulled into the garage of Mark's condo and parked next to his BMW. He had told her he would leave the garage door open. That way, her car wouldn't sit in his driveway all weekend, just in case a coworker happened by.

As she got out and grabbed her bag from the backseat, the garage door closed. Mark met her at the stairs leading into the kitchen.

"Hey you." He swept in for a kiss.

He took her bag and stepped aside. A trail of steam rose from the spout of a pan on the stove, and the savory scent of garlic and oregano suggested Mark could cook a mean Italian dish.

"You can cook?" She looked over her shoulder as he stepped behind her and wound his arms around her waist. Her heart fluttered.

"Oh, yes, Karma. I can cook," he said against the side of her neck before kissing it.

Easy jazz played from somewhere in the living room, lending a classy ambience to the atmosphere. She took a seat on one of the barstools and watched him make his way around the kitchen with the swift confidence of an executive chef. He lifted the lid off a skillet, releasing a plume of steam, then dipped in a spoon, raised it to his mouth and tasted, licked his lips thoughtfully, then sprinkled in a dash of salt before replacing the lid and opening the oven in one fluid motion. He pulled out a tray of thick slabs of buttery garlic bread, barely golden brown, and set it on the counter. It was an entertaining dance between man and cuisine.

"You sure know your way around a kitchen."

"Cooking is sort of a hobby." Using a fork, he plucked a piece of spaghetti from the boiling water, blew on it, then dropped it in his mouth.

"I didn't know that." She leaned on her elbows and crossed her forearms on the granite countertop. Learning these nuggets and nuances was like opening small gifts. Each one revealed something precious, something expressly hers.

Using a kitchen towel, he lifted the pan and carried it to the sink, where he poured the contents into a metal colander. "I love to dabble in the kitchen. It eases my mind." He set the empty pan on the counter, lifted the colander, and shook off the excess water. "When I'm stuck on some part of a project, or when I get stressed, cooking always seems to clear my head. It's kind of like my doodling. It occupies my thoughts in a way that just feels simple so my subconscious can work on other things."

"Do you make up your own recipes or follow others'?"

He used tongs to lift the noodles from the colander and twisted them into a spiraled bundle on a nearby plate. "I usually make up my own, but sometimes I see something I like, get the recipe, and alter it my way."

"You're a real Gordon Ramsey."

He twisted a second pile of pasta on another plate. "Nah, just an amateur who has a way with food." He carried the plates to the stove, lifted the lid off the skillet, and ladled a large spoonful of thick, rich sauce that smelled heavenly onto each mound of pasta. Two giant meatballs topped them off. Then he added a piece of garlic bread and placed one plate in front of her and the other at the setting beside her. "Wine?" He lifted a bottle of red.

"Please."

Very impressive. This was the first time a man had cooked for her. The first time one had gone through so much trouble to seduce her. Mark didn't have to go to such lengths. They both knew what tonight was about…what this entire weekend was about. He could have simply ordered takeout, fed her, and whisked her off to bed. Instead, he took his time, easing into the moment. Despite their steamy exchanges at the office today, Mark was in no rush to reach the evening's denouement.

The first bite of her meal sent an explosion of flavor through her senses. This was Italian with an attitude.

"Oh my God." She turned toward him as he sat beside her.

His modest grin did little to hide his pride. "Good?"

She nodded then changed her mind and shook her head. "No. Not good." She turned back to her plate. "This is orgasmic."

He had just taken a drink of wine and nearly spit it out. He coughed, dabbed his napkin on his upper lip, and cleared his throat. "Well, I wasn't expecting *that*."

She grinned. "This is really good." She sliced her fork through the steaming meatball and slipped a chunk into her mouth. "Mmmm, heaven." Flavors crashed against her tongue. "Is this your recipe? You didn't replicate someone else's?"

He nodded once and took a bite. "My own."

"What's in it?"

He winked. "It's a secret."

"I want this recipe," she said.

"If you're good, I'll think about it." He nodded toward her plate and flashed a wicked grin. "Now eat. You need your strength."

It was his first allusion to what was in store for her this weekend.

"I'm sure I do." She turned to her Italian heaven-on-a-plate and dug in. If he wanted her to eat, she would eat. And if he wanted her to do other things later? Well, she would just have to do those, too.

After dinner, Mark took their plates to the sink then returned and wrapped his arms around her from behind. "Why don't you take a bath while I clean up the kitchen?"

"Why do I get the impression you've already made that decision for me?" She slid off the barstool.

He simply smiled, picked up her bag, and led her upstairs to the loft bedroom.

The small desk lamp was the only one on in the room, but evening light still spilled through the western-facing windows. He set her bag on the king-sized bed, which was dressed in burgundy satin with enormous throw pillows resting against the leather headboard.

She followed him into the bathroom.

He turned on the water and started filling the large, oval tub.

"Vanilla okay?" He held up a bottle of bubble bath.

"Yes." It was more than okay. Everything—the whole evening, all of it—was perfect. She had hit the romantic jackpot. Was Mark even for real?

He poured two capfuls of bubble bath into the running water.

Mark had gone to great lengths to make tonight special. First dinner, now a bubble bath, and not just any old bubble bath in any old ho-hum bathroom. A vanilla bubble bath set among a romantic oasis. Three large bouquets of pink and white roses created ice cream colored decadence on the counter and on the deck of the ivory tub, along with a dark red candle. A second candle rested on the opposite end of the counter from the flowers.

"Cinnamon?" She gestured toward the candles.

He smiled, lit them, then moved toward her like a cougar on the hunt. "Did you know vanilla and cinnamon are powerful aphrodisiacs?" His gaze danced over her face, and his arms circled her waist.

"No."

He nuzzled her neck, leaving a trail of kisses. "It's believed that vanilla is arousing for both men and women, but especially so for men." He kissed the corner of her mouth. "And cinnamon produces heat in the body and increases the sexual appetite."

She glanced around his temple of seduction. "You've thought of everything, haven't you?"

"Yes." He looked over his shoulder at the bubble bath. "The only thing you have to do is relax in the tub. I'll bring you a glass of wine in a few minutes." He kissed her before departing.

Was this what it would be like if she were really, honestly Mark's girlfriend and not just an affair with an expiration date?

Her gut told her that this was just how Mark was. That he wasn't putting on some act. He believed in romance and the *art* of seduction. And with Mark, it *was* an art. Other men could lure women into their beds with a look, a nice meal, or a well-placed compliment, but for Mark, seducing a woman involved evoking her senses, pleasing her, making the seduction about *her*.

She retrieved her bag from the foot of the bed and set it on the floor by the bathroom counter. Inside was the white baby-doll nighty and thong. A few months ago, she wouldn't have dreamed of wearing something so sexy, but now she couldn't wait.

After undressing and pinning up her hair, she eased into the tub. The water's temperature was perfect. Hot, but not scalding. A bevy of vanilla bubbles enveloped her, covering her entire body except for her head and shoulders.

Aaaahhhh. Sinking into the bubbly bed was as decadent as pouring melted chocolate over her skin. Lifting one arm through the vanilla-scented film, she skimmed her hand up to her shoulder. The bubbles made her skin slick, almost as if she were covered in oil. Only Hollywood royalty was treated better than this.

A few minutes later, Mark knocked lightly then entered. He held a glass of wine and a bath pillow. "Enjoying yourself?"

"Mm, yes. Very much," she said lazily. Between the vanilla and cinnamon scents, she felt like she was in a bakery, but without the calories. And what woman didn't like the idea of smelling like a cinnamon roll?

He set the wine beside her on the edge of the tub, nestled the pillow behind her head, removed a pink rose from the vase beside her, tore off the flower, and then sprinkled the petals over the white blanket of bubbles. She lifted one foam-covered hand and slid one of the petals into her palm. It felt like silk-covered velvet.

"I still can't believe you removed your panties at work," he said, dropping his hand into the bath. His palm caressed her inner thigh.

She played the rose petal through her fingers. "Me neither."

His hand slid all the way up her thigh and back down, making her catch her breath. Dark shadows filled his gaze, and the lines of his face softened. For several seconds, he continued to gently caress her leg. It felt like a hundred naughty thoughts passed between them in the space of only a few seconds. Finally, he smirked and pulled his hand out of the water. "I should stop that or I won't be able to." He reached behind him for one of the plush, cream-colored towels and dried his arm.

"I didn't mind." She felt like a lamb caught in a wolf's sights, only she wasn't scared.

"Don't worry, we have all weekend to play." He bent, kissed her, then stood and turned for the door. "I'm almost finished downstairs, but don't rush. Take your time. I'll be waiting when you're done." He stepped out, quietly closed the door behind him, and left her with her wine, her hot bath, and a warmth in her lower belly that had nothing to do with the water's temperature and everything to do with the lingering burn of his touch.

It took Mark five more minutes to finish in the kitchen, then he shut off the light and went back upstairs. The bathroom door was still closed, and he heard the quiet burbling of water as Karma shifted in her bath.

She had looked surprised and pleased when she saw the setup he had prepared, but he wanted tonight to be special. Giving her that little taste of luxury was the least he could do.

He turned on some light jazz through his computer and changed into a pair of light blue pajama pants and a white T-shirt. His semi-erection tented the cotton pants, but there was nothing he could do about that. He had been in an aroused state the better part of the day from all the teasing and flirty texts.

He left on the dim desk lamp and pulled back the satin comforter to reveal matching burgundy sheets. He'd bought them especially for tonight. There was nothing quite like making love on satin sheets, and Karma's pale skin would look beautiful against the dark red shade.

Once everything was ready, he climbed into bed, propped himself against the wall of pillows against the headboard, and let the sounds of Chris Botti's trumpet carry him away as he waited.

Karma looked at her reflection in the mirror. She didn't fill the bust of the lacy baby-doll as well as the model on the Yandy website, but she still looked good.

Her pale nipples were barely discernible above the opaque swath of satin that covered the lower half of her breasts under sheer lace. The gathered skirt hit just below her hips, barely covering the G-string she wore underneath. The delicate lace eyelets that extended six inches up the skirt, as well as the tight gathers from the waist, helped conceal enough to ease her nerves a little.

Deep breath. She was ready for this. She wanted it. After tonight, there would be no going back. *Good-bye, little lamb.*

She placed her hand on the doorknob, took one more deep breath, and opened the door.

Mark opened his eyes…and promptly forgot how to speak.

If he had thought Karma looked like an angel before, she epitomized the definition now. Dressed in white and backlit from the candlelight in the bathroom, all she needed was a pair of wings and a halo. Her silhouette under the gauzy film of fabric was an erotic shadow of sex appeal that lit his soul on fire, and his gaze devoured her inch by slow inch, from her pretty face all the way down to the sexy pink tips of her toes.

Speechless, he turned and sat on the edge of the bed, his feet on the floor. She shifted her weight and curled the toes of her right foot over the top of her left.

"Is it okay?" she said.

Finding his voice, Mark licked his lips and nodded. "It's very okay."

When had he ever seen anything sexier? White. Good choice. The color of innocence. It was perfect for her. Any other color would have been a sacrilege. At least at this point. Later, when they had spent more time together, he would like to see her in something red, or maybe black, but right now, white was perfect, especially given the style of the almost Victorian-looking chemise. She looked ready for the cover of a historical romance novel.

"Come here," he said, unable to make eye contact as he stared at her outfit…or, rather, her lack of one.

She did as he requested and walked tentatively toward him then stopped less than a foot away. "Do you like it?"

His hands disappeared under the hem, and he skimmed the tips of his fingers up the backs of her thighs to the lower curve of her bottom. "Yes, I like it very much." He smoothed his palms over the bare cheeks of her ass.

Her plump lips parted and a soft breath escaped.

"I underestimated you," he said, grinning. "I didn't expect this." Her smooth skin warmed his palms, and the firmness of her rump boosted his erection.

"I hoped you would like it."

"I do." He drove his hands up her back then down to her ass again. "You're not uncomfortable?"

Her hands rested on his shoulders as she took another small step forward. "Not anymore."

In other words, his reaction had emboldened her and erased any insecurity she might have felt before she stepped out of the bathroom. Who would have thought that the woman in the sexy red dress that had stolen his sense of reason would be even sexier in a white negligee?

His breath came in shallow draws. He knew tonight was as much about himself as it was about her. He had tried to tell himself it wasn't, but now he knew better. By giving her pleasure, he gave pleasure to himself.

"You're beautiful." He hooked his fingers inside the strap of her G-string and tugged it down her hips.

Her grip briefly tightened on his shoulders then loosened.

Slowly, so slowly, he dragged the wisp of fabric down her legs. "Lift your foot," he said. She stepped out of the thong, and he nearly fell to his knees to kiss her lovely feet but didn't. Instead, he sat back up and pulled her forward so that his knees were between her thighs. She lowered herself onto his lap as he pulled off his T-shirt.

"Now what?" she said

"Now I give you a night to remember." He wrapped one arm around her waist and pulled her with him onto the bed, ready to deliver on his promise.

Chapter 39

Sex is as important as eating or drinking and we ought to allow the one appetite to be satisfied with as little restraint or false modesty of the other.
-Marquis de Sade

Karma had heard people use the term surreal before, but she had never quite understood what they'd meant. Now she did. Mark's mouth lavished her everywhere, and his arms secured her like a prison she never wanted to escape, and the only word that came to mind?

Surreal.

Surely, this was happening to someone else, not her. Or maybe she was dreaming. It certainly felt like a dream. A very erotic, lifelike, sexual dream. The kind she had been having more of since meeting Mark. Sometimes she even awoke as she climaxed. They say that if you die in your dream, you die in real life. Well, the same could be said of orgasms, because when she came in her dreams, she often awoke in the throes of orgasm.

Never in a million years had Karma thought something like this would happen. That a sexy, hot man who could have any woman he wanted would want her. But here she was, with Mark, and he seemed to more than want her. The way he held her, kissed her, looked at her, and the way his hands ranged down to her butt and squeezed as he moaned appreciatively was proof.

Maybe this was life's way of repaying her a karmic debt. For so long, life had given her nothing but hell when it came to relationships, so now maybe karma was making up for it by giving her Mark. How funny was that? Karma was paying Karma a debt. But she would take it from her namesake.

Mark rolled her to her back and settled on top of her, his erection a thick rod between her legs. He rotated his hips so that it massaged her in just the right spot, and she moaned inadvertently, closing her eyes as his lips teased her neck.

And then he slid lower, dragged his mouth over the lacy fabric of her nighty, and still lower.

Oh, God! He was going to put his mouth on her. Down there! She'd never experienced that.

"You smell like vanilla," he said before lifting the nighty and kissing her stomach.

Her muscles quivered, and her bottom lip trembled. The tense anticipation was like a building inferno.

"Mmm," Mark murmured. "I like that." He lightly traced his fingertips over her stomach, making her quiver again. "I like how you respond to me."

Karma moaned as his touch danced over her stomach yet again. Her fingers twisted into the satin sheets, and she squirmed beneath him.

A dark, shallow chuckle bubbled out of his throat as he continued his journey south, trailing the tip of his tongue down one side of her torso then the other. Lower and lower. Sensual, full-lipped kisses dotted her hips, across her belly, down the tops of her thighs, up again to the juncture where her body and legs met.

She almost couldn't breathe, lost to the spiraling sensations spinning like a tornado in her core, growing bigger and stronger with each moment, each touch of his mouth. His hands pressed against her inner thighs and slid up to her hips, opening her. Karma couldn't look, couldn't even keep her eyes open. If she did, she would come. That's how close she was. Right there. On the cusp. And he hadn't even touched her *there*, yet.

Mark seemed to sense how near she was to orgasm, but instead of giving it to her, he prolonged the suspense. He dragged his lips up her inner thighs, lightly licked the sensitive skin at the creases between legs and body, and let his warm breath tease her flesh. Ever closer he drew, always to retreat, making her writhe.

If she didn't come soon, she would pass out. The sensory onslaught was almost unbearable. She had been without him and without release all week, and she had been in an aroused state every day, especially today. She needed an orgasm. And she needed Mark to give it to her.

"Mark, please..." she whispered, her voice shaky. She licked her lips and dared to glance down her body.

He was watching her, and the moment their eyes met, his tongue flicked her clit.

Her body lit up like a torch, and a tight, high-pitched groan bit out from her throat as she threw her head back on the pillow. In an instant, he closed his mouth over her clit and swirled his tongue around and around, not too fast, not too slow, but oh-holy-hell just fucking right!

Without thinking, she clamped her hands on his head, buried her fingers in his hair, held him in place as she rotated her hips against his mouth. Instinct had taken over. She lost conscious control of her body and succumbed to whatever it wanted. The pressure in her lower belly quickly built. She was going to come. Any second, it was happening…right now!

"Mark!" Her back arched violently off the bed as she came. Every muscle shuddered and pure pleasure ripped through her body.

She was lost to euphoria. Her first orgasm with a man's mouth on her. And it was better than any she had ever given herself. Within seconds, she began laughing then crying, and then Mark was beside her. He scooped her into his arms and cradled her against his body as if he knew she was going through an emotional cleanse and simply needed to be held.

Her body still sang with pleasure even as she continued to cry. Her orgasm still echoed and pulsed inside her, and she couldn't get close enough to him, even though he held her tightly and her arms latched on like they'd been welded to one another.

Closer. She needed more. He was too far away even though he was right there, holding her, pressed against her.

"Reach into the nightstand and grab a condom, honey," he said, rolling with her toward the nightstand so she was on top of him

Yes, yes. That was what she needed. Him inside her. Now!

She wiped tears off her cheeks then yanked the drawer open and reached inside. Her hand landed on a book and she searched farther toward the right. Nothing.

"On the left," he whispered, caressing her back. His voice held an edge of urgency.

She found the box and managed to open it one-handed, tearing the thin cardboard. She dug out a condom and practically threw it into his hand.

"Lift up for me," he said, tearing the packet open. She did, then his hands were between her legs, and she felt his erection tap against her inner thigh then against her overly stimulated clit as he put on the condom.

She looked over her shoulder at his legs. At some point, Mark had taken off his pants, but she had been so caught up in what he'd been doing that she hadn't noticed.

Then he flipped her to her back. She bounced on the mattress as he surged on top of her.

Yes, more! Now!

For over a month, she had waited for this day to come. They had teased about it, talked about it, even come close to doing it a couple of times. There were no more secrets keeping them apart, no dads to walk in and interrupt them. It was just her and Mark, and with the sensations of the orgasm he had just given her still ricocheting like unfinished business through her body, she was ready for the moment to finally happen.

"Make love to me," she said, gripping his shoulders.

"Oh, I plan on it." He found her lips with his and scorched her with a volcanic kiss. Mark had never kissed her with such primal fury. It was like a promise that declared he was about to rock her world in a way it had never been rocked, and she had better get ready.

The hard length of him slid forward and back, up and down against her, teasing, making her ache, filling her belly with viscous warmth that trickled numb tingles up her thighs and into her center.

Forever. The pleasurable ride seemed to last forever, driving her stark raving mad. She couldn't hold still. Her legs brushed up and down, her hips drove against him, seeking him, wanting him inside.

"Please," she finally whispered as she came up for air.

In answer, his hand brushed down between their bodies until his fingers parted her.

Her nails dug into his back, just below his shoulders.

With the tips of his fingers barely inside her, he used his hand to guide his erection to the very place she wanted. As he extracted his fingers, the head of his cock glided in to replace them.

He was inside her. Just a little. Not all the way. But still! God, Mary, Jesus, and the Holy Spirit! She felt like she should pray. Give thanks. Sing praises to heaven. Yes, this was what she had been missing only minutes ago. This was what she needed. This felt right. And he was thick. Thicker than the fourth dildo.

She sighed heavily and lifted her gaze to meet his as he held his breath.

"Are you ready?" he said.

Licking her lips, she nodded. "Yes."

Ever so gently, he pressed forward, sliding inside her just a little. There was a pinch of tightness, and she tensed and whimpered.

He stopped. "Ssshh, take your time." He gave her a moment to breathe, and then began filling her again once she relaxed.

Slowly, inch by inch, he encroached then withdrew before driving himself a little deeper, until finally he was in. All of him. And it felt so good. So damn good...and full. He filled her completely, and her vagina pulsed with anticipation, making him groan.

"You feel good," he said.

"So do you." Oh God, it was happening. It was finally happening.

His body shifted against hers, and he rotated his pubic bone against her clit.

A bolt of sensation zinged her, and she gasped. "Oh!" She had just had an orgasm a few minutes ago but was already on the verge of another. Or maybe this was the same one and it wasn't finished and just needed a little coaxing to fully spend itself.

He rotated himself against her clit again, more insistently, with similar results.

With an emphatic nod, she panted and dug her blunt nails into his back. "More."

He took a slow rhythm then gradually increased the tempo, maintaining the deep connection between them. The head of him buried as far as it could go.

The result was unreal. She had never felt anything like this. The pleasure, the way that simple contact took her to a place of physical rapture, was the stuff of fantasies. She was the heroine in a romance novel, and Mark was the supernatural hero able to show her magically intense pleasure like none she'd ever known.

But this was no fantasy, and she wasn't some character in a novel. This was real. Oh God, was it ever real. And within minutes, she wasn't sure she would ever be able to take a normal breath again.

So intense was the euphoria he coaxed in and out of her body, from head to toe, she could no longer speak, only breathe. High-pitched moans tore from her throat on each exhale, her body merely a vessel to receive and amplify every joyous, shallow, persistent stroke.

On the edge. That's where she was. He had pulled her to the precipice, and she hung, gazing down at the churning waters below, ready to fall, ready to be swallowed by the pending deluge.

So close. A second release was right there. Looming but just out of reach.

She had never come like this—without touching herself—and yet Mark had her precariously on climax's doorstep for a second time in less than fifteen minutes.

But that's as close as she came to release, because she remained rooted, her orgasm budging not an inch further.

Damn, the frustration. She was right there. So close to coming, but unable to. Out of desperation, she began to wend her hand between their undulating bodies, despairing, her proverbial back against the wall. Maybe if she used her fingers, that would help unleash her orgasm.

Mark grabbed her hand and thrust it down beside her. Their joined fists slammed against the mattress.

"No!" He grunted the word between clenched teeth. "Not like that."

She threw her head back and wailed from both the unbelievable pleasure and the frustration.

"You will come with me." Each word punched out like his voice was making love to her, not his body.

She writhed, furiously trying to unbind her orgasm from whatever shackled it. "I can't."

"Yes. You can." He slowed his pace and took deep breaths. "Relax, baby. Breathe."

She did as he said, as hard as it was with the threat of what felt like a volcanic climax bound tightly inside her belly.

His rhythm slowed further, and he gently slid in and out of her. In and out, in and out. And he lifted on his arms. His skin glistened with perspiration.

Her body cooled as air touched her damp skin through the lacy lingerie.

For at least a minute, maybe two, he stayed like that, supported on his arms, suspended over her body, his hips drawing back and driving slowly forward, over and over with extreme patience and care. From the looks of it, he was going to drag her orgasm out of her if it killed him.

The explosive sensations taking up residence in her body didn't diminish, but she was finally able to breathe almost normally again.

"That's it," he said, lowering himself once more. "Breathe. Deep breaths. And put your arms around me. Lay your legs out straight on either side of mine. Yes, just like that. Now…keep breathing." He pressed in, driving deep once more.

Oh! Now that was different. Mmm, yes.

Again, he rocked his hips forward, and again, and again. And oh! This was better. When his mouth found the side of her neck, it was like a mainline blasted into place between her neck and her vagina, and the most…*astonishing* flame licked to life deep inside, where his erection made contact with her G-spot.

The response felt similar to how it had felt when he sucked her nipples while fingering her the night he removed the Ben Wa ball, only this was ten times stronger.

"Yes," she said on a gasp. "Yes, God yes. There. Don't stop."

He wasn't stopping. If anything, his thrusts became more elongated, deeper, more powerful.

Karma lost all sense of herself as her eyes rolled back in her head. She couldn't breathe. Not because Mark was lying on her, but because the mounting, winding pleasure wouldn't allow it. His tongue laved her neck, and then he closed his lips against her skin and sucked with tiny nectar bites. Somewhere in the distance, the sound of a jazz piano played a deceptively fragile melody for the rising passion about to let loose a whole lot of oh-my-God-and-then-some in the room.

She didn't think her body's response could inflate much more, but she was wrong. My God! What was happening? What was this? She had never orgasmed like *this* before. Not even on the night Mark had freed her from Ben Wa.

Just when she didn't think she could take much more, an impulsive cry ripped from her throat as her entire body fell into uncontrollable convulsions.

When had she ever come this hard? When had the intensity been so great that she couldn't control her vocal chords *or* her body? Dear Lord! For a moment, the room went dark, even though her eyes were open. She had almost blacked out.

Breathe!

She sucked in a vast gulp of oxygen by sheer force of will, and another involuntary moan stuttered over the spasms in her throat.

She became vaguely aware of Mark slamming into her with a grunt, his entire body going stiff as he growled out, "I'm coming, I'm coming, oh *fuck!*"

And deep within, against that magical little spot he had found with the tip of his erection, he throbbed, filling the condom.

Long moments extended into blissful oblivion, until finally, breathless and spent, Mark gave a final shudder and relaxed into her arms, his face buried against her neck.

The drought was over. She had graduated. She had finally experienced a *real* orgasm, and Mark had been the one to give it, as promised. Cleansing tears streamed from the corners of her eyes as more of the emotional weight she had shouldered for so long eased away, disappearing into the shadows where Old Karma now resided. Where all her old habits, injurious behaviors, and self-doubting thoughts were tucked away. Where the shell she had lived in since junior high quickly filled with cobwebs and dust, because she had shorn that hiding place weeks ago.

Finally, Karma felt like a real woman. The training wheels were off and she stepped into the world changed, mature, all grown-up. This was what it felt like to be with a man who cared about her. A man who respected her and put her pleasure before his own.

"Fuck the chocolate chunk brownie," he said, out of breath, panting hard against her. "That was a chocolate *explosion*."

Karma was too depleted to laugh, but she offered an airy chuff. "You don't say."

His cheeks rose against her skin, so she knew he was smiling. "Told you I would give you one."

A satisfied grin spread over her face. "You could have warned me."

He carefully lifted off her, rolled her to her side, and eased behind her. "And ruin the surprise?" He kissed the back of her shoulder.

"Oh, I doubt anything could have ruined *that*." Every muscle in her body was loose, warm, and satiated, and she smiled as she snuggled against him.

"Now you know why I wanted you to abstain this week."

"Why?" She wasn't sure she saw the connection.

He nuzzled her neck. "Have you heard the expression that absence makes the heart grow fonder?"

"Yes."

"Well, abstaining makes the orgasm stronger." He kissed her ear. "And since I imagine you've faithfully been doing your Kegels, I suspected—correctly, I might add—that if you abstained, you would have one hell of an orgasm tonight."

"You really are a Jedi Master of the Sexual Force, aren't you?"

He chuckled. "Feel the Force moooove inside you." He tried to speak like Yoda but failed. He burrowed closer and nibbled her ear.

"Oh, I felt it."

He squeezed her and kissed her shoulder, the back of her neck, caressed her arm and hip, and played with the fabric of her baby-doll, which she was still wearing. Finally, he laid his head on the pillow behind her and said, "So, will it be Hank or me? It's time to choose."

This time, she did laugh. "Let's put it this way: Hank who?"

His arm tightened around her waist. "That's my girl."

Yes, that she was. His girl. After what they had just done, she had a feeling she would be "his girl" forever, even after he left and went back to Chicago. But now wasn't the time to think about that. Later. She could think about that later. In this moment, all that mattered was that he was here with her now.

An hour later, while watching a movie in bed, Mark peeled Karma out of her lingerie and made love to her one more time before curling her against his body and dozing off, his head tilted toward her as if he could watch her even in slumber. Before he fell asleep, he pulled her arm over his stomach, and his hand lay on her wrist as if he wanted to keep her there.

His chest rose and fell deeply, and the longer Karma watched him sleep, the heavier her eyelids became. She had slept uneasily all week, looking forward to tonight. Now, with the excitement behind her and her body feeling as content and lazy as a cat napping in the sun, the restless nights finally caught up.

Within minutes, with her head nestled on Mark's chest, she was asleep.

Chapter 40

No guts, no glory.
-Major Gen. Frederick C. Blesse

Saturday morning, Mark awoke with his lips resting against the top of Karma's head. He blinked drowsily and smiled.

Last night had been amazing. She had come three times and responded to him better than he'd anticipated. He had expected her to be nervous, more bashful. Instead, she had eagerly and willingly embraced the entire experience, pushing herself into the unknown without a blink, even asking for more at one point.

He brushed his fingertips over her face to push back her hair. Even tousled with mascara rubbing off on her eyelids, she was gorgeous. It made her look sexy. Like a woman who'd just been fucked silly and had lost all inhibition. What a turn-on.

She twitched, and her eyes eased open.

"Oh wow," she said.

"Sleep well?"

She stretched and groaned. "Too well."

"You must have been tired."

She snuggled closer and burrowed her face into his chest, and didn't that just make him feel all warm inside. "Very tired."

"What do you want to do today?" He secured his arm around her waist and held her against him.

Without hesitation, she said, "What we did last night."

He grinned. "I think that's a given." Most definitely. He wouldn't let the day end without a replay of the prior evening.

She sighed and looked up at him, her slender hand flattening against his chest. "What are my choices?"

"Well, I think I need to make you breakfast first. Then shower." His gaze burned into hers. "Hopefully, you'll join me for that so I can show you a few more things worth learning."

Her mouth widened into an expectant smile. "Sure."

He paused a moment as the weight of showering together sank in then said, "I don't want to keep you inside all day, but obviously, going out around here is out of the question."

"Obviously."

In Clover, the odds of running into one of her coworkers were greater. It wasn't worth the risk.

"So, I thought we could drive down to Brown County," he said. Brown County State Park in southern Indiana was large and remote enough that they could spend the day hiking or shopping in the small nearby tourist town of Nashville and not bump into anyone they knew. "The weather's supposed to be beautiful, and we can make a day of it."

"Sounds perfect."

He tapped her bare bottom under the covers. "Okay then. I'll make us breakfast." He kissed her forehead, slipped out of bed, and pulled on a pair of sweats. Then he stepped into the closet and pulled a white box with a pink ribbon around it from the shelf. "This is for you." He sat on the edge of the bed and handed it to her as she sat up and held the burgundy satin over her chest.

"What is it?"

"Just a little something I thought you could use this weekend."

She untied the ribbon and lifted the lid off the box. Inside was a pink and cream satin robe. "Thank you."

"You can wear it for breakfast." He kissed her cheek. "I'll see you downstairs."

Karma watched him go then eased from under the covers. Her whole body hummed. Every muscle ached and sang at the same time, and in such a glorious way. As she slipped her arms through the kimono sleeves of the robe and shrugged the airy material over her shoulders, she pattered to the bathroom.

Her eyes shot wide when she got a look at her reflection. The hair on one side of her head was mashed to her scalp, and flaked-off mascara darkened her eyelids, giving her mock circles under her eyes.

How embarrassing.

Kneeling beside her bag, she dug out her facial cleanser and cotton wipes, cursing herself for falling asleep before removing her makeup. In a flurry of agitation, she washed her face then hurriedly brushed out her hair before securing it with a scrunchie.

Much better. Not as scary.

When she joined Mark downstairs a couple of minutes later, he was ladling pancake batter onto a griddle. Bacon sizzled in an iron skillet.

She sat at the bar. "Smells good. Do I smell peanut butter?"

He set the bowl of batter to the side and wiped his hands on a towel. "Mm-hm. Peanut butter pancakes. It's kind of a specialty."

The man never ceased to amaze her. "I suppose you won't give me the recipe?"

"We'll see." He winked at her then turned the bacon.

After breakfast—and yes, the pancakes were amazing—he took her back upstairs, turned on the shower, pulled the scrunchie from her hair, and helped her out of her robe.

She wore nothing underneath.

"How about that shower?" he said.

She was pretty sure she was about to get her first taste of shower sex, especially when he grinned mischievously and pulled a condom from the drawer under the sink.

He set the condom on the shelf that held bottles of shampoo and soap, took her hand, and tugged her under the cascading water.

"Let me guess," he said, "you've never had sex in the shower."

"No."

"Do you want to?" His gaze fell to her breasts as he swirled the tip of his index finger around her nipple, making it form a tight peak.

Water spilled over his chest, and the hair flattened against his skin. "Yes."

His mouth widened into a pleased grin then he bent and took her nipple between his lips.

She dipped her head back and dug her fingers into his wet hair. Now that they had opened the gates to this new dimension of their relationship, it was as if they'd been together forever. Touching him was easy. Being touched by him was easy. Letting him see her naked was as normal and effortless as breathing. In less than twelve hours, she had overcome almost all her inhibitions.

"Turn around for me," he said, straightening and nudging her toward the wall.

She did as he said, and he eased her forward.

"Put your hands on the wall." He took hold of her wrists and lifted her arms.

"What are you doing?" She glanced over her shoulder and saw him rip open the condom.

A moment later, his left arm circled her waist and he pressed in closer behind her. "You'll like this."

"This?"

Then his fingers were on her, parting her, guiding his penis into place. "Yes, *this*." His voice sounded hot, gruff, on the verge of breaking.

In one smooth glide, he was inside her, and his hands gripped her hips. Oh, now this was different. She immediately felt the contact with her G-spot. Now she knew what he meant by *this.*

"I feel it," she said, closing her eyes as he penetrated her again and rocked her forward.

"And what do you feel?" His voice came from right beside her ear. His whiskered chin scratched her shoulder.

"My G-spot," she said breathlessly. "You're hitting my G-spot."

He thrust into her, a bit more forcefully, making her gasp as he hit her special place again.

"That's right," he said. "Taking you from behind allows me to stimulate you better, especially when you tilt your hips this way." He applied pressure with his hands and angled her hips so that her back arched, showing her what he meant. When he surged into her again, the contact was harder, more direct. And a bolt of pleasure rippled viciously down her legs.

"Oh!"

"You like that?" He thrust again, then again before she could reply.

"Yes. God yes." She slapped one palm against the wet tile wall.

"Was Hank ever this good?" He practically pounded himself inside her.

"No!" In no time at all, her body was on the verge of something cataclysmic, her legs shuddering, her muscles quivering.

"I told you I would take care of you, didn't I?" He was practically growling.

"Yes! Oh my God!" Over and over, his erection assaulted her pleasure zone. Each thrust awakened another set of nerve endings, lighting up her body on its way to another blinding climax.

"I promised I would make you come." His grip on her hips was almost brutal, but she didn't care. If he bruised her, at least the bruises would be shaped like his hands.

"Yes!" She practically saw stars, hovering over yet another soul-rupturing, Mark Strong-induced orgasm.

He released her hips and clamped his hands down on her breasts. His fingers pinched both nipples at the same time he closed he lips over the side of her neck and laved her with his tongue.

Explosion!

The invisible fuse from her vagina to her neck and breasts ignited, and a snap later, as she shrieked in pleasure, every muscle in her body contracted at once then blew apart. Her legs spasmed as Mark continued pumping relentlessly into her, stimulating her beyond comprehension, then he, too, shuddered with release.

He grunted against her neck, his arms once more secured around her waist.

Moments later, breathing hard, her cheek pressed against the wall, she opened her eyes. Mark's forehead rested on her shoulder, his soaked hair hanging over his face. She could still feel him pulsing inside her.

After another few seconds, he opened his eyes, blinked drowsily, smiled, then lifted his head. "*Now* it's a good morning."

That it was.

An hour later, Karma sat in the passenger seat of his BMW as they hopped on the interstate. A cooler filled with water, a container of green grapes, and turkey and lettuce sandwiches on Italian bread sat on the floor of the backseat. The drive to Brown County was long, but by eleven o'clock, they arrived, ate lunch, and spent the next three hours hiking. Of course, Mark had chosen one of the more challenging trails, which required climbing up and down a few ridges. They spotted a pair of eagles, a fox, and a doe with her fawn. Eventually, they made their way to the horse barn and took a thirty minute guided ride.

After spending a few hours in the park, they drove into Nashville, wandered among the quaint shops, had a dinner of roasted chicken, mashed potatoes, and fried okra, and ordered biscuits and apple butter for dessert at a cozy country café decorated with blue and white checkered walls and wood tables. Mark liked the apple butter so much that he bought a dozen jars to take home, promising six to Karma.

By the time they left for the two-hour drive home, it was after seven o'clock.

Once back at his condo, Mark carried in their things while she went upstairs and took a bath. He showered downstairs then joined her in bed.

"I think you got a little sunburned," she said, noting his reddened cheeks and nose.

"So did you." He pulled her on top of him and pushed the tips of his fingers under the back of the tank top she was wearing.

"I had on sunscreen, so it's not that bad." She settled against him.

He kissed her. "No, not that bad." His hands roamed more freely as he pulled her down.

She rested her head on his chest, listening to his heartbeat. Like the rest of him, the cadence was full and strong.

For a while, he simply caressed her back, saying nothing, but she could feel him getting harder. Her breathing deepened. He smelled clean but outdoorsy, his subtle masculine scent breaking through that of his soap.

"I was wondering," he said a couple of minutes later, "when you might like to show me what you've learned from those books you've been reading. You know, about how to give a man pleasure."

Was he asking her to go down on him?

"Is it too soon?" he pushed against her shoulders, making her sit up. He searched her face, his gaze hopeful yet cautious.

She nibbled her bottom lip. "Um…"

His palms smoothed up and down her back. "I like when you touch me with your hands, but I'm wondering how good your mouth would feel." He brought his hands around to her thighs. "Am I asking too much?"

She wanted to do this. Wasn't that why she had read those books in the first place?

"Right now?" Her eyes met his.

"I'll even turn off the light if it makes you more comfortable." He reached over and clicked off the lamp on the bedside table, throwing the room into darkness except for the night-light plugged into the wall by the bathroom door.

Nerves fluttered in her stomach. Mark would be the first man to experience her naïve oral talents. But if she hadn't planned on giving him a blow job at some point, she wouldn't have bought those books on how to give stellar head. The only problem was she had zero faith in her amateur abilities. And what if he came in her mouth? Was that what he expected? She wasn't sure she could do that.

"You're overthinking it, honey."

She met his eyes. "I'm sorry. I just—"

"I won't come in your mouth, if that's what you're worried about."

She blushed and looked away, embarrassed, before meeting his eyes again. "How did you know I was thinking about that?"

His lips curved into a sympathetic smile. "You looked apprehensive. So I assumed."

With a lift of her eyebrows, she nodded. "I am…was…am. A little."

He placed his hand over his heart. "Well, I promise to be good and not do that. I just want to feel you."

She bit her bottom lip, considering the situation. Finally, she said, "I trust you. I'm just nervous."

"I'll help." He took her hands and kissed each one before lowering them to the waist of his sweats.

She scooted down between his thighs, and he lifted his hips off the mattress. With his help, she maneuvered his sweats and undershorts off his legs then took a deep breath as she situated herself on her knees and took his erection in her hand.

He drew in a sharp breath, almost as if he hadn't been expecting her to touch him so quickly.

She smiled sheepishly. "Sorry."

"No…it's okay." He took her wrist and held her hand in place before she could pull away.

"I'm not very good at this." She hung her head. Seriously, her confidence in giving good fellatio was about a negative five on a scale of one to ten. Even with all her reading, she was still just a newbie. Book smarts didn't make up for real world experience.

"I'm a man, Karma."

She met his shadowed gaze. "What do you mean?"

Another of those award-winning smiles closed the distance from his heart to hers. "It means that any head is good head. Men don't distinguish between good and bad when it comes to blow jobs. If a woman's mouth is on it, it's good. Trust me."

Well, since he put it that way.

He must have sensed that she was still unsure, though, because he wrapped his hand around hers. "I'll help you. Would you like that?"

His strong fingers slipped between hers, and his palm gripped her hand securely as he pulled her fist up his shaft to the head.

"Yes," she whispered, fascinated by the smooth, velvety feel of his skin over such a hard interior.

His penis didn't look as smooth as it felt. Veins protruded the length from the base to the ridge that separated head from shaft, but other than the natural feel of edged muscle, engorged with blood, he was as smooth as a tube of sugar cookie dough.

His erection was curved, too. Not perfectly straight as she'd thought. It arced slightly like a bow, as if the head wanted to curve back toward him. Was that why he felt so good inside her? Did he hit her differently because he was curved? Perhaps in a way that helped her achieve orgasm more easily? It was like his curved penis was made to hit her just right inside. Not that the curve was that pronounced, but she had to wonder if penis shape had anything to do with her own pleasure, given all she had read about the different types of penises and how each shape had a different effect.

"Slow and easy," he said, bringing her mind back to him. "Not too much pressure." His fingers loosened, indicating what he liked, and she in turn slightly loosened her grip.

"Like that?" She watched his face closely, looking for signs that she was doing it right.

"Yes. Perfect." His chest rose, and his pecs rippled. Then he breathed out a contented sigh. "I like a little manual stimulation before…"

"Before oral stimulation," she offered.

A distracted chuckle rumbled from his throat. "Yes."

For another minute more, he helped her stroke him in long, even caresses.

"Give me your other hand," he said, reaching out.

She did, and he directed her below his erection and placed her palm on his scrotum. Without saying a word, he manipulated her fingers, rolling the healthy twin weights against her palm.

"Mmmmm." He closed his eyes. "I like that, too. A lot."

His erection grew more rigid against her palm, and she licked her lips. His reaction made her naturally want to take him further. Without even thinking, she leaned forward and, taking the cues he'd given, she simply brushed her lips over the head. Just a simple, slow, back and forth motion.

His entire body lifted, tensed, and then relaxed as he groaned. "Yeeesss. God, that's perfect."

The glans felt just as velvety soft as the rest of him, smooth and firm. Parting her lips, she closed them again in a series of sensual, pouty kisses. Feeling his body's shuddering reaction, and hearing the way his breathing increased and the way he groaned his approval, she continued the slow build and outlined the ridge between tip and shaft with her tongue, licking one long, luxurious line all the way around before closing her mouth over the top inch, just the way her books had taught her.

"Fuck." The word bit out like the snap of a rubber band, and he let go of her hands and reached for the lamp. The light on the nightstand came back on, and he drove his fingers back into her hair, pushing it off her face.

When she looked up through her lashes, his chin was on his chest, his mouth open, eyes glazed and hungry.

"That's good. Very nice." His hips pressed forward involuntarily, but only a little, not enough to drive him deeper into her mouth. "Use your hand and mouth together," he said. "As you take me in, stroke down. And when you pull away, stroke up. Please?"

Well, since he said please.

She did as instructed, taking things slow to get the feel. He seemed to like it slow, because he nodded, letting her know she was doing it right, and his hands gripped her scalp more firmly as his hips got a bit more involved.

"Is this okay?" He said between clenched teeth.

She nodded, her mouth too busy to answer as she hollowed out her cheeks and applied a touch of suction.

"God. Damn. Karma." His shoulders and arms flexed and bunched, and his chest tightened.

Okay, so she was better at this than she thought.

"Stop," he said, pushing her as he gasped. "You need to stop. Oh God."

She sucked her mouth off the end with a pop. A moment later, with his face scrunched tightly, he groaned as semen shot out and landed on his stomach. His erection jerked in her hand, over and over, as he continued to come. It was sensual and fascinating the way his body convulsed and twitched, the way his breathing hitched, the way his hands fisted the sheets as he shivered through each wave.

After a long moment passed, Mark opened his eyes and grinned. "Sorry. I didn't mean to—"

"No, it's okay. I liked it." Watching him come—from just her mouth—was thrilling. Arousing.

He blew out an unsteady breath. "I wasn't expecting that." With his eyelids barely parted, he exhaled again then licked his lips. "You give undeniably good head."

Pride bloomed in her chest. "I do?"

He grabbed a tissue and smirked as he wiped off his stomach. "Duh." He tossed the tissue on the floor and took her hand. "Come here."

She slid up his body and laid her head on his shoulder.

He kissed her temple. "Give me a few minutes to recover and I'll pay you back."

"A few minutes?"

An amused rumble rolled in his chest. "Okay, maybe fifteen or twenty. That was pretty damn good."

Yes, it was. She had enjoyed giving him head. Such power. To hold him literally in the palm of her hand, inside her mouth, and lift him to the height of pleasure with her lips and tongue was more erotic than she could have imagined.

She was beginning to think there was nothing she couldn't do now that Mark was paving the way.

Chapter 41

"Nothing happens by chance."
-Paulo Coelho

Over the next few weeks, Mark and Karma thoroughly explored each other's bodies. For the time being, both seemed content to keep the sex simple. Nothing too acrobatic, too wild. Mark explained that first they needed to become comfortable with one another. Then they could become more inventive.

Karma's relationship with her dad remained strained, but she made it clear she didn't want her time with Mark to end until it had to. To be honest, Mark didn't, either. The more time he spent with her, the more time he *wanted* to spend, and as their affair evolved and she became more comfortable making love to him, the more eager he was to see her.

So, when Mark heard about the Fourth of July celebration in downtown Indianapolis, he decided to make the holiday, which landed on a Saturday this year, even more special and reserved a hotel suite in the Marriott, making sure with the reservation clerk that the room faced the direction of the fireworks.

Everything was set, and the weekend promised to be perfect.

The Thursday before the holiday, after spending the night with Karma, he arrived to work late—something he had never done before meeting her, but which felt perversely thrilling—Mark turned the corner at the top of the stairs, smiling as she came into view.

Her gaze lifted secretively to his, and color touched her cheeks, making her look like she had a sunburn. Even after reaching the pinnacle of intimacy with one another, he could still make her blush.

"Good morning, Karma. You look rested this morning."

"I feel rested, thank you."

He smiled, stopped at her desk, and gazed down appreciatively at the ensemble she had put together while he lay in bed and watched her get dressed. Her new skirt revealed more leg than usual, and the blouse she had bought to go with it exposed more of her modest cleavage. A few months ago, he imagined she never would have worn such an outfit.

Lisa appeared from around the corner, carrying a coffee mug. "Good morning, Mark. How are you today?" Lisa had become a stalwart ally in helping them maintain their secret relationship, and he had grown fond of her.

"I'm well this morning," he said. "You look nice."

She glanced down at her patterned summer dress, which hung almost to the floor. "Thank you. Karma and I went shopping last weekend." Lisa winked at Karma as she dropped a file on her desk. "Well, I should be getting back to my office. Just wanted to bring by some paperwork for Don." She pointed to the folder. "I'll talk to you two later."

"Bye, Lisa." Karma stood and motioned in the direction of the coffee station. "Coffee?" she said to Mark.

"Yes, please."

Don was already in his office as Mark passed by. "Good morning, Don." He waved in.

"Morning, Mark."

Today, he and Don needed to review a few personnel issues. The time to start making some hard decisions was fast approaching.

As he pulled out his laptop, he glanced over as Karma brought in his coffee.

Will that be all?" she said coquettishly.

"No." He kept his voice quiet.

"What else do you need?" She dropped her voice, as well.

He licked his lips and let his gaze drop to her skirt, which hit above the knee. "I need to know what you're wearing under your skirt, *Miss Mason.*"

She bit her bottom lip for an instant before smiling and whispering, "You already know. You watched me put it on this morning."

He narrowed his eyes and skimmed them down her body. "Well, tell me, anyway."

With a lick of her lips, she grinned and said, "I'm wearing a thong. A black, lacy one. Does that work for you?"

He leaned in and grinned. "Yes, that works for me just fine, thank you."

"Thought so." With that, she turned on her pretty black high heel and swished her slim hips as she returned to her desk.

Don entered the conference room a few minutes later, closed the door, and sat down across from him.

"Okay, so we're getting to the hard part," Mark said, shifting his mind from Karma's black thong to the meeting.

Don nodded. "Yes."

Mark had been alluding to the pending personnel discussion for over a week.

"This is the least favorite of all my tasks." Mark tapped a key on his laptop and brought up the report. "And, just as a reminder, this is only a preliminary discussion."

"I saw that Karma's name is on the list," Don said, concerned.

There was no way Karma was going anywhere. After observing her aside from their extracurricular activities, it was clear she was too valuable to the company.

"This report automatically lists administrative staff. You'll see that Nancy and Jolene are also on the list, as well as Phil's assistant." Phil was Solar's owner, president, and CEO.

Not that the list was long. There were only ten out of nearly a hundred employees pointed out for suggested termination. He figured six of them would need to go. Karma, Nancy, Phil's assistant, and one other, a member of IT, would stay, so long as Nancy was willing to take on extra responsibilities. Right now, she was underutilized but more productive than Jolene. And Jolene needed to go for a lot of reasons. Other than making too many mistakes and possessing an atrocious work ethic, she was also too much of a gossip. Karma already did the brunt of Jolene's job because the sales and marketing staff had little confidence in Jo's abilities. And if Jo even knew what the term confidential meant, Mark would be surprised. And, lastly, sleeping with your married boss, who happened to be the son-in-law of the company's president, was too out-of-bounds even for Mark's tastes, and he thought of himself as pretty nonjudgmental about other people's personal lives.

Mark leaned forward and threaded his fingers together. "Don, I can see you're worried. Trust me. Karma's not going anywhere. I'm very good at what I do, and I can see how valuable she is. Believe me. I know what's going on. I know she does half, if not more, of Jolene's job."

There was a moment of silence before Don spoke again. "You're going to recommend Jolene's termination?"

Mark nodded. "Yes. She's not pulling her weight, she spends too much time stirring up gossip and spreading rumors, and she's just not contributing. She's dead weight, Don. She's dragging the company down."

"Jake will fight you."

"He already tried."

"You've already spoken to Jake about this?"

He had stopped by Jake's office a few weeks ago when Jolene had been exiting. She had looked guilty, and both of them had been flushed, their clothes rumpled. Jake and Jo could take a lesson from him and Karma about how to have a proper office romance. Rule number one was never fuck at work unless you knew you wouldn't get caught or could hide it well. Jake and Jo had failed on both counts.

"Yes."

"And…?"

"Like you said, he resisted at first, but he eventually agreed." All Mark had needed to do was drop a subtle hint that he knew about Jake's inappropriate relationship with Jolene to convince him that releasing Jo was the right decision. Jake was more worried about not letting his wife and Phil find out he was screwing his admin than he was in sticking his neck out on Jo's behalf.

So much for those good looks Jolene relied on to get her out of troubled waters.

Don nodded and sighed as he crossed his arms and rocked back in the chair. "He does like Jolene." He sounded like he was choosing his words carefully, as if he, too, knew about Jake and Jo's relationship. "But when it comes to getting the job done, he prefers Karma."

Mark leaned back, his hands still linked in front of his body. "Do you have a problem sharing Karma with Jake's department?"

Don shook his head. "No. But that's a lot of work for one person to do."

Mark explained his idea to redistribute the administrative tasks to incorporate Nancy more in higher level functions, which would loosen Karma's schedule.

"That could work nicely for all involved," Don said. "I think that's more than do-able."

"Karma's a valuable employee. She's smart, efficient, resourceful." He knew her passion rested in writing, but she was good at her job here. "She's a real asset."

"I've been very pleased with her," Don said.

"Likewise." That sentiment held dual meaning for Mark. "She's quite capable. I think she just needs a subtle nudge, and the possibilities are endless."

"I can tell you've been working with her," Don said, his eyes shrewd. "Since you arrived, her confidence has really improved. I've never seen her so eager to dig into new projects. You've been good for her, Mark."

He smiled, thinking of all the ways Karma had changed in the last two months. "I just recognize talent, and I enjoy bringing the best out of people. It's been fulfilling to watch her grow."

Don nodded emphatically. "Yes, it has. In two years, I've not been able to tap in to that talent the way you have in less than two months. She just seems so much more confident now. Everything about her has changed." Don met Mark's eyes in such a way that gave Mark pause. He was an expert in body language and nonverbal communications, and he could swear from the look on Don's face that he was aware of what was going on between him and Karma. If he was, he didn't pursue it. Maybe Mark was just overreacting.

A bit ill at ease, Mark averted his gaze and quickly forged ahead. "Well, rest assured, I plan on recommending her to stay, and I am also going to suggest a healthy raise. She deserves it, especially since we'll be loosening up salaries by letting a few others go. Would you agree?"

"Definitely."

"Good. We can discuss that when the time comes." Mark glanced down at his report. "Okay, let's talk about Ken." Don's demeanor had unnerved him, and he was eager to move on. "Ken is—" His cell phone rang, cutting him off. One look at the caller ID made him frown. Chicago Police Department? Why would he be getting a call from the CPD?

"Excuse me. I need to take this." He held up his index finger. "Hello?"

"Hello. Is this Mark Strong?"

"Speaking."

"Yes, Mr. Strong. This is Captain Cole from the Chicago Police Department. There was an incident earlier at your apartment. How soon can you meet us there?"

Mark stood and paced toward the window. "What kind of incident?"

"Someone broke in. One of your neighbors found the door forced open. Our guys are there now."

Was this a joke?

"What? Wait a minute. Are you saying someone broke into my apartment?"

"Yes. We're investigating now, but—"

Mark began gathering his things. "There are officers at my apartment now?"

"Yes."

Great. His apartment was crawling with police and he was over two hours away. How the hell had someone gotten inside his apartment? His building was secure. "Is everything okay? Is anything missing?"

"We don't know. Place has been tossed. Can you come home and take a look around?"

"I'm in Indianapolis on business, but yes, I'm leaving right away."

"I'm sorry about this, Mr. Strong."

"Not your fault, Captain. Thanks for calling."

He hung up and continued shoving papers into his bag. "I have to go. Someone broke into my apartment."

Don was already on his feet. "So I gathered. Everything okay?"

"The police are there now." He shut down his laptop. "My apologies, but we'll have to finish this next week." Damn it! He'd have to cancel his date this weekend with Karma, too. Their special night downtown…and all the planning and reservations…all of it ruined by some idiot who had decided to play cops and robbers.

"Don't worry about it, Mark. Get home. Make sure everything's okay."

With a brisk nod, he hefted his bag over his shoulder and marched toward the door. As soon as he opened it and set eyes on Karma, he knew she could tell something was wrong.

"I'll see you week after next, Miss Mason," he said, willing her not to behave out of character.

To Karma's credit, she adjusted quickly. "What's wrong? Is everything okay?"

"I've got an emergency back in Chicago. Someone broke into my apartment."

She gasped. "Oh no. Is everything all right?"

"I'm on my way to find out," he said.

"I'm sorry." Disappointment touched her pale eyes, but she quickly replaced it with concern.

He paused for just a heartbeat. "I'm sorry, too."

He was sorry for having to cancel, for not being able to be here, for having to bail on their weekend.

He tore himself away before he revealed too much of his feelings and hurried down the hall.

Once in his car, he typed out a quick text to Karma. *So sorry about tonight. Was looking forward to it. Call you later.*

He started the engine and pulled out into traffic as his phone dinged. At the stoplight, he read her reply. *Was looking forward to it, too. But this is more important. Talk to you later. xo*

He smiled at the xo. Before the light turned green, he sent another text. *Will make it up to you. Promise. Xoxo.*

Then he called Rob to ask him to go over to his place and hold CPD until he got there.

So much for best-laid plans.

Chapter 42

Don't look back. You're not going that way.
-Marcia Wallace

By the time Mark arrived home and met Rob and Captain Cole at his disheveled apartment, CPD had caught the suspects: a couple of teenagers who lived in the building and apparently got bored and took a dare from a friend to break into one of the apartments.

Lucky Mark. He couldn't win the lottery, but he could be the one in a hundred chosen at random to be robbed.

The kids had left his place in shambles, but they had taken only three items: a gold watch, a diamond necklace, and a pair of matching wedding rings from where they had been tucked and forgotten inside the small, wooden chest on his dresser for the last six years, otherwise, he would have secured them in his safe.

After the kids apologized profusely and returned what they'd stolen, Rob headed out, and Mark spent a couple hours looking around for anything else that was missing. He also called his bank and all his credit card companies to request new accounts and to close the old ones. His files had been rifled through, and he didn't want to take the risk. After he was sure everything else was covered and okay, he tossed the stolen items in his duffel, along with a pair of sweats, tennis shoes, and a T-shirt, and headed over to Rob's, leaving the building superintendent to secure the door, which the building manager had agreed to replace tomorrow. Mark had told him to add an extra deadbolt. He wasn't taking chances.

By the time he reached Rob's place, it was after eight o'clock.

"Hey," Rob said, opening the door to his brownstone and standing aside. "Everything back to normal at your place?"

"Getting there. They've got a special lock on my door. The super will install a new one in the morning. By the way, thanks for coming over and helping." He dropped his duffel on the couch and plopped down beside it as Rob took the recliner across from him.

"No problem."

Mark rubbed his palms over his face. "I can't believe two stupid kids caused this much trouble. Because they were *bored.*" He gave Rob an exasperated, can-you-believe-that-shit look.

Exhaustion wilted his shoulders. The drive back had been long and tiring, and he was angry with the kids for taking him away from his job, Karma, and their weekend getaway. He couldn't abide chaos or having his routine fucked with like that.

"Did you find anything else missing?" Rob picked up the remote and turned down the volume on the TV.

Mark let his hands fall to the side as he slouched. His voice sounded as tired as he felt. "No. Just my watch, the diamond necklace I bought for Carol, and our wedding bands."

As angry as he was with the kids for messing up the normalcy in his life, he was angrier that they had reawakened old memories from a time he had worked hard to forget. Just seeing that necklace again, and especially those wedding bands, had seriously fucked with his head.

Rob seemed to sense this and got up, went to the kitchen, and brought back a pair of Budweisers.

"Good man," he said, taking one and twisting off the cap.

"I ordered food, too." Rob checked the clock. "Should be here any minute."

Mark tipped back his beer and drank. When he pulled the bottle from his lips, he said, "Very good man. I'm starving. Haven't eaten since breakfast."

"I figured."

For a while, neither of them said anything, keeping their eyes glued to ESPN and the baseball game.

"You doing okay?" Rob said.

"Yeah, sure." Mark frowned and absently fiddled with the label on his bottle. "Why wouldn't I be?"

Rob shrugged. "No reason. Just that your apartment was broken into, you had to drive back from Indy to deal with the fallout, and what those guys took was pretty personal. I mean, your wedding bands and—"

Mark held up a hand. "I'm fine. I don't want to talk about her." Or the necklace. Or the rings. He wanted to think about Karma, not Carol.

Rob held his hands up in surrender. "Okay, okay. I'm sorry."

Silence fell again, and Rob seemed to get real interested real fast in the baseball game.

But Mark's mind was short-circuiting down memory lane to the day six years ago that had changed everything.

He had been standing at the altar. His hands had been clasped in front of him, and he had been eager to begin the rest of his life with the woman he loved.

He remembered looking proudly over his shoulder at Rob, his best man, who grinned and nodded back. The minister stood in front of him, smiling benignly, a genial expression plastered on his face, his Bible tucked against his torso inside folded arms. Nine white candles flickered in a silver candelabra, which was shaped like an arrow pointing toward heaven and was set on the high altar behind the minister. More than three hundred guests chattered quietly as they prepared for the ceremony.

This moment had been all Mark could think about for months. The life he had planned was finally going to become reality. Today, he and Carol would become man and wife, and after their honeymoon in Mexico, they would buy a house. Carol didn't know it, yet, but Mark had already been working with a realtor and had a line on the perfect four-bedroom two-story with a basement in the richest suburb of Chicago that would go up for sale in the next couple of weeks. It was perfect for their family. After getting settled in their new home, he would focus on his consulting career, and Carol would continue competing, then in two years, they would have their first child. Maybe even get a dog. A golden retriever. And two or three years later, they would have their second child, and their kids would go to the best schools. Mark had it all planned out.

He fought to contain the almost giddy feeling bubbling inside him. Most men didn't get this excited about their wedding day, but Mark wasn't like most men. He had never walked the beaten path and wouldn't start now. He proudly admitted his love. Carol was beautiful, smart, and his parents' star pupil. She had just won her first national dancing championship, and she was poised to rule the professional dance circuit for many years to come. Not a day went by when he didn't tell her he loved her, and the two of them would become one of Chicago's top power couples.

The organist started playing "Here Comes the Bride," and Mark exchanged smiles with Rob once more as the guests rose in a whoosh of movement and turned toward the back of the church.

Seconds ticked by, and Mark stood tall, shoulders back, his excitement rising the longer the wedding march played.

Time stretched, and the guests began looking at one another, frowning, questions in their eyes, but Mark ignored them and kept his gaze locked on the foot of the aisle, waiting…waiting for his bride to appear. He didn't want to miss his first glimpse of her in her dress. She would be lovely, more beautiful than he could imagine.

The music suddenly cut off, and Mark frowned and looked toward Rob, whose brow crinkled as he set his jaw.

What was going on? Where was Carol?

The maid of honor, a friend of Carol's named Stacy, hurried around the corner and walked briskly up the aisle, her face red, her eyes skittish and filled with pity.

A low murmur sprouted throughout the church as the guests glanced around, looking for the happy bride-to-be, and then turned concerned eyes toward him. A sinking feeling tore at his heart. Something wasn't right.

Stacy finally reached him, leaned forward, and whispered, "I'm sorry, but Carol isn't coming."

"What?" He didn't understand. "What do you mean? Is she okay? Has something happened?" Surely, he misunderstood. Stacy must have meant to tell him Carol was simply delayed, not that she wouldn't be there at all.

Stacy took a heavy breath and looked away. "I'm sorry, Mark, but..." Her shoulders sagged. "She told me to give you this." She haphazardly shoved a lavender envelope into his hand then hurried back down the aisle and out the door.

He stared down at the envelope and dread sank into his soul. It was Carol's stationery. He turned away from the guests as Rob joined him.

"What's wrong?" Rob said.

"I...I don't know." Mark couldn't fathom what was happening. He ripped open the envelope and pulled out a folded piece of lavender notepaper.

The rumble in the church began to strengthen, and Mark's parents left their seats at the front pew to investigate, but Mark didn't hear their questions. His brain was too busy trying to process the note in his hand.

Mark,

I'm so sorry, but I can't marry you. I thought I could make it work, but I can't. I'm so, so sorry, but I'm in love with someone else. I should have told you, but I couldn't. I'm giving back the ring. I never should have accepted it in the first place. I'm so sorry. So very sorry about all of this. I hope you can forgive me.

Carol

He reached into the envelope and pulled out her engagement ring. The one with the fat diamond he had given her eight months ago.

In an instant, the life he had so meticulously planned, which had seemed so perfect and within his grasp only a couple of minutes ago, disappeared. And not just disappeared, but exploded with such force that Mark felt it all the way to the soles of his feet. It was like a bomb had blown up in his chest.

In front of everyone, Carol had left him standing alone, to tell their friends and family that she didn't love him…didn't want him. God, he felt like a fucking reject. An idiot.

The minister's merciful smile almost made him sick, and the flames on the candles stung his eyes like needles. Or maybe that was just his tears. He couldn't be sure. Rob, his parents, the minister, and so many others gathered around him, imploring him about what had happened, but he couldn't hear a word they said. Distress wrapped itself around his heart. An inconsolable sorrow so profound that he didn't think he would ever recover wormed its way into his soul.

What had he done wrong? Why had Carol left him on their wedding day?

He closed his eyes and tried to breathe. He had failed. Somehow, in some way, he had failed her. And now the life he had so carefully planned was over.

It was supposed to have been the happiest day of his life, and instead the day became his own personal apocalypse.

He had never seen the freight train coming, and then there it was, cutting him down and slicing him into pieces.

He turned toward Rob and held out his hand. "Give me the rings."

Rob pulled the box from his pocket and handed it over. Mark opened the lid, set the diamond engagement ring inside, and snapped the lid closed.

Then he glanced at the faces on her side of the church. How many of them had known the truth? Her parents. Had they known? Her mom didn't look too surprised. How many knew that she didn't love him and wanted someone else? Why hadn't they told him? Couldn't they have cared enough to save his feelings and all this fucking, goddamn humiliation? He had become the butt of a cruel joke. A laughingstock to be pointed at and ridiculed, just like he had been in school. Only this hurt a hundred times worse, because his greatest disgrace came at the hands of the woman he loved.

He looked back at Rob. "Can I borrow your keys?"

Without question, Rob pulled them from his pocket and handed them over.

Dishonored and shamed, he cleared his throat and addressed the crowd. "I'm sorry for the inconvenience, but there isn't going to be a wedding today."

He regarded Rob and his parents then stepped down from the raised platform at the front of the church, marched up the aisle, and right out the door to Rob's car. His was at the hotel where he and Carol were to spend their wedding night before tomorrow morning's flight to Cancun.

He had to talk to her. Had to find out what had gone wrong and why she had done this. What had happened? Where had he failed? He had to know. Maybe if she told him, he could fix this and win her back. He couldn't imagine his life without Carol. He loved her, and he had already planned their entire life together. They would be married, buy a home, and in a couple of years start a family. He already had names picked out for their kids, as well as for the golden retriever that would be the family pet. The next ten years were all planned. He couldn't lose her now, and especially not without a fight.

Arriving at the brownstone she had insisted on keeping even when he suggested they move in together, he didn't bother knocking. He barged in. He had every right to. She was his fiancée, and she was supposed to have been his wife. When he didn't find her downstairs, he climbed the stairs two at a time and threw the door open to her bedroom…to find her in bed with Antonio, her dance partner. The man her parents had partnered her with a year-and-a-half earlier. She was *fucking* the guy when she was supposed to be getting married, and her wedding dress lay discarded on the floor. Talk about your slaps in the face.

"Mark!" She grabbed the blanket and pulled it over herself. Antonio at least had the decency to look ashamed. Small consolation given the circumstances.

Mark staggered backward and slammed into the wall outside her room. He was going to be sick. He ran to the bathroom and fell to his knees over the commode, hanging on while his stomach emptied. He loved her. Loved her so damn much. How could she do this? Why hadn't he seen the truth? What had he done wrong to push her into Antonio's arms?

"Just give me a minute," he heard her say to Antonio. Then he heard the sound of her pretty feet beating on the floor as she hurried down the hall toward the bathroom.

He was still heaving air when she entered and shut the door.

"What are you doing here?" she said.

Not "What's wrong?" Not "Are you okay?" Not "I'm sorry." But "What are you doing here?" As if he were to blame for her duplicity. As if *he* had been the one to jilt *her*. "Didn't you get my note?"

Was she serious?

"Yes, I got your note!" He was finally able to swallow and looked up at her. The last tears he would ever cry trailed down his cheeks. "Why the fuck else do you think I'm here, Carol? For fuck's sake, I thought…I wanted…what the FUCK! You left me standing there like a fucking fool!"

She looked affronted but at least chagrined. "I…I'm sorry, Mark. I truly am, but…" Tears formed in her eyes, and she averted her gaze. "Mark, I don't love you. I don't, okay? I'm sorry. I love Antonio. I want to be with him, not you." She bowed her head and crossed her arms tightly over her robe as if hugging herself.

"Thanks for waiting until our WEDDING DAY to TELL ME THAT!"

"I'M SORRY!" Tears fell to her cheeks. Then she cowered as if trying to rein in her emotions. "Okay, Mark? I'm sorry," she said more softly. "I didn't know how to tell you."

They remained in silence a long time. Mark crouched next to the toilet. Carol hugging herself by the door.

Empty suffering expanded inside his chest. "How long, Carol?" His gut told him he wasn't going to like her answer, but he had to know. He lifted his gaze to hers. "How long have you and Antonio been together?"

She blanched and pulled her robe more tightly around her as if he had never seen her naked. "Mark, let's talk about this later, okay?" She glanced toward the door.

"No. I want to know right now, Carol. How long has this been going on?"

She gulped.

He stood. "Tell me!"

She jumped and looked away, fighting back tears.

He grabbed her arms and shook her. "How fucking long have you been fucking your partner, Carol!"

Her gaze jerked around at his harsh tone. "Since the beginning!" She shoved him away. "Since the beginning! Okay? I've been seeing him since he became my dance partner!"

He stumbled back and nearly fell into the tub. If there had been anything left to upchuck, he would have tossed the rest of his cookies all over the floor. As it was, all he could do was dry-heave.

"I'm sorry! Damn it, but I didn't know how to tell you." Carol started crying in earnest. "I tried, but I just…I couldn't."

"Why?" Mark struggled to breathe. That one three-letter word began looping through his mind. Why? Over and over. "Why, Carol?"

Never before had he felt such pain in his chest. He had to be dying. Had to be losing his heart. He couldn't breathe. Everything felt numb and lost its luster. Carol had lied for a year and a half. All this time, she hadn't loved him.

Beautiful Carol. The first and only woman he had ever truly loved. And she had never loved him back.

The only answer Carol gave him was silence, and he was too fucked in the head to give a damn.

Without another word, he vowed never to fall in love again, and he meant it. He was the type who, once he set his mind on something, followed through, and right now, his mind was set on never losing his heart again. He would never set himself up to be burned so badly ever again. He left her home, quit his parents' studio for good, and turned his attention wholeheartedly toward his young career as a consultant…after a brief bout with depression, of course.

That had been six years ago, and until those stupid kids had stolen the necklace he had planned on giving to Carol on their honeymoon, as well as the wedding bands and the engagement ring he had tucked away, he had been doing a decent job forgetting the worst part of his past.

Sure, Karma had begun to awaken old ghosts weeks ago. But never like this. Never in such a painful, heart-splitting way. Those damn kids had stirred old emotions, old fears. The fact they had broken in and tossed his home was inconsequential in the face of deeper wounds.

Now, sitting on Rob's couch, nursing a brew, it was like not a day had passed. The pain was just as raw, and the memories much too fresh.

A part of him died that day. Or rather, he had tucked the details of that day away where they couldn't hurt him anymore. Now, a barrier existed around his heart. One that he steadfastly guarded. He was as committed to his vow to keep hold of his heart as much today as he had been in Carol's bathroom. He couldn't risk letting go again. He couldn't let himself fall in love. The price was too great. Look what Carol had done to him, all because he had trusted and loved her.

It had taken months to recover, but really, he never had. Even now, he suffered what felt like post-traumatic stress disorder any time he entered a church. He had to take a Valium just to attend a wedding. Without it, his heart raced, he broke out in a cold sweat, and panic gripped every cell in his body.

That would never be him. Not again. The thought of putting himself out there like that was too painful. Some wounds never healed. They just scarred over. But the damage was still there, under the scar tissue, wreaking havoc.

The doorbell rang and jarred Mark out of his biting reverie.

Rob hopped up. "That's dinner." He hustled to the door.

Mark reached inside his bag and pulled out the velvet-lined box that housed the rings. He had held on to them because, at the time, he couldn't even look at them. Tucking them at the bottom of the small chest on his dresser had been about as much as he could stomach. After a while, he had forgotten about them lying dormant like landmines waiting to be triggered.

Today, those fucking kids had triggered them, and his heart was exploding all over again.

Rob set a couple of pizzas on the coffee table and went to the kitchen to retrieve two more beers, plates, and napkins. While he was gone, Mark pulled his ring free from the velvet slot inside the case. The decoratively etched silver was dull, as was the ribbon of gold that ran all the way around the center, but when he slipped it on his ring finger, it still fit.

"What the hell are you doing?" Rob stopped dead in his tracks as he re-entered the living room.

Mark looked up and yanked off the ring. "Nothing. I..." He frowned as he stuffed the ring back into the box and tossed it inside his bag. "I just..."

"You know how long it took for you to get over that bitch, Mark. Don't go there. Okay? Just...you should get rid of those damn rings." He sat down and handed him a plate before opening one of the pizza boxes. "Sell them to a jeweler or some shit. Or toss them into the fires of Mordor. Whatever works."

Mark scowled and grabbed two slices, dropped them on his plate, and sat back. "I'm fine. I'm not fawning over the past and wishing for a fucking do-over or anything."

"I hope not, for your sake. That woman is poisonous." Rob tipped his beer bottle in Mark's direction. "Take my word, she's like poison ivy and you're severely allergic. Do *not* go there. Even in your mind.

Or you'll be scratching for months"

"I'm not, Rob. Trust me." But where Mark's thoughts were taking him was a place just as dangerous, because he was imagining what would have happened if he and Carol had never met and he and Karma still had. Would he have had his chance at happiness then? With Karma? Because then he wouldn't have been damaged goods.

But he didn't need to get soft and think he and Karma had a future, no matter how much he liked her. That was perilous territory for his mind and heart.

After dinner, Rob disappeared to his bedroom and changed. A few minutes later, he came back to the living room and stopped by the couch. "I'm meeting a friend for drinks. You want to tag along?"

Mark was in no mood to go out. Not only was he bent ten ways to Sunday, but he was also dead ass tired. "No. I'm beat."

"You know where everything is." Rob grabbed his jacket. "Don't wait up." Then he pointed to Mark's duffel. "And leave that shit alone."

"Don't worry. I'm fine. Just don't bring anyone home and we'll be square. I don't think I could take it tonight." Mark tried to smile, but he wasn't feeling it.

He could have spent the night in his own place, but the apartment was completely trashed, and he really needed a break.

"Don't worry. It's not that kind of meet-and-greet." Rob left, and Mark clicked through the channels until he came across a replay of one of last season's games on the NFL channel. For a while, he simply stared, unmoving, trying not to think about the break-in, Carol, and the six-year-old rings sitting in his duffel bag.

What he did want to think about was his sweet, precious Karma, even though he knew doing so was seriously risky business with the haphazard tumble of jagged memories ripping his mind apart.

He took out his phone and dialed.

"Hello?" Karma's voice immediately made him smile, and he relaxed for the first time in hours.

"Hi," he said.

"How's your apartment?"

"A mess."

"How are you?"

He smiled. "I'm a mess, too, to be honest."

"Why? What happened?"

He couldn't admit he was thinking about Carol and that his mind was in a state of waste. "It's just this whole ordeal." He sighed and lay back on the couch. "My place was pretty much trashed." He rubbed his palm down his face. "I had to call all my banks and credit card companies and cancel all my accounts. It's been a crazy afternoon and evening."

"I'm sorry," she said, "Did they catch whoever did it?"

"It was a couple of kids who live in my building."

"Oh wow. Did they take anything?"

"Just some jewelry." No need to tell her that wedding bands and a diamond necklace that had been meant for another woman were part of the loot. "How are you doing?"

"Okay." She sounded lonely.

"I'm sorry about this weekend," he said. She had taken tomorrow off so they could get an early start on their time together since he had planned to spend next week in Chicago. He had a couple of meetings to attend with his boss and needed to give a progress update on Solar. And now he needed to add handling the fallout of today's break-in to his to-do list.

"Don't worry about it," she said. "Things happen."

"Is there any way you can come up to Chicago next week so I can make it up to you?" Since the holiday fell on a weekend, Solar had given the employees both Friday and Monday off, but he knew that Karma hadn't taken vacation like a lot of the other employees had to take full advantage of the long weekend while their kids were on summer break.

"I wish. But I have to work. Jolene already took the week off, and there's a quarterly review coming up in a couple of weeks I need to do the presentation for, so I have to be here."

Mark laid his head back against the cushions. "What are you doing right now?" He imagined her lying on her bed.

"I just got off the phone with my dad and was about to sit down to read."

"And how's Dad?" He loved how her eyes always lit up when she talked about her father. They had a close relationship, even if it was strained now because of him. "Are you two getting along better?"

She laughed quietly. "He's still not keen on the idea of me seeing you, but he doesn't hassle me about it anymore. But we're going fishing on Monday, and my parents invited me to their house this weekend for fireworks and a cookout."

Her plans sounded relaxing and peaceful. He could use some of both after the day he'd had.

Mark turned off the TV and sprawled on the couch. "Sounds nice.

I'm not much of a fisherman, though."

"I can teach you."

"Oh? Are you good?"

"Good enough. But don't ask me to tie any fishing knots. I suck at them."

"I doubt you suck at anything."

She laughed. After a moment, she said, "So, what are you doing?"

"I'm at a friend's house, thinking about all the things I haven't taught you, yet."

"There's more? And here I thought we were doing pretty well."

He felt much better now that he was talking to her. "We are, but yes, there's always more. And there's certainly a lot more in those books you've read about how to please a man that you haven't shown me, yet."

"Do I not please you?" she said flirtatiously.

"You please me just fine. More than fine. I think I've become quite addicted to you, actually." It was the truth. Karma was something special. "You've just teased me so much about all this reading you've done that I think I need another demonstration soon so I can examine your technique firsthand. You know, so you can show me something new."

She giggled and warmth untied the remaining knots in his neck and shoulders. "I'll see what I can do the next time I see you then. How's that?"

"I can't wait."

"I hope I don't disappoint."

"There's no way you could disappoint me, Karma." He smiled. If not for Carol, he could easily have given Karma his heart.

They talked idly for a while, just small talk, nothing too deep or serious. Hearing her voice, her laughter, the smile in her tone, Mark felt at peace for the first time since this morning. "Well, I should let you go," he finally said nearly an hour later. "But thank you for cheering me up. It was a rough day."

"I know it was, and I'm glad I could help," she said. "Is there anything else I can do?"

"Come to Chicago tomorrow." The words were out before he knew he'd spoken them.

She laughed. "What?"

"I know you can't." If only she could, but it was out of the question. "That's just wishful thinking on my part."

"I guess, but don't say such things. I might think you're serious."

"I'm dead serious," he said. "but I know you can't."

"Well, it's a nice thought."

"Yes, it is. I'll let you get back to reading. Good night, Karma."

"Good night, Mark."

He hung up and set the phone on the coffee table before grabbing his duffel and heading to the bathroom, where he changed into his sweats and brushed his teeth. Then he made himself comfortable on the couch.

Somewhere around eleven o'clock, he fell asleep.

And dreamed about Karma.

And wedding rings.

And happiness.

Chapter 43

Once something is a passion, the motivation is there.
-Michael Schumacher

Karma passed a sign that said the Chicago exit she needed to take was in two miles. She had white-knuckled the steering wheel like the reins on a bucking bronco for the past thirty minutes. Chicago area traffic was a major suckfest. Cars whizzed by, even passing on the shoulders, which she had never seen done before, and her nerves were almost shot. She couldn't believe she was doing this. What had gotten into her?

Mark. That's what.

If he hadn't invited her to Chicago, she never would have gotten the half-cocked idea of pulling up a Yahoo! map to see how to get to his apartment building. And then she wouldn't have contrived the idea to surprise him, which had become an idea to pack an overnight bag, which had led to her printing off a series of maps and plugging his address into her car's GPS, which had ended with her heading north on I-65, Chicago-bound.

Somehow—miraculously without getting in a wreck or killed—around two thirty in the afternoon, she arrived at his apartment building in one piece. Flustered, yes. Relieved to park her car and shut off the engine in the parking garage below his building, absolutely.

Taking a reassuring breath that she had made it through the wicked world of Chicago's crowded streets, she got out, grabbed her overnight bag from the backseat, and checked the slip of paper she had written his address on.

Apartment number 902.

Ninth floor.

Now to find her way to the lobby.

Mark had the balcony door open to let the breeze in while he and Rob finished straightening his apartment. The new door had been installed that morning, along with an extra deadbolt. He was feeling better than he had last night, but then he'd slept eight hours. He rarely got that much sleep. Apparently, he had needed the rest.

The phone rang.

"Hello?"

"Mr. Strong?" It was building security. "You have a guest, a—"

"Just send them up." It was probably another police officer. The chief of police had alerted him that officers might stop back by.

"Yes, sir."

Mark disconnected and got back to work.

"Where do these go?" Rob held up a stack of books.

Mark pointed down the hall. "In my office."

As Rob disappeared, Mark's phone chimed from the kitchen counter. He snagged it and smiled when he saw a text from Karma. *Hey you. Are you busy?*

He typed out a response. *Not really. Just getting my apartment back in order. What are you up to?*

He set the phone down and grabbed a couple of bottles of beer from the fridge. One for him and one for Rob.

His phone chimed again. *Nothing much. Just walking down the hall.*

His brow furrowed. Walking down the hall? What an odd thing to say. Before he could type out a response, his phone dinged again. *Who's that at your door?*

He looked up. He hadn't heard a knock. Wait a minute. What was going on? He typed out a reply. *At my door?*

Yes. At your door. I could swear I heard a knock.

What had she done? Had she sent him flowers? A gift? Balloons? A maid to help him clean? Maybe his visitor wasn't CPD after all.

He set down his phone and went to the new door, unlocked the dual deadbolts, and pulled the heavy thing open…and found Karma, her hair pulled into a ponytail, phone in her hand and a smile on her face, standing in the hall.

"Could you use a hand in there?" she said, slipping her phone inside her purse.

He stepped out, his heart melting, and wrapped one arm around her waist. "No. But I could use two." He pulled her inside, shut the door, and drew her into a hug. "This is a pleasant surprise."

Rob came back into the living room. "Hey, who's this?"

Mark stepped aside with his arm still around Karma's waist. "Rob, this is Karma. Karma, meet my best friend, Rob."

She stepped forward and extended her right hand. "Hi, nice to meet you."

Rob eyed Mark for a second then took Karma's hand. "My pleasure. Mark's talked a lot about you."

"He has?" She looked at him. Mark could only smile back,

dumbfounded that she had come to Chicago.

"Oh yeah," Rob said. "All good, of course."

"I'm glad." Her cheeks pinked, and she looked around at the remaining mess. "It doesn't look that bad." She glanced at Mark. "The way you talked last night, I expected a lot worse."

With Rob's help, Mark had managed to get almost everything back where it belonged. He only had a few more stacks of files and books to go through.

Rob smiled knowingly at Mark. "You didn't tell me you called Karma last night," he said a little too dramatically.

Mark ignored the jab. "We've been cleaning all day," he said to Karma. "It's a lot better than it was."

"Can I help?"

Her just being there helped, but he didn't want to say that in front of Rob. "Sure."

Rob checked his watch. "I actually have to cut out."

"What? You've got another hot date?"

"Something like that." Rob grinned. "But it's been nice finally meeting you, Karma."

"Same here," she said.

Rob headed for the door. "Keep this guy out of trouble while you're here, okay?"

"I'll try, but he can be a handful."

"Ain't that the truth?" Rob waved and left.

As soon as the door closed, Mark wrapped his arms around Karma and kissed the top of her head. "Thank you for coming."

She buried her face against his chest, then pulled away and glanced around. "Where can I start?"

He pointed to his lips. "How about right here?"

She smiled. "I think I can manage that." She rose up on her toes and pressed her lips to his. She smelled like vanilla and tasted like peppermint.

And just like that, his weekend went from elephant dung to sweet-smelling roses. Vanilla-and-peppermint-scented roses at that.

After cleaning for another hour, Mark plopped down on the couch. "Okay, that's it. No more work today."

Karma smiled then spied his gym bag and basketball in the hall. She picked the ball up and flipped it around in her hands. "How about you show me your moves?" She tossed him the ball.

"What? Now?"

"Sure." She sat next to him and took the ball. "I used to play, remember. I think I told you that."

"You want to play with me?" Why did that sound so dirty?

"Baby, I want to play with you so bad." Her flirtatious gaze sent a lick of heat between his legs.

He took back the ball. "Are we talking about basketball or something else?"

Her left brow arched. "Both?"

He regarded her for a moment through narrowed eyes then nodded. "Okay, you're on."

A few minutes later, they were in his car heading to the gym.

"You look good in my sweatshirt," he said. She hadn't brought a jacket, and in Chicago, even in the summer, the wind off Lake Michigan could make for chilly days and nights. And despite it being Fourth of July weekend, today was unseasonably cool.

"I feel good in your sweatshirt," she said.

They arrived at the courts and only had to wait a couple of minutes for one to free up. After a few minutes of warm-up shots, he passed her the ball. "Okay, show me what you've got, little lady."

"It's been a while since I played. Don't expect much." She dribbled the ball.

"Isn't it like riding a bike? You never forget how?"

"I think you're thinking of something else." She watched the ball as if getting familiar with the feel of it in her hands again.

"Like what?"

She smirked. "Like riding a bike." She stepped up and shot.

The ball bounced off the front of the rim. He leaped for the rebound, and then went in for an easy layup.

"Two-zip." He passed her the ball again.

"Oh, so we're keeping score now?"

"Of course."

She began dribbling, faked to the left, and cut around to the right, pulling up for a short jump shot. The ball bounced off the backboard, rolled around the rim, and then out.

"Damn!" She huffed and ran for the rebound, but Mark beat her to it.

As he dribbled away from her, she rolled her eyes. "You do know you have, like, an entire foot on me, right?"

"You're exaggerating." He bounced the ball back and forth, from left to right. "I can't be more than six inches taller than you are."

She jumped forward and tried to steal the ball. He took the opportunity to dribble around her and made a break for the net. By now, they were both breathing harder, and small beads of perspiration were already breaking out over his forehead.

Karma unzipped his sweatshirt and crawled her way out of the sleeves. "Yeah, six inches taller," she said defiantly. Her nipples peaked under her T-shirt against the cool breeze. "But with the wingspan of a gorilla." She tossed the sweatshirt to the bench as if she was getting serious.

"A gorilla?" He laughed. "Did you just call me a gorilla?"

She smacked the ball out of his hands and cast him an over-the-shoulder glare as she walked away. "I sure did. You gonna do something about it, big guy?"

Mark tugged at his sweatpants. Perspiration dripped down his thighs. "Time-out." He pulled off his sweats so that he was only in his T-shirt and nylon shorts.

"Are you done getting undressed?" she said, getting snarky. "Or are we gonna play some ball."

"Oh, baby, you have no idea." He clapped his hands once to show he was ready.

She dribbled, and the hint of a smile played over her lips. She was obviously enjoying this as much as he was. He loved that she wasn't intimidated by all the men on the other courts, or that he was obviously more practiced than she was. Karma gave it all she had. He liked that competitive fire in her belly. Few women had it. At least that he'd seen.

She bulldozed toward him, rushing the net.

He planted his feet and slid in to block her, but she barreled right through him, sending the ball up. It came down through the net.

"Foul!" he said. "Charging!"

"Charging my ass," she said, snagging the ball on the bounce. "You stepped in front of me."

He took the ball. "Oh, I see. That's how you're gonna play, huh?"

"It was a legal move. Quit crying about it like a little girl."

He laughed. "Little girl?"

"If the shoe fits."

He got up in her personal space, grinning like he had the best hand in a game of poker. "You are in so much trouble."

"Promises, promises." She stole the ball out of his hands, turned and dribbled for the goal, making an easy layup.

She caught the ball and passed it to him. "Your ball."

He passed it back. "No. I'll let you take it out again." This was too much fun.

With a coy smile, she traded spots with him. "If you insist." She started dribbling, creeping up on him. Just as she was about to make her move, he grabbed her around the waist and pulled her against him.

She yelped as he picked her up, laughing. "Foul!" She pretended to blow a whistle, and then they both broke into laughter before he gave her a breathless kiss.

A quiet moan broke in her throat, and he pulled back.

"I think that was a technical." Her face flushed and lit up like a kid who had just run down the stairs at breakneck speed on Christmas morning.

"Am I ejected?" He let his hand drop to the upper curve of her rump, where he gave her a little finger pat.

"Nah. I like the way you foul." She pulled away and darted after the ball.

They played for another thirty minutes, which really ended up being more like thirty minutes of competitive foreplay than basketball, then they packed it in. On the way home, they stopped at a corner store for a few things then picked up sandwiches at Mark's favorite deli.

"That was more fun than I've had in a long time," she said as they settled on his balcony with their sandwiches.

"Same here." He felt invigorated and alive in a way he hadn't felt in years. It was almost as if he were ten years younger. But that was the Karma Effect. This was what she did to him, and he couldn't deny he loved how he felt when they were together.

They ate in comfortable silence, with only the breeze off the lake and the sound of distant traffic to lull them into an easy ambience.

After she put away her last bite, he invited her onto the lounge chair with him. With the sun behind his apartment building, casting them in shadow, it got chilly fast, and Karma readily snuggled into his embrace.

He absently linked his fingers between hers and lay back, closed his eyes, and enjoyed her presence. He was usually so tense, even when he didn't appear to be. There was always something to do, a job to work on, a date to plan, memories to avoid. His mind was always going, going, going. It never stopped. Until now.

For the first time since he could remember, he didn't think about anything at all. Not his assignment at Solar, not about Carol, and not about how his apartment had been a ransacked disaster twenty-four hours ago. His mind was free and clear, completely in the moment and at peace. A glassy, tranquil pond covered with early morning mist in the heart of summer. And it was because of the woman lying beside him, tucked into the crook of his arm.

"This is nice," she said softly, as if she knew he relished the serenity she gave him and didn't want to disturb it.

"Mm-hm." Mark opened his eyes and gently rocked her against his side as he kissed the top of her head. "Are you getting cold?"

"Just a little."

"Come on," he said, sitting up with her. "Let's go in, get cleaned up, and turn off the phones. He stood and wrapped his arms around her waist. "I want to be with you and only you tonight."

"Me, too."

He followed her inside and closed the sliding glass door, ready to put yesterday and all the bad memories behind him.

Chapter 44

There's just some magic in truth and honesty and openness.
-Frank Ocean

After soaking in a relaxing bubble bath for twenty minutes, Karma wrapped herself inside the fluffy terry robe Mark had loaned her and vacated the master bath so he could take a shower. While he did, she brushed out her hair and tied it back in a ponytail then knelt beside her bag, which sat next to his duffel on the bedroom floor, and fished out a pair of flannel pajama pants and a T-shirt. She stood, slipped out of the robe, pulled on the T-shirt, and began to put on the pants when something sparkly caught her attention from inside Mark's bag.

She frowned and peered inside as she cinched the drawstring around her waist and tied it in a bow. Then she bent down for a closer look. Were those diamonds? She gasped and reached inside his bag to pull out a necklace that looked like it had cost a fortune. So many diamonds. Then the velvet box caught her eye, and she took it out of the bag and opened it.

Oh my. Was that an engagement ring? And were those wedding bands? They were. She sat on the edge of the bed, wondering what Mark was doing with a set of wedding bands, and pulled the diamond engagement ring out of the box. Of course, she had to try it on. What self-respecting woman wouldn't want to put on a fat diamond like that just to see how it looked and felt on her hand? It was just a tiny bit too big, but otherwise looked fabulous on her, and she smiled. What lucky girl had been destined for this ring?

Wait a minute. Mark said he didn't do commitments. So, what was he doing with wedding rings?

After the expected jolt of hope vibrated her heart, she remembered with disappointment their conversation from several weeks ago when he had mentioned a woman named...what was her name? Karen? No, Carol. That's right. Karma looked at the diamond on her finger and frowned. Mark had suggested Carol was the reason why he couldn't commit, but he hadn't gone into details about their relationship. Was this supposed to have been Carol's ring?

The bathroom door opened, and she glanced up. Mark wore a towel around his waist and rubbed another over his hair as he turned for the dresser.

"I was thinking that tomorrow we could—what are you doing?" Mark stopped in his tracks when he saw the ring on her finger.

Icy awareness licked down her spine as a chill blasted through the room. Clearly, he hadn't meant for her to see the rings. Maybe not even the necklace. Uh-oh. What had she done?

Quickly, she took off the ring and dropped it back in the box, but not before Mark closed the distance between them and snatched it and the necklace away from her as if they were poisonous relics that only he could handle.

"I—Is that the jewelry that was stolen?" she said warily, trying to defuse whatever firestorm she had awakened inside him.

"I don't want you touching these." He marched to the dresser, tossed them inside a wooden chest, and slammed the lid closed.

"I'm sorry. I didn't think—"

"I can't believe you went through my things, Karma." Mark spun on her. Anger and something darker—anguish or fear, maybe—roiled over his face. She had never seen him angry and didn't know how to respond, but she knew she had to say something.

"I wasn't going through your things. I was getting dressed and I saw the necklace. That's all. I wasn't intentionally snooping."

Standing akimbo, head down, Mark took several deep breaths. "Those weren't meant for you to see, Karma. You never should have touched them. They're not yours. You should have left them in my bag." The tone of his voice sent knives into her heart. He made it sound like she had purposely snooped. Well, to hell with being accused of something she hadn't done.

"Oh, I'm sorry," she said, standing up. "I guess I didn't see the sign that said, 'Hands off, Karma. You can only look where I tell you to look and touch what I allow you to touch.' My mistake."

He frowned. "That's not what I said."

She swiped her hand toward his duffel bag. "If you didn't want me to see that stuff, then you shouldn't have left your bag open right next to mine. Or you should have put it away so I wouldn't see it." Tears stung the backs of her eyes. She felt betrayed and wounded, but worst of all, she felt like an inconvenience. Not even thirty minutes ago, she had felt like she belonged here, comfortable and welcome. Now she felt like an intruder.

Mark was still frowning but didn't say anything.

"Great." She threw up her hands and turned away so he wouldn't see her cry. "This has turned into a great trip. Thanks for the awesome time, Mark." She grabbed her bag, zipped it up, and turned for the door.

"Where are you going?" He took an urgent step forward then stopped, scowling at her bag.

"I'm going home. At least there I don't have to worry about poking my nose into the wrong nook or cranny." She shoved past him.

"Karma, wait. It's getting late. You shouldn't—"

She spun and held up her hand. "Thank you for your concern, Mark, but I found my way here just fine. I can find my way out, too."

"Karma—"

But she didn't stick around to hear what he had to say, and, after figuring out the deadbolts on the door, swung it open, stormed out, and slammed it shut behind her. This had been a side of Mark she had never seen, and she hadn't liked it. His accusations had stung and made her feel like she was somehow inferior.

That Carol woman must have been some kind of special for him to guard her engagement and wedding rings more acutely than a lioness guards her cubs.

Karma stepped into the elevator and choked back a sob. At least now she knew where she stood. For all his words to the contrary, she was nothing more than a post to scratch his itch on. It looked like her dad had been right about Mark after all.

Mark stared numbly at the door. Had Karma really just left?

When he had come out of the bathroom and seen Karma wearing Carol's engagement ring, a dreadful chill iced his blood. She shouldn't have touched them. She was too pristine to be tainted by such poisonous objects. To see them touching her skin had been like seeing a cobra bite her.

But he had handled the situation terribly. Fear had rushed out as blame. Being caught off guard had made him react defensively, and he had accused her of putting herself in harm's way even though it was his fault for not taking enough care to protect her. Would he ever learn? Was he forever destined to fail with those he treasured most? First Carol, now Karma. He had let them both down.

Obviously, he still wasn't ready to try for forever again. Not that he needed proof. When it came to matters of the heart, he would never be ready to give himself completely to another. He would always mess up. Somehow, in one way or another, he would always fall just shy of being everything a woman deserved. His behavior tonight had confirmed that. He would always pull then push.

But he couldn't let Karma leave under these circumstances. It was late, she wasn't familiar with Chicago, and she was upset. Because *he* had upset her. He shouldered the blame entirely. But he could apologize. He could bring her back and convince her to stay. He didn't want to lose her over something like this. He wasn't *ready* to lose her. Not even close.

Moving fast, he dressed and grabbed his phone as he darted out the door.

Karma couldn't find her damn car. She had been so excited just to arrive in one piece this afternoon that she hadn't paid attention to what level of the parking garage she had parked on. After circling for nearly five minutes, she got back on the elevator and went down one more floor then stormed out just as her phone dinged.

A flicker of hope danced in her heart even though it shouldn't have. She didn't want to hear from Mark right now. Nope. She didn't. Not at all.

I'm not even gonna look.

Ugh. She stopped and fished out her phone, unable to resist her heart's demand.

Don't go. Please.

Her heart smiled. Too bad she was listening more to her brain right now.

Why should I stay? She hit *send* and set back out on Car Quest.

Her phone dinged a moment later.

Because I'm an ass and I'm sorry.

Well, okay then. That's a start. Karma's quick steps lost some of their gusto.

At least you're honest, she sent back.

Please stay. I promise not to be an ass. I'll even sleep on the couch. Just please don't go.

Karma slowed almost to a stop as she typed. *You don't have to sleep on the couch.*

Then you'll stay?

She rolled her eyes, tried not to look at her phone, determinedly picked up her pace briefly then stopped, sighed with defeat, and typed her reply. *Fine. I'll stay.*

Where are you?

She looked around and realized she was standing next to her car.

Great. Good timing now that she had decided to stay. She found a sign.

Parking garage. Level 3.

Resigned, she turned around and began the walk back to the elevator. Mark had gotten to her, already so deep inside her heart that she was amazed she'd been able to leave at all. But she had. Over a stupid ring.

As she approached the silver elevator doors, the red down arrow lit and dinged. Then the doors opened.

Mark rushed out then stopped when he saw her. His wet hair stuck out in all directions, he wasn't wearing shoes, and the few buttons he had fastened on his shirt were buttoned crookedly, making one shirt tail longer than the other.

If they hadn't just had a fight, she would have laughed. This was so not the typical Mark look.

"I'm sorry," he said. His chagrined expression tugged at her heart.

She joined him in the elevator, and he took her bag.

They rode in wary silence back to the ninth floor. It was as if Mark didn't know how to act around her right now, and it seemed as though he were wrestling with a thousand thoughts, all of which he kept to himself.

Once they were back inside his apartment, he led her to the bedroom, set her bag back on the floor where it had been earlier, and took her hands.

"I owe you an explanation," he said.

"And I'd like to hear it, but first…" She tore her hands from his and brushed her fingers through his still-wet hair, making some sense from the chaos. Then she began unbuttoning his shirt. "We need to make you look a little less insane."

Brow furrowed, he glanced into the mirror then down at his shirt's placket as she rebuttoned it, this time so that the buttons and holes aligned properly.

"I guess I was in a bit of a rush to catch up to you." He grabbed his brush and finished making sense out of his hair.

"I guess." Some of the steam had evaporated from her anger, and she sat down on the edge of the bed.

Mark set his brush on the dresser. "Okay, explanation." He sat down beside her and peered at her sideways. He offered a smile that didn't reach his eyes. "I was engaged once."

Now they were getting somewhere.

"Her name was Carol. I mentioned her before."

For the next forty-five minutes, Mark poured out the details of what had happened. How he met Carol, how they got engaged when he was twenty-three, how, on their wedding day, Carol never showed, and how he had gone to her home afterward to find her in bed with her dance partner.

"I fell into a horrible depression," he said. "I began drinking a lot. A functional drunk, I think is what they called me. I could work, and I got the job done well enough, but as soon as the workday ended, I drowned myself in a bottle."

Karma took his hand and scooted a little closer.

"Rob sat with me every night, talking me down from the ledge of full-blown alcoholism, until finally, some of what he said got through. After a while, the bite of what Carol did stopped hurting quite as much, and then, gradually, it faded to the point I only felt it when I thought about her." He looked at her. "I messed up with her. Somehow, I screwed things up and she left me."

"How so? What did *you* do to chase her away?" From what Mark had told her, she didn't see any of this as his fault, but for whatever reason, he blamed himself.

He shrugged. "I don't know. I never found out. She never told me. But it had to be something." He met her gaze. "So, I started working on making myself a better man. The kind of man…"

"That Carol would want." Karma let go of his hand and looked down. This Carol certainly was a special lady. Karma would kill to have Mark love her as much as he loved Carol.

Mark quietly cleared his throat and slowly reached for her hand again. He folded it inside the warmth of his. "At the time, I'll admit I wanted her back. That's what motivated me. But then she married her dance partner, and it became clear she would never want me back, no matter how much I changed." He shrugged. "But I still wanted to make myself a better man."

"Why? If you don't want long-term, committed relationships, then why is being a better man so important?"

He paused and shook his head. "I don't have a good answer for that. All I can say is that part of me still hopes that someday I'll be good enough to try again, but another part of me is too terrified to try." He glanced away. "I just can't seem to get past what she did. I keep thinking that if I could just find out why, then I might be able to go on, that I can fix it, but she never told me why, and I can't let it go."

"Why don't you just ask her?"

He looked to the floor. "I can't. I can barely be in the same room with her without feeling the trauma all over again." He shook his head, closed his eyes, took a breath, then met her gaze with an air of shame. "She was at the benefit. The night you and I met. She was there, and do you want to know what I did?"

The pain in his eyes nearly throttled her. "What?"

"I threw up." He smiled sadly. "I left the benefit, went to my room, and threw up." He sighed. "Not because I still want her, but because I can't get over what she did. Because she's pregnant now, and that was supposed to have been my life. I always wanted children." He hung his head.

What a sad story. Here was a man who Karma thought was perfection in every way. The perfect boyfriend who would make the perfect husband, and yet he had been so severely traumatized by his ex-fiancée that he had all but taken himself off the market.

Carol was in his past, and he didn't seem to have any illusions that he belonged with her, but clearly she still sat first and foremost in his thoughts, even if only subconsciously. Carol affected every decision he made. Like a chronic case of indigestion, Mark couldn't exist without thinking that at any moment, Carol would rip at his insides and lay him to waste again. He had been through hell because of her, and her memory tore at him like a relentless succubus.

And here Karma thought *her* past was painful. Even though she and Mark shared a similar childhood, Mark had her beat hands down in the relationships department. Carol had splayed his heart and filleted it like nothing more than yesterday's catch, leaving behind a man's body in which resided a scared and wounded little boy. A little boy Mark worked hard to protect by putting up walls and donning a shell of armor. He held his share of insecurities, but he hid them well behind his successful, confident, and controlled façade.

What a shame he couldn't get past what Carol had done, because he was a remarkable man. One any woman would be lucky to call her husband. He unjustifiably shouldered the blame for her leaving, and he had ventured out on this quest of becoming a woman's ideal man to prove he wasn't the loser he accused himself of being. It was a vicious Catch-22. No matter how close to perfection he became, in his eyes, he would always be a failure.

"I think you would surprise yourself if you gave yourself a chance, Mark," she said. "For the record, I think you're pretty terrific."

He inhaled and squeezed her hand, almost as if to reassure himself more than her. "The fact is—especially after what you just witnessed...my behavior...my complete meltdown—I think you would agree that this is all I'm capable of right now. I can't give more, and I'm not sure I'll ever be able to."

She stared, speechless. He was confirming what he had told her from the start, but this time it sounded like he wished he *could* give more, as if he wanted to give more to *her*.

"I'll understand if that's not enough for you and you want to end this now. I don't want to hurt you, Karma. The last thing I want to do is hurt you. You're such a sweet, lovely woman. One who deserves better than this." He let go of her hand, stood, and gestured toward the door. "Like I said, I'll sleep on the couch tonight…give you some space to think." He grabbed a blanket from the closet then stopped in the doorway and looked over his shoulder. "But I want you to know how sorry I am for the way I treated you earlier. It had more to do with me than you. What happened wasn't your fault. It was mine. I never should have gotten angry."

She knew that now. "I know."

"I just didn't like seeing that awful ring on you. It's cursed, and you're too good for that." He smiled sadly, looked away, and quietly closed the door behind him, leaving Karma alone with her thoughts and a blanket of compassion for the remarkable man who had just poured out his soul.

Mark was a truly troubled man, but then, in her way she was a truly troubled woman. But Mark had begun to change all that. He had helped her discover how beautiful she was, both inside and out. Did that mean she was cured? No. But it did mean she was a better woman because of him. There would always be ghosts of her past to haunt her. She would never completely cast out Johnny's and Jo's and all the others' taunts, but now she could minimize their effect. Mark had shown her that. He had given her the tools to deal with her past. Wasn't there something she could do to give a little back?

She lay down. Surely there was, even if it was only a small token.

Mark lay on the couch, unable to sleep, even though both his mind and his body were weary. The quiet ticking of the clock wasn't even enough to lull him.

How had the night gone so wrong so fast? He had made a wreck of an evening that had been meant for savoring. Karma was sleeping in his bed, and he should be in there with her. Instead, he was on the couch like a kicked-out dog.

For what felt like the hundredth time, he closed his eyes and tried to force himself to sleep. A minute later, he heard the snick of the bedroom door as it opened, and then Karma's silhouette glided around the corner.

He propped himself on his elbow as she approached. "Is everything okay?"

"No," she said, dropping to her knees on the floor beside him.

Shit. How badly had he screwed things up?

"Because you're not in bed with me," she said a moment later.

Wait, what? He blinked several times, not sure he understood.

His confusion must have shown even in the darkness, because she smiled softly. "I know this is all you're capable of, Mark, but I want it. Whatever you can give, for however long you can give it, I'll take it."

He sat up, and she shifted so she knelt between his knees.

"What are you saying?" He brushed her hair off her face.

She rose so that her lips were barely an inch from his. "I'm saying that I want you to come back to bed with me." The way she said it left no question what she was asking for.

His body sprang to life, and gratitude flooded his veins. Even now, faced with the truth of his past, she still wanted to be with him.

She took his hand and stood.

He let her lead him back into the bedroom, where she pushed him onto the bed, undressed, and crawled on top of him. "I came to Chicago to be with you, Mark. Nothing has changed that." Her mouth crashed against his, and all he could do was hold on, still shifting gears to catch up.

Once he finally did, he gripped her arms and rolled over, pinning her to the mattress as her feet hooked inside the waist of his flannel pants and pushed them down his thighs. Her gaze pleaded with him to make love to her, awakening that primitive part of him that needed a physical outlet for all the fear, worry, and anxiety of the last two hours.

"Do you know what the best part about fighting is?" he said.

Her bright eyes sparkled from the city lights. "No. What?" She bit her bottom lip as the corners of her mouth turned upward.

"Make up sex." He shimmied the rest of the way out of his pajamas and snagged a condom from the bedside table.

Her lips spread into a coy smile. "Is that so?"

More than ever, he needed the physical connection. After what had happened earlier, being with her, making love to her, feeling her warm body against his…that would make everything right. That would help heal his heart and reconnect them to one another.

He pulled back and positioned himself on his knees between her thighs. "Yes." He lifted her legs and placed her ankles against the front of his shoulders.

"What are you doing?" She smiled up at him as he hoisted her legs higher and held them against his torso.

"Giving you the best make up sex you'll ever have."

"Is this even...oh!" Her eyes shot open and her hands slapped down on his thighs as he thrust inside her. "I see what you—OH!—mean."

Lifting higher, he crossed her ankles over the front of his neck, making the connection between them tighter, more snug.

"Mark!" Her nails dug into his thighs as he pumped harder.

In this position, her G-spot was in his direct line of fire. Every thrust hit it head-on. Every rock of his hips connected the most virile part of his sexual anatomy to the most receptive part of hers. He knew without her saying so that he was about to deliver a shot of pleasure that would split her nerve endings wide open.

"Don't stop don't stop don't stop!" Desperation filled her gaze.

With a death grip on her thighs, he drove in and out of her, teeth clenched. What they had was magical. She made him feel things he had never felt. She made him want to be a better person, not just as part of some plan to be perfect, but because he truly wanted to be. Karma was his own personal guardian angel, and his only wish now was to make her happy. To make her feel good.

"Harder." She gasped as he gave her what she asked for. "Yes, yes!"

How beautiful. To see her unraveling so quickly was almost spiritual.

She held her breath, her mouth opened in a silent plea, and then...

"MARK!" She cried out, throwing her head back on the pillow, thrashing as her body fell into stunning spasms that made her breasts jiggle.

Not even close to finished, he grabbed her arms and pulled her up and onto his lap as he sank to a kneeling position. Her arms flopped onto his shoulders and she threw herself against him, gasping over and over as he wrapped his arms around her and pounded into her.

It was the hardest he had taken her, but he couldn't hold back. It was as if the harder he made love to her, the closer they grew.

The bed squawked in protest, banging against the wall.

Sweat poured down his body, his muscles screaming.

"Yes, yes, more...I'm coming again." She threw her head back, her hair swaying and rocking as he approached climax and fucked her harder.

"Karma!" He slammed into, falling into orgasm as a long, guttural groan streamed from his throat. Their bodies crashed together again as he thrust once more, and then again, draining himself.

Loose and breathless, Karma sagged against him, her arms slung lazily around his shoulders.

He took her face in his hands, brushed back her hair, found her lips with his, and devoured her as the end of his orgasm echoed through his body.

"You're amazing," he said, gazing into her eyes.

"So are you."

They had given each other all they had, and Mark was in awe.

With the flames of their passion still burning the air around them, they collapsed against the mattress. She curled into his arms and he buried his nose in her hair.

"Thank you," he whispered, pulling the blankets over them.

She made a quiet, happy noise, as if she were smiling, and snuggled more securely against him.

With his arms around her and the warmth of her body giving him comfort, he closed his eyes and finally drifted into a peaceful sleep.

Chapter 45

There is no end. There is no beginning. There is only the passion of life.
-Federico Fellini

With their connection re-established, Mark spent Saturday showing Karma around Chicago. Nothing more was said about Carol or the argument they'd had the night before, which was fine by Karma. It was done and over, in the past where it belonged. All that remained were the two of them, and she was ready to get back to enjoying what little time they had left.

It was the Fourth of July, and the city bustled with activities. They enjoyed a couple of hours of the annual music festival in Grant Park, grabbed barbecue sandwiches and bottles of water for lunch from a street vendor, and milled through the crowds in Millennium Park before waiting for over an hour to be seated at a very packed, very popular Giordano's for dinner. After devouring a small deep dish, it was almost eight o'clock, and they headed back to Mark's place, where they watched from his balcony as the fireworks were shot off Navy Pier.

"I had fun today." He stood behind her, arms around her waist. He smelled of soap and shampoo from the shower they had just shared.

A red firework turned the night sky pink.

"Me, too."

They watched the rest of the fireworks in silence, then after the finale returned inside and sat on the couch. Mark exhaled heavily. "What a day. I'm beat."

Karma played with the ends of her red scarf, which was wrapped loosely around her neck. "Not too beat, I hope."

His eyes narrowed on her. "Why? What did you have in mind?"

"Hold on." She hopped up and went to the bedroom, where she fished the Truth or Dare game from her bag. They hadn't played since that first time. She returned to the living room and handed it over as she plopped back onto the couch. "I brought it with me just in case."

He grinned and opened the box, apparently interested in her idea. "Just in case of what?" he asked.

She shrugged. "Oh, I don't know. Just in case we wanted to have a little fun." She had come a long way since playing Sexual Truth or

Dare that first time. It would be fun to see just how far by playing another round.

He shuffled the cards then placed them face down on the table. "You first." He gestured toward the deck.

Karma picked up the top card. "Truth or dare?" She scanned both options.

"Oh, why not?" Mark said with a flippant wave of his hands. "Since our first venture into this game was all about the truth, I say dare."

She read off the card, "Drop down and give me ten push-ups…shirtless."

Mark rolled his eyes. "Lame." He peeled off his shirt and walked around the coffee table.

Karma's gaze ranged his muscled, lightly hairy chest and abdomen. "Not from my perspective."

He hesitated on his way down to the floor and grinned. "Well then, in that case, I'm happy to oblige." He got into position. "Count off."

"With pleasure." She sat forward. "One…two…three…" Interesting. She had never thought that watching a man do push-ups could be so sexy, and yet, mmm, yes, she could get used to this. The muscles of his arms popped into defined peaks and lickable crevices that reminded her of pictures of hot men she had seen on Facebook. "five…sex—I mean, six—seven…"

Mark bobbled on "sex," paused briefly, chuckled, then got back to pushing up…and down…and up…and down…

"Nine…nine…nine…"

"Hey!" Mark stopped and rose to his knees, laughing. "I'm on to you." He pointed an accusing finger, making her laugh.

"I'm sorry, but I just didn't want that to end." Watching him get physical had been a surprising turn-on.

He stayed on the floor and reached across the table for a card. "Uh-huh. We'll see if I can make you change your tune, little lady. Truth or dare?"

She jutted out her chin. "Truth."

"Awe, you're no fun." He grinned and read the card. "What were you thinking when you first saw me naked?"

"Damn!" she said without hesitation.

He frowned, confused. "Are you saying that's what you thought, or is that your way of saying that you don't like the question?"

She laughed. "That's what I thought. 'Damn!'"

It had been that first night at his condo. She had been too keyed up to notice much the first time he made love to her, but then he stood, went to the bathroom, discarded the condom, and she had gotten her first glance at just how incredibly built he was. It was obvious he was serious about weight training. His butt was tight and the perfect shape. Some men have bubble butts if they work out a lot, but Mark's wasn't. It was just the right size and roundness to grip during sex, which she had done later that night, at his insistence, of course. And his legs were strong and lean, with a perfect teardrop above each knee.

But it was the upper half of his body that made Karma's knees week. The six-pack abs, the thick biceps and chiseled triceps, the strong forearms, and of course, that pumped chest. The treasure trail—she had never known that was what the line of hair below a man's belly button was called until she started reading her books—below his belly button created a thin, faint line to his penis. Even now, she couldn't quite bring herself to call it a *cock* or even a dick without blushing. But even penis didn't sound right...not impressive enough for its length and girth. Mark's penis needed a better name. One that had impact. She would have to work on coming up with one.

"That's all?" he said, grinning from ear to ear, obviously pleased with her assessment of his naked body. "Just 'Damn!'?"

She considered for a moment. "Well, there was one other thing I thought." Her face warmed and scrunched with embarrassment.

"I can tell this is going to be good."

She giggled and slapped her hands over her face. "I thought, 'How did *that* fit in *there*?'"

He laughed so hard he fell over. She buried her face against the arm of the couch, giggling uncontrollably.

Propped on his arm, he wiped a tear from under his eye. "Well, thank you. I take that as a compliment that my *junk* is notably sized."

She made an "okay" sign with her fingers. "I definitely approve of your...er...*junk*." She wasn't sure that was the word she was looking for, but it worked for the moment. She caught her breath and grabbed a card. "Okay, your turn again. Truth or dare?"

"Dare."

"Bring your lips as close as you can to mine without touching them. Stay that way for two minutes and imagine all the hot ways I kiss you. If you kiss me, we have to start over." She set the card back on the table and glanced at him expectantly.

He sat up and lifted onto his knees between her thighs, bringing his mouth less than an inch from hers.

"Like this?" he said

"You're good at this." She gazed into his intense, grey-green eyes and lifted her hands to his chest.

"I try."

"I can tell."

"Are you timing me?"

Her gaze flicked sideways but she couldn't see the clock. "Sure."

"So, are you having a good weekend so far?"

Their noses bumped, and she smiled as his cheeks rose and tiny laugh lines broke at the corners of his eyes.

"Yes, and you?" She was beginning to think this dare was harder for her than him. All she wanted to do was pull him to her and kiss him.

He blinked. "I'm having a fabulous time. Did you enjoy the fireworks?"

"Yes. They were nice."

"You have lovely eyes," he said out of the blue.

"Thank you. So do you."

"You're blushing."

"Are you surprised?"

"No." He circled the tip of her nose with his. "Eskimo kisses don't count, do they?"

"Eskimo kisses?"

He nudged her nose with his again. "Yes. Didn't you know this is how Eskimos kiss? With their noses?"

"I didn't know that."

"Do I have to start over? Because technically I just kissed you."

"But not with your mouth."

"Ah, so Eskimo kisses are okay." He tapped her nose with his again.

"Stop that."

He grinned. "Why?"

"Because you're cheating."

"I'm not cheating. You said they don't count."

"You're so difficult."

"Only because I really want to kiss you." He blinked. "How long has it been?"

Her gaze slid to the side. She still couldn't see the clock. "I don't know."

"What do you mean, you don't know?" His brow crinkled.

"You're not timing me?"

"I can't see the clock."

His eyebrows lifted.

She huffed. "Hey, it's not my fault. Your big head is in the way."

He laughed. "My 'big head' is in the way?"

"Yes. You have a very big head."

One of his eyebrows arched. "Do I now?"

"Yes." Then she quickly added, "But it's a very handsome big head."

"Nice save."

"Thank you."

"So, do you think my two minutes are up?"

"I'm not sure."

"How about now?"

"Mark."

His left eyebrow arched. "Hey, it's your fault. You were supposed to be timing me."

"Well, I'm not."

"And now I have to suffer because of it."

"Poor baby."

His eyes narrowed. "This is hard."

"That's the point."

His gaze dropped to her mouth. "I really want to kiss you."

"You can't."

"I'm going to."

"Mark..."

He rocked forward.

"Mark!"

"I wasn't going to kiss you." He rocked back, but his face was still within a couple inches of hers.

"Can't you just sit there quietly? You're supposed to be imagining my hot kisses instead of talking."

"I can multitask."

"Whatever."

"Has it been two minutes, yet?"

"I don't know!"

"Well guess!"

"Fine. It's been two minutes."

He pushed forward and locked lips with her, stealing her breath. His tongue danced over hers, and his teeth nipped her lip, then he pulled away and sat back down on the floor, grabbing the next card.

"Truth or dare?" he said as if he hadn't just blown off her toes.

"Give me a minute." She held up her hand then fanned herself. Fire still coursed from her lips to parts south of her waistline.

He huffed sarcastically as if she were wasting his time.

"Hey!" She leaned forward and smacked his arm.

He laughed and sat back down beside her on the couch, giving her knee a playful shove. "Did I fluster you?"

"A little, yes. You don't play fair." She sat back, took a deep breath, then said, "Okay, truth."

"What outfit of mine gets you really worked up? Explain exactly what you like about it."

"This is an easy one. You have this navy blue suit with pinstripes that you usually wear with a white shirt and dark red tie."

"I know the one." His grin cut through her soul.

"I like that suit. It fits you very well and always turns me on when you wear it. But you look good in suits, in general. I love seeing you in a suit."

"Good to know. I'll keep that in mind."

"I hope you do." She picked up the next card.

"Dare," he said.

She giggled when she read what he had to do. "Rub your chest, paying special attention to your nipples, for thirty seconds."

"What?" He shot forward, snatched the card from her hand, and read it. "Oh, hell." He disgustedly flipped the card to the table.

Karma snapped her fingers. "Come on, Mark, show those nipples some love."

"Have I mentioned that I'm going to get you for this?"

"No."

"Well, I am." He sat back and, as if it was the last thing he wanted to do, lifted his hands to his chest and began rubbing. "Are you timing this?" He gave her a look as if to warn her that she had better be watching the second hand on the clock this time.

She coughed out a laugh and nodded. "Yep." She checked the clock.

"You should be doing this for me, you know." He swirled his fingers over his nipples and made a face. Out of nowhere, he said, "Do I make you randy, baby?" in his best Austin Powers voice.

Karma howled with laughter, waving her hand in front of her. "Stop! Just stop!"

He dropped his hands from his chest and fell into laughter with her. "Was that good or what?" He reached forward and picked up the next card on the deck. "I sounded just like him."

"Not," she said.

"Hey, I thought it was pretty good." He looked at the card. "Austin Powers rocks."

"And, just like that, the sexy moment of a few minutes ago is gone."

With a smirk, he said, "Well, let's get it back. Truth or dare?"

"Dare."

"Oh, now…I *do* like this one." Mark trailed the tip of his finger across his bottom lip and sat forward. "Starting at my lips…" he paused and met her gaze. "Kiss your way to your favorite part of my body."

This could definitely bring back some of the sexy mood his Austin Powers impression scared away.

Mark set the card down and settled into the cushions, one arm slung over the back of the couch. "I wonder what the lady's favorite body part is?" He tapped his fingers on his leg.

She slid to the floor between his knees, hands on his thighs. "I guess you'll find out." She kissed his mouth, lingering for an extra few seconds, then pulled away and kissed the side of his neck.

"Where will she go? Where, oh where?" His voice rumbled quietly.

Down his neck to his shoulder, she left a trail of soft kisses. She continued to his biceps, where she nipped him with her teeth before skimming her tongue to the crook of his elbow, where she licked back and forth along the crease. Then she kissed down the underside of his forearm to his wrist and finally to his hand. As she swirled her tongue against his palm, she lifted her gaze and found him staring glassy-eyed at her, his eyelids heavy and his lips parted. She turned over his hand and kissed the back of each of his fingers.

"Who would have thought my hands were an erogenous zone?" he said huskily.

She smiled and sat back on her heels.

"So, my hands are your favorite body part?" he asked.

"Yes."

He grinned. "Do you want me to show you what my favorite part of your body is?"

"Isn't it my feet?"

"Well, there is that, but no. There's another part of you I like just a little better?"

"My butt?"

He sat forward and rested his elbows on his knees, shaking his head. "No. Come here." He lightly grabbed her shirt and pulled her forward. "It's this." He lifted his mouth to her eyelids. As she closed them, he kissed one then the other. She opened them again, and they shared an intimate moment, gazes locked, and then he gestured toward the cards. "Your turn, honey."

He had started calling her "honey" and "baby" lately, and she liked it. He didn't say it like Daniel did. When Mark called her "honey," it came out sounding as easy as a breath, and just as tender.

"Truth or dare?" she asked.

"I'll try dare again. It's got to be better than the last one."

She giggled. "Don't be so sure."

"What? Come on, don't do this to me."

Her giggle turned to outright laughter. "Pull your shirt up and do a sexy belly dance."

He flopped back on the couch. "Oh good God!" Sighing, he stood and quickly shimmied his hips then sat back down and grabbed the next card.

"Hey! That wasn't a belly dance." Karma smacked his leg.

"That's as good as it's gonna get, sister. Truth or dare?"

"Fine. Truth." She sat back and crossed her arms.

"What's a sex position we've never attempted that you're dying to try?" Smug satisfaction oozed over his face as if he were opening his mental Karma file and preparing to amend it.

"Well…" She nibbled her bottom lip. "There is this one story I read in one of my books that's kind of stuck with me."

"Oh? And what position did the participants in this story engage in that made you like it so much?"

She lowered her voice and cringed with embarrassment. "Doggy style."

Mark's eyebrows shot high into his forehead. "Oh really. Is that so?" He sat forward, suddenly fully interested in the conversation.

"Yes." She flopped sideways to the floor and buried her burning face in her hands.

His dark chuckle suggested he was definitely amending his Karma file. "I'll have to see what I can do about that. I'm actually kind of surprised I haven't shown you that, yet. Wait. What about that shower we shared at my place? Doesn't that count?"

He had taken her from behind in the shower, but she didn't count that as doggy style since she hadn't been on all fours. "I want it on a bed." Something about being held face down on the bed while he took her from behind just…well…it really—as in *really*—worked her up.

"I see."

Karma was still lying on the floor, covering her face, when she felt the edge of a card flick against her fingers. She drew her hands away and saw that he had picked up the next card for her and was waving it in front of her face, his gaze dark and mischievous.

She took it and sat up with a resigned sigh. "Truth or dare?"

"I'm banking on dare." He crossed his fingers. "This time I'm catching a break. I can feel it."

Karma read the card and burst into laughter. Mark groaned and threw his head back on the couch.

She cleared her throat. "Speaking of doggy style…your dare is to get on all fours and playfully spank your booty in a naughty way."

"Oh, Christ!" He slapped his hands over his face. "Are you kidding? I can*not* catch a fucking break with this game."

"Giddyup, little pony!"

Mark slammed his palms on the cushions on either side of his hips. "You'll get yours."

"You keep saying that, but so far it's not happening. Now get down here and smack that ass, Mark." She scooted out from between his feet to the other side of the coffee table.

Grumbling under his breath, Mark joined her on the floor and reluctantly got on all fours, smacked his butt a few times, then sat down cross-legged. "Happy?"

"I'll accept that. You have been getting some pretty lousy cards."

"Thank you, and yes I have." He picked up the next. "Truth or Dare?"

"I'll take dare this time." Hopefully it would be another good one.

A slow grin crept over Mark's face, and he looked like he had just discovered the secret of the Holy Grail. "This one card makes all the shit cards I've received worth it." He licked his lips. "Are you ready for this?"

This was either going to be very good or very embarrassing. Possibly both. "Sure. Bring it." She waved him on.

"Using only your *feet*," he said with a pop of his eyebrows, "caress your way from my ankles to my inner thighs and back again."

The reason for his excitement became glaringly apparent. As much as he loved her feet, he had never asked her to do anything fetishy. But now he was going to get his dream come true, all because of this sexy game.

"How do we do this?" she said, taking off her socks, determined to give him the best fetishy foot feast she could. This game had been her idea, hadn't it? And this one dare would prove just how far she'd come in her quest to shed her old, shy ways.

He gestured toward the couch. "You might find it easier if you sit on the couch." He pushed the coffee table out of the way while she hopped up and took a seat. A few seconds later, he slipped out of his sweats, leaving on his undershorts. Then he situated himself in front of her and opened his legs, wearing a hungry smile. The revitalized tent in his shorts expressed his eagerness.

She had never done anything like this but was willing to give it a shot if it turned Mark on. "Okay, like this?" She pressed her toes to the insides of his ankles and smoothed them up his calves.

"Mmm, yes." He heaved a heavy sigh and leaned back on his arms.

She pushed the soles of her feet past his knees and curled her toes against his inner thighs. His erection bobbed and briefly strained the cotton fabric of his boxer briefs. He liked this more than she anticipated. She continued the upward climb along his inner thighs and pushed her toes under the bottom hem of his shorts, making him groan.

"I know it's not part of the dare," he said, "but I'd love it if you would keep going."

"Keep going?"

He pushed the waist of his shorts down and blinked almost drunkenly.

"You want me to put my feet on you?"

"Please…yes." His muscles flexed and bunched under his skin, making his body appear to be in constant, fluid motion. And it was damn near the sexiest thing she'd ever seen. But then Mark himself was the damn sexiest man she'd ever met.

Cautiously, she lifted her right foot and gingerly placed it at the base of his cock. Yes, she was beginning to like that word a bit better for his *junk*.

Mark moaned low and deep and dropped his head back.

She liked the way he responded. She spread her toes and rubbed up his shaft, her big toe and second toe massaging up either side, all the way to the head, where she rubbed her toes around and around. Something slippery coated the bottoms of her toes, and she spread it down the shaft. Mark groaned and stared, eyes hooded.

"Am I doing okay?"

"Better than okay." He sighed and squirmed, watching her foot rub slowly up and down.

After a couple more minutes, he gently pushed her foot away and pulled his shorts back up. "Thank you, but I think I have to stop you."

"Why's that?" she flirted. "Getting to be too much for you?" She skimmed her toes down his calves.

"Something like that, yes." He picked up the next card on the deck, sat forward, and handed it to her. "The next time we do that, we're using baby oil." He kissed her. "By the way, dare. My luck has to get better at some point."

She grinned, looked at the card, and read, "Place steamy kisses all over my face…except on my lips."

"Finally, a good one." He pulled himself to his knees, pushed her legs apart, and leaned in to kiss the tip of her nose. "Now this I can do."

He left a blazing trail of kisses all over her face. Her nose, her cheeks, across her forehead, even her eyelids again, then he kissed along her jaw. Pressing near to her ear, he said, "Dare me."

"But you don't have a card," she whispered. Her pulse hammered in her veins.

"I don't need one."

"Dare then." She was game for improvisation.

He licked her earlobe then said softly, "I'm going to whisper one sexy command into your ear. You must follow it."

"Okay." The timbre of his voice hinted of wicked decadence.

"Go into the bedroom," he whispered, "take off your clothes and lie down on the bed." He kissed the tender place just behind her ear. "Then wait for me to join you." He rocked backward, took her hands, and pulled her off the couch as he stood.

With one final heated glance his direction, she tore herself away and went to the bedroom. She closed the door, stripped, and then crawled into the center of the bed and lay down on her back.

A check of the clock on the nightstand showed they had been playing their naughty game for almost an hour. An hour of foreplay. And didn't Karma know it. Her body was alive and tingling, and her muscles quivered with anticipation. A pool of moisture slicked between her legs in the most debauched way, and abandon ruled her emotions. She was a woman quickly becoming lost to the pleasures Mark showed her, but which for so long she had thought would never be hers.

The door opened a few seconds later, and her anticipation spiked. He was naked, and his ruddy erection stood high and proud.

Without a word, he took her scarf from the pile of folded clothes on the dresser and slowly walked all the way around the bed, his gaze devouring her from every angle as he played the fabric through his fingers. Then he returned to the foot of the bed and stopped, playing the gauzy material loosely around one hand before unwinding it and placing it on the foot of the bed.

"Roll over for me." His rich voice purred.

She did as instructed, and he rubbed the soles of her feet. The mattress shifted as he climbed behind her and smoothed his hands up her ankles, calves, thighs, to her butt. His weight pressed forward as his hands continued up her back, to her arms, and then finally to her hands before skimming their way back along the path just traveled as he sat up and straddled her hips. His erection rested against her backside.

"Lift your head for me," he said.

She did, and the scarf came down over her eyes, blocking out the light coming in through the wall of windows on the east side of the bedroom.

"What are you doing?"

"Trust me." He knotted the scarf at the back of her head. "Too tight?"

"No." It was just right. "What are you going to do to me?" She had never been blindfolded and had to admit it excited her. With any other man, it probably would have scared her, but this was Mark, a man she had come to trust. She knew he wouldn't do anything she didn't want.

He kissed the back of her shoulder. "I'm going to give the lady what she said she's always wanted, but first…" He rolled her onto her back again. "A little fun."

She felt the mattress shift as he left.

With her sense of sight taken away, all her other senses were on high alert. And had he just said he was going to take her from behind? Was that what he meant by saying he was going to give her what she wanted?

The sound of ice clinking in a glass caught her attention, and she turned toward it. What sounded like a plate or bowl was set down on the nightstand, and the bed shook again as Mark rejoined her.

"What is that?"

His mischievous chuckle rumbled in her ear. "That's what you have to tell me."

Was this another game?

"What do you mean?"

His tongue—at least she thought it was his tongue—licked her shoulder. Yes, it was his tongue. She felt the subtle rasp of his whiskers.

He moved then went still. A moment later, something lightly touched her lips, making her jump. He rubbed the object more firmly back and forth. "Tell me what it is," he said.

Concentrating, Karma focused on what he pressed to her mouth. It was smooth but a little prickly, and she frowned behind the blindfold. No, prickly wasn't the right word, but it was definitely not a perfectly smooth surface. She licked her lips and picked up the faint flavor of…what was that? She smacked her lips together. It was fruity, sweet.

"Strawberries?"

"Mmm, good. Take a bite." He nudged the berry between her lips.

She bit off the end. Juicy sweetness slid over her taste buds.

Mark brushed the wounded berry over her lips, spreading the juice, then kissed her and licked it away. A moment later, the berry unexpectedly swirled around her nipple, and she sucked in her breath. His mouth followed and sucked off the juice, then he repeated on the other nipple. Then she heard the quiet crunch of him biting into the berry and chewing it.

"More?" he said.

She nodded and licked the taste of strawberries off her lips. "Yes."

She heard the sound of a spoon inside a glass jar. A familiar smell infiltrated her nose. "Peanut butter?" she said.

He chuckled. "Not quite, but you're close. Open."

She did, and something thick and sticky rubbed her upper lip as he slid the spoon gently into her mouth.

"Oops," he said. "Looks like I made a bit of a mess. Leave that for me." His quiet laughter made it sound as though he'd missed her mouth on purpose.

She swirled the buttery, nutty matter on her tongue. It wasn't as thick as peanut butter, and there was a hint of something else, cocoa maybe? "I don't know. What is it?" She finally said, giving up.

The mattress shifted, and then his mouth was on hers. He sucked in her top lip and licked off what he had smeared there, making her moan. God, he was a good kisser. A few seconds later, he released her lip. "It's gourmet espresso almond butter."

She giggled. "Oh gee, how did I not guess *that*?" She had never even heard of almond butter. But now that she had, she would have to buy some. It was pretty good.

"Stick out your tongue," he said.

"What?"

He pinched her nipple, which made her jump and sent a jolt between her legs. "Stick your tongue out for me."

She did as he said, and something sweet and syrupy dribbled onto it. Honey.

Before she could swallow and tell him what it was, he squeezed more on her left breast, circling her nipple. A moment later, his tongue lapped it up, and his teeth grazed the tight peak that formed.

Now, this was what she called playing with food. When she'd been a kid, she had sculpted mountains from her mashed potatoes and turned peas into torpedoes, which she flicked from the table to behind the refrigerator. Her aim had gotten pretty good, too. Of course, her fun had ended when ants invaded the kitchen and her parents discovered her spent arsenal when they moved the refrigerator. There was no more warrior princess of the pea after that. But now Mark was reintroducing her to the lost—but fine—art of food play. She needed to take notes. This could come in handy in the future.

The bed rocked again, and his legs straddled her body. "Stick your tongue out for me again."

More honey? She liked honey. She opened and offered him her tongue. But what she received wasn't more honey. A warm, rounded object settled against her tongue instead, and an instant later, he groaned.

"Fuck me, but that's sexy." His voice was an erotic rumble.

That's when she realized what he had put on her tongue.

Mark gazed down at the head of his cock resting on Karma's pretty pink tongue. He drizzled honey from his bear-shaped squeeze bottle onto the head and over her lips. Not much, just enough to make it sticky and slippery.

She lifted her hands to his hips as if she wanted to make exactly sure where he was, and then she drew them around to the front. One hand found his scrotum, which sent a wave of heat up and down his back and into his thighs, and then her other hand wrapped around his shaft at the same moment she closed her mouth around him.

Groaning, he capped the honey, tossed it aside, and grabbed hold of the headboard as he bent forward and watched the tip of his cock disappear inside her warm, sticky mouth. She was exceptional at fellatio. The way she touched him—the way she worked her tongue around the head and along the length—was by far the best oral sex he'd ever had. Was it because she was so inexperienced and had no preconceived notions about what he wanted? Was it because she didn't try to be an oral acrobat like some women he had known? Or was it something more, something deeper and more intimate. Whatever the reason, she could go down on him all night and he would be in heaven.

He pumped forward and back in shallow thrusts, being careful not to invade her mouth too deeply. That would be a betrayal of the trust she had granted him, and he wouldn't do that, no matter how intensely lust-driven he was. He gripped the headboard, clenched his teeth, and forced himself to maintain control as she licked and sucked away all the honey. Sweat broke over his face and chest from his self-imposed restraint, and he bit back a curse as pressure built inside his balls.

He abruptly pulled out of her mouth. "Roll over." As she did, he reached into the nightstand, grabbed a condom, and hastily rolled it on. "Lift your ass." He grabbed one of the pillows, thrust it under her hips, and lay down on her back. She moaned as he ground his cock against her backside. "Is this what you want?"

She nodded, breathing hard. "Yes."

"You want me to fuck you from behind?" He took hold of his cock and positioned it at the juncture of her body, using his fingers to find and part her lips.

She nodded again, more insistently. "Yes. God, yes."

After all their play, the blindfold, their growing intimacy, and yesterday's near-disastrous fight, they had finally come to a place of complete and total honesty with one another. Karma was more turned on than he'd ever seen her, and he was more keenly connected to her than he'd ever been.

The head of his cock breached her, and she gasped. He buried himself inside, and she moaned. And when he began pumping in earnest, she found his hands, planted on either side of her head, and gripped them tightly as she issued a protracted crescendo of exclamations for more and cries for harder.

This was how man and woman had been made to mate. So primal, so raw. Prudence and social acceptance were abandoned as instinct took over. The man's body craved the woman's, and logic had no place here. All there was, was desire and need. The need to sow and the desire to revel. Coupling like this, with such primitive intentions, was a religion. A spiritual experience. A testament to the dawn of man and the invisible forces that drew one man to one woman and compelled them to procreate.

Karma was a vessel of perfection. The way she lifted her head and pressed it against his shoulder, the desperate cries that ruptured from her throat, the way she clutched his hands like she was holding on to a life preserver in choppy water. All of it called to his base needs like a siren's song.

In this moment, she was his. All his. And he was hers. And as her body shattered into an earthquake of orgasm and a thousand aftershocks, Mark held on tight and let himself fall into her abyss. Pleasure erupted. Reality shifted. And for the moment, he wanted for nothing other than her. Her touch, her scent, her taste, the sound of her voice, and the sight of her beautiful, haunting eyes. For as long as he lived, he would never forget her eyes.

The spiritual moment gently faded as he lay against her back, spent, breathless, and drenched in sweat. Beneath him, she breathed heavily, just as swept away by their passion as he was.

He let go of her hand and untied the makeshift blindfold. She turned her head, blinked against the city lights breaking through the wall of windows, then looked over her shoulder.

"Where did you go just then?" she whispered.

So she had felt the magical transcendence, too.

He licked his lips and kissed her. "Nowhere. Nowhere but here with you."

Chapter 46

Honesty is the first chapter in the book of wisdom.
-Thomas Jefferson

At one o'clock in the morning, Karma slept the sated sleep of a woman well-tended, curled in Mark's arms. After their intense loving, they had taken a quick shower to rinse away the sticky remnants of juice, honey, and almond butter, made love one more time, and then she had drifted into sleep.

Her steady breaths were a stark contrast to her cries of pleasure earlier, but he liked both equally. Even now, he wanted to touch her, caress her face, wake her with kisses, and start all over again and lift her to the peak of pleasure just so he could watch her angelic face twist with passion and hear her cry his name.

She had turned out to be such a surprise. At every turn, she threw him a curve. With the women he dated before, he had anticipated their every move, gauging their reactions to the second. He had known when they would balk and when they would embrace. With Karma, he never knew. All he could do was make his best guess. Sometimes his guesses were on target, sometimes not.

Like tonight. She had taken to his game without a blink. Without resisting, she had let him blindfold her and put unknown objects in her mouth. He'd had no intention of tricking her or giving her something he thought would disgust her, but she hadn't known that. And yet she had accepted everything without question.

Trust existed between them. A kind of trust that only came with honesty and full disclosure. Last night he had finally come clean about his past and why he was the way he was, and instead of pushing him away and telling him this was all too much for her, Karma had bravely forged ahead. She knew the risks, and she knew he would leave and why, but that didn't deter her. She still wanted him for however long they had together, and that spoke highly of her spirit and courage, because he knew parting ways would be hard. For both of them. But that was how it had to be. He couldn't give her the future she deserved, and he couldn't risk letting go of his heart again. But there *was* a middle ground, and that's where the two of them now existed...in the thin sliver between the proverbial rock and a hard place. This was where the past and the future held no sway, where he could hold and cherish her before his inevitable departure. For now, this was enough, and from the way it looked, it was enough for her, too.

He grinned fondly as he watched her sleep. He was happy. With her, he found a measure of contentment he hadn't found with anyone else, not even Carol. But then he wasn't the same man he had been six years ago.

Karma's hair was tangled and knotted after their lovemaking, but the imperfection endeared her to him rather than made her appear flawed. Her lips were parted almost seductively even in slumber, urging him to kiss her. But he wouldn't. She needed to sleep.

If only he weren't so emotionally damaged, maybe they would have stood a chance. But a long-distance relationship would only end badly and destroy all the good memories they'd made during these few precious months. Trying to force a relationship would be a costly mistake, and he didn't want to do that to either one of them.

Still, everything about her seemed custom-made to fit, just like one of his tailored suits. Every inch of her molded perfectly to every inch of him. She was like a favorite sweater, warm and comfortable.

He stared at her, somnolent, ready for sleep but not wanting to miss a moment.

Closing his eyes, he listened to her soothing, deep breaths, felt the gentle rise and fall of her body against his, and let her warmth ease his mind.

Carol had ruined everything. She had taken away his confidence and his ability to give away his heart.

But she hadn't taken away this night. She hadn't robbed him of this one perfect, almost spiritual evening with his Karma.

His Karma.

Tonight, she belonged to him and his heart was hers.

"I love you," he whispered.

Just this once, in the magical silence of his bedroom, with her fast asleep in his arms, Mark admitted the truth. He did love her, and while he allowed himself this brief indulgence of honesty, he would never utter the words again. This was his moment, and now that he had said the words, he would hold them in his heart forever. He would set her free when the time came. He would. It was the right thing to do.

But for now, loving her was right. He sighed contentedly, burrowed his nose into her still-damp hair, and finally allowed himself to sleep.

Chapter 47

Sex is emotion in motion.
-Mae West

Mark rose with the sun, Karma still in his arms. Carefully, he pulled himself free, got out of bed, closed the curtains so the sunlight wouldn't wake her, and rubbed his palms up and down his face as he walked barefoot to the bathroom and closed the door.

After a quick shower, where he replayed the memories of last night like a favorite movie, he returned to the bedroom and quietly pulled on a pair of boxer briefs, nylon sweats, and a faded blue T-shirt that was so old the collar was frayed. The shirt was one of his favorites, and despite its tattered appearance, he had never been able to get rid of it.

He was funny like that. When he found something he loved, he simply couldn't throw it away. He still had cassette tapes from when he was a kid. Old classic rock stuff he had inherited from an uncle at the age of six. Even though he had no means of playing them anymore, he kept them for nostalgia. Every time he ran across them while digging through his things, good memories flooded his mind. That alone was enough to make him hang on to those antique cassettes.

He glanced at Karma, sleeping so peacefully, and smiled as he picked up his phone from the dresser. Aiming it, he took a picture and then a second, closer one. This was how he wanted to remember her. Tousled and glorious after their night of passion. Just like his old cassettes, he wanted to hold on to his memory of Karma long after their affair ended, and years from now, he would open these pictures and remember how, for a short time, he'd had it good. So wonderfully, perfectly good.

With another glance toward Karma to make sure she was still asleep, he quietly rummaged through her bag and found a pair of shorts, which he gently set on the foot of the bed. Then he scrounged one of his T-shirts from the closet, placed it beside her shorts—because he did enjoy seeing her in his clothes—and quietly slipped out of the bedroom, latching the door with a snick.

He made a pot of coffee, set out tea and a cup for when Karma woke, grabbed the Sunday paper from the hall, and took his coffee and paper to the balcony, where he parked in the early morning sun. A refreshing breeze blew off Lake Michigan.

About thirty minutes later, Karma joined him, holding her cup of tea and wearing a sleepy grin.

"Good morning, sexy," he said, setting his paper aside.

"Morning." She blew over her tea and gingerly sat in the chair beside him as if her body wasn't quite operational, yet. After last night, she was probably all kinds of achy, but in a good way.

Her hair was a mish-mash of combed tangles, and she was wearing his shirt and the shorts he had set out. Sleep still hung in her eyes, but he had never seen anything more beautiful.

"Come here." He held out his hand.

She set down her tea and slid from her seat into his lap, where she snuggled against him.

"Sleep well?" He brushed his palm down her hair. She smelled like mint toothpaste.

She nodded. "Uh-huh."

"Still tired?"

Again, she nodded. "Uh-huh."

"You hungry?"

Without preamble, she lifted her head and kissed him, catching him by surprise, and chiseled a crack into the concrete wall around his heart.

Her mouth was refreshingly cool and tasted of mint, and his reaction was instantaneous. His head drifted back, his arms encircled her, and he pulled her closer, greedy for the feel of her taking control. She held his face in her hands, her palms pressed against his cheeks, her thumbs crisscrossed under his chin, and her lips opened and closed in tender, hungry pulls against his mouth in a dreamy, affectionate display.

He could wake up to this every morning. He really could.

All too soon, she drew back and licked her lips, her cheeks flushed. "I could eat."

He smiled, his body ready for hers again. "You know, making love in the morning is a beautiful way to wake up."

She inhaled sharply, albeit quietly. "I wouldn't know."

It was the perfect thing for her to say at the perfect moment.

He pushed her off his lap, stood, and took her hand. "Then I think it's time you learned."

He led her back to the bedroom, left the door open, and pulled her down into bed on top of him, ready to savor her a little bit more before she left.

Chapter 48

Being honest may not get you a lot of friends, but it'll always get you the right ones.
-Author unknown

Mark stepped onto Rob's back patio. The radio was tuned to B96, and the backyard was full of people. A volleyball net was set up in the back part of the yard, and half a dozen guests were batting a white ball back and forth. Still more stood in cozy pockets around the patio.

Karma had left right after breakfast, leaving a gaping void, and he just didn't feel right without her. Maybe being around the festivities at Rob's house would lift his spirits.

A spread of appetizers and finger foods were set out on the table, shaded by a large umbrella, and a couple of giant, ice-filled coolers teeming with bottles of beer, water, and soda sat nearby. He grabbed a Budweiser.

"Hey, Mark." Rob spied him from the grill and headed over.

"Hey." The two clapped their right hands together and pulled each other in for a brief man hug, and then Mark stepped back and glanced around. "Lot of people."

"Yeah. I invited some of my coworkers." Rob's gaze swept around the yard. "Hey, by the way, I've got somebody I want you to meet."

Mark held up his hand defensively. "No. No fix-ups today, Rob." Rob had a habit of springing women on him at parties like this, and he wasn't in the mood to entertain some strange, random woman tonight. Not when the woman he really wanted was back in Indiana, over two hours away.

"This isn't a fix-up." Rob held out his hand as a pretty blonde approached. She took his hand and let Rob pull her in. "Mark, this is Holly. Holly, this is my best friend, Mark."

Rob was seeing someone? The prodigal bachelor was in a relationship? When had this happened? The guy had stars in his eyes and tiny hearts dancing around his head. Rob couldn't even tear his gaze from Holly, and that goofy, cheesy grin said plenty about his feelings.

"Hi. Nice to meet you." Mark held out his hand.

Holly had a firm, confident grip. Just like Karma's. Cue the tug at his heartstrings again.

"Nice to meet you, too," she said. "Rob's told me a lot about you." Holly had a smooth voice and spoke with clear enunciation.

"Holly is the director of marketing for a web marketing firm," Rob said proudly, clearly smitten.

For the next couple of minutes, they talked about work and careers…typical, first introduction type stuff.

"Holly! We're up!" Someone from the makeshift volleyball court called.

Holly waved over her shoulder. "Okay. Hold on." She turned back. "Good meeting you, Mark. Maybe we can talk more later."

"Absolutely." Mark tipped his Bud in acknowledgement.

With a smile, she stood on her tiptoes and gave Rob a quick kiss.

As he slid his arm around her waist, he said, "Go get 'em, tiger."

"I'll be back." An intimate look passed between them.

Mark knew that look. It was the same one that had passed between him and Karma about a hundred times the other day while playing basketball. The same one they gave each other every morning when he came around the corner at the office and every time she greeted him when he went to her place.

As Holly jogged off to the volleyball court, Mark followed Rob back to the grill, taking a swallow of beer.

"So, when did you two start dating?" he said.

Rob was still staring after Holly. "About three weeks ago."

Three weeks, and Rob was already this enamored? "Looks serious."

Rob spun around and tried to wave him off. "Nah." But that same cornball grin remained on his face, saying otherwise.

"Whatever you say."

A pair of barbecue tongs tipped with charred remains swung his way like a finger and waggled up and down. "You're one to talk."

Mark frowned. "What are you talking about?"

A long hard stare answered him as Rob's brow rose knowingly. "You know what I'm talking about. That cute little thing that came by your apartment Friday. Karma." He looked around. "Why didn't you bring her? I assumed she was staying the weekend."

"She needed to get back home." Just the mention of Karma's name did something to his ability to breathe, and he cleared his throat and looked away. "And you know what the score is with her. We're just having fun, remember? Nothing serious." What he felt for Karma was more serious than anything he had ever felt. Saying otherwise was like knifing his own gut.

"Bullshit, Mark. Don't try to pass that line of crap on me. I've known you too long. So, you can ride my ass all you want about Holly, but I'll just ride yours right back." He shook the tongs again, a smirk on his face. "I promise you that."

In an effort to defuse the conversation, Mark took another drink and backed into a nearby lounge chair.

But Rob wouldn't let the topic go. "Besides, if things aren't that serious, why did she drive to Chicago to see you?"

Sprawling open-kneed in the chair, Mark rested his Bud between his thighs. "It's not like that, okay? I've already told you…I just…I don't know…I like her. She's different." They were the same old tired excuses he'd been using for weeks, but nothing new came to mind. And he refused to go into the kiss and tell. Not about this. Not about Karma. Some things were too sacred to tarnish by blabbing about them to others, even his best friend.

"Yeah, you've told me." Rob gave him a dubious look. "I hear your words, Mark, but your actions are telling another story. But hey, that's cool. You like her. Nothing wrong with that." He paused. "But you're still going to say good-bye, aren't you?" He shook his head disapprovingly.

Mark collared the neck of the beer bottle between his index and middle fingers and lifted it to his mouth, averting his gaze. Rob was a smart fucker. He could see through Mark like he was made of glass.

"Tell me about Holly." Mark glanced back at his friend to see that lovesick grin plaster on his puss again.

"Nice change of subject, Ice Man." Rob looked over his shoulder at his new girl. "Holly's great. Beautiful, smart, funny."

"Sounds perfect." *Sounds like Karma.*

"Yeah, yeah." Rob fidgeted as he turned the smattering of meat on the grill.

"So, what? You gonna marry her or some shit?" Mark had meant it as a joke, but when Rob turned serious eyes on him, it was clear he wasn't laughing. Not even close.

"I think I will."

Mark puffed out an incredulous breath. "You can't be serious." Rob, the consummate single man. The guy who said he would never get married.

Rob looked over his shoulder again to make sure no one was within earshot. "I can't explain it, Mark, but…yeah. She's *it*. Holly's the one."

"I thought you said you'd be single forever." Why did this news unsettle Mark so much? He should be happy for Rob, but instead, he was agitated and quickly reminded of the empty loneliness of his own life. If Rob got married, it would grow even lonelier. Rob was screwing up the whole friendship dynamic. He was rearranging the terms and jacking up the feng shui of their relationship.

"Things change," Rob said. "People grow up." He glanced toward Holly. "And when you find something precious, you grab on and don't let go." He gave Mark a pointed look. "You might do well to remember that."

"If you have something to say, just say it." Irritation grated Mark's nerves. He was getting unusually aggravated by this conversation.

Rob twirled the tongs in his hand. "You've been through hell, buddy. I know that better than anyone."

Mark shifted uncomfortably, tension mounting in his neck and shoulders.

"But at some point," Rob said, "you need to move on. This isn't healthy, man. Karma obviously means more to you than—"

"Goddamn, Rob, you just won't drop it, will you? She's just another woman. I'm not in love with her." *Liar.* "I'm only with her while I'm working in Indy. And when I'm done there, we're done, too. End of story. You know how this goes. You know I'm not interested in anything serious."

"Yeah, and I also know that you're the most uptight, plan-your-life-to-the-millisecondest motherfucker I know. You planned your whole life with Carol before she even said 'I do,' and when she bailed, you unraveled. You didn't know which fucking way was up, and you nearly drowned yourself. Goddamn, loosen up and live a little. Stop living life like you're on a schedule. You're just pre-destining yourself for failure."

"Why? Because I refuse to let myself go through that shit again? It's called protecting myself."

"Protecting yourself, my ass." Rob flipped a burger with a little extra aggression. "Shit happens, Mark. It's part of life. You get up, dust yourself off, and move on. But in your case, Carol threw you so badly off your pre-defined timetable that you've never been able to get back on track." He nearly tossed a pair of hot dogs off the side of the grill. "So what? She didn't want you. Better you learned that before you exchanged vows than after, right? Consider it a blessing she gave you an out before tying you down, squeezing out kids, and taking half your shit in an ugly divorce." He pointed the tongs at Mark. "That, my friend, would have been truly disastrous and reason to drown yourself, given how much you're worth." He turned back to the grill.

"I don't need your glass-half-full bullshit right now, Rob." He loved Rob like a brother, but the guy was seriously grating his nerves.

"Yeah? Well, too bad, because I'm gonna say what needs to be said." Rob shut the lid of the grill and glared at him. "If you like this girl, grab her. Maybe fate made Carol leave you because the forces at work in the universe knew that she wasn't right and this girl is. I mean, look at her name, for God's sake. Karma. After the shit you went through as a kid, and after what Carol did to you, maybe her name is a sign that karma is coming back around to give you something good for a change." Rob paused then added, "What if you're pissing away God's gift to you, Mark, all because of some stupid vow you made to yourself about never letting your heart get hurt again?

"Life is about getting hurt, Mark. Without pain, we don't grow. But in your case, you shut down. You're still shut down. You've let Carol completely derail you. It's like she's still fucking you over six years later. Pick up your sorry ass, dust yourself off, and let yourself be happy again. Don't you think you deserve to be happy?" Rob held up his hand. "Oh wait, that's right, you've planned *not* to be happy so there's no way you could possibly let yourself deviate from your plan because then you would have to create a whole new schedule for the rest of your life. One that actually includes things like happiness and hope. My bad."

It was the most Rob had ever said about Carol at one time in six years, and it was the only time he had ever dared encroach on Mark's personal life in such an in-your-face way. "Shit, Rob, why don't you tell me how you really feel." Mark looked away and downed a heavy swig of beer.

"Man, you need to get out of your own way and give yourself an out clause from this self-imposed contract of yours." Rob looked over his shoulder toward Holly. "Life is not a contract we negotiate with ourselves. You and I both swore we would never get married, and now look at me." He grinned as Holly whacked the volleyball out of bounds and started laughing at herself. "Only three weeks in, and I'm ready to pop the question. I can't see my life without her. Is that crazy or what?"

Mark scowled from Rob to Holly and back. "Yes, it is. And I'm not you. So drop it." This conversation needed to end. Now. Before Mark lost his mind, got in his car, and drove back to Indy so he could see *her* again. His Karma.

Rob held his arms up in surrender. "Fine. But Mark, maybe it's time you grabbed on and didn't let go." Knowing eyes penetrated him to his soul. "That's all I'm saying, man. Maybe it's time to make some new promises and throw out the old ones that no longer serve you…draw up a new contract with your soul."

Rob returned his attention to the grill without another word. Conversation over. Thank God.

Mark wandered to the fence, away from the crowd, where he leaned against it and hung his beer over the other side. From his vantage point, he could just see beyond the houses to Lake Michigan. A yacht trolled slowly along the blue surface.

If only he were on that boat. With Karma. Just the two of them. Then he wouldn't feel so damn lonely.

Chapter 49

Worry is like a rocking chair. It gives you something to do but gets you nowhere.
-Erma Bombeck

Monday morning, Mark stood on his balcony, drinking coffee, gazing at the red sunrise. *Red skies in the morning, sailor take warning.*

Karma was supposed to go fishing with her dad today. Hopefully, they would have good weather.

Mark took out his phone and tapped out a message. *What are you doing?*

A minute later, his phone chimed. He smiled as he opened the message. *Good timing. I was just sitting here thinking about you.* She had attached a picture of a lake.

Another message chimed in from her. *What are YOU doing? :-)*

He smiled, lifted his phone, and took a picture of Lake Michigan and the sunrise. *Funny. I was just thinking about you, too,* he typed, attaching the picture.

Her next message warmed his heart. *Jinx. Buy me a Coke. We're both looking at water and thinking about the other. Why do I suddenly have to pee?*

LOL. Clever girl. Good to see you're comfortable enough to discuss bodily functions with me, though.

Ew. LOL.

You started it.

I know, and now I'm ending it.

Are you enjoying your day off with your dad?

Yes, but I miss my "teacher." I had a good time with him this weekend.

Mark's brow quirked, and he grinned. *Your teacher? Maybe I can meet him sometime.*

I'll ask him, but don't get your hopes up. He's kind of private. Likes to keep me to himself.

Smart man.

Eh, he's a'ight.

He laughed. *Just a'ight?* he typed.

LOL. Okay, so maybe I lied. But I don't want to bruise your ego.

No. Please. Bruise me. Tell me about him. He was having too much fun with this conversation. As he always did when he and Karma texted.

You're incorrigible.

And you're stalling.

Guilty.

Are you not going to answer my question, Miss Mason?

Oooo…you're using your teaching voice.

If that's what it takes to get you to spill, then yes I am.

He waited for what felt like an hour but was only a couple of minutes, and then his phone chimed again.

Fine. Be that way. It's your ego. If you must know, my teacher is to other men like a warm, chocolate chunk brownie swimming in hot fudge, with marshmallows, and drizzled with warm caramel is to a bite of milk chocolate. Both are nice, but one makes me moan and gives me goose bumps when he enters a room, while the other just makes me smile. And sometimes the other doesn't even do that. My teacher makes me feel beautiful, and he has shown me things I've only imagined, and for however long I have with him, I will be eternally grateful for all he has given me.

Speechless. She had rendered him speechless. For at least a minute, he could only stare at his phone and re-read her message, until finally he lifted his face against the wind and rubbed his palm and fingers over his pursed mouth as he stared out over the lake. Another crack formed in the wall around his heart, and he took a deep, shaking breath.

After a long moment when his emotions churned and threatened to overwhelm him, he typed out his reply.

I'm sure I can speak for him when I say that you are truly a remarkable, stunning, and glorious woman. Be assured, you bring out the best in him, as well. And wherever he is right now, I bet he's wishing he was with you instead, so he could thank you for your kind words in person.

He leaned against his banister and gazed out at the blue expanse of the lake, at the red sunlight reflecting off the waves that rolled and rippled toward the shore.

When his phone chimed, he eagerly read her message.

I hear he's standing on a balcony, somewhere in Chicago, looking at Lake Michigan.

And there came another crack in his armor, and his heart melted a little bit more. What was happening to him?

I miss you. His thumb hovered over the send button, but when he re-read what he had written, he frowned. He couldn't send that. Not *that* message. It was all wrong. But felt so damn right. But if he went down that road, it would lead him away from the control he coveted and longed to retain, putting it right back in her hands.

This relationship wasn't about love and emotion, or commitment, or missing her, or of anything permanent. To tell her he missed her would only set them both up for inevitable pain. Well, more pain than what they would both already feel when he said good-bye.

He backspaced the message and started over.

And I hear he is very much looking forward to seeing you again.

That was much better. The personal component was gone, and he was still telling the truth. He hit the send button.

Me, too, came her reply.

His breath caught, and suddenly, all he wanted was for her to be there, with him as she had been this weekend, both of them looking out at the lake, his arms around her waist and his nose buried in her hair.

I'll see you soon. I have to run. Some of us have to work today. Enjoy the rest of your day off. He set the phone on the small patio table and sat in his lounge chair in his sweats and T-shirt, one arm crossed over his torso, his other hand pressed to his chin.

When his phone chimed, he glanced over and read the message.

Work hard. Talk to you soon.

He closed his eyes and leaned back. His apartment already felt desolate without her. After just a couple of days, she had completely invaded his space. He couldn't look around his apartment and see one place that didn't remind him of her. He didn't even want to wash the shirt she had worn, which still held a touch of her scent.

This assignment needed to end. And soon. Because he was becoming emotionally compromised with this one. From a rational perspective, he needed to pull back, but every time he tried, he found himself drawn further in.

And he had no idea how to stop the train from careening off the tracks.

Karma tucked her phone into her hip bag.

"What are you smiling about?" her dad asked, coming back from his truck and dropping their tackle boxes beside her on the bank.

"Nothing." But she couldn't wipe the goofy grin off her face. If anything, it got bigger. And for the cherry on top, her face heated.

"I saw you over here on your phone." He frowned. "Were you talking to that *boy*? Mike or Mark or whatever his name is?"

"Mark," she said. "And yes. I was." She busied herself with her tackle box.

"Is that where you were this weekend?" He began loading the boat. "Why you didn't come over?"

She sighed and stood, fishing pole in hand. "Yes, Dad. I went up to Chicago to see him."

He shook his head but didn't say anything as he checked the truck, locked it, and waited for her to climb into the boat. He got in, used one of the oars to push them away from the bank, and started rowing through the water. She wiped perspiration from her forehead. A humid mist clung to the water's surface.

"I don't like you with that boy," Dad said.

Tell me something I don't know.

"He's not a boy, Dad. He's a man."

"He's a boy to me." He continued rowing them to their favorite spot. "A man wouldn't behave the way he is. And don't tell me you think he's going to stick around when his job here is done."

"I don't think that." She stared ahead, refusing to meet her dad's eye. Knowing that Mark would leave soon was bad enough. She didn't need her dad rubbing salt in the wound.

"What you need is some smart fella who'll treat you right and not skip out when he's done using you."

"Dad!" She spun around and scowled at him. "Mark is not *using* me, and he's not going to *skip out* on me, either. He's good to me, and I like him, okay?" She turned back around, her good mood of a few minutes ago spoiled like month-old milk.

"Honey, if he was really good to you, he wouldn't be doing what he's doing." The oars dipped into the water and gurgled as he rowed. "Nice boys don't mess around with the girls they work with."

Were they still having this conversation?

"Maybe when you were younger that was how things were done, Dad, but that's not how it is, anymore. More and more people meet their spouses at work now. It's a proven fact." She crossed her arms and kept her gaze straight ahead on the misty water.

"Yeah, and look at how many people end up getting divorced." Dad harrumphed. "I'll stick with the old ways."

"Are we really going to spend the day talking about this?" She shot him a glare. "I thought we were going to spend a nice day together."

"We are." Dad shrugged innocently. "I'm just looking out for my little girl is all."

"Well, stop it. I've got this, Dad. Trust me."

And she wasn't a little girl, anymore, either. She needed her dad to get on board with that idea immediately. Mark was *her* problem, not her dad's, and she could handle him without her dad's help.

The thing was after this past weekend, Mark was an even bigger complication than before, because she had finally realized she was, in fact, in love. Hopelessly, unbelievably, and irrevocably in love. But, like it or not, Mark was going to leave.

And therein lay the biggest problem of all.

Chapter 50

I think that sexuality is only attractive when it's natural and spontaneous.
-Marilyn Monroe

More than half the office was out on vacation for the week after the Fourth of July.

When Karma returned to work on Tuesday morning, she sat in a veritable ghost town. Don was out. Jolene was out. Lisa was out. All but two members of Sales and Marketing were out. A quick trip through the war room, where the project teams worked when they were in the office, revealed that only Jasper and Courtney were working in the office this week. The rest who hadn't taken time off were working from home.

Karma meandered back to her desk. As she passed the conference room, she flicked a despondent glance at the empty chair where Mark usually sat when he was there.

But he wasn't this week.

He, too, had taken the week to work from Chicago and finish getting his affairs in order after the break-in.

Tuesday remained quiet all day. She made major headway on the upcoming quarterly presentation, but by the end of the day, she actually got a little bored. With no one in the office, the workload was lighter than she thought it would be.

Wednesday was more of the same, and by the end of the day, she was finished with the presentation and had cleaned out her files, her e-mail, and had played with some ideas for a new presentation template for October's quarterlies.

On Thursday morning, she stopped at the store and bought a smattering of magazines, *The New York Times*, and the local newspaper before heading in to the office. She needed something to keep her mind busy, and since she was all caught up—a rarity to be sure—having some reading material on hand was a must.

Feeling like a whole lot of ho-hum-I-wish-I-were-in-Chicago, she made her way up the stairs to her desk. At the foot of the hall, her steps faltered. Something was different this morning. The air held a different spark. A familiar scent, ever-so-subtle, touched her nose. Trying not to appear overly eager, she hurried down the hall and came out on the other side just as Mark emerged from the conference room as if he had felt her presence, too.

They both stopped, and she sucked in her breath. He was beautiful, as always, even though he was only wearing simple charcoal grey trousers and a dark blue pullover.

"Can I see you for a minute, Miss Mason." He turned back around and disappeared inside the conference room.

She dropped her bags and magazines on her desk and tamed her excitement enough that she didn't fly into the room behind him.

"Yes?"

"Close the door," he said without looking at her.

She did as he said, and the door latched quietly.

He turned around, and she couldn't quite place the look in his eyes, but it caused her heart to race.

"Lock it."

Obediently, she did as he commanded. The week had just gotten very interesting.

In four long strides, he was on her, his hands lifting her skirt. "How has your week been, Miss Mason?"

"Boring." She loved when he called her Miss Mason. It made her feel like they were strangers or mere acquaintances, and in light of how familiar they were with one another, his using such a formality often added to their intense chemistry.

He pulled off her panties. "Boring?"

She nodded as cool air washed over her bare flesh. "Until now."

His lips quirked and the jangle of his belt preceded the sound of his zipper opening. "Lesson," he said.

Already flooded with desire so intense she could barely stand, Karma could only nod, ready to learn. But, clearly, this was a very specific lesson, with hands-on application.

A square cellophane packet appeared in her hands as if by magic.

"Office sex can be a good thing," he said. "Under the right circumstances." He nodded toward the condom. "Put it on me."

She had never put a condom on a man before. Mark had always taken care of that. "I don't—"

He shushed her as he backed her toward the wall. "I'll help."

She tore the packet open and took out the latex sheath.

He flipped it in her fingers. "It goes on this way, so that it unrolls down my cock." He helped her position it. "Leave a little at the tip and gently roll it on me."

She did as he instructed, then he lifted her up and pressed her back against the wall.

And then he was inside her.

Oh God. She was hot. So hot. So needy. She hadn't realized how much she'd missed him until just now.

"Office sex must be fast," he said, grabbing her hips and taking her harder than he had last weekend. "And quiet."

"Uh-huh." She clung to his neck, already feeling herself climbing toward release.

"Can you be quiet, Miss Mason? Can you come without screaming my name?" He sounded just as close as she already was.

With a shuddering breath, she nodded.

"This is not making love, Miss Mason." He grunted between clenched teeth as he drove into her. "*This* is fucking."

Just hearing him growl the dirty word pushed her toward climax.

"There is a time and a place for both." His fingers dug into her flesh.

Hell yes there was!

The whole act lasted maybe three minutes from start to finish. Quick, dirty, hard, and furtive. As she came, with her lips against his in a silent kiss, she shuddered violently and whispered his name at the same time he sighed hers on a tense breath and climaxed.

Still breathing heavily, he quickly pulled out, peeled off the condom, and pulled up his pants as she straightened her skirt and blouse as if they had done nothing more than run through a sales report, except her legs were still trembling and her insides were still pulsing through the tail end of her orgasm.

She had never had office sex, so dirty and almost panicked in its pace. At any moment, someone could have knocked on the door and discovered them. But that hadn't happened. They had done the deed and no one was the wiser. Not that there were many in the office to interrupt them. Which had made this the perfect time for such debauchery.

Mark had defiled her, corrupted her innocence, and seduced her into the most depraved act she had ever committed.

A smile crept over her lips as she took her panties from him and pulled them back up her legs.

"Why are you smiling like that?" he said, stepping close and wrapping his arms around her waist as she finished situating her clothes.

"I was just thinking about how fun that was."

"I thought you would stop me."

She laughed. "Are you surprised I didn't?"

"Yes, but glad."

"Me, too."

With an affected shake of his head, he said, "You continue to surprise me, Karma. Just when I think I know how you'll react, you go the complete opposite direction." He kissed her. "I like it. Keeps me on my toes."

"It's your fault. I was never like this until you came along."

"Well, I'm glad I came along then."

After another quick kiss, he pulled away, ran his hands down his shirt and gave her the once-over to make sure she was put together before unlocking the door. As he opened it, he said, "Thank you for getting right on that, Karma."

That was her cue to pull the façade back into place. "Absolutely."

As she was leaving the room, he stopped her. "Could you grab my coffee, please?"

She looked around. It was just the two of them. Casting him a coy look, she leaned close and whispered, "Get your own damn coffee, *Mr. Strong.*"

His hearty laughter as she spun and sashayed away on unsteady legs was like a symphony, and a moment later, as he passed her desk with his mug in his hand, heading in the direction of the coffee station, their eyes met. Amusement lit his face.

"Just you wait, Miss Mason. I'll make you pay for this."

"Ooo, promises promises."

He winked and disappeared around the corner.

Thursday was looking up. And so was Friday.

Chapter 51

I've been out with some extremely beautiful women who have had no sex appeal whatsoever. It really is a lot more than skin deep.
-Rod Stewart

Sitting at the conference room table, Mark swiveled in his chair and glanced at the wall where he and Karma had made love. Or, rather, fucked. He hadn't expected her to go through with it. He really hadn't. But, as usual, she had surprised him. She had a way about her that threw him into a tailspin. Like a surprise ending to a movie, she always gave him something he didn't expect.

Maybe that was why he was here now. Because he wanted more of those surprises. He was becoming addicted to them.

He wasn't supposed to be in Indiana this week. He had planned to stay in Chicago. But he had been slowly going stir-crazy. All he could think about was getting back here to see her, touch her, kiss her.

He pulled out his phone and typed out a text.

I'd like to see you tonight.

Her phone chimed at her desk, but he refused to glance at her.

A moment later, she replied. *I'd like to see you, too.*

He smiled and could feel her eyes on him.

7:00? Dinner? My place?

He buried his face in the reports on his laptop, and a moment later, she appeared by his side, a fresh mug of coffee in her hands. He turned, surprised to see her there.

"You looked like you could you use a fresh cup," she said, leaning down. "What are you working on? Anything I can help with?"

Turning back toward his tablet, he said, "Always." Little did she know, but he had plenty she could help him with, both professionally and personally. Another round against the wall would be fabulous, but he wouldn't risk that again.

She inched closer, and he closed his eyes as her lips pressed against his ear. "Dinner at seven o'clock at your place would be perfect," she whispered.

Then she pulled away, stood up, and walked back out. Just that quickly, Karma stole his concentration and another chunk of his heart.

As she retreated to her desk, he stared after her in amazement.

The student had become the teacher, and just that quickly—just that easily—control shifted back into her hands. Once more, the power was hers, even though he had been trying so hard to keep it within his grasp.

He sent her another text. *Make sure you bring an overnight bag, Miss Mason. You'll be spending the night.*

This time, he looked at her as her phone chimed. Her cheeks turned red as she typed out a reply. His phone signaled the arrival of her text just as she met his gaze with a shy smile. *I had a feeling. Want me to bring my Truth or Dare game?*

He chuckled and tapped out his response. *No. I have another game we can play.* He had plenty of fun ideas to keep them entertained.

Another game?

Yes. Now, get to work. I hear you've got a consultant in your office who's watching everyone like a hawk. Some more than others.

A moment later, his phone beeped. *Yes, we do. And he's seriously distracting me right now.*

How so?

By being the sexiest thing I ever laid eyes on.

He had never had this much fun with anyone he'd dated. *Rest assured. He's just as distracted.*

Why's that?

Because he can still smell the scent of you on his body from when he fucked you against the wall this morning. He's in a terrible state.

His message was intended to shock, and when he glanced her way, he got the response he wanted. She gasped and shot a wide-eyed look at him, her mouth open in silent surprise.

Gotcha. He grinned and chuckled as he typed out another message. *I love how you react when I play with you.*

Maybe we should take the afternoon off and play back at your place.

His brow quirked. Not a bad idea. *Think anyone would notice we're gone?*

A moment later, he received her reply. *You're not even supposed to be here. And I haven't had anything but a presentation to work on (finished, btw) for two days with two-thirds of the office out. What do YOU think?*

Mark leaned back in his chair and glanced toward her. She arched her brow as if challenging him. Making his decision, he stuffed his files in his bag and packed up his laptop and tablet. Then he rose, pushed his chair under the table, and shut off the lights.

"Miss Mason, I'll be working from home the rest of the day. If anyone needs me, you can reach me on my cell."

She nodded, and a mischievous grin spread over her delightful face. "Well, enjoy the rest of your day then."

He leaned on her counter and whispered, "I'll see you soon."

She winked. "Yes, you will."

He turned on his heel and headed for the stairs. Thank goodness he had come back to Indianapolis a few days early.

Chapter 52

The only limits you have are the limits you believe.
-Wayne Dyer

Karma's back arched off the bed so violently, Mark had to latch on with his mouth, trying for dear life to hold on as an abandoned shriek tore from her throat.

"I'm-coming, I'm-coming!"

Her thighs clamped around his head, her fingers dug into his scalp, and she cried out again. He actually felt the tiny contractions of her tender flesh against his mouth and fingers as he held her swollen clit against his tongue.

This after only thirty minutes of playing Strip Chess.

After some time had passed, the convulsions rippling her body ceased, her breathing evened out, and she relaxed. Her legs unlocked from around his head, and, with a soft kiss against her vulva, he crawled up her body then lay down beside her, pulling her against him.

"Are orgasms always stronger when the Ben Wa balls are in?" She lifted on one elbow and peppered his chest with kisses.

"So I hear." He had been pleasantly surprised to feel the twin metal balls inside her when he entered her. He'd been so excited that he hadn't been able to last and had come before she could join him, which obligated him to go down on her so she could finish.

"Then I need to wear them more often." She lowered herself and rested her cheek on his chest.

"You won't hear any complaints from me." He lazily brushed his fingers up and down her arm.

For a while, neither spoke, relishing the quiet stillness that always wrapped around them after sex, then Mark said, "I met with my boss yesterday."

"Oh?" her fingers pressed more firmly against his skin.

"Yes. My assignment is entering the final stage. Things are progressing well." Bad choice of words, because the better his assignment progressed, the sooner it would end and he would leave.

"I see. How long?"

"A month, two at the most."

She huddled closer.

"Hey, I'm not going anywhere, yet." He kissed the top of her head.

"I know." Her voice sounded fragile. "I'm fine."

"No, you're not fine." He rolled her to her back and pinned her down. "And I'm not, either." There. He'd said it.

"You're not?"

"Of course not. I like you. I'm having a very good time with you."

"So am I."

He lowered onto her body and sighed against the side of her neck, praying the weeks would pass slowly. "I just wanted you to know so you weren't surprised. We have plenty of time left, okay?"

"Okay."

But they didn't have plenty of time. Mark knew it and Karma knew it. But it would have to be enough, because as much as he wanted to take Rob's advice and let go of the past and embrace a new future, he couldn't.

He just couldn't.

Chapter 53

Everything that has a beginning, has an ending. Make your peace with that and all will be well.
-Buddha

Karma tried not to think about Mark's looming departure, but each day brought the end of their relationship a little more into focus, and the weeks passed faster than she could keep track. She took advantage of every opportunity to spend time with him.

Mark seemed just as motivated to make the most of their time together, as well, because after that night he never brought up his eventual return to Chicago again. It was as if he wanted to focus on what little time they had together instead of the brick wall looming in the distance.

But she knew the end was coming. An hourglass sat over their heads, and grain-by-grain, time slipped further away. The nights spent together, the laughs, the way they seemed so perfect together. All of it would eventually cease.

Karma lay in bed and stared at the ceiling. It was now the first week of September. She and Mark had been together four months. Four incredible, magical months. In one respect, it felt much longer than that, but in another, it felt like they had only just met.

It was a rare night when they weren't together. She slept as many nights in his bed as her own, and when she was in her own, he was usually with her. Not that they always made love. Three or four nights a week, he had business dinners or work to do after regular hours and showed up at her place a little before bedtime. Or he would call her from his place to let her know he was home and invite her over.

And then there were the nights he was in Chicago and she was here. Sometimes they would talk on the phone, and sometimes they only texted back and forth, but no matter how she sliced it, she and Mark either saw each other or communicated in some way at least once every day. He had become the most dominant force in her life, and she had never felt so confident and purely feminine.

It was hard to believe that only four months ago she had been a different person. Thanks to Daniel and that red dress, he had unknowingly thrust her into Mark's path, and she had found her true self through his eyes. She smiled into the darkness. Four months ago, she had been a naïve mess, lost, confused about what she wanted and who she was, and a little self-conscious. But not anymore. She was still a good girl, but now she was the type of good girl who embraced a little sexy, a little bad. She had become good-but-a-little-naughty Karma.

Her phone chimed on her nightstand. It had to be him. He was the only one who would text her after ten o'clock, and even then, he didn't do it often.

She picked up her phone and read his message.

Hey, beautiful. Are you sleeping?

She grinned and texted back. *No. Are you?*

LOL. No. Want company?

Do you have to ask?

A knock came at her door less than a minute later as if he had been waiting outside in his car.

She darted into the living room. "That was fast," she said, pulling the door open.

He was on her so swiftly she didn't even have time to blink. Strong arms pulled her in as he kicked the door shut behind him. Without a word, he lifted her, his mouth hot with kisses so blazingly intense, he stole her breath. Within record time, she was back in her bedroom, on her bed, her pajamas discarded wherever he had thrown them.

The sex consumed her, his body almost desperate with urgency as he sank inside. Something was different tonight. Something raw and almost frantic dwelled inside his coiled muscles as he rolled and surged above her.

"Come with me," he gritted between clenched teeth.

They had found that rhythm long ago. After making love so many times, he knew her body better than she did, and simultaneous climax wasn't something they struggled with. But tonight he seemed especially keen on the two of them hitting the end together. It seemed important. Almost crucial.

Barely hanging on for the ride, Karma hooked her arms under his and gripped his shoulders from behind, crying out with each urgent thrust. She was close, and she wouldn't disappoint him.

"Hurry!" Desperation gripped her body. Whatever drove Mark tonight, she was on board and ascending with him, unable to hold back as he unleashed a torrent of pleasure that invaded her senses.

"I'm close." A long, ragged groan rumbled in his throat, and he repositioned himself so he could meet her gaze and hold it. That connection, that link between them. No one before and no one ever again would claim this mastery over her. She was all his and always would be.

"So am I," she whispered urgently.

"I'm about to come." Duress tightened the skin around his eyes. His jaw clenched, but his gaze stayed locked on hers. He wouldn't even blink.

"Don't stop don't stop!" She was about to come, too.

"Now, Karma!"

Both of them let loose a guttural cry of release, their bodies hitting the height of the crescendo simultaneously, shredding them with jarring spasms that rocked them to their souls.

For several long moments, not a word was uttered, just the shuddering sounds of breathing mingled with broken moans. And then he fell on top of her, driving his arms around her, crushing her to him as if he would never let go.

They stayed like that for a long time. So long that Karma began to worry that something was wrong.

Just as she was about to ask if he was okay, Mark sighed, kissed her neck, and eased away.

"That was…" she began.

"Good," he said, filling in the blank.

"I was thinking more along the lines of intense."

He grinned, but the gesture didn't quite touch his eyes. Something was bothering him. "Intense is good."

"Yes, it is." She combed her fingers through the dark hair on his chest.

Tonight hadn't been about a lesson plan or what he jokingly called hands-on teaching. In fact, as the weeks had ticked by, it seemed like, more and more, their time together had become more about just that: spending time together. The level of comfort between them was more like that of a bona fide couple, not two people having a temporary affair.

He got up, went to the bathroom to discard the condom and clean up, then returned to the bed. He sank onto the mattress and pulled her into his arms. "I had a conference call with my boss tonight," he said quietly as his fingers tickled her arm in a feathery, affectionate dance from her shoulder to her elbow and back up.

A momentary pulse of fear jolted her. Without hearing him say it, she knew their time was up. The inevitable end had come.

"And…?" she said.

He sighed. "My assignment's over."

So the hammer fell.

"Oh." That was all she could say, because her mind went blank.

They hadn't talked about this moment since Fourth of July weekend, as if both had refused to risk damaging their magical dynamic. No sense talking and worrying about an ending they couldn't do anything about, right?

Well, they had to talk about it now. And Karma wasn't prepared. Like a speech she hadn't practiced beforehand, all she could do was stand at the front of the room and stare blankly at all the eyes looking at her. She had no notes to refer to, no experience to pull from, nothing at all to help get her through this.

So she said nothing.

"All the reports are done," he said. "The analysis is complete. Recommendations have been made and accepted." Mark's fingers continued caressing her as if they weren't playing from the same program as his words. "All that's left to do is pull the trigger."

What an appropriate expression, because right now, it felt like someone had shot her in the chest.

"How long will that take?" She had finally found her voice, and now survival mode kicked in.

He answered the real question. "Next week is my last week. Don will be telling you tomorrow, so I wanted to make sure you knew in advance so you weren't caught off guard."

In other words, he wanted her prepared so she didn't behave inappropriately when Don told her, lest she let the cat out of the bag about their relationship.

"Oh." She was back to one-syllable responses.

Silence engulfed them for several minutes, then, out of the blue, he said, "Come to Chicago with me this weekend." He spoke as if he hadn't just dropped a weapon of mass destruction in her bedroom. "Spend one last weekend with me where we don't have to hide from everybody."

The fact he wanted to take her away for a weekend brightened her spirits a little. She had one more week left with him, and it wouldn't do any good to mope around and waste that time. It was a much better idea to embrace these final days and make them count. But count for what? She didn't know, she just knew she needed to make them count.

"I'd like that," she said. She forced a fake smile, but who was she fooling? She was hurting so badly. This was heartache. Now she knew why people called it that, because her chest felt like an elephant was sitting on it.

"Me, too." His voice took on a clinical tone. "We'll drive up tomorrow night after work, if that's okay."

Tomorrow was Friday. Doomsday, as far as she was concerned. "Sure. After work is fine."

She suddenly didn't know how to talk to him. The walls that had dropped around him over the past couple of months seemed to have fully reformed, and she couldn't seem to bridge the divide already pushing them apart. He already seemed to be pulling away.

She recognized his behavior as a defense mechanism. Of course he would have one. Maybe she needed to get one, too.

He rolled to the side of the bed and sat up. "I need to get going."

"Okay. Yeah, it's late."

Normally, he would stay, but not now. The magic was over. He was leaving in a week. The carriage was turning back into a pumpkin, and her prince was stealing her magic glass slipper. Only, in her case, it was her heart.

He found his pants and pulled them on, taking away her view of his muscular thighs and backside. And then he fumbled with his shirt, turning it right-side out. Within seconds, his perfectly sculpted six-pack and the lightly hairy chest she had grown so fond of were stolen from sight, too.

Everything was different now.

They had spent a beautiful summer together. One she would never forget. Ever. Because you didn't forget men like Mark. He had transformed her from a girl to a woman, taking her from gawky, geeky, and insecure to comely, confident, and self-assured. The man was a miracle worker. He had delivered everything he had promised.

And that was where it ended. No extras were thrown in. She would receive no gold stars for being an honor student. There would be no happy, surprise ending.

After he sat down on the edge of the bed and pulled on his shoes, he leaned down and kissed her, but there was no passion in his lips. Not like there had been when he swept through her door not even an hour ago and stole her breath with an urgency that screamed into the depths of her soul.

"Good night," he said.

"Good night."

He got up and walked out of her room, and a moment later, she heard the front door open and close.

And a moment after that, she rolled over and buried her face against her pillow.

And cried like she never had before.

Until she finally cried herself to sleep.

Mark drove back to his condo in a stupor. The ache in his chest gnawed his sternum like an army of carpenter ants devouring a fallen tree.

But he refused to give in to the pain.

He pulled into his garage, parked, walked calmly inside, grabbed a bottle of water from the fridge, drank the whole thing, trudged up the steps to his loft, and got undressed.

The pain magnified the longer he tried to ignore it. He would not give. He wouldn't. He couldn't. He was doing the right thing—what he had promised from the very beginning.

Entering his bathroom, he flipped on the faucet, leaned over, and splashed cool water on his face.

Splash-splash.

But the ache continued to intensify. He tried taking deep breaths. He tried closing his eyes. But nothing helped.

Bile rose in his throat, and he gagged. No. He was in control. He was. He shook off the wave of nausea, doused his face again with more water, took several deep, shaky breaths, then gazed at his reflection.

Oh God. This wasn't happening. Not again.

Falling to his knees in front of the toilet, he tried to keep it down. He fought, he swallowed, but it was useless. He couldn't fight his anguish any longer. He threw up, sobbing even as he continued to wretch. When the gagging stopped, he threw his arm over the seat and rested his forehead against the front edge, lost to wracking sobs that tore at his raw throat like the tines of a fork. Tears splattered the tile floor.

It had been six years since he'd cried—truly cried. But this time it wasn't Carol who had forced his emotions to overflow.

It was Karma.

More specifically, his feelings for her.

He loved her. In his heart, he knew the truth, no matter how much he tried to deny it.

But his relationship with Karma was over.

And there was nothing he could do about it.

Chapter 54

Welcome to the Karma Café. There are no menus. You will get served what you deserve.
-Author Unknown

The next morning, after applying ice packs to her dry, swollen eyes, which felt hot to the touch, and willing herself not to cry anymore, Karma gathered herself, got ready for work, and headed in to the office.

She had to act unaffected when Don told her. Talk about a poker face. She'd never been good at poker. And that made her think about blackjack, which made her think about Mark, and she was crying again.

She pulled over, dried her eyes, and touched up her makeup, but who was she kidding. She looked awful. Maybe no one would notice. Then again, what if she couldn't hide how upset the news made her that Mark's assignment with Solar was up? Somehow, the idea of dropping to her knees and praying that he wouldn't go seemed like it would give things away.

Just a tad.

Inevitably, her short drive to work came to an end, and she faced the longest walk of her life. Steeling herself, she got out, threw Mark's BMW a mournful glance, and headed up the sidewalk.

As she walked in, Nancy was already situated at the front desk and caught her eye. "I think something big is happening today," she said in a hushed voice.

Karma forced a perplexed, I-wouldn't-know-a-thing-about-it look on her face. "What do you mean?"

Nancy waved her over. "Mark was in early. Don's already with him. And HR has been in and printing off documents since seven o'clock."

Nancy looked at her as if she was fishing for information.

"I guess we'll find out what's going on soon enough," Karma said, trying to act clueless.

If only Nancy knew, what was about to go down today was nothing compared to what had gone down last night. Call her selfish, but Karma wasn't feeling too sympathetic or compassionate to the plights of those who may or may not be losing their jobs today. Maybe under better circumstances, or maybe pre-Mark Strong, she would have given a damn about the fate of her coworkers, but with her own problems to worry about, which felt like the weight of the Rocky Mountains on her shoulders, there wasn't a whole lot of energy left for anyone else. She needed to save her strength to endure the natural disaster about to occur in a week when Hurricane Mark finally moved back out to sea and left her in a state of emergency.

Karma left Nancy at the reception desk and headed upstairs. Mark and Don were already in the conference room poring over a stack of papers. Mark already had his coffee.

Disappointment throttled her. Apparently, she couldn't even get his coffee, anymore. The transition back to being Mark-less had begun.

Silly girl. It had begun last night when he left her apartment instead of staying. Screw that. It had begun the moment she wore that brooch to work back in May. She had known then that this day was coming.

She set down her bags, resisting the urge to stare at Mark's perfect profile. And failing. He looked tired, his shoulders rounded instead of squared.

"Karma. Ah, there you are. Could you step in, please?" Don said, turning to see her sitting there.

Mark didn't even flinch.

"Uh, sure." She got up and hurried in. At least, she hurried as much as she could, being that she felt like a giant ball of lead.

Mark finally turned and met her gaze as she entered. His eyes were bloodshot, and when he spoke, his voice was full of gravel, as if his throat was irritated. "Don and I will need your assistance today," he said. Then he cleared his throat as he glanced down at his paperwork and lifted his mug of coffee for a sip. "We'll be talking to some of the employees and will need you to call them in for us."

"Yes, of course." She frowned. "You sound like you're catching a cold."

He kept his eyes averted. "Allergies. Seems the dry summer finally caught up to me."

Hmm. He had seemed fine last night. Better than fine, actually. Not a hint of the sniffles.

A moment later, Kathy, the HR director, walked in with a file folder in her hand.

Don gestured for Karma to have a seat then shut the door. "We thought we would start with you," he said. "Get it out of the way, so to speak, so you wouldn't sit and worry all day."

She wanted to ask, "Get *what* out of the way?" But given her conversation with Nancy, she was pretty sure *what*. And based on Don's proud smile, she was one getting good news today.

If only he knew that all the good news in the world wouldn't make up for the one bit of bad news she had received last night.

She sat down and laid one hand over the other on the polished wood.

"Karma," Don began, "Mark and I have discussed your future with Solar quite extensively in the past few weeks."

Her gaze flicked to Mark, who met her eyes for only a second before he looked back down at the piece of paper in front of him.

"Mark seems to think you've got a tremendous amount of potential," Don said. "He advises that your talents extend far beyond what even I was aware of."

The tops of Mark's cheeks reddened, and he cleared his throat again.

Was he thinking the same thing she was? That if Don knew about the personal time they had spent together, he would rethink his phrasing? Because knowing what she knew, Don's comment was almost comical. Or would have been under less depressing circumstances.

Don continued. "We're creating a new position for you. One in which you will not only function as my assistant, but also take on more responsibility from the sales team, among others. We've worked up a new job description for you." He slid a piece of paper in front of her.

She read her new title: *Coordinator of Administrative Services and Logistics.*

As Don went down the list of responsibilities and highlighted a few of the key changes to her role, all she could think was that this had been Mark's doing. He had given her this new title. He had seen something in her beyond their personal time together and had recommended her for this new position.

"Of course, we're prepared to offer you a salary increase," Don said. "We consider this a promotion."

Kathy passed another piece of paper to Don, which he placed in front of her. He rattled off some percentages and numbers, but all Karma saw was the bold number at the bottom of the page. Her new salary nearly made her choke on her own saliva. This was no chump change. And there was an option for quarterly bonuses based on company performance.

She remembered something Mark had told her early on. He had been given carte blanche where the personnel was concerned. His human resources recommendations were sacrosanct.

Suddenly, those private conversations between Mark and Don seemed more important than anything else. He had spoken of her. To her boss. And his words had helped decide her fate. And all this time, she had thought their relationship went no further than their time outside the office.

But that wasn't the case. He had taken care of her. Mark had seen fit to leave her better than he had found her in more ways than one.

Maybe this was his way of showing her how much he cared. He couldn't give her his heart, but he could give her this gift to let her know that, while he couldn't stay in body, he could at least stay in her thoughts as the one who had set her up for success and a future she hadn't dreamed possible. One in which she made more money than she ever had, and which stuffed her resume with experience that could take her even further if she ever chose to leave Solar and pursue her writing career. Yes, she still wanted to be a journalist, but in the meantime, she didn't have to scrape to get by. This was his way of letting her know she was special. That's what she chose to believe, whether it was true or not. Because believing that made his leaving just a little bit easier to stomach.

Don went on about how they wanted to cross-train her in all operational tasks, including project management, as a means of furthering her potential and possibly allowing her another departmental move into an even more encompassing position if she wanted, and then they were finished.

She signed the appropriate documents and returned to her desk with a list of all the other employees scheduled for a visit with the three of them this morning. It was Karma's job to call each person in and keep the door revolving. Some of those employees would be like her and keep their jobs, but she was certain that some would come out of the conference room not wearing such happy faces.

Jolene was one of the names on the list, and as the door closed behind her after she went in, Karma was certain that she wouldn't come out happy, and she was right. A few minutes later, she exited with tears in her eyes and glared at Karma as she passed her desk, Kathy beside her.

"She should be the one being let go!" Jo pointed at her. "Not me. She's—"

"Enough, Jolene," Kathy said sharply. "Don't make this any harder on yourself."

Whatever Kathy held over Jo's head was enough to shut her mouth, and they disappeared around the corner as Jolene let out a quiet sob.

After their falling out over Memorial Day weekend and during the weeks before, Karma really wasn't surprised by the show of aggression. If anything, Jo should have seen this coming. All the signs had been there, and even Johnny had said anyone in administration should be looking for new work. But oh well. Jo wasn't Karma's problem, anymore.

Jo had tried to stir up trouble for her and Mark, and who knew what she would do now. She could still make waves if she wanted to, but it didn't really matter. Mark was leaving.

Today was going to be unsettling for everyone, and come Monday, the landscape would look a lot different around Solar.

Mark had barely slept last night. He had been too sick with misery, which felt like it might be translating to actual sickness. He could see his weekend with Karma slipping away, but he would fight through it. He didn't want anything to ruin their last weekend together.

"How are you feeling?" Don asked during the short break between employees. "You sound worse."

"I'll be fine." It was a lie, of course. He was so far from being fine that he wasn't even in the same zip code. If only things could be different. If only he could take her with him instead of leave her behind. If only Carol hadn't torn his emotions to shreds. If only. Because then everything would be different, and he wouldn't be so wary—no, terrified—of letting himself fall in love again.

He needed to stop considering alternative options.

It. Was. Over.

Period.

Karma was a sweet, wonderful, magnificent woman, but she would have to be someone else's perfect match, because there were simply too many things that stood in the way between them.

One more weekend together, and then next week, he would start packing up and make the necessary arrangements to leave.

Kathy returned to the conference room and dropped into the chair beside him.

"*That* was fun," she said sarcastically.

"I didn't think Jolene would take her dismissal well," Don chimed in.

"I'm not surprised. I pegged her early on as one who would cause trouble." Mark riffled through the last four letters in his stack. "Let's bring in the next one."

Don glanced out the door. "Karma, we're ready for the next one on the list."

By the end of the day, long after the last terminated employee had been escorted from the building, Mark was feeling slightly better. His throat wasn't as raw, and at last check, his eyes weren't quite so bloodshot.

He picked up his phone and typed out a text. *You're still coming to Chicago with me this weekend?*

A moment later came Karma's reply. *Yes. If you still want me to.*

Yes, I do.

The screen on his phone lit with another message from her. *In that case, count me in, Mr. Sicky.*

He looked up and caught her eye as she grinned secretly without meeting his gaze. Even now, with the end looming, he found such joy in the simple act of texting her.

He looked back down and typed out a response. *I'm not sick, but you can still feed me chicken soup and herbal tea…play nurse with me.*

Do I get to take your temperature?

He chuckled. *That depends,* he typed.

Are you worried about where I'll stick the thermometer?

Now he laughed. *You must be psychic.*

Nah. Just very good at my job.

That you are, Miss Mason. You're good at ALL your jobs.

He looked up and met her gaze. Then she glanced down, and he could tell she was typing out a response. His phone dinged with her message a moment later.

Thank you. And thank you for whatever you said to Don. Today was such a surprise.

A welcome one, I hope. That was the intent.

Yes. Very. It means a lot to me. I can't thank you enough.

You already have, Karma. Believe me. You've given me more than I ever imagined. So much so that I feel I should be thanking you. And you deserved that raise.

hug

Mark smiled at the simple message, and quickly tapped out his answer. **hug and kiss* I'll pick you up at 6:00. Bring your dancing shoes and a nice dress.* He would take her dancing this weekend. It had been years since he had taken a woman dancing, but it just felt right with her.

He began to pack up his things but stopped as another message came through.

And a thermometer.

He heard her stifle a giggle, surely because she had just seen the goofy, amused look on his face. His fingers danced over his phone's touch screen.

Perhaps I should take YOUR temperature, Miss Mason. But I won't use a thermometer if I do. ;)

It took a few seconds for her to get it, but when she did, the resulting gasp was music to his ears.

As morbidly as the day had begun, it was ending on a much nicer note. And even though by next Friday he would be gone, they still had one last weekend together. Two more days to forget about the rest of the world and enjoy one another.

On his way past her desk, with his bag over his shoulder, he gave her a secret wink.

For a few more days, she was his.

And he wouldn't waste one more second of the little time they had left dreading the inevitable moment when he would leave for good.

Chapter 55

The best proof of love is trust.
-Joyce Brothers

They arrived at Mark's apartment around ten o'clock after getting a late start out of Indy. On Saturday, Mark started them off early with breakfast at a quaint bakery near Grant Park, and then took her to Navy Pier and Shedd Aquarium. After lunch, they laid in the grass in Millennium Park, and Mark took a couple of selfies of them together. One of them straight on and smiling, and one of her kissing him on the cheek as he laughed from her tickling him.

Around four o'clock, they returned to his apartment to get cleaned up for a night out.

While Mark showered, she took the red dress she had worn the night they met out of the garment bag and laid it on the bed. She hadn't worn the Jimmy Choos since that night, either, and she placed them on the floor with thoughtful precision, as if she were setting chinaware on a table.

She blew out her hair and brushed it smooth. Mark exited the bathroom as she was applying her mascara. He stopped, and Karma turned to see him smiling at the dress. He glanced at her, nodded once, and bowed his head as he walked into the closet.

When he came out, he was buttoning the cuffs of a sleek, almost shiny charcoal grey shirt. She had just pulled on the dress.

He stepped behind her, wound his arms around her waist, and kissed her bared shoulder. "Thank you for wearing this."

She leaned into him. "I thought it was fitting."

He nudged her toward the edge of the bed. "Take a seat."

She did, and he knelt, lifting her foot in his hand as if it were made of delicate crystal. After reverently caressing the top of her foot and her red-tipped toes, he picked up one of the Jimmy Choos and, like the prince to Cinderella with the glass slipper, slid it on her foot and nimbly fastened the clasp. Then he did the same with the other, stood, and took her hand to help her up.

"You're beautiful."

"Thank you. So are you."

He took her to a romantic dinner at Boka then to The Joynt where they danced to jazz music and sipped high-priced libations for a couple of hours.

A little after eleven, they returned home.

As she eased out of her red scarf and jacket, placing both over the arm of the couch, Mark turned on some easy jazz and shut off the lights.

"Hi," he said, stepping in front of her and sliding one arm around her waist as he lifted her other hand into his. This was seductive Mark. The man who always made her knees weak and her heart race, even now, after months together.

"Hi." She lifted her face and gazed into his steamy, hooded eyes.

"Can I have this dance?"

She nodded and fell into step with him.

"Did I tell you how beautiful you look tonight?" He rocked her gently from side to side.

She rubbed her lips together. "I think you did mention that once or twice." She let go of his hand and let her fingers skim down the placket of his shirt, unbuttoning it as she went. She slid her hands under and against his skin. He was smooth and warm, firm. And then her fingertips found that handsome sweep of sparse hair that flowed to his sternum and led down the center of his torso.

"You're absolutely stunning. The most beautiful woman in the city tonight." His grip on her waist tightened.

"And you're the most handsome man." She fondled the opened collar of his button-down.

The appreciative grin that spread over his face drew a blaze from the kindling in her belly, as if a gust had blown over hot coals and fed a burst of flames.

For a while, they merely danced. He pulled her close, held her, rocked her, swayed to the lazy tempo and muted trumpet as if part of some old-time romantic movie. The air crackled between them. Electricity intensified the longer they danced in the darkness, and blurred shadows joined them from the subtle light breaking through the window that overlooked the lake.

And then Mark's hands began to roam with a controlled urgency that lit Karma's internal inferno for good.

"Take off my dress, Mark," she whispered.

With barely a second of hesitation, his fingers pinched the fabric at her waist and tugged upward. Once the hem reached her hips, he slid his hands underneath and carefully lifted the dress off her body, leaving her in a red strapless bra and matching lace panties.

"Tonight is all about you, Karma." He kissed her bare shoulder.

"Your dreams." His lips slid up to her ear. "Your desires." His whispered words sent warmth through her abdomen...and down lower, between her legs. The tip of his tongue flicked the place just behind her ear. "Your fantasies."

He tightened his hold around the small of her back, his seduction merciless and calculated. The effect he had on her was not unlike the effect a feline in heat had on a tomcat. She would do anything he asked. Her breath came in heavy gulps, and moist heat slicked her most intimate flesh.

Mark bent and leisurely trailed his lips from the left side of her neck to the right, sweeping down and across her collarbones as he spoke. "So what would you have of me tonight, Karma?" Mark's lips dazzled her skin, leaving tiny crackles in their wake. "Where do you want me? Anything you want, tonight it's yours."

She knew by now that Mark was not one to come right out and say what he wanted. Every intimate action he perpetrated was part of a game. A seductive, sexy, playfully erotic game that she was more than willing to play, because she was beyond ready to feel him inside her after their long day of foreplay.

"I want—" She cut off on a moan as his mouth closed at the tender place between her neck and shoulder and applied gentle suction. Fireworks exploded under her skin as he drew her flesh between his teeth and into his mouth. Heat raced to her nipples, followed by a detonation of butterflies springing to flight low in her belly.

"Yes? Tell me, Karma." His whispered words in the darkness were hushed and languid, falling over her like decadent, dark chocolate. "I'm yours tonight. All yours." He kissed her neck again. "Whatever you want from me, I'm willing to give. Just for you. Just for tonight. Say the word, and I'll be anything you want."

She tilted her head back, dug her fingers into his thick, soft hair, and sighed up to the ceiling. "Mark..."

Firm yet gentle lips placed measured caresses up the column of her neck, over her chin, and finally to her mouth, where they hovered a hair's breadth away. "Tell me what you want."

God, how his hands and mouth worked together with the precision of a surgeon, laying her bare, undoing her, dispatching all rational thought from her mind.

"I want *you*," she said on a breath that wafted gently from her mouth in a slow tumble of surrender.

His arm encircled her, flowing like fluid strength, a constant dance of movement as he shifted his hold, adjusted against her, and swayed her to one side. "And what do you want from me?"

If desire could be defined with motion, their bodies, pressed together, gently swaying, with arms caressing and lips teasing, would be the definition.

She lost herself in the music, his embrace, his soft-as-silk kisses, the warmth emanating from his torso, and the heat of his breath on her skin. Even as she realized this was their last real night together, the evening seemed right. The entire day had been perfect. Once more, Mark had granted her another beautiful, unforgettable good-bye gift. She knew even now that she would never forget this night. Ever. Even if she grew old and senile, this one night would stay cemented in her memory, no matter what other memories faded with age.

"All of you," she said, not holding back. He was hers, at least for now, and she would take all she could, live hard in the moment, and leave nothing to regrets. Because when next Friday came, and he left for good, she didn't want to look back and wish she had done more, said more, been more. It was now or never with Mark. "I want all of you, Mark. Right now. Just for tonight." She wanted him to remember tonight, too. She wanted it burned in his memory forever, so that he knew for the rest of his life that no other woman could give him what she could.

In that moment, Karma felt an invisible barrier around her shatter. The young, shy, innocent, do-gooder she had always been fell away once and for all. She was now and forever a changed woman. It was one more gift Mark had given her. He had brought her completely out from her shell. She was the sexy woman she had always fantasized being, but never knew how until he taught her. All their time together—the lessons, the time spent flirting with strangers, the naughty stories, the training—all of it had been for this moment. Right here. So she could become her true self in Mark's arms and show him what he had given her.

With a surge of newfound confidence, she ran her hand down his bare stomach to the waist of his pants, paused for just a heartbeat to say a final good-bye to the last, lingering vestige of the little girl making her final retreat into the shadows, then let her hand drop past his belt to the bulge pressing against his zipper.

As her palm gently caressed the length of his erection, empowerment and determination surged to the surface. She looked up at him through her lashes. "I want this," she said, sweeping her palm back up his length to the tip, where she let her fingers rest.

Mark's chest rose and fell heavily, and he blinked as if drunk and swayed toward her.

"Karma…" he whispered, eyes shimmering.

Fortified by his reaction, Karma lifted to her tiptoes and dusted her lips softly across his, taking complete control. Their gazes locked. "I want this," she said again, more forcefully, closing her fingers around the cylinder of hardness under her palm.

He lightly gasped and shivered then drew her top lip into his mouth, slowly slid his tongue across it, then drew away almost drowsily. "It's yours." He repeated the kiss on her bottom lip. "I'm yours." Then he placed his hand over hers and held it against him. His cock pulsed against her palm. The subtle jerk was just a single, tiny hiccup, but it pulled a dreamy moan from his throat. "You can have all of me…all night."

Karma nudged him toward the couch, using her free hand to push his shirt off one shoulder. He shook it from the other and let it fall to the floor.

With a shove against his chest, she pushed him to the couch. "Take off my panties."

He hooked his fingers around the waistband and drew them down her legs while she unhooked her bra and let it land beside his shirt. All she wore were her gold, strappy high heels.

As she straddled his lap, she pulled her red scarf—the one he'd used to blindfold her on the Fourth of July—from the arm of the couch. "Do you trust me?"

Mark was in awe of Karma. She was in control. He had never seen her like this, with such a dominant edge. She was a transformed woman in every way, and the power shifted completely into her hands.

For a moment, as he stared at her scarf, which she waved side to side like a hypnotic pocket watch, he almost said no. But then he gazed into her eyes, into a well of honesty, and knew, no matter his fears, he could trust her.

"Yes." He breathed the syllable even as his heart began to race.

He had never let a woman blindfold him. Doing so made him too vulnerable, but he had promised Karma that he would be anything she wanted tonight, that he would give himself completely to her for these last precious hours.

She lifted the scarf to his eyes, covered them, and his pulse quickened. His breathing picked up tempo as panic threatened to consume him.

"Sshh," she said, kissing his forehead. "Trust me." Her lips dotted his skin to his cheek, along the slope of his jaw to his chin, and finally to his lips.

He exhaled through his nose as her mouth closed against his, and he gripped her naked hips. Without his eyesight, everything was heightened. Her lips scorched his mouth and lit a fire so hot under his skin that he feared he would lose control. When she raked her blunt nails down his torso, he hissed as flames burned through every muscle in his body.

Mark had never felt anything like this. So fiercely intense and extreme. Vivid colors lit behind his closed eyes as her tongue left a sinuous trail down the center of his stomach. He gasped for air, dug his fingers into her hair, and fought to maintain their physical connection as she left his lap and settled between his legs.

She pulled off his slacks and pushed his knees apart, and then her mouth found him.

"Oh fuck…" He laid his head against the back of the couch, inhaled sharply, and surrendered to desire so acute and all-consuming he couldn't recall ever feeling more alive.

Her tongue swirled around and around the head, her hand working him up and down. Without his sight, the feelings amplified. Every stroke of her hand, every flick of her tongue, the way her moist lips brushed the sensitive head…every wicked sensation exploded times the power of ten.

It was better head than she'd ever given him. "Damn, Karma," he whispered on a breath.

He found her face with his hands, slipped his fingers into her hair, and sank further into the couch.

Her mouth was a combination of fire and ice, making him shiver and melt all at once. When she finally closed her lips over him and sucked him in, he knew he was a goner.

"Karma…" He tapped the top of her head. He was going to come. So fast, so hot, like lightning. But he couldn't hold back.

But she didn't stop. If anything, she swallowed him more enthusiastically.

"Karma…" Fuck, but he was about to shoot. "Karma, I'm going to…oh, fuck…I'm going to come. Stop. You need to stop if you don't want it in your mouth."

She doubled her efforts, taking him deeper and moaning.

Jesus! She wanted him to come in her mouth. She'd just blown his mind again. Pumping his hips, he gripped both sides of her head, seized fistfuls of her hair, clenched his jaw, and held his breath as his orgasm advanced like a tidal wave. He had never come this hard, and he hadn't even released, yet.

"Karma! Fuck!" His breath shuddered from his throat as he grunted and spilled into her mouth in vicious, uncontrollable waves.

Before he was even finished, he was ready to go again. He had never experienced multiple orgasms, but Karma, the blindfold, and her merciless onslaught had other plans for him.

Her mouth released him. Then her weight shifted as she climbed back onto his lap and found his lips with hers. He tasted himself, the salt of his offering, and it only made him want her more. For a woman to swallow a man's release like that was damn near the most erotically intimate act in the universe, and Karma worked her way a little further into his soul.

Still hard and in need of more, he gripped her hips and thrust himself against her. He needed to come again. Needed to feel her quiver around him as he did.

"More…" He sounded like an addict begging his dealer.

"Already?"

"Yes." God, he needed inside her. Now.

He felt her lean to the side, heard the sound of ripping plastic, felt her nimble fingers roll the condom on, and then her hand guided him inside as she sank down onto his lap.

He groaned. Yes, that was what he needed.

"Make love to me," he said, wrapping his arms around her.

He was still blindfolded, but he could feel, and he could hear. Her breasts mashed against his chest, her nipples hardened pebbles. Her palm pressed against one side of his neck, her face against the other. Her urgent gasps as she rode him bathed his skin in warmth, igniting his blood.

Gasps became hard breaths. Moans morphed into demanding groans. Urgency quickly became desperation, which reached criticality soon thereafter. Her body was a storm, riding in on the atmosphere like a squall line, picking up strength, power rising into the heavens. Her fingers dug into his shoulders, her breasts pressed against his chest, and she cried out with every breath. All Mark could do was hang on in an effort not to be blown away.

And then she grew deathly silent, the calm right before the storm. She tensed and held her breath. A moment later she blew apart just as she reached around and untied the scarf. It fell around his neck, and he blinked his eyes open to the visual feast churning and crying out on his lap. Karma's head was thrown back, her body convulsing. She clung to his neck and shoulders.

So close. He was so close. Thrusting into her, he rode the path she had left for him, and within seconds, he slammed into her as she cried in orgasm a second time, harder than the first.

As he came, he forced his eyes to remain open, not wanting to miss a moment. He wanted to experience this, all of it, the deep yearning, the incredible heights she had taken him. Then he pulled her close and buried his face against the side of her neck. He waited until the last shuddering spasm coursed through his body then slowly pulled away. Opening his eyes, he looked into hers, which glistened from the dim light coming through the windows.

She had given him a far greater gift than any he'd ever received. One greater than any he had given her or ever could. She had shown him he still had the capacity to trust. She had blindfolded him and led him through his fear to show him more pleasure than he'd ever known.

He pulled her against him once more and kissed her shoulder, her neck, and finally her lips, holding her so tightly he didn't think he would ever be able to let go.

"Thank you," he whispered.

"Thank *you*." Her fingers combed through his hair.

If only they had more time together. But he couldn't think like that. He didn't have any more time. This was it. Their time was almost up. But he still had tonight, and he would remember it forever.

Chapter 56

Grief is not a disorder, a disease, or a sign of weakness. It is an emotional, physical, and spiritual necessity, the price you pay for love. The only cure for grief is to grieve.
-Earl Grollman

Twice more, they made love before falling into a sated, exhausted sleep, then again in the shower the next morning. Neither talked about the end of the week, choosing to hang on to the magic as long as they could, but soon enough it was time to return to Indianapolis, where they spent Sunday evening lost inside each other at Mark's condo before falling asleep in each other's arms.

Mark's boss came down Monday afternoon and spent two days with him at the office, and on Wednesday night, Don took him to dinner with the other members of the executive team, so it wasn't until Thursday night that he got to see Karma again.

"Are you going to be okay?" he said, spooning her after they made love for the last time. This was it. Their last evening together.

She nodded. "Yes."

He heard the hurt in her voice.

"Are you sure?"

She nodded again and sighed, then turned to face him. Her eyes glistened with unshed tears. "I'll miss having you around. It already feels strange to look into the conference room and not see you there."

"I know. I'm sorry. I never meant for our good-bye to be this hard on either of us, but especially not on you."

One of her tears finally dropped to her cheek, and he lifted his hand to her face and wiped it away with his thumb.

"Good-byes are always hard, anyway," she said, working up a sheepish smile. "It's not your fault. I knew this day would come from the beginning."

"And yet you got involved with me anyway." He smiled and gingerly kissed her. "Brave girl."

She coughed out a truncated laugh. "Or a glutton for punishment."

He hugged her close. "Or that, too."

But he was just as gluttonous. He had let his heart slip into Karma's possession just as willingly as she had entered into the arrangement with him, and that was something he hadn't counted on. Unlike the other women he had dated, he would actually have to get over Karma.

His relationship with her was different. It didn't feel finished. He wanted more. But his time was up, and that meant whether he thought he was ready or not, he had to go.

That was how it worked. That was what he had promised her. And that was what he had promised himself after being *Caroled:* never to lose his heart again. Mark was steadfast in his conviction if not somewhat obsessive about it, and he couldn't make exceptions, not even for Karma.

He turned her face up to his with a brush of his fingers on her cheek so he could look her in the eyes. "When you get married, make sure you send me an invitation." His grin held every ounce of sincerity he could muster. "I wouldn't miss that for anything, Karma. You deserve to be happy. You deserve a good man who will worship you as the cherished angel you are." He held her face in his palm and stared into her lovely green eyes. "You. Are. Precious. Promise me you'll never forget that."

"Damn you," she said as tears flowed down her cheeks. "Now look what you've done. You've made me cry, and I promised I wouldn't cry tonight."

She reached to wipe the moisture from her face, but he pushed her hands away, leaned forward, and kissed the tracks of her tears. Teary brine dampened his lips, but he didn't care. They were *her* tears. Tiny, liquid diamonds. Her very essence.

"Promise me, Karma. Promise me you'll never forget how special you are."

She swallowed down a sob that tried to escape as she nodded. "I promise." She lifted up on her elbows and hit him with a serious stare. "Just as long as you promise not to forget the same."

The sentiment caught him off guard. "I'm beyond redemption, Karma." His mind drifted to the past that he couldn't let go off. The pain, the heartache, all of it. "My fate is already sealed."

"You're wrong," she said with certainty. "You have so much to offer. I hope someday you see that and can let go of the past to share yourself again. You deserve happiness, too."

He thought back to their conversation about Carol two months ago. Karma hadn't missed a thing in that conversation. She knew just how badly Carol had affected him and all the repercussions of her betrayal. Still, he nodded. "I'll try." He kissed her brow. "I promise."

She nestled back down against him, her cheek on his shoulder, her fingers lazily combing through the hair on his chest. He loved when she did that, as if she wasn't even thinking about it. Her fingers had a mind of their own and combed back and forth, back and forth. Occasionally, she would lightly tug a small thatch of hair between her thumb and fingers. The gesture was endearing, soothing, and all Karma.

For a while, they remained like that, one against the other, silent, simply existing in each other's presence, but he was only putting off the inevitable, because he couldn't spend the night.

He wanted to, but it was better if he left.

After fifteen minutes of silent comfort, he sighed. "I have to go, Karma."

"I know." But she didn't move.

This was harder than he had intended.

Another minute passed, and then she reluctantly slid away. He sat up, and swung his legs off the edge of the bed.

"Come here," he said over his shoulder, reaching for her hand.

She snuggled up behind him, and he took her hand and pulled her arm around his waist as her lips met the back of his shoulder in a tender kiss.

"I had fun," he said. "With you."

"So did I." She kissed his shoulder again and squeezed him as if she could hang on forever. "Thank you."

"No. Thank *you,* Karma. This was…" He glanced around her bedroom one last time, committing it to memory. "Nice. Very, very nice. Totally unexpected."

She smiled against his skin. "Yes. It was. I'll never forget you."

At that, he grinned and raised her hand to his lips. "Nor I you," he said, and then kissed each knuckle in turn. "You're unforgettable."

With one final squeeze of her hand, he let go and forced himself to pull out of her arms, retrieve his discarded clothes, and get dressed.

She walked him to the door, wearing the pink and cream robe he had bought her, which had remained at the condo until this week as he began packing up. After a final, lingering good-bye kiss, he reluctantly walked out of her life.

As he drove away and glanced in his rearview mirror, he could just make out her silhouette in her window, her hand against the glass.

It took a will greater than God's to keep his foot on the gas, but somehow, he fought through the lump in his throat and held his emotion at bay until he got home and collapsed, still dressed, in bed.

Only then did he allow himself to break.

And break he did.

Karma refused to take a shower. She wanted Mark's scent to linger on her skin as long as it could. And she didn't think she would ever again wash the pillowcase he had used.

In fact…

She pulled it off the pillow, neatly folded it, and tucked it into her keepsake box. It was Mark's pillowcase now, and like a T-shirt autographed by every member of the Beatles, it would never meet detergent nor water for the rest of its existence.

Of course, crying was a given. Now that he had left, and his pillowcase was safely stowed, she collapsed in a heap on the floor and cried harder than she ever had in her life.

Their affair was over. He was all but gone. She would probably never see him again, and if she did, it would likely be too painful to bear, because she knew he was moving on. Talking to him after tonight would just cut deeper and hurt worse, because he would never be hers. And she would never be his. Not anymore.

There was no way she could go to work tomorrow, either. Going in on Monday would be hard enough.

Mark. Was. Gone.

Gone!

And nothing could change that.

Or make her feel any better.

They say that misery loves company. Well, Karma had a new bedmate. She and misery were going to get good and acquainted, because she had a feeling they would be together for a good, long while.

And damn it. If her dad said "I told you so" just once, she would punch him.

Chapter 57

If you love someone, set them free. If they come back, they're yours forever. If they don't, they never were.
-Author unknown

"I wish Karma could be here to say good-bye, Mark," Don said, shaking his hand. "I know she hates missing your last day."

Mark didn't blame Karma for calling in sick. He would have done the same in her shoes.

It was better this way. Seeing her here would have made it that much harder to leave, and he wasn't sure either one of them would have been able to hide their disappointment.

"Yes, I hate not getting a chance to say good-bye to her," he said truthfully, even though he had said his good-byes last night. "Tell her I wish her well in her new role."

"I will." Don gave his shoulder a reassuring pat. "Thank you for all you've done for us, Mark. You've left us in better shape than you found us, and I think all of us are grateful."

There was one person in particular who had been left in better shape than all the others, as well as worse.

Karma.

She was no longer the shy, timid woman he had met in Chicago, trying to be someone she wasn't. She was well on her way to being the woman she was born to be, but because of the time they had spent with one another to help her achieve that status, she was now worse. Hurting the same way he was.

"Just doing my job, Don. And I'm happy I could help." He shook his hand again. "Make sure to contact me if you need anything else. I'm just a phone call away."

"That goes both ways," Don said. "My door is open any time you're in town, so don't be a stranger."

Mark made his rounds then ventured down to the lobby.

"Good-bye, Nancy." He waved to the receptionist.

"Bye, Mark." She flashed him her best sexy eyes, and he smiled.

"If only it could have worked between us, Nancy," he teased.

Nancy had made no secret about how attracted she was to him during his stay.

"Story of my life." She rolled her eyes and laughed. "Will we see you again?

He shook his head. "Not if you play your cards right."

"Well then!" She got a glint in her eyes. "I'd better get started screwing things up."

He laughed at her. "Be careful, or they might send someone else next time."

She sighed. "It was worth a try."

He waved and walked out the door.

As soon as he got in his car, he pulled out his phone and typed out a message. *Missed you at the office. I hope you're okay.*

He refused to go until she replied. He didn't want to be driving when her message came through. He needed to be ready.

So he waited. And waited.

And waited some more.

Karma?

Was she okay? Why wasn't she answering? He tried again.

If you don't reply, I'll be forced to stop by your apartment to make sure you're okay. In a way, he hoped she wouldn't reply, because that would give him an excuse to see her one last time. But if he saw her, he wasn't sure he could leave. But maybe that was what needed to happen. Maybe this was a sign. Maybe God or the powers that controlled the universe—or however Rob had described it on Fourth of July weekend—were trying to tell him something. That he couldn't go. Not without her.

He closed his eyes. "Please, please, God," he muttered under his breath, suddenly desperate. "If this is a sign, let me know before I make the biggest mistake of my life." Maybe he *could* try a long-distance relationship. He could come down one weekend a month, and she could go to Chicago once a month, and then they could figure things out later. But first, he needed a sign. And if she didn't answer him and he had to go see her, that would be it. That would be the sign he needed to know that God wanted him to take a chance again on love.

He was about to put the car in gear and drive to her apartment when his phone chimed with a message. All hope dissipated in a blink.

Good-bye, Mark.

The finality of her text kicked him in the gut and brought him back down to earth. Even though they hadn't been spoken, the words drove like a dagger into his heart, and the message was clear. She was moving on, and this was her way of telling him to do the same.

He had gotten his sign. So then why was he so disappointed?

Clearing the emotion from his throat, he typed out a final text.

Good-bye, Karma. I wish you well. Stay in touch.

As much as he hoped she would, he knew she wouldn't. He tucked his phone away and pulled out of Solar's parking lot for the last time. And even though every instinct screamed at him to turn into Karma's apartment complex as he drove past, he set his jaw and drove on.

She needed to move on without him, and he needed to do the same without her.

Their chapter was over.

Karma sat in the parking lot across the street and watched him leave. Tears flowed like twin rivers down her face and dropped off her chin. One even splattered on the screen of her phone as she lifted it and re-read his last message for what felt like the tenth time.

After twenty minutes, with tears still streaming her face and blurring her vision, she finally dropped her phone in her purse, backed out of the parking space, and drove home.

Her apartment felt empty. *She* felt empty.

She would hurt for a while. Maybe even get depressed now that he was gone. But in time, she hoped the edges of the pain he left behind would dull, and she could move on.

But as she lay on her couch, the morning turned to afternoon, then to evening, and she began to fear the worst. She would never get over Mark. She would never forget his kisses, or the way his fingertips felt on her face, or the way he turned to mush at the sight of her black high heels as she slipped her feet into them.

Maybe she shouldn't have responded to his text. The one in which he threatened to come to her apartment if she didn't reply. She could have raced home and seen him one last time, because she knew he would have followed through on his threat. But that would have just made his leaving that much more unbearable. She needed to rip off the Band-Aid and let the wound heal, and seeing him again would have only delayed the healing process.

The longer she lay on the couch, though, the more she knew that no other man would ever fill his shoes—because no other man was Mark. No matter how many men she dated or slept with for the rest of her life, none would ever truly make her happy.

Why?

Because she was in love with him.

She had fallen in love with Mark Strong.

And now he was gone. She had let him leave without so much as a fight.

Now it was too late.

At seven o'clock, her phone chimed. She jumped up and grabbed it off the table, eager to see his message. She deflated in an instant. It was a message from Lisa.

Daniel and I are on our way.

She texted back. *K.*

A few minutes later, Karma opened the door. Daniel held a pizza and a bag of Ben & Jerry's. Lisa held a box of Kleenex, flowers, and a DVD.

Karma broke down in uncontrollable sobs and fell into Lisa's arms.

"Sshh, sweetie. It'll be okay. We'll get you through this."

Daniel ushered them inside, set down the pizza and ice cream, took the flowers and Kleenex from Lisa, and the three of them made a hug circle, with Karma in the middle.

She needed her best friends now more than ever…because the best thing that had ever happened to her was gone.

Epilogue

Never give up on something you really want. However impossible things seem, there's always a way.
-Sophie Kinsella

Six weeks later…

"And for all her efforts to transition operations through our recent changes, employee of the month goes to…Karma Mason." Don gestured toward Karma while the rest of the employees took a break from their Halloween luncheon to applaud.

Karma ducked her head as her face heated.

This was Mark's legacy. The employee of the month program had been his suggestion, and how fitting was it that she should be its first recipient?

Don handed her a gift card. "Congratulations, Karma."

"Thanks." She tucked the fifty-dollar card into her pocket. She didn't know what she would spend the money on, but in time, as the clouds lifted from Mark's absence, she would figure it out.

Lisa nudged her arm. "Way to go, girl. I knew you'd get it this month." She was in charge of the fledgling program. "Here, have some chocolate to celebrate." She grabbed a piece of Dove chocolate from inside one of the small plastic pumpkins decorating the tables and set it in front of Karma.

"Uh…" Karma frowned at the piece of chocolate that reminded her of her favorite lesson with Mark and pursed her lips as a jab of pain knifed her chest.

"Oh, um…I'm sorry." Lisa quickly removed the blue square of chocolate, tossed it back inside the pumpkin, and fished out a Snickers instead.

Karma sighed, took the bite-size bar, and offered Lisa a wan grin. "It's okay," she said. "I have to move on eventually, right?"

Lisa stroked her arm. "You want to come over to my place for Halloween tomorrow? We could make popcorn, watch scary movies, and pass out candy to the trick-or-treaters. And you can help me decorate the front yard. It'll be fun. What do you say?"

"I don't think so, Leese. I'm just going to stay home."

Lisa sighed and nodded sympathetically. "Okay. Let me know if you change your mind." She stood with her empty plate. "I'm gonna get back to work. Congratulations again." She smiled warmly then headed off.

Back at her desk, Karma's gaze strayed to the empty conference room Mark had made his office over the summer. Another stab of sorrow cut into her heart. Where was he now? Was he standing on his balcony, looking at Lake Michigan? Had he taken on a new assignment in another state? Had he met someone new? Someone he could teach all his lessons of love to the way he had her? Did he even think about her, anymore? She still thought about him every day.

She had thought that, with time, the sadness would diminish, and in some ways it had. She no longer cried herself to sleep every night, but she still couldn't look at a Dove chocolate square or a brownie without tears prickling the backs of her eyes. She still couldn't wear her red scarf or her peep-toe pumps, either. And she hadn't touched her stack of books since he'd left. They still sat on her dresser, right where they were the last time he was inside her apartment.

But getting through her days was getting easier. Baby steps, right?

"Hey, Karma."

She looked up as Jasper stopped in front of her desk. "Hey, Jasper. What's up?"

Jasper was one of Solar's project managers. He was about her age, slim but fit, with straight brown hair that always hung a little over his eyes. He brushed it aside and smiled. He had a nice smile. She had never noticed before.

"We need another girl for tonight's softball game. You interested?"

Softball? She really wasn't up for softball or anything else. "I'm not sure, Jasper. It's been a while since I played, and—"

"That's okay. We just do it for fun. I have an extra mitt if you need one."

"No, I've got my own mitt." She hadn't used it in years, but she had one.

"Come on. It'll be fun. We go out after for burgers and drinks at the Stacked Pickle. You should join us." His brown eyes sparkled with an interest that was deeper than his desire to fill a vacancy on the team.

Jasper was an attractive guy. Karma had never paid him much attention before, but now that she really got a good look, he was sort of handsome. Was he boyfriend material? Was he worthy to replace Mark in her heart? Probably not. But she would never know if she didn't give him a chance. Didn't he deserve at least that?

"Well…okay. I suppose I can help out. Sounds like fun." As with her affirmations, if she said it enough, eventually she would begin to believe it. And she had to start somewhere. *Baby steps, Karma. One step at a time, one day at a time.* If she kept that in perspective, before long she wouldn't have to remind herself to have fun. She just would.

"Great." Jasper nodded, grinned, and held her gaze for a long moment before saying, "We meet at the Midwest Sports Complex around five thirty. Game starts around six." He hesitated. "You can ride with me if you want."

She shook her head. "No. Thanks, anyway. I know where it is. And I have to go home and change first."

He looked a little disappointed. "Oh, that's right. Okay."

"But I'll be there."

He brightened. "Then I'll see you at five thirty. Thanks, Karma."

She watched after him as he headed off to the war room. Then she glanced back into the conference room. Mark was gone. He wasn't coming back. She needed to move on, even if it hurt like hell to pull him from her heart and give someone else a shot. Life couldn't be put on hold just because Mark had vacated hers. She needed to find her way toward living again. Filling in on the company softball team was a good first step, but she could do even better.

She grabbed her phone and dialed Lisa's extension.

"Hey," she said when Lisa answered. "About tomorrow. I changed my mind. What time should I be at your place?"

Baby steps. Little tiny baby steps.

Mark carefully removed the bandage from his chest, a little left of center, where the hair had been shaved. He inspected his new tattoo, a pair of Asian hieroglyphics inside a three-inch-diameter circle. It looked like a stamp, which was fitting given its meaning and placement. His skin was still red and irritated, but the black oriental symbols looked good. Clean and crisp.

Karma. That's what the symbols stood for.

A nostalgic smile touched his lips. The tattoo was his way not only to brand Karma on his body but also to honor the promise he had made to the universe while driving back to Chicago six weeks ago. Leaving her had been the hardest thing he'd ever done, and, more than once, he had almost turned around. Finally, halfway to Chicago, when, once again, he had almost pulled off the interstate to go back, he struck a bargain with God…or whatever higher power controlled fate.

"Okay, I'll make a deal with you, God." He gripped the steering wheel and pushed his foot a little harder on the accelerator, passing the exit to Merrillville and continuing toward Chicago. "Maybe I misunderstood before. I'm not adept at reading signs, and I know I kind of threw that one at you last minute back there, but let's try this again." He sounded like he was negotiating, not praying. Was this how asking for signs was done? He took a deep breath and nodded to himself, determined to see this through, even if he sounded like a negotiator instead of someone desperate for another chance at the best thing that had ever happened to him. "I'll go back to Chicago. I'll go back to my life. But if I'm meant to be with her, bring her back to me. I don't care how or when." He stared out the windshield at the stretch of gray, double-laned pavement. "Well, I do care when. The sooner the better, but I'll take what you can give me."

What was that old adage? *If you love someone, set them free. If they come back to you, they're yours forever. If they don't, they never were.* Well, he was setting Karma free.

"If we're meant to be together, God, then bring her back to me. If you bring her back, I'll know we're supposed to be together forever." He needed a sign. One that came from outside himself, because he couldn't trust his own feelings. His heart tugged him in one direction, and his head pulled him in another. He was at odds with himself, wanting two things that sat on opposite ends of the spectrum. His heart wanted Karma, but his brain reminded him what listening to his heart before had gotten him: a lot of pain and suffering.

So he released responsibility over the decision altogether and gave it to God and the universe. Let fate decide. That was best. That was easiest.

But what if God did bring her back and gave his heart what it wanted? How would he get past his aversion to long-term commitments, and how would the two of them make a long-distance relationship work?

No! Stop thinking, Strong.

He forced himself to shut down the questions whirring through his mind. His future was out of his control now. This was how signs worked, right? Not that he'd ever believed in all this kismet stuff before, but in principle, you asked for a sign, put yourself into Fate's hands, and went about your business. If you got the sign you asked for, then everything else automatically fell into place, one way or another, because you wouldn't have gotten what you asked for if it wasn't meant to be.

So he had sent his request into the universe and returned to Chicago. Still, it hadn't felt like he had done enough. That was when he got the idea to tattoo "karma" on his chest, right over his heart, thus branding himself as hers forever, no matter whether God answered him or not.

He stared fondly at the fresh ink then pulled up the picture he had taken of the two of them together in Millennium Park. The one where she had been kissing his cheek while they lay on the grass. He looked at that picture at least once a day. He had been so happy then. Happier than he was now by about a mile. Maybe ten. Hell, maybe a hundred.

He sighed, set his phone on the bathroom counter, and grabbed his antibacterial soap as an ache set up shop in his chest, right behind the tattoo…deep inside his heart, which now belonged to Karma.

He carefully cleansed the tattoo, let it dry, and then gently rubbed the ointment the tattoo artist had given him over the glyphic symbols. He would care for this tattoo the way he should have cared for the woman that was its namesake. And if given the chance, and God saw fit to answer his prayer and fulfill His end of the bargain, Mark wouldn't make the same mistake twice.

If Karma came back to him, he vowed to take care of her forever.

Turn the page for an excerpt from Coming Back to You, book two in the Strong Karma Trilogy, to be released winter 2014

Karma sat in her car in Solar's parking lot, staring at the diamond ring on her finger. She had never seen the proposal coming, and yet, yesterday, at her parents' Labor Day cookout, Brad had surprised her.

Everyone had just finished chowing down on burgers, baked beans, and potato salad around the large patio table when Brad had addressed her dad.

"Mr. Mason, I'd like to ask you something."

"Please," her dad said, "Call me John."

Dad liked Brad. At least he acted like he did. Karma thought he was just happy that she'd finally moved on from Mark, which was why he was overly welcoming when she'd shown up with Brad. Her dad had heard about him for months, but this was the first time he'd met him.

Brad offered a deferential smile. "John then, I'd like to ask you something."

"Sure, ask me anything."

Across the table, her brother Johnny, who had learned how to behave himself since last summer, bounced his one-year-old daughter on his knee. She'd just awakened from her nap. Johnny's wife, Estelle, looked on. Both had been surprisingly quiet and polite, but Karma knew the peace could only last so long. Johnny would eventually show his ass again.

Brad took her hand and squeezed. "I've been dating your daughter for six months." He paused as she turned and gave him a quizzical look. What was he doing? "I love her very much, and, with your permission, sir, I'd like to ask her to marry me."

Thud! Marry him?

Her mom uttered a soft squeal and covered her mouth as her eyes lit up. Johnny stopped bouncing his baby. A slow grin spread over her dad's face as he clasped his hands under his chin.

"Brad, I can think of *no one better* to marry my daughter." He pointedly met her gaze, his meaning clear. He was ready for the Mark Strong chapter of her life to be officially over. Marrying Brad would guarantee that.

Brad pulled a diamond ring from his pocket, scooted back in his chair, and got down on one knee. "Karma, with your dad's blessing, and in front of your family, I'm promising my love to you." His whole face beamed as he poised the ring at the tip of her finger. "Will you do me the honor of becoming my wife? Will you marry me?"

She stared at him. She felt her hand in his. Everything about this moment was perfect, and she glanced around the table at her family.

This was what she wanted, right? She wanted to be married. She wanted a husband, a family, and a life where she was no longer alone.

As she took a deep breath and nodded, a tiny niggle of alarm vibrated in her soul. She brushed it aside, forcing herself to leap forward rather than stay rooted in the past.

"Yes, Brad. Yes, I'll marry you."

He slid the diamond onto her hand and hugged her.

She was engaged. She was striding forward, furthering herself a little bit more from her memories of Mark.

Her phone chiming inside her purse broke her from thoughts of yesterday, planting her back inside her car, sitting in Solar's parking lot.

She quickly gathered her purse and bag and hopped out. She'd sat so long recalling Brad's proposal she was now officially late.

Oops.

She rushed up the sidewalk and into the lobby as her phone began ringing again.

"Good morning, Nancy," she said, rushing past the reception desk. As she took the stairs to the second level, she fished through her purse for her phone.

At the top of the stairs, she finally pulled her phone free and checked the screen.

Lisa? Why was Lisa calling her?

Darting down the hall to her desk, she slapped her phone to her ear. "Lisa, what's up? Sorry it took so long to answer. I'm running late. God, I need to talk to you." She had yet to tell Daniel and Lisa that Brad had proposed.

"Karma! Will you shut up! I need to tell you something."

Sheez! What was up with Lisa?

Karma dropped her bags on the floor at her desk and booted up her computer. "Fine. Sorry. What?"

At that moment, the door to Don's office opened.

"Ah, there she is," Don said, gesturing toward her.

Lisa was still talking in her ear. "Karma, don't freak out, okay, but…"

Everything fell into slow motion. The earth slowed to a near standstill on its axis. Lisa's voice sounded like she was talking through molasses. And Karma was sure her chin must have hit her desk as her mouth fell open.

"Mark's here!" Lisa said. "In Don's office. Right now."

Karma almost dropped her phone as her gaze met Mark's for the first time in a year.

"I know," she murmured and hung up.

And just like that, in the time it took for a light to come on once the switch was flipped, all her efforts to get over him during the past year faded in a blink.

He was back. Mark was here.

About the Author

Donya Lynne is the author of the award winning All the King's Men Series. Making her home in a wooded suburb north of Indianapolis with her husband, Donya has lived in Indiana most of her life and knew at a young age that she was destined to be a writer. She started writing poetry in grade school and won her first short story contest in fourth grade. In junior high, she began writing romantic stories for her friends, and by her sophomore year, they had dubbed her *Most Likely to Become a Romance Novelist*. In 2012, she made that dream come true by publishing her first two novels and two novellas. Donya has many more novels and novellas planned for years to come.

For more information on Donya's books or just to say hello, visit her on Facebook or swing by her website.

https://www.facebook.com/DonyaLynne

www.donyalynne.com

Made in the USA
Middletown, DE
27 November 2020

25352521R00255